PRAISE FOR LUCIANA CAVALLARO

The Labyrinthine Journey, Book 2

The storyline was refreshingly original, and there are certainly enough plot twists to keep the reader engaged. This is one adventure you don't want to miss.

— MARY ANNE YARDE | AUTHOR

Five out of five for its sophisticated and inventive retelling of the well-known and widespread story of Christ.

— LITERARY TITAN

A truly epic saga written with a gold-tipped pen!

— WISHING SHELF BOOK REVIEW

MINOTAUR'S LAIR

MINOTAUR'S LAIR

SERVANT OF THE GODS
BOOK THREE

LUCIANA CAVALLARO

Mythos|Publications

Mythos Publications

https://www.luccav.me

Publisher's Note: This is a work of fiction. Names, characters, places, and incidents are a product of the author's imagination. Locales and public names are sometimes used for atmospheric purposes. Any resemblance to actual people, living or dead, or to businesses, companies, events, institutions, or locales is completely coincidental.

Cover designed by Damonza.com

Ordering Information: Quantity sales. Special discounts are available on quantity purchases by corporations, associations, and others. For details, contact the "Special Sales Department" at the address above.

Minotaur's Lair/ Luciana Cavallaro. -- 1st ed.

978-0-6452726-3-5

The gods love to punish whatever is greater than the rest.

— HERODOTOS

ALSO BY LUCIANA CAVALLARO

Accursed Women

SERVANT OF THE GODS TRILOGY

Search for the Golden Serpent

The Labyrinthine Journey

Minotaur's Lair

COIN OF TIME SERIES

The Guardian's Legacy

For my Family, who encouraged me to keep persevering and writing.

Minotaur's Lair
Book 3
Servant of the Gods

Luciana Cavallaro

CHAPTER 1

T he Dark Master walked through the debris of the throne room of
the king of the Atlanteans. He glanced at the faded crimson walls
and the embossed tableau of griffins—lion-like creatures with the heads
of birds—interspersed with lilies. Diffused sunlight penetrated the
entryway of four large doors, creating a dappled effect on the dirt-
encrusted floor. He followed the trail of the speckled light to the one
object in the room not damaged from the floods and earthquake that had
razed the mighty house. Embedded in the wall was a throne, made from
alabaster stone, once white, now a dirty yellow-brown, stained and
marred over the millennia.

Kronos sat down. The seat, carved to accommodate a person's
haunches, was a comfortable fit. To his right and left were stone benches
that ran along the length of the wall, once a rich and vibrant saffron,
now faded and concealed by rubble and detritus. The tsunami and
earthquake that had shattered the coastline a thousand years ago had
caused the former formidable thalassocracy—once a supreme naval force
of the region—to flounder and dissolve. Prior to the land's destruction,
the Atlantean kings had ruled and wielded authority from this very

location, safe in the knowledge of their dominion. Until Zeus and his siblings had interfered.

His face darkened.

He closed his eyes and took a deep breath. Now was not the occasion to lose control. He was so close to accomplishing his mission and ultimate victory. Kronos stood, rubble and dust particles swirling at his feet, and strutted towards a series of broad steps that led into a pit. Here, he would sacrifice the Atlanteans, one by one, the High Priestess powerless to stop him. The thought of the beautiful mouthpiece of the Mother Goddess titillated him. His breathing came fast, his blood roaring through his veins; his plans for her warmed and aroused him. He would make her bend to his will and cower before him. Kronos moaned and he panted; his rapture reverberated in the room. His knees trembled at the anticipation of coupling with the High Priestess. And when she had borne his spawn, he would send her discarded remains to the Mother Goddess.

Exhilarated by that thought, he materialised onto the central court. Fragments of rocks and painted shards glimmered under the sun. Here, on this great expanse, the irrevocable act of vengeance would take place. The Mother Goddess on her knees to him, the bodies of Zeus and the Olympians strewn in bloody carnage, weeping and broken. That wasn't all he had intended for her. He would return her children from whence they had come and rejoice at her screams, and then she would feel the suffering he had endured.

'Oh, the glory of it!' he said in a booming voice, arms spread out, and he spun in a circle, his scarred face tilted skywards. Birds tittered and fluttered, bursting into flight. His amber eyes glittered, tracking the frightened birds as they scattered in disarray across the blue sky.

'What will you do if Evandros does not accept your offer?' asked Eris, descending to the ground.

Kronos whirled, angered at her intrusion and her ludicrous question. 'He will! No insignificant mortal can resist the power of sovereignty and the gift of immortality.' His lip curled at the sight of her pet, the monstrous Ekhidna—a dragon with the head and upper body of a woman and the tail of a serpent.

'Yes, most mortals would, but Evandros is not like any other human,' she said. 'He is ... unique.'

'I am confident he will accept my proposition. However, if he chooses not to, he will meet the same fate as his companions.' Kronos drew his cowl further over his head, casting his face into darkness. 'Is it done?'

Eris nodded. 'All is in place. The males are enjoying their sojourn with the Amazons, and the queen is aware of the consequences if the men recover before you accomplish your plans.'

'Good. Leave and take your ... creature with you.' He sniffed and turned his back on them.

The Dark Master, so engrossed with devising his next task, did not hear the Titaness mutter or see the look of hatred on her face. He needed to waken and coerce the one who protected the location of the final sacred object—the Minotaur. Repulsed, he shuddered, loath to enter the lair and communicate with such an abomination. He had informed the Goddess of Discord that such repugnant beings could not exist in his new world order and that their extinction was nigh. He almost chortled out loud at her pleas for him to reconsider.

The goddess had become a problem, her demands having grown greater, and now he regretted releasing her from Tartaros. At one time, he had contemplated rewarding her with the esteemed role of sacred motherhood, but her affection for the beasts and her meddling ways were repellent. Once he destroyed the Atlanteans, he would cast her out along with the dissolution of the gods and Gaia.

He crossed the length of the court, ignoring the decimation of the upper floors of the palace impacted by the volcanic eruption and the violent implosion felt from the island of Thira and ravaged a century and a half later by the marauding Sea Peoples. The Dark Master veered towards the fringes of the palace, the target an intact building. He stomped inside and ventured into the murky bowels beneath the palace, his cloak blending with the surrounds.

His nose crinkled at the musky and unpleasant scent, and another odour—death. The decay of thousands of victims steeped within the cavernous walls. He moved ahead with sure steps, heading deeper into obscurity, swallowed by the labyrinthine confines.

CHAPTER 2

A tall, striking blonde woman, her face glowing with love, lit up when he smiled at her. She spoke to him and then frowned when he didn't respond. She took a step into the room, talking. Evan tugged his ear, but he couldn't hear what she was saying. His eyes bulged as she crumpled to the floor, blood spurting from her neck. He rushed to her side, placing his hands on her neck to stem the flow of blood. The thick, warm inky-dark crimson fluid seeped through his fingers and soon drenched the bodice of her white khiton.

Evan looked around, calling for help.

'Her sacrifice was essential,' said a voice.

'Help her!' he implored. 'You can heal her, Zeus.'

'It is too late. The quest has begun. I brought you home to fulfil your destiny and ours. You, my son, are the only one who can stop Kronos and his intention to bring forth the birth of the Messiah, for if you do not, we—the Olympian gods—and you will die. It is your knowledge of the future that provides you with the strength and ability to succeed against the Titan. That is why I hid you in the twenty-first century, to learn and ensure your safety.' Zeus rocked back and forth on his feet. 'Use the gifts I have endowed you with to lead your companions in retrieving the Mother Goddess' sacred icons, for without them, you cannot succeed and our sovereignty is lost.' Zeus shimmered.

'Wait! You cannot let this woman die!' he shouted at the fading blue nimbus. 'Zeus! Come back!' Evan's chin dropped. The woman's sightless glassy eyes were fixed on his face. He sat back on his haunches and gazed at his bloodstained hands, choked back a sob and squeezed his eyes shut, rocking back and forth.

When he opened his eyes again, Evan noticed he was sitting at a desk, staring at a large rectangular computer monitor with drawings of a Greek-style temple, the rendering in 3D and rotating from front view to side and bird's-eye. He touched the crisp sky-blue shirt he wore and inhaled, and with it the fresh scent of lemon from the material. He rubbed his hand on his legs and saw he was wearing dark denim jeans, his feet shod in steel-capped work boots.

He whirled around on his desk chair, dazed.

Evan got up from his chair and walked to the window. The Swan River, the Narrows Bridge and the city's national park dominated the view. Cars of various shapes and sizes, motorbikes and trucks sped along the freeway. To the east was the casino, and the redesigned Victoria Quay, sprouting the brand-new Hilton Hotel. Evan leaned his forehead against the cold glass and watched the scene below.

'Evandros!'

Evan moved away from the window and turned around. No one was there. He sighed and returned to his desk.

'Evandros ...'

'E vandrosss ...'

He stirred.

'Evandrosss ...'

He woke with a start, his body sheathed in sweat, his mind jumbled and muddied. The woman next to him in bed murmured, rolled onto her side and fell silent. The blonde-haired woman from his dream he was certain he knew but could not recall from where. And Divine Zeus was there and refused to help the dying woman. He stared at the wooden ceiling, the thick beams blackened from years of smouldering torches. Evan thought he heard a female calling for help. The voice sounded familiar, but who was she? He frowned, trying to remember—he was sure he knew her name, but it eluded him.

His companion stretched her supple golden limbs, body toned and athletic, as if she spent a considerable deal of time exercising. Evan's brow furrowed, the lines etched deep as he pondered his confusing and disturbing dream. Strange images filtered through his mind, many of which made little sense. Towering structures with mirror-like walls, contraptions on wheels that moved with remarkable speed and yet did not resemble a chariot. Large birdlike creatures that flew in the sky, though they were not birds. Then there were the strange clothes he wore. He could not conceive that such objects existed; however, a gnawing feeling in his gut told him otherwise. What was it that Zeus had said in his dream state—that he had placed him in the future to learn about the past? What did it all mean? He rubbed his forehead as if it would erase the hallucinations.

'Are you still having those dreams, Evandros?' The woman searched his face, caressing his cheek, her grey eyes filled with concern. 'Allow me to have our healer give you an elixir to help quieten those apparitions.'

Evan kissed her palm. 'Antioche, no amount of sleeping

draughts or concoctions will improve my sleep or rid me of the visions. The gods are sending me these messages for a reason, and I can't ignore them. They are trying to tell me something and until I work out what it is, I will not take any medication.'

'I do not care what the gods want—you cannot continue to have sleepless nights. My physician asserted it is not good for the mind nor the body if one does not sleep well,' said Antioche, voice rising and eyes welling.

'You spoke to the healer without my consent?' He glowered at her. 'You did not have my permission to do that. I decide what is best for my health.'

Antioche vaulted upright, breasts heaving, face flushed and hands clenched tight. 'I have every right! You are the queen's consort. I will do what I must and seek advice to help my companion.'

Evan took in her dishevelled honey-blonde hair and the tears welling in her eyes. He sat up, drew her into his arms and cradled her. 'I love you too.'

He felt her hot tears as they wet his neck and tightened his arms about her, his stomach clenching. The thought of Antioche being so distressed bothered him, as did the idea that he caused her pain. She was always collected and steadfast. He kissed the top of her head as she clung to him. Then an unexpected revelation popped into his mind, and his heart skipped a beat.

'Antioche,' he said, holding still in expectation. She sniffled at the mention of her name. 'Are you pregnant?'

She calmed down and quietened.

'It's not normal for you to react with intense emotion, and I wondered if you might be pregnant. It would explain your fluctuating moods.'

Antioche lifted her head and gazed at him in wonder. 'I … I never … or thought … it's been months, I didn't believe I …'

He smiled and kissed her. 'Why don't we call the healer and let her examine you? Then we'll know for certain.'

'I ... yes.' She nodded, wide-eyed.

'Go to the baths. You'll feel refreshed, and I'll send a guard for your healer,' Evan said.

'Yes, I think I will.' Antioche slid off his lap and stood by the bed. She faced the wall with a vacant expression. He got out of bed, took her by the shoulders and sat her down, wrapping the blanket about her naked body.

'I'll get one of your handmaidens to assist you,' Evan said. He pulled a khiton over his head and walked to the door.

Two guards posted outside in the hallway stood to attention.

'Bring the queen's handmaidens to the room,' Evan said, pointing to one of them, 'and you,' he told the other, 'summon the healer here.'

The guards hesitated.

'Now!' he said, raising his voice. 'Your queen requires their help.'

They acknowledged him with a slight bow, then scooted down the passageway and veered in opposite directions at the T-junction. He re-entered the chamber and sat next to Antioche, embracing her. She leaned against him and shivered. He rubbed his hand up and down her side, kissing her brow. If his mind had been chaotic earlier, it was in a worse state now. A baby. What did he know about babies? Or how to be a father? He bit his lip. When the queen had taken him as her consort, her intention was to become impregnated. After a few months, they'd realised nothing was happening, and even with the healer's remedies to increase the possibility of pregnancy, was ineffectual.

The queen should have replaced him with another man, one capable of succeeding where he had failed, but she had refused to consider taking a different lover. Her advisers and healer had insisted she find a substitute—'one more virile and fertile,' they'd said—but Antioche had ignored their counsel. He tightened his arm around her and choked back the bubbling anger brewing in his veins. The image of Antioche being with some other guy, in this chamber and in their bed ... he swallowed, unable to contemplate the prospect. He would step aside, if she wanted him to, and not hold any grudges. He'd do it for her.

'Evandros?'

'Yes, Antioche?'

'Will you stay with me?'

'Of course.'

~

While the handmaidens attended to Antioche, Evan slipped out of the room to use the bathing facilities. He did not wish to loiter too long in the baths, knowing Antioche needed him and not wanting his absence to upset her. He had just stepped into the water when Dexion, a twelve-year-old Sicilian boy, showed up.

'Master Evandros, I have important news to tell you,' he said, his dark brown eyes almost black from the shadowy circles beneath.

'Not now, Dexion. I need to return to the queen as soon as I have finished washing,' he said.

The boy's face fell.

'I'll come find you when the queen no longer needs me.' He gave him a reassuring smile. 'I promise. All right?'

Dexion nodded and, with head lowered, left him to bathe. As Evan watched him leave, he had a premonition of the boy and his friend Phameas standing under a tree, ten metres away from where he stood in front of a building, with fast-moving contraptions blocking their way to cross the wide, dark strips of land. He blinked, and the vision vanished.

What in the name of the gods does it all mean? He cupped his nape.

'Master Evandros, the queen is requesting your presence.'

Evan jumped, his musings disrupted. He cast a brief glance at Antioche's handmaiden hovering in the doorway. 'I'll be right there.'

When he re-entered the queen's chamber, the physician and her attendants were fussing about her. He sat next to her, and she clutched his hand.

'I would not let the healer begin until you arrived,' she said, voice wobbling.

'I'm here now,' he said, kissing her on the cheek. He bit his tongue, seeing the healer's disapproval and the irritation etched on her face.

'My queen,' she said, 'may I state again that it is not our practice to have a man in the room while I conduct an examination.'

'I am the queen, healer, and my companion stays.' She waved a hand at her handmaidens. 'Leave us. I will request your assistance if I require further help. Evandros is here to care for me.'

Her attendees departed with a sniff, the door shutting behind them with a definitive loud clank.

'You need to disrobe so I may examine your breasts, belly and aidia—your womanhood,' said the healer, ignoring Evan.

Antioche pulled off her khiton.

'Lie down,' the physician ordered.

He observed the healer poke, press and probe Antioche's body, and he winced when she spread the queen's legs and prodded below the waist. The healer straightened and washed her hands in the basin by the window. Antioche dressed and sat next to him, clutching his hand, waiting for the healer to speak. A slow smile crept across the woman's face.

'I am certain you are with child, though to confirm my

findings I will need you to urinate in this bowl.' She thrust a clay dish at the queen.

'What will you do with it?' he asked.

'Pour the urine over wheat and barley. I will collect more from you over the next few days.'

'Why wheat and barley?' he couldn't help asking.

'If the wheat sprouts, it's a girl; if the barley grows, it is a boy.' The healer sniffed.

'And if nothing happens?' he asked.

The minute smile on the healer's face faded. 'Then there is no baby.'

CHAPTER 3

Evan waited until Antioche fell asleep before leaving the room and sending a guard to collect her handmaidens to wait with her. He did not want her to wake up alone, not after receiving the news of her pregnancy. The prospect of being pregnant delighted and excited her, as it did him, after months with no positive results. He'd mentioned to Antioche that Dexion had sought him out earlier, wanting to talk, and that he'd speak to the youngster after the healer finished. Her response was not what he had expected. She had forbidden him to see the boy. When he'd asked why, she would not give him a reasonable answer but had insisted he not visit Dexion. The strangeness of her behaviour and impassioned reaction added to his disquiet.

He strode along the colonnade and reached the staircase, the sunlight streaming and blinding him. Evan's vision blurred. He gasped as if drowning, and his arms and legs became weightless. He began to choke and sputter and found himself descending into darkness, unable to breathe. His hand hit a hard object. Evan spun around, seeing debris surrounding him, splintered wooden planks and the remains of a mast sinking. He clutched at a nearby floating timber and clambered aboard. He stared across the sea and a memory niggled at him. A vague yet familiar recognition of being amongst the remains of a ship.

Evan stumbled and almost fell headlong down the staircase. He reached out for the pillar and clung to it, the remnants of the illusion fading. He gulped in air, the sound of his heartbeat thundered in his ears. Evan drew a shaky hand across his mouth. There was no way he'd mention this episode to Antioche. She'd insist the healer check him over, and he would not have that woman examine him. He composed himself, shaking off the feeling of uneasiness, and straightened his khiton. He sucked in a deep breath and exhaled, shook his hands and legs.

Evan took the first step down the staircase with trepidation, and then another until he reached the bottom and crossed the courtyard to the accommodation where the servants slept. He paused, collecting himself, before entering a small room, expecting to find Dexion, but he wasn't there. He went into the next chamber.

'Hello, Homer. Have you seen Dexion?' he asked.

Homer grunted. His head almost touched the ceiling and his broad shoulders prevented Evan from seeing if anyone else was in the room. Homer reached for his wax tablet lying on the floor and scribbled in the Linear A script, a series of pictograms, characters that each represented a syllable.

He may be at the stables. He spends a lot of time there with the stable master.

'Ah, yes.' Evan nodded. 'I'll check there.' As he was about to leave, he had second thoughts and spun around on his heel, the question dying on his lips. A pretty young brunette's head poked out from beneath the woollen blanket. He scowled. 'I sent a guard to fetch you and the others to sit with the queen in my absence.'

'I will go to her now,' she said in a meek tone, throwing off the cover, revealing her naked body.

Evan cast an appraising look at Homer, who shrugged in response. He left the big man's room and marched along the walled courtyard until he came across a gate and unlatched it. He walked quickly, trying not to dwell too much on the incident. Using the steps cut into the slope of the acropolis, he strode to the northern gateway, where sentries acknowledged him. A few metres ahead were the stables, protected by the rocky outcrop on the western side and surrounded by ten-foot-high walls. He detected voices and laughter coming from a stall and veered towards the joyous interplay. Evan stood back, witnessing their interchange as the playful horse snuffed at the boy's hair. The stable master laughed and shook her head, stopping short at seeing Evan at the stable entry.

'I didn't mean to interrupt.' He entered the stall. 'I was searching for Dexion and was told he'd be here.'

The youngster ignored him and kept rubbing down the horse's flanks.

'I'd like to take him with me,' he said to the stable master.

The woman shrugged. 'He's completed his chores here for the day.'

Dexion stroked the horse's snout, at which the animal snickered. He handed the brush to the stable master and joined Evan. They left the stables and the overpowering musk and excrement of the equines.

'You and the horse seem to enjoy each other's company,' he commented.

Dexion kicked at a rock. 'Boreas is a calm and good-natured mare.'

'Boreas?'

'She can be windy on some days, and you don't want to be in the stall during those moments,' Dexion answered.

Evan chuckled. 'No, I imagine it would be most unpleasant being stuck in the stall when that happens.'

On re-entering the citadel, Dexion went straight for the water cistern. He reached for an earthenware mug and dipped it into the cold, fresh water.

'Master Evandros,' he offered.

He smiled and shook his head. 'You first.'

After Dexion had his fill, he passed the mug to Evan and wiped his mouth with the back of his hand.

While Evan drank, he noted how the boy could not stop fidgeting.

'What did you want to talk about?' he asked, setting the empty cup on the rock-hewn rim of the reservoir.

'Do you remember how we arrived on the island?' Dexion asked, peering up at him.

Evan clasped his neck, his skin crawling, trying to make sense of the images in his mind. 'We were sent here,' he answered, his mouth dry.

Dexion's face brightened. 'Yes, by the Goddess of Discord. She instructed the Cyclopes and the Stymphalian birds to attack our ship. The High Priestess was knocked out by the broken mast.'

'No ...' Evan said, pressing his lips together. 'The Elders sent us here to mate with the queen's women. As for the High Priestess, she's on Atlantis, attending to the needs of the Mother Goddess and fulfilling her duties as an Elder of the Senate.'

Dexion's chin dropped to his collarbone, his mouth downturned. 'No! That is not what happened. The Cyclopes created a storm and damaged the *Argo*, smashing the mast and setting us adrift. Our friend Jason piloted the ship to the nearest island—this one, the Isle of Hephaistos. The High Priestess is here, in the palace, treated by the healer. The queen and her healer have given you a potion to make you, Phameas, Homer, Leander, Hektor, Jason and the Argonauts forget everything.'

He shook his head. 'All the men, myself included, are here by choice.' As he spoke, refuting the boy's allegations, he could not dismiss the unease and uncertainty he felt or the dejection on Dexion's face.

'They made you believe it to be true through the drug,' said Dexion, eyes imploring. 'If the High Priestess is still on Atlantis, why did you, Homer, Leander, and Hektor leave? What is the reason for you to be here?'

His scalp tingled. *What if Dexion is right?* It might explain the strange dreams and illusions he was having.

'Master Evandros, your father, Divine Zeus, brought you here, to prevent his Family, your Family, from dying. If you do not find the last sacred object of the Mother Goddess, then our lives will change forever. You must stop the birth of the Messiah. You told me about this man and the terrible deeds that follow his death.' Dexion touched his arm.

Evan's tongue stuck to the roof of his mouth. The word *Messiah* struck a chord, and yet he could not fathom why. A vision flashed through his mind in which he was standing atop a mountain, looking over a desert where hordes of people were gathered and waited for a man holding a staff as he negotiated a path on a steep incline.

'Master Evandros, do not drink the wine the queen gives you, and you will see I speak the truth!'

Evan pursed his lips. 'That is enough, Dexion. I will not hear any more of this. You must not repeat this or seek me out to discuss it any further. The queen is pregnant and I will not leave her.'

Dexion's shoulders slumped. Evan clenched his teeth, calming the inner turmoil. His queen needed him and he would not let her down; however, Dexion's words kept ringing in his ears, and the visions he was having were becoming much more frequent.

CHAPTER 4

The sun filtered through the small window, brightening the otherwise dingy room, the beams of light falling across a motionless body that lay in a bed. The shallow sounds of inhalation and exhalation broke the unnatural silence. The woman's shrivelled and fragile frame, covered by a grey woollen blanket, exacerbated the pallor of her face and her long, limp, dull locks. Her eyelids quivered as the sun's rays caressed her face.

'Alexina, wake up,' whispered a gentle voice.

The High Priestess' fingers twitched under the covers.

'My dearest daughter, you must awaken. Your brother and companions need you—they are in trouble. But you cannot help them if you do not waken.' The speaker paused and then in a firmer, deeper tone said, 'Alexina! Open your eyes. *Now.*'

A thickset body blocked the sun's light and cast a shadow over the reposed form of the High Priestess. Her eyelids fluttered open, sensing a familiar presence. She was oblivious to her surroundings, her ice-blue gaze transfixed by the dark timber slats of the ceiling. Her mind was awash with strange images, random pictures that she could not comprehend.

'Whe …' she began, but no words came out. She tried to swallow, her mouth and throat as dry as the woollen-spun coverlet. She opened and closed her mouth, as a baby did when hungry. 'Wh … where … am I?' she breathed.

The older woman spun around, startled.

'Goodness, you are awake.' She moved closer to the bed and gawked at Alexina, dumbfounded.

'Where … am … I?' Alexina repeated, voice hoarse yet clear.

'You are in the palace of Queen Antioche,' the woman replied, laying a hand on her forehead.

'Who are you?' Alexina asked, the words coming out in breathless spurts, as if she had just sprinted the one hundred stades.

'I am the queen's physician.' The healer stepped back to the table, her hands moving, though Alexina could not see what she was doing.

'Why … am I … here?'

'Do you remember anything?' the healer asked, glancing back at her.

Alexina's ice-blue eyes clouded. 'No.'

'Your ship capsized during a storm and you struck your head, which left you unconscious. The damage to the ship made it impossible to sail, and the winds brought you here to the Isle of Hephaistos.'

'How … long … have I … been here?' Alexina asked, her stomach twisting. The odd pictures were now making sense— they were fragments of memories of what had happened since she'd left Atlantis, and of their errand as set by the gods.

'You have been a guest of the queen for five full moons.'

'What?' She tried to sit up but collapsed back onto the bed, puffing. 'It is imperative I see my brother and companions.'

'That is not possible.' The healer moved to the bedside with haste. She shook her head at Alexina and took her slender, pale hand. 'You are unwell, and if you were to stand, you will fall. First, we must build your strength, and when you are stronger, then you may see your brother.'

'Bring my brother here,' Alexina said, her lips trembling. 'I must speak to him.'

The healer smiled and patted her hand. 'There, there, my dear, please calm yourself, I will summon your brother.' She placed Alexina's hand on the bed, moved to the table and grabbed an earthenware cup. 'Drink this, it will help you get better.'

With the woman's aid, the High Priestess drank the bitter-tasting liquid and sank back onto the bed, exhausted.

'I shall return with food and news of your brother,' she said, setting the cup back on the table behind her. 'But for now, I want you to rest.'

Alexina's eyelids were getting heavier, and she tried to resist the drowsiness that threatened to overcome her.

'What was … in that b … b … beverage?' she asked, slurring her words, her tongue thickening and sticking to the roof of her mouth.

'It's a draught to help you sleep.' The older woman's voice sounded far away. 'It will aid your recovery.'

The healer sped through the palace grounds and towards the megaron. Theories as to the High Priestess' remarkable recovery ran through her mind. She stumbled, her heart quickening at the thought of explaining it to the queen. She had been a physician for countless years and had witnessed many of her patients recuperate; however, the miraculous awakening of the High Priestess unnerved her. No one had ever woken from such a potent sleeping draught.

She slowed on nearing the throne room, paused on the

threshold and carefully regarded the queen. She had been glowing and smiling a great deal in the last number of months. Not unusual, given the recent news of her pregnancy. However, the healer was at a loss as to the queen's affection for her consort. Many of the queen's previous companions had lasted one or two weeks, with a few fortunate to last out an entire month. This man was the exception. The Atlantean's sexual prowess must be extraordinary—why else would the queen keep him?

She breathed in, her ample bosom rising, exhaled and approached the throne, squelching any apprehension she felt before stopping before her ruler. Queen Antioche acknowledged her with a slight nod and continued to speak to her advisers.

'When the Persian captain next docks, have him bring more silks for the purple clothes they so desire. If the bargain is not to his liking, then tell him we will take our trade to our Hittite neighbours.' The queen thrust the document at an adviser.

The others nodded, busily scribbling her instructions. She gave additional directives, at which her bursar interjected with a few questions and acknowledged the queen's response before making a notation. The queen dismissed them with a wave and laid a hand on her flat stomach. She smiled with such content that the healer felt inclined to leave.

Almost.

'Are you here to see how my baby fares?' the queen asked.

The woman wrung her hands. 'The High Priestess is awake.'

The queen sprang to her feet. 'What? Is that possible?'

The healer mopped her sweaty brow. 'I hadn't expected so, but she has roused.'

'The Goddess of Discord assured me the draught would keep the High Priestess asleep forever. Given she hasn't eaten food throughout these months, I assumed she would never wake again.'

'She is a high priestess. Perhaps she has powers that we cannot even fathom.' The healer swallowed, and bit her lip.

'Double the dose.' The queen sat back down on her throne.

'She is weak, and if I increase the amount, it may kill her,' the physician said. 'Given she is a high priestess, and someone who is favoured by the gods, is it wise to precipitate her death?'

The queen pursed her lips, tapping her fingertips on the armrests of the throne. She followed the smoke from the hearth as it escaped into the cloudless blue sky through the opening in the roof. Her jaw tightened, and she closed her eyes for a moment. She finally replied, 'No, I do not want to incur the wrath of the gods by slaying their high priestess. What do you suggest we do?'

'Provide her with sustenance and I will continue to administer her the sleeping potion,' the healer answered.

The queen nodded. 'And what of our stores? How do we fare?'

'There is very little left of both elixirs. If we maintain the same dosage for all the men, I expect to run out of our supplies by the end of this next full moon. I don't need as much of the sleeping draught, and given the patient is very thin, it may only last a few new moons.'

'This is unfortunate news.' The queen sighed. 'How many Amazons are pregnant?'

The healer beamed. 'At least three-quarters of the women who have come to me have missed their cycle in the past four full moons.'

'That is very good.' The queen smiled. 'Is there anything else you wish to discuss?'

'No, my queen.' The healer bowed her head.

'Keep me apprised of our guest's condition.'

'Of course,' the physician acknowledged and left the megaron.

CHAPTER 5

Alexina awoke to the tantalising smell of roasted lamb, the heady aroma of caramelised onion and another mouth-watering scent she did not recognise. She witnessed the healer carrying a steaming bowl into the room.

'That smells wonderful,' she said in a hoarse voice. Her throat ached and she found it difficult to form words after not speaking for many months.

'Oh, good, you are awake.' The healer put the bowl on the table. 'You need to sit up.'

Alexina nodded. Her arms shook as she struggled upright, and small beads of perspiration glistened on her forehead. Her chest heaved, and she panted. The simple effort of sitting took all her strength. She swayed from side to side, her head swimming, and slid sideways, unable to stop the momentum. Alexina felt the steady, powerful arm of the healer about her shoulders. She closed her eyes against the rising tide of light-headedness.

'Perhaps you should lie back down,' the healer said, brow furrowed.

'No! It will soon pass,' Alexina said in a firm voice. She

clutched at the woollen blanket, her hands trembling, took a long, steadying breath and opened her eyes. She maintained strong eye contact with the healer, lines etched on her face and around her mouth. 'I am fine now,' she told her.

The healer tut-tutted.

'Mistress Healer, I can sit on my own,' Alexina said, shrinking away from the woman's support.

The older female blew through her nose and lowered her arm but did not move until Alexina sat without wobbling. Only then did she pick up the bowl of soup.

'Now,' she said, 'take a little sip at a time. Your throat has become lazy and needs to remember how to swallow.'

She held the bowl out to Alexina, whose hands trembled, the contents sloshing over the sides.

'Here, let me help you.' The healer steadied the dish, Alexina's thin, bloodless fingers a sharp contrast to the healer's thicker tanned ones. Alexina's taste buds tingled and her mouth watered at the anticipation, and she took a mouthful of the warm, flavoursome liquid. She coughed and spluttered. The healer patted her on the back.

'Try again,' said the physician. She held the bowl to Alexina's mouth. 'That's better, nice and slow.'

She fought against the clicking and shutting of her throat as it resisted the smooth, tasty broth. The more she drank, the easier it became. She felt the warm liquid slide down her oesophagus and pool in her stomach. She let her hands slide from the bowl.

'Enough,' she said and flopped back onto the bed.

The healer patted her hand and straightened. 'I will bring more after you have rested.'

She did not hear the woman leave as she drifted off to sleep, but she wondered why her brother and the others had not yet come to see her.

When she next woke, it was dark and she saw stars glittering like jewels in the night sky through the window. She inspected the bare room. The objects on the table captured her interest. She pushed herself upright, threw off the blanket and gasped. She had lost so much weight; bones stuck out and her skin was almost translucent, the blue veins as clear as the lines on a map. Alexina swung her limbs over the side and shivered, the chill seeping from the stone floor through the soles of her feet. She leaned forward and heaved herself into a standing position. Her legs quaked, and the tremors grew stronger, her entire body shaking. She collapsed onto the bed and lifted a tremulous hand to brush the hair from her face. She glowered at the moonlit ceiling and banged a fist against the bed. She forced herself to sit up again.

Alexina attempted to stand once more. Her limbs shook like an inner earthquake, but she refused to give up and remained standing until her legs buckled. With a small triumphant smile, she slumped onto the bed, exhausted. She hoisted her legs and snuggled under the woollen blanket, sinking with relief into the soft folds, where sleep soon enveloped her.

Next time she would walk.

The sound of people talking in low voices roused her into wakefulness. Not wanting to alert them, she kept her eyes closed. As they continued speaking, she realised it was coming from outside. She popped open an eye and peeked through the crack of the doorway. She didn't see anyone but recognised the healer's voice. From the healer's deferential responses, the other person commanded authority. She strained to listen to what they were discussing.

'What I want to know is how much longer she can live if you are to keep administering the potion?' the woman demanded.

'If she continues to eat when awake, the likelihood is greater. However'—the healer's tone changed—'I am concerned she may die if not given enough nourishment.'

'We cannot allow that to happen, not one so close to the gods. My concern is her growing power, and there is no telling what she is capable of once she has regained her strength.'

'It's possible she does not have any powers, Your Highness,' the healer said.

'Yes, then there is the risk she still has them. She is a high priestess. How can I jeopardise what we have accomplished on that possibility and not incur the wrath of the gods?' the queen said. 'I must also consider Evandros, and although his recollection is altered, he hasn't forgotten his sister or companions. I want to avoid testing his memory. It would not serve me well if he does start to remember.'

Alexina tensed hearing Evandros' name. *What is wrong with his memory? And why hasn't he come to see me?*

'What is it?' snapped the queen.

Alexina shook off her thoughts and concentrated on the conversation.

'Is it time to let these men and the High Priestess leave and find other male sources, ones that are expendable?'

'That is not an acceptable option.'

'We may not have a choice, your Highness. This female is held in tremendous esteem by her people and they are Atlanteans, who are favoured by the gods.'

There was a lengthy pause. 'Make the High Priestess comfortable until I make a decision. There is much to consider.'

'I will await your decision, Your Highness.'

Alexina's ears pricked when the queen left and she shut her eyes, hearing the healer enter the room. Her heart pounded as she tried to maintain her composure, pretending to be asleep. She felt the healer's proximity from the warmth of her body.

'You and I have much to discuss,' the woman whispered. 'I would like to learn about your methods used for cures.' The healer patted her hand with affection. 'I will come back with food. We need to strengthen you.'

When Alexina was certain the physician had left, she opened her eyes. The healer's last comment was not one of chance. Could the woman have known she was awake, and that she might have overheard their conversation? She bit her bottom lip. Perhaps the healer was going to help her. She needed to contact Evandros and the others. It had to be soon, for she did not know how much time she had before the queen announced her decision.

CHAPTER 6

Alexina studied the filtering sunlight that cast strange shadowy shapes on the uneven surface of the ceiling. An odd pattern disturbed her concentration. She tilted her head to one side and then the other. The harder she concentrated, the more familiar the pattern became. The refracting light grew larger and brighter. She raised a palsied hand to shield her eyes. When that didn't help, she squeezed her eyes shut, and even then her eyelids glowed within. The brilliant luminescence faded as quick as it had begun.

'Open your eyes, daughter.'

She gawked at the figure at the foot of the bed. 'Mother!'

The Mother Goddess was silent and stood as still as a statue. She squirmed under Mother's unrelenting scrutiny.

'Alexina.'

She flinched at Mother's voice reverberating in the small room.

'I have placed you in grave danger, and now my greatest and strongest of all high priestesses is too weak to fight back.'

'Mother?' she asked, puzzled.

The Mother Goddess' visage darkened.

'Evandros needed to fulfil a prophecy, but it has gone on long enough.'

She struggled into a seated position.

The Mother Goddess' eyes grew black.

She wheezed as she leaned her skeletal frame against the wall. 'I do not understand.'

'Eris interfering and changing the direction of the *Argo* was fortuitous. However, you being harmed was not. I hoped you'd recover sooner, given the powers you received from the high priestesses of the past, and when you did not waken, I encouraged the healer to reduce the potion she was giving you,' said the Mother Goddess.

The lines on her forehead deepened. 'What did Evandros need to do? Is that why he has not come to see me?'

'He has fulfilled his duty. It sets the bridge between the two worlds.'

She tried to make sense of the cryptic message, but unable to decipher what the Mother Goddess meant, she instead pondered the second revelation. 'I understand it was not only wisdom I acquired communing with the high priestesses.' She recalled being cold, and the omnipotent essences of the ancient high priestesses, their voices whispering, imparting vast aeons of experiences and knowledge to her, their energy melding with hers. 'I could not ignite their power, and an unknown force shut off access to my mind.'

'Now you have wakened, harness the combined abilities of those who came before you. First, build your strength and leave this place.' The Mother Goddess cocked her head. 'The healer is returning.' The goddess shimmered.

'Wait!' Alexina beseeched, hand outstretched. 'Why didn't you help us to escape and heal me?'

'Evandros hadn't accomplished what I needed him to do; I did not take into account how the time shifting would affect his physiology.'

'"Time shifting"?' *Why is the condition of Evandros' body important to Mother?*

The hair on her arms stood on end. She remembered one of the old high priestesses mentioning the same phrase, and how the gods harnessed it to move mortals through the ages.

'You have always known Evandros was different,' said the Mother Goddess.

'I knew it! He's an impostor!'

The Mother Goddess shook her head. 'No, he is your brother. Your blood is the same. His exceptional abilities come from the experiences he has had and are why he was chosen to lead. He is essential to fighting the Minotaur and defeating the Dark Master. You, my dear daughter, are the one to restore the way of the gods.' The goddess shimmered. 'Remember the lessons of the high priestesses, for in them you will find answers.'

Alexina drooped and slid against the wall, seeking its strength from the masonry. What had happened to Evandros? Why was he different to the brother she had grown up with? There were vestiges of his mannerisms and words she recognised in him, yet there were elements of his behaviour, the darkness of his psyche and odd statements that were not the brother she knew and loved. Where had the gods sent him to change him so?

She let herself drift into a slumber, her mind pulled elsewhere and deeper until she could no longer hear the noises outside. She floated along in a dreamlike state until she arrived at the cavern on Thira. She entered the dark cave, seated herself on the stone floor and waited. One by one, the old high priestesses came to her and recounted their stories and words of enlightenment. She jolted awake hours later and bolted upright, the woollen blanket falling aside to crumple at her emaciated waist. Her ice-blue eyes sparkled, a striking contrast to her wan face.

'I know what to do! Thank you, Mother and my dear sisters. The restoration and unification of Mother's gifts with her tree is the solution.'

Alexina lay back and fell asleep, smiling.

CHAPTER 7

The following day, Alexina waited for the healer to leave, but the woman was fussing and making sure she ate everything in the bowl. She then helped her bathe and settled her back into bed.

'I must admit,' the healer was saying, 'it was a surprise to learn there were survivors from the destruction of Atlantis. The waters in the region were impassable for centuries. I recall the legends of ships swallowed whole after sailing too close to the turbulent seas. Old travelling storytellers told how day became night, and when the earth shook for many days, and where an entire island sank into the sea, engulfing humans and animals.' The healer tucked the blanket around her. 'How did your people escape, and where did they go? No such stories were told about anyone surviving the terrible cataclysm.'

'It was written in our historical annals. The High Priestess knew of the coming tragedy—she learnt of the impending devastation through a portent. For many months the earth trembled and shook. She instructed the citizens to flee and sail to Krete. While a flotilla left Atlantis, numerous remained, and then the island stopped shaking. They repaired damaged homes and toiled the land to prepare for sowing. During this period of stability, the inhabitants who had fled went back to the island. Soon after, the mountain of Hephaistos exploded without warning and sank into the sea. The ships closest to Thira overturned in gigantic waves and were never seen again. My ancestors, those of my companions and others escaped. The impetus of the heaving swells drove the ships westwards. Divine Poseidon guided them beyond the Pillars of Herakles and to an unfamiliar land. We have lived there since, obeying the wishes of the gods and building a new Atlantis.' Alexina swallowed a lump in her throat at the memory of her parents and sister priestesses.

'You must miss your home.' The healer picked up the bowl.

'What we are doing is critical and takes precedence over personal needs and feelings.' She felt hollow. Everything they had endured and suffered had been for nought. 'Why has the queen held us captive?' It was a question she had wanted to ask since awakening.

The healer avoided eye contact and her gaze flittered over the High Priestess' head, gripping the bowl so tight Alexina thought it would crack. 'You must consider the queen's position. Each year, fewer babies are born, and our numbers are declining. When she learnt there was a ship heading for our island filled with males, she did what any leader would do to ensure our existence.'

Alexina sat up. 'How did she know about our ship and that we would shipwreck here, on this island, out of so many?'

'The Goddess of Discord visited the queen and told her about Atlanteans being on the ship and to keep you here until such time the men failed to be productive.'

'Eris,' she hissed. 'I should have known. She and the Dark Master will do anything to prevent our success.' She grabbed the healer's hand. 'You must help me free my brother and companions.'

The woman pulled her hand from Alexina's. 'I will not betray my queen.'

'I am not asking you to conspire against your queen, but if we remain here, what you have striven for is fruitless and the entrapment of men won't matter.'

'Explain yourself. What do the Goddess of Discord and this Dark Master seek, and why do they want to stop you from leaving here?' the healer asked.

'The Dark Master, Kronos, once ruled, as Divine Zeus and his Family do now. After the Titanic war between the Titans and younger gods, Divine Zeus cast him into Tartaros, and he has since escaped. He plans to bring another god, one to replace the rule of our gods, and he and his son will become the sole immortals of this world. Divine Zeus and his Family have charged us with preventing the birth of this new god. As to Eris, she sided with him over a squabble with the other gods when she did not get invited to the wedding of Peleus and Thetis. She has meddled and caused much mayhem, impeding our progress.' The words rushed out of her mouth as she tried to press the importance of their quest.

'What must you do to stop the Dark Master?'

She reclined against the stone-cold wall and shivered. She gathered the blanket around her shoulders. 'We must restore the sacred relics of the Mother Goddess on the island of Krete, her and my people's ancestral home. There is one left to find. If we succeed, then the reign of the gods continues. If we do not, this life we cherish ceases to exist.'

The healer sucked in a sharp breath. 'Are you certain of this?'

'Divine Poseidon visited the Elders and explained what was to transpire, instructing a select group to prevent the machinations of the Dark Master. Later, we learnt the Oracle of Delphi had foreseen this event and given her prophecy to a philosopher of repute, who we met in Athens. He confirmed our arrival was part of the premonition and we were to stop the birth of this new god,' she replied.

'Why were you chosen and not the Amazons, or warriors from Greece or the Hittite soldiers?'

'The gods chose us by virtue of our lineage.'

'Are you saying you're of divine blood?' The physician's eyes grew large, the whites surrounding the irises stark and luminous as the moon.

She nodded. 'My ancestors coupled with the gods, siring a new Atlantis, a practice that has continued through the centuries. Many of us owe our parentage to the gods. My siblings, Evandros and Homer, and companions, Leander and Hektor, were fathered by an Olympian God.'

The colour drained from the healer's face. Alexina lurched forward and took the woman's hand, giving it a reassuring squeeze.

'What have we done? We've duped and ensnared the children of the gods! They shall punish us for our impiety. I must tell the queen.'

'Wait!' She clung to the healer's hand.

'I must go!' The healer tried to yank her hand from Alexina's grasp.

'The gods will not harm you, for the Goddess of Discord tricked you into capturing us.'

'We have shamed Divine Hephaistos and Artemis!'

'I will tell the gods you were unwitting victims in a larger scheme, set by the Dark Master. But first, please explain why my brother'—she hesitated, the pain in the back of her throat growing —'Leander and the others have not come to see me.'

The healer's shoulders drooped, and she sat with a heavy thud on the edge of the bed, the timber frame creaking. 'They have forgotten you.'

Alexina's heart skipped a beat. 'Wha ...?'

'It is not of their doing,' the healer added in a rush. 'We have given them an elixir to make them forget—not their names but what they were doing. The Goddess of Discord told the queen about the serum, where to buy it and how much to give.' The older woman lowered her head. 'I've been providing the concoction for the men and one for you.'

She rubbed her eyes and swallowed back the tears that threatened to spill. 'What of the boy, Dexion?'

'He is unharmed and given tasks to keep him away from the others.'

'I would like to see him,' said Alexina.

'I'll arrange it.' The other woman stood.

'Is there an antidote to the potion you have been giving my brother and the others?'

'Not to my knowledge.'

'How long would it take for the elixir to be dispelled from their bodies, if you stop giving it to them?'

The healer pursed her lips and replied, 'They've been taking it for many months, and it may take as long for their bodies to be free of the effects.'

'Now that you know what is happening, will you stop making the memory loss potion?'

'I will do my best to convince the queen.'

Alexina nodded. The healer, with head lowered, shuffled out the door. Alexina lay back on the bed, trying to make sense of what she had learnt from her discussion with the Mother Goddess and the Amazon. The mystery centred around Evandros. The question was, why? He was pivotal to the quest—for what purpose, she could not determine. Not yet.

CHAPTER 8

Alexina ran her fingers through her long black hair and wished for a mirror. Not that she was vain, she just wanted to see the effects of the drug they administered her. She sighed and then straightened her drab apparel and ironed out the invisible creases on the woollen blanket. Her ears twitched at the sound of muted voices approaching. She took a long steadying breath and placed her hands on her lap, fingers interlocking. The chatter grew stronger, one voice younger than the familiar tones of the healer. She fixed her gaze on the doorway and forced herself to remain still and poised. A shadow paused on the threshold, and all talking ceased.

'High Priestess!'

Before she could react or speak, a skinny, wiry body catapulted across the room and flung themselves into her arms. She clung to the boy, unable to stop weeping. She clasped his face and smiled, relieved to see him. Dexion sat on the edge, eyes sparkling.

'I am so glad you are alive!' he said. 'I didn't know where they kept you.'

She wiped the joyful tears from her cheeks. 'As am I.' She took his tanned hands, a sharp contrast to her white, thin, almost skeletal ones.

'You must be quick,' said the healer, rubbing her palms up and down her hips. 'The chief cook will miss the boy if he doesn't report to her for kitchen duties.'

'Dexion, have you had any communication with the gods during our time here?' she asked.

He pursed his lips. 'I've tried many times, but I cannot sense their presence.' His smile faded.

'It is not of your doing.' She gave his hand a reassuring squeeze. 'The Dark Master has somehow blocked our ability to reach out to the gods.' She leaned forward and murmured, 'Mother came and announced there was a reason we had to come here, but now we must leave.'

'How?' he whispered. 'The queen has guards everywhere, and Master Evandros and all the men have lost their memories. I've tried to speak to Master Evandros, but the queen keeps him in her chambers.'

'What do you mean the queen keeps Evandros in her room? Is he her prisoner?'

He shrugged. 'I don't think so. When they are not in her room, he remains at her side much of the time.'

She pressed her lips together as she digested his news. *Of what purpose and importance is the union between Evandros and the queen?*

'What is it?' he asked, seeing the troubled expression on her face.

'I am uncertain. Whatever the significance of our being here, it's over. Dexion, you are my link to what is happening outside this room, and I need you to find a way for us to leave.'

'I have been exploring the palace for a secret passage for us to escape,' he said. 'I've searched everywhere.'

'I am confident you have, but keep seeking in every part of the palace. There must also be a way to break the spell the men are under.' She paused and beckoned the healer, who hovered by the door, wringing her hands. 'Is there a way out of the fortifications without being seen?'

The physician hesitated and bit her lip. After a lengthy pause, she answered. 'There are rumours of a secret passage in the north wall that leads into the forest. However, no one has ever found it.'

'I will find it,' he said, sitting straighter, with a gleam of certainty in his eyes.

'The boy has to leave, *now*,' the healer hissed, her eyes darting from the two occupants in the room to the exterior.

Alexina gripped his hands. 'I believe you will, and when you do, return here and tell me. In the meantime, we must devise a plan to escape.'

'The guards will come to search for him if he doesn't depart this instant, and he'll be locked away,' said the healer in a low, urgent tone.

'Go on, Dexion. Find the passage, and please come back soon.' She squeezed his hands and then let go.

He nodded and without a word slipped out of the room, dashing past the healer. From the strained appearance of the woman's face, Alexina thought she would collapse. The healer's body sagged, and the lines around her mouth and eyes deepened and became more hollowed.

'I cannot allow the boy to visit again,' she said, her voice flat and low-spirited. 'If the queen was to learn I brought him here, she would stop me from nursing you and order your demise.'

'As queen, she must be reasonable and perceptive when dealing with matters of the state and dignitaries,' said Alexina. 'I am sure once she learns the significance of our quest, she'll let us depart.'

'The queen's first and foremost duty is the security of her people, even if it means the sacrifice of those who intend no harm.

She is fulfilling that obligation, or our world will cease to prevail,' said the healer.

'I understand your plight, and the measures taken to keep your bloodline alive. However, the quest of the gods is more important than your problems. If we cannot continue our mission to prevent the Dark Master from being victorious, our gods cease to exist.' She closed her eyes. 'I am tired. I would like to rest now.' She slid under the blanket and rolled onto her side, facing away from the healer.

CHAPTER 9

D exion felt hopeful for the first time since landing on the
island. He had watched on powerlessly as his friends had
become bewitched and enslaved by the queen and her Amazons.
The queen had been very hospitable during the early days of their
arrival, offering food and beverage to half-starved men who had
battled against the catastrophic and tumultuous waters produced
by the Cyclopes. It was a miracle they had made it to the Island of
Hephaistos, and a day he would never forget. These hardened
mariners, who had seen the most terrible of things sailing and on
land, reduced to mere sheep at the sight of attractive female
warriors. His companions, having fought and killed to stay alive,
he had not expected to see comply and be commanded. Not even
Master Evandros, someone he admired—he knew no other as
clever or resourceful.

The queen invited them to the palace, and from then on, he
noticed a strange transformation within the men. At first, there
was nothing too obvious in their behaviour to suggest something
untoward was occurring, but as the days stretched into weeks, he
saw the steady progression of forgetfulness, lethargy, and wanton

sexual activities. He approached Master Evandros to ask when they would return to the beach to fix the *Argo*. What he got in response disturbed him. The man he knew and idolised had forgot about the quest and that he was from the future. Dexion had realised in that moment that they were in trouble.

After seeing the High Priestess, Dexion spent what time he had searching the palace for a secret passage, but as yet, it remained undiscovered. He was in the kitchen washing dishes when he overheard that the queen was leaving the palace to attend to business at the port. As soon as he finished his chores, he raced to his room and grabbed the board game Senet. He headed for the queen's quarters and found the tall, muscular man in the garden, lying on the grass, arms crossed under his head and staring up at the cloudless blue sky.

'Master Evandros,' he called out. The Atlantean turned his head, and Dexion held up the board game. 'I thought we could play a few rounds of Senet. It has been a while since we've had a game.'

His friend grinned and sat up. 'A good idea, Dexion, and it will help pass the time until Queen Antioche returns.'

Dexion placed the cedar board on the grass between them. He withdrew the sticks and fourteen pieces hidden in a drawer on the side of the board and passed seven pawns to his friend. He then pulled out two more game pieces as Master Evandros reclined back onto his side, his head propped on a hand.

'Would you like to go first?' he asked.

'Hmm ... I am going to need all the advantages I can get since you are the grand master of this game.'

Dexion rejoiced at how Master Evandros remembered the many games they had played and asked the goddess Mnemosyne to help his friend regain his memory. He gave him two coloured sticks, both sides etched in dots showing the number of moves a player could make. His friend threw the rods and moved his pawn five places. Dexion had his turn. They played in silence, concentrating on the strategy of the game and who could outwit the other's tactics.

'Ah ... you win!' His friend laughed. 'Why don't I learn that a stupid move across the House of Water will cost me the game every time?'

Dexion grinned. 'Perhaps you are expecting a change of position before I withdraw my piece from the House of Happiness.' He gave him an eager smile. 'Another game?'

'Why not? I may just beat you this time,' Evandros replied with a laugh. He sat up, crossing his legs, and studied the board as Dexion made his first move. The Atlantean then tossed the rods and moved his piece.

'May I ask you a question, Master Evandros?'

'Always, Dexion.'

He threw the sticks and placed another pawn on the board. 'Do you remember how we met?'

His friend threw him a quick and easy grin. 'How could I forget? You rescued me from two prostitutes.' He shook the sticks in his palm and dropped them, then moved his pawn forward.

'Can you recall how you got there, to the port of Hippo Regius?' Dexion asked, sliding his pawn across to block further attempts.

'I ... I arrived on a merchant ship,' came the hesitant reply.

He gave a brief nod. 'That is right. However, that is not all. A sailor on a merchant ship spotted you floating on debris and thought you were dead until they rescued you. You became a member of the crew and that is how you met Phameas. Afterwards, your ship landed at Hippo Regius.' He cocked his head to the side. 'Do you remember that?'

Something flickered across the Atlantean's face. 'Why was I unconscious?' he asked.

'Your father, Divine Zeus, put you there.'

'Why would he do that?'

He plunged into the story, words gushing from his mouth. 'Divine Zeus brought you back from the future, a time you called the twenty-first century, where you are an architect. He brought you here to locate the sacred objects of the Mother Goddess and to preserve the way of the gods.' His elbows dug into his thighs as he leaned towards the board game. His friend's face paled. 'You, Phameas and I got off at Carthage, where you uncovered a riddle in a scroll housed in the library. You solved the puzzle and learnt we needed to go to Aegyptos to get an object, a golden serpent. Before we left, Divine Zeus ordered you to rescue your sister, the High Priestess and Masters Leander, Homer and Hektor. We sailed to the city of Kyrene, where the king held them prisoner. This was when Master Homer was beaten up by the king's soldiers, his throat so badly damaged he lost the ability to speak ever again.' He gulped, catching his breath. 'You saved the High Priestess and your companions, and we continued our voyage to Aegyptos.'

'Ah ... there you are.'

Dexion and the Atlantean jumped to their feet as the queen of the Amazons wandered over.

'My queen, you have returned.' He took her hand.

'Yes, and I missed you,' she said, smiling up at him. Her attention was then diverted to the object on the ground. 'What is the game that you are playing?'

'It is called Senet, a game from the lands of Egypt,' he replied. 'Dexion helped me pass the time while you were away.'

'You have been to the mysterious deserts of the pharaohs,' she said, her face clouding.

'Hmm ... yes, perhaps so,' he said, glancing down at the game, 'not that I can recall travelling there.'

'Well,' she said, spinning on her heel with a sniff, forcing him to let go of her hand, 'I need your presence, if you have finished playing your little game.'

'Yes, we have,' he acknowledged with a slight bow of his head. The queen sashayed away, ignoring Dexion.

His friend winked at him. 'Bring the game back here tomorrow, just after noon. We will play again.' He caught up with the queen, and with her entourage of royal guards, they disappeared through the gateway and into the queen's private quarters.

The following day, Dexion went back to the garden and set up the game while he waited for his friend. Just as he finished, the tall man entered the enclosed grounds, carrying a plate of fruit.

'I thought some food might help as we played,' he said, setting the laden dish down.

Dexion reached for a fig and bit into it, grinning.

'I must admit, the story you told me yesterday sounds unbelievable,' he said, sitting on the grass. 'In particular, the part where you said I am from the future. I keep having strange dreams. Images of contraptions that soar in the air and big ships made from strange grey material other than wood monopolise my mind … it is not possible such things exist.'

'Not here and now they don't,' Dexion said, throwing the sticks and moving his pawn. 'They do where you come from. You even drew a picture of a plane—that's what you called it—for Phameas, Homer and me while we were in Corinth. It soars through the air like a bird.'

The Atlantean rubbed his forehead. 'No, no. Not probable.'

'Master Evandros, do you remember what I told you about how we arrived here, on the island?'

He pursed his lips, and his brow furrowed, etched in deep lines. 'We … um … someone shipwrecked our ship!'

Dexion nodded and pressed him further. 'What else?'

'Ah … we hit a sandbar,' he replied, though it sounded more like a question than a statement.

'No, Master Evandros, the Goddess of Discord sent the Cyclopes and the Stymphalian birds to attack our ship and set the *Argo* off course,' Dexion explained. 'We were adrift for many days and the High Priestess was knocked unconscious in the terrible storm, and we landed here. The High Priestess is being nursed by the queen's healer.'

'Why would the Goddess of Discord want to harm us?' asked the Atlantean. 'It makes little sense. We are loyal servants of the gods.'

'She sided with the Dark Master, Kronos, who wants Mother's sacred objects to destroy the gods and replace them with a new god. You called him the "Messiah".'

He noticed a spark of familiarity flicker across his friend's face.

'What happened after we arrived in Egypt?' Evan asked in a quiet voice.

Dexion's heart lifted and he struggled not to sound too excited or eager as he answered the question. 'We sailed for Thebes, and that's where you found the golden serpent. The gods warned us only the High Priestess could touch the objects, and when the High Priest of Ra tried to steal it, the serpent killed him. Afterwards, we sailed back up the Nile to Naukratis, where you bargained a fare for our passage on a ship to Krete. However, divine forces altered our destination and we arrived at Pylos. We remained guests of the king for many weeks, until the High Priestess gifted his wife with a son. From there we travelled to Messene and when we left, a boy called Theodoros, who sought adventure, followed us. Brigands who hunted Theo attacked us, and one of them stabbed you.' He pointed at the Atlantean's side, and Evandros winced, touching his ribcage.

'The Mother Goddess saved you, and by morning we

journeyed to Tegea to find people who would take Theodoros back to his family in Messene. We then travelled to Corinth, where a princess driving a chariot almost ran us over. You berated her, at which she was not pleased, and she fled in anger. She later came back with her father, the king of Mykenae and his warriors. That's when the High Priestess used the red light to protect us.' He paled. 'What happened next was awful. As the horsemen and soldiers advanced towards us, they walked into the red shield. It burnt off their limbs.'

The Atlantean swallowed.

'I will never forget their screams,' Dexion said. His mahogany-brown eyes grew darker against the complexion of his face. 'We continued to Corinth with no further problems and gained passage on the *Argo*, captained by Jason.'

'Jason! He and his men are here with us!' his friend said, eyes brightening.

'Yes.' Dexion nodded. 'He sailed across the gulf and the harpies attacked and killed one of his crewmen. You jumped after the harpy where you both fell into the sea. You fought the harpy, who drowned, and mermaids saved you. We made it to the other side and left Jason and his men to go to Delphi, where you met Pythia, who told you about the Minotaur and where to find the other relics.' He hesitated, noting the struggle of recognition on the Atlantean's face, but when he didn't get a further response, he continued.

'On leaving Delphi, we got caught in an earthquake, and you fell into the chasm. Homer, Hektor and Phameas saved you from falling into the abyss. Afterwards, you led us to Athens using the maps the king of Pylos gave you. There, we met Plato, who helped us and let us stay at his home, then guided us to Piraeus. We reunited with Jason and his men, who took us to Thira, where we recovered an object that you must use against the Minotaur. Just as we set sail to leave Thira and go to Krete, Skylla, a sea monster, attacked our ship. The Goddess of Discord sent her. The monster killed two of Jason's men, but Divine Poseidon and Ares came to help and stopped her. It was when we were sailing to Krete that the Cyclopes first arrived and set the *Argo* off course. They attacked again and a third time, when we crashed here.'

Dexion fell silent and examined his friend, who was staring at the board game, holding a pawn, forgotten in the story's telling.

The Atlantean set the piece aside, dragged a hand over his mouth and blinked at him. 'It all sounds absurd, but'—he swallowed—'in my heart, it feels true. Why can't I remember any of it?' Troubled, he gave the unfinished game a once-over, the pieces on the board facing off against each other in a stalemate. With a finger, he pushed over one of his pawns in defeat.

'You and the other men are being given something to forget,' replied Dexion. 'There is a secret passage somewhere in the palace, and I am going to find it so we all can leave, and your memories will return.'

His friend stood. 'Do you think I will forget what you have told me?'

'I don't know,' he said, shrugging. 'You remembered to come back today and what I said yesterday.'

'Yes, that is a positive sign.' He made to withdraw. 'Good luck in your search.'

Encouraged by the Atlantean's words, Dexion left the garden, dropping the game in his room before making his way to muck out the horse stables. He thought of a plan for their escape and knew it must work, or they'd never leave.

CHAPTER 10

Hephaistos limped up the gilded steps of the throne room, the massive golden doors swinging inwards as he alighted the top step. He narrowed his eyes and crossed the opaque marble floor, his sole interest centred on the couple who sat at the head of the thrones.

'Good Hephaistos, what is the ma ...?' Hestia's words faded as she took in the stormy countenance of the God of the Forge.

He halted at the foot of the dais, legs planted wide, swinging his hammer back and forth as he eyeballed the King of the Gods.

'I wish for you to explain why we waited so long to help Evandros and his companions while the Amazons incarcerated them?' he asked. The lame god tossed his head and added, 'I have just arrived from Krete, and the Minotaur stirs. Had we intervened earlier, Evandros would have slain Minos' beast before it wakened. Now, the Minotaur will regain his strength when they arrive on the island and be difficult to maim or kill.'

Zeus' ice-blue eyes flashed, then darkened for a split second before returning to their normal hue. Hestia spoke before he responded.

'I must agree with Hephaistos. However, I find it unusual that you have allowed the transgression of the Amazons to continue without some *intervention.' The Goddess of the Hearth eyeballed Zeus, her penetrating icy gaze spearing him to the seat.*

'They have wasted precious time on Lemnos with the Amazons,' *Athene said, shuddering and shaking her head in distaste.*

'And where is Poseidon?' *Ares asked with a raised brow, pointing at the Sea God's empty throne.* 'He is always the voice of opposition, not the saccharine Hephaistos.'

'It was Mother who wanted the Atlanteans to remain on the island. She mandated that Evandros fulfil a prophecy, and they had to remain with the Amazons until he executed his part,' *he replied.* 'As for Poseidon, he is making sure the Argo and everyone on board arrive on Krete without further interruptions.'

'Prophecy? What prophecy did your spawn need to complete?' *asked Hera, surprised.* 'Why wasn't I informed?'

'There is no point worrying about the welfare of the Atlanteans and the Argonauts. We should direct our efforts to ensuring they reach Krete free from further problems and calamities. These delays could have been avoided if we had provided guidance from the start of their journey,' *Hades expressed in disapproval.*

'Hades' argument is sound,' *said Ares with a churlish snarl.* 'What was it you declared ... that we cannot interfere or administer aid for it will alert Kronos as to what we are doing? And now it's fine to do so? We are fools for relying on feeble mortals to do what we should have done, rather than wait for them to find Mother's objects.'

'Enough!' *Zeus stormed to his feet, and lightning flashed overhead, followed by rolling thunder, sending shock waves across the earth.*

Ares narrowed his eyes, crossed his arms and huffed. Aphrodite and Demeter took a step back, while the others stood tall and thrust their shoulders back under the glower of the towering figure of Zeus.

'I need not justify my actions!' *Zeus drew in a deep, angry breath.* 'We cannot underestimate Kronos or Eris. They are formidable opponents and together, they can destroy all we have worked for and created. It is as important to learn why Eris arranged such an elaborate* scheme to ensnare Evandros and his fellow companions and keep the High Priestess unconscious as it is to find out how dreaded Kronos intends to use Mother's possessions. What we must prepare for is the ultimate battle between Evandros, the Minotaur and Kronos.'

'If Evandros survives the bout with the Minotaur, which I don't believe he can, but if he does, how is he to destroy Kronos? He is a Titan and powerful,' asked Athene.

'The probability of Evandros surviving the might of Kronos is remote,' said Apollo, tone as cold as the snow on the peak of Mount Olympos. 'The fact is, the Minotaur will kill him. What is the point in using this mortal who cannot defeat an immortal?'

'When I created the Race of Silver, I intended that they would honour us with supplication and tributes, but greed and aberrant behaviour saw to their demise. Then we produced a new specimen of man, the Race of Bronze, to right the wrongs of their forebears, but once again we could not permit these mortals with their fractious antics to live. The Atlanteans, neither Man of Silver nor Man of Bronze, are the union of the best elements of the two races. For thousands of years they flourished and ruled with piety until they discovered wealth and the fortunes and influences prosperity brought them.' Zeus scrutinised each Olympian. 'We chose this race to do what no other mortals can achieve, and I selected Evandros, for he can harness the dark force he holds within to fight Kronos.'

'And then, what happens to Evandros?' Demeter asked, her fine-textured brow crinkling. 'If he cannot withstand the duration of the battle or the power of Kronos, he will die. There must be another way to act against the Titan without causing your son's demise.'

'This is the only course of action,' Zeus said, face as rigid as marble. 'Or our existence ceases—and our survival is far more essential than a mortal's, even if he is of my own bloodline. We will aid Evandros in the fight against Kronos.'

'A pity, and I was just beginning to become fond of Evandros,' Hera said with a careless shrug.

CHAPTER 11

Alexina sat on the edge of the bed. The bones in her arms and legs protruded like sticks on a dying tree. She brooded, hands curling into fists, enraged by her confinement, her weakened state and the entrapment of her brother and companions. She felt stronger, though not well enough to leave the room. It had been weeks since Dexion's visit, and while the healer gave her food, the woman was evasive, presenting excuses as to her promise to gain an audience with the queen. All Alexina wanted was to persuade the queen to release them, or they would fail to stop the Dark Master.

She shivered as a cold draught swept by the doorway. Particles of dust and leaves caught in a whirly wind rose and then dropped as soon as it had begun. She pulled the woollen blanket around her shoulders, trying to dispel the chill that seeped through to her core. Perhaps this was what death felt like, an unbidden coldness that seeped into your body and psyche. She had hoped to see her brother but was resigned to the prospect that this might never happen.

'Do not despair, High Priestess, your time to leave is at hand.'

She shielded her eyes against the brightness of the blue nimbus and gasped as the light faded. She bowed her head.

'Divine Hermes, you honour me with your presence. Have you come to escort me to the realm of Hades?'

Hermes chuckled, his eyes glinting with mirth. 'I come with news from the King of the Gods. He instructed me to convey information to aid Evandros and the others to remember the quest of the gods and leave the isle of the Amazons.' The Messenger God regarded her for a moment. 'Centuries ago, the sorceress Kirke took a man called Odysseus captive and plied him with a potent narcotic to make him forget his home of Ithaka, his wife and his son so he would never abandon her. She kept him imprisoned for many, many years.' Alexina's mouth fell open, but she clamped it shut when he continued the story. 'Father Zeus sent me to assist him in recovering his consciousness and returning to Ithaka.' He leaned towards her. 'There is a noxious flower called Moly, and it contains a compound that clears the mind and restores memory.'

Her heart skipped a beat. 'Does such a flower grow on this island?'

Hermes smiled. 'Indeed, and it grows in abundance on a nearby mountain.' The Messenger God went on to explain where to find the flower and how to create an antidote. He then left in a flash of blue.

She closed her eyes, clasping her hands. It was time to leave. She searched through the lessons the ancient high priestesses had imparted to her in the cave on the island of Thira and fixed an image of Dexion in her mind.

'Dexion?' she called out in a soft voice. 'I need you. Please come.'

She slumped back onto the bed. The effort to communicate via metaphysical means was foreign and taxing. She did not know if it would work, for no Atlantean had used this form of communication since the destruction of their ancestral home. The ability and skill had been forgotten, never written about in the historical annals. From what she had learnt, only Atlanteans had developed the ability to use telepathy. She hoped Dexion's gift of receiving messages from the gods enabled him to hear her. If he did not come in the next day or two, she would implore the healer to bring the boy to her.

The next few days came and went, her only visitor the older woman. She waited and listened for the healer's footsteps to recede before thrusting the blanket aside and swinging her legs over the side of the bed. With feet planted on the cold stone floor, she propelled herself upright. She swayed, and her limbs shook. Alexina gritted her teeth and took a step, then another. She aimed for the door, the hint of the waning daylight filtering through the gap between the door panel and the floor. She shuffled a few more paces. A shadow blocked part of the light. Her heart thudded and she froze. The shade reversed direction, receded, and minutes later was back. Then the door nudged open. Her breathing was shallow and rapid.

'High Priestess?' whispered a voice.

'Dear Mother Goddess!' She clutched her hands at her chest. 'You gave me a fright, Dexion.'

Alexina tottered back to the bed and plopped herself down, panting. He slid through the narrow opening and closed the door.

'I'm sorry. I had to wait until the healer left.'

'I am so glad you are here.' She seized his hand and beamed at him.

He tilted his head to the side. 'I had a feeling you needed to see me, so I came as soon as I could.'

She squeezed his hand. 'You were correct. I have something for you to do, but first, how fares my brother and the others?'

His face changed. 'I am trying to help Master Evandros remember while playing Senet.'

'That is very good.'

'As we played, I told him about how we met, the journey from Hippo Regius to Carthage, how we rescued you. Hektor, Leander and Homer from the bad king, and of the many occasions our ship had changed course away from Krete, and how we landed at Pylos. I talked about our journey through Messenia, Tegea, Corinth, meeting Pythia and Plato, and finding the sacred labrys.'

'Well done, Dexion.'

'I can see he remembers some things when I describe the various locations we've been to and what we have achieved, but he struggles to recall details.'

'What of the others?'

His shoulders drooped. 'It's as if they have forgotten everything.'

She peered at him. 'How is it that you avoided the fate of Evandros and the others?'

'I was able to convince the queen's attendants that I'd only known the men a short time and had no idea that they were on an important quest for the gods,' he replied. 'I will keep talking about all the places and people we have visited to help Master Evandros,' he added with confidence.

'Very good, you must keep trying to make my brother remember,' she said, patting his hand. 'Now for my bit of news—I had a visit from the Messenger of the Gods.'

Dexion's eyes widened.

'He told me there is a flower that can restore their memory. It grows on a mountain close by, west of the palace. The flower has white petals, and the root is black. I need you to find this flower and bring back as many as you can. When you pull the flower out of the ground, the root needs to be intact. Try not to snap or break it, for the plant's sap is poisonous. Dexion, be careful, and be vigilant the soldiers do not follow you.'

'Don't worry about me, High Priestess. I have since located many secret passages in the palace and they have not caught me,' he boasted with a grin.

CHAPTER 12

Before the sun rose the next day, Dexion stole into the kitchen and took a loaf of bread, a chunk of dried meat and some apples. He filled his water bag, stored the items in a knapsack and sneaked out of the palace grounds, using instincts honed by living on the streets as he set forth towards a long-forgotten tunnel. He had stumbled across the passageway during his exploration of the palace, soon after meeting the High Priestess.

He climbed, nimble and sure-footed as a cat, over the fallen debris that shielded the small opening from even the most discerning observer. He scrambled through the narrow, darkened passage, relying on his instincts and prior knowledge of the tunnel's layout. Dexion thought about the High Priestess held prisoner and his friends drugged to forget the errand of the gods. It was up to him to help them, as they could not do so themselves. He quickened his pace, determined to find the flower.

Lots of it.

'Almost there,' he said to himself, spying soft light that penetrated the gloomy interior.

He slowed, coming to a stop at the opening, and monitored the grounds outside. He took a step and glanced up. The exit of the tunnel came out under the palace's eastern defensive walls, where the guards patrolled the ramparts. He admonished himself for his carelessness the first time crossing the open land. The warriors had nearly seen him. His heart plummeted, realising that the sun's position made it difficult to determine the soldiers' location. If he couldn't see their shadows, then he did not know where they were standing and on the lookout.

I should have left when it was dark, Dexion thought, pursing his lips.

He looked to the left, then to the right. Still no sign of telltale shadows. The walls curved for two to three stades each way, following the curvature of the cliff face. Straight ahead, about half the length of a stadium away, were trees, scant in density, but they would provide ample coverage for a boy of his size. He bit his lip. He had to cut across the meadow without being seen. Dexion crouched and sized up the distance between his position and the woods. From his vantage, they gave the impression of being near, yet after a quick mental calculation of how fast he'd have to run, he realised the trees were much further away than he'd expected.

Though the sun had not fully risen, there was sufficient light for discerning eyes to catch sight of movement. He couldn't delay, and he didn't want to let the High Priestess down. He stood and rubbed his hands up and down his thighs.

'Thank you, Mother.' He beamed.

The embankment on the edge of the cliff face on his right became shrouded, where only moments ago sunlight had bathed the craggy wall. He sidestepped along the wall, sticking close to the hillside, his arms prickling with goosebumps from the coolness of the shade. He scanned the lengths of the ramparts and then bolted. His heart hammered against his chest, his breathing loud to his ears as he inhaled and exhaled. He pounded the ground with sandal-shod feet, expecting shouts and arrows. Dexion dared not check to see if the sentries had seen him escape, racing to the perimeter of the trees. He skidded and dove behind a tree, shimmying out of sight.

He lifted his face to the sky, panting, and gulped. He then peeked around the tree.

'Thank you, Mother.' He closed his eyes and took a deep, steadying breath.

He got up and started walking west, and by mid-morning he caught sight of the mountain. He ate and drank as he walked, not wanting to waste time. A little while later, he spotted a path leading towards the mountain. If he followed the trail, he would get there quicker, but there was a risk of encountering patrolling Amazons.

'I will run away from them,' he said aloud and with more confidence than he felt.

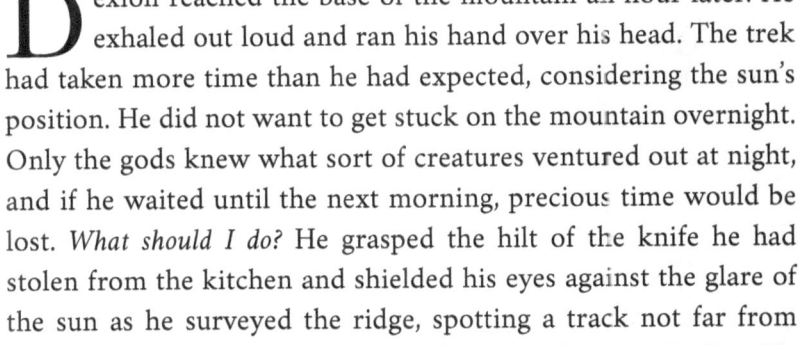

Dexion reached the base of the mountain an hour later. He exhaled out loud and ran his hand over his head. The trek had taken more time than he had expected, considering the sun's position. He did not want to get stuck on the mountain overnight. Only the gods knew what sort of creatures ventured out at night, and if he waited until the next morning, precious time would be lost. *What should I do?* He grasped the hilt of the knife he had stolen from the kitchen and shielded his eyes against the glare of the sun as he surveyed the ridge, spotting a track not far from where he stood, meandering up the length of the steep incline. He followed the trail until it disappeared around a bend.

He scrunched up his face and hoped he didn't have to climb all the way to the top to find the flowers. Before going up the trail, he trekked over to a line of trees, located a young but supple sapling and tested its strength by bending it as far as he could. Satisfied, he sawed it at the base with the dagger and sharpened one end.

Dexion had been out only for a few hours on previous escapades. This time, he'd be out far longer and prayed the Amazons would not detect his absence. Not, at least, for a number of hours he hoped. They regarded him as a slave, and being a boy was an advantage. This allowed him to move around the palace grounds without being hindered, exploring whenever he wanted, as long as he had completed his chores. He had learnt at a very early age when to be visible and when not to be.

The initial stage of the track was even and the incline steady, but as the path grew steeper and more treacherous, he used the butt of his newly made spear as a staff to aid his hike. His calf muscles and thighs strained with every step he took. He stopped and wiped the sweat from his face with his khiton before reaching for his water bag. He checked back from where he had come and saw he was an eighth of the way up the mountain and no sign of the flower.

After a second hour of climbing, he heard an echo of mewling. Dexion stalled to listen. *Must be the vibration of the wind*, he thought and kept going. A few steps further, he heard it again. He angled his head towards the noise. The whimpering was coming from further ahead. Dexion increased his speed, ignoring the pain in his legs. He wondered what sort of creature made such a noise. The mewling grew louder as he sidled closer, and then it ceased. He hesitated and gasped, not realising how high he'd ascended, so intent on finding the animal that it overshadowed his search for the flowers. He shivered at the cool mountain breeze, the perspiration on his face and arms and damp khiton adding to the chill. Dexion pulled out his woollen cloak from his bag and flung it over his head, the coarse material soon warming his body. His eyes detected a speck fluttering on the ledge and he marched over.

'Thank the gods!'

Jutting out from the craggy face of the mountain was a cluster of white-petalled flowers. Dexion lay on his stomach and leaned over the edge to inspect the bunches. It resembled the blossom the High Priestess had described. As gently as possible, he tugged at the stem of the flower, but it would not budge. He pulled out the knife and dug at the dirt, the black root of the flower emerging. Minutes later, he removed the bulb, the root looking like a large black onion. He laid it on the path next to him and went on to the next flower. He kept going until he had retrieved all the flowers.

Dexion groaned. From his lofty position, he could see across the valley and noted the steady advance of nightfall creeping over the land with stealth and determination. He squatted to wrap the plants in a tattered rag. Time to leave.

Dexion stowed the precious items in his bag, moving quicker, and grunted at hefting the sack over his shoulder. The weight of the collection was greater than he had expected. Conscious of the late hour, he returned to the trail, making his way back to where he had started when he heard the same squeal. The sound came from above. He examined the rock face and saw a glimmer of movement. He slipped the pack from his shoulder and onto the ground. Dexion scaled the cliff face until he reached a small ridge and the source of the crying. His mouth fell open in surprise at the young creature, a bundle of white fur. Its grey-blue eyes blinked at him.

'How in the gods did you get here?'

The ledge was so narrow it was a miracle the pup was on it. He reached to seize the animal, but it yelped and backed away. The pup's hind legs slid over the edge. Dexion snatched at its tail, the pup wailing, its shrill echoing across the valley.

He checked back to see how high he had climbed. If he jumped, chances were he would break a leg or knock himself out, and then he would be no good to the High Priestess or the pup. His arm trembled and his legs shook. If he remained clinging to the rock face much longer, odds were he would plummet to the ground. He could tuck the pup into his girdle, but if it loosened, the pup would fall out.

His clawlike fingers stretched and tensed further as he gripped the ledge. He bit his lip and grimaced. It was then he remembered his cloak had a hood. He took a mouthful of the material and pulled it across his chest. After an excruciating length of time, and with a sore jaw, he dropped the pup into the hood. He scaled down, and when his feet touched the ground, his legs shook with such intensity he had to sit. It reminded him of the time when the earth had trembled and torn apart and Master Evandros had plummeted into the chasm. He inspected the hood of his cloak, where a pair of eyes probed his.

'What am I going to do with you?'

He pulled out the pup. Under his hands he could feel the animal's heart beating at a rapid click and thought he would die from fright. The pup's fur was thick and soft, and though his coat was snow-white, he had silver-grey flecks on his tail.

'Ah ... so that is how you came to be on that ledge,' he said.

He lifted the pup's lame leg. The poor creature had no chance of survival and was easy prey for an eagle or a hawk.

'Well, I have to take you with me.'

The pup's eyes never left his, and though he did not make any further noises, his heart still beat fast. 'I guess you must be hungry.' He settled the pup onto his lap and pulled his bag closer. He rummaged through it for the remaining dried meat and broke off a chunk. The pup gulped it down. Dexion grinned and fed him another piece, which vanished as fast as the previous morsel. He gave the rest of the meat to the pup while he ate the fruit he had packed for the journey.

'Time to get off this mountain or we will freeze up here.'

Dexion placed the pup into the hood and wrapped the cloak around his shoulders. He picked up the bag and his spear and began the trek down the mountain.

CHAPTER 13

A preternatural silence greeted Dexion on his return to the palace. He peeked out of the tunnel to find torches set around the perimeter of the courtyard, lighting up the area. It was empty. He knew sentries were on patrol every night and during the day. He took a step and froze. Dexion slipped back into the darkness and crouched behind the debris as the sound of clinking neared. He popped his head over the stones just as two warriors neared the obscured opening. He ducked, his pulse thumping as fast as a rabbit's wayward paw. Their footfalls loomed, the soles of their sandals slapping against the stone floor, loud in the night's quietness. He remained as still as possible, beads of perspiration trickling down the side of his face.

'What was that?' asked a warrior.

Dexion stiffened.

'Sounds like it came from over there.'

With his heart in his mouth, he scooted back into the inky passage, the pup whimpering. He peered over his shoulder and hastened further into the cavernous corridor as a light materialised in the small aperture of the tunnel.

He tried to calm the pup with gentle strokes. 'Shh ... it will be all right.'

'It is as black as a mother's womb,' a soldier commented. 'Pass me a torch. The commotion is coming from down here.'

'What can you see?' asked the other woman.

'Nothing but darkness.'

'What do you think the noise was?'

'Whatever it was, it's gone.'

'Shall we investigate?'

Dexion held his breath.

'I am not going down there!' replied the warrior.

He monitored the shadows of light as they played across the roof.

'Besides, we would not fit through the opening. We'd have to remove the stones and they are too big to shift. It's likely to be a puny creature that has crawled its way into the cavity and can't get out,' finished the same warrior.

'Well ...'

'If you want to go, go ahead. I don't think it is worthwhile investigating what in all probability is a dying animal.'

Dexion heard the other soldier mutter. 'That makes sense ... I guess.'

'Good, now let's continue with our patrol.'

The light faded, and the tunnel fell into pitch blackness. His shoulders sagged and he let out a gigantic sigh. He lifted the pup so they were eye to eye.

'You must be quiet, or we will be in terrible trouble if they catch us.'

He cradled the pup in his arms and scurried forward, keeping low. On reaching the opening, he searched the grounds for the guards. The courtyard appeared to be empty. Before he lost his nerve, Dexion sprinted across the square and headed for the propylaea. He slid to a stop and hid behind a thick, colourful column. He waited to see if anyone heard him.

No one came.

Face set in grim determination, he rushed down the steps and towards the slaves' quarters. He grinned and slipped into his room unnoticed, setting the pup on his bed and dropping the knapsack onto the floor. The pup gazed up at him.

'You almost got us into trouble,' he scolded, tossing his cloak aside.

The pup yawned and lowered his head onto his paws.

'A good idea. Time to sleep and in the morning, we will figure out what to do.'

He was asleep as soon as his head touched the pillow.

Dexion woke with a start. The pup he had rescued from the mountain cliff lay nestled against him and was staring at him. His grey-blue eyes belied intelligence that gave the impression he saw beyond his physical presence and into his soul.

'I have a feeling the gods sent you for a reason, and I will wait until they reveal why.'

The pup blinked and stretched. His lame paw lay immobile.

Dexion sat up and swung his legs over the side of the bed. 'I will check your paw—but first, breakfast. You must be hungry. I know I am. I'll bring us food. Please do not make any noise while I am away.' He patted the pup on the head and left.

He entered an old and disused path that led to the palace kitchens. After being housed in the slaves' quarters, he had taken to searching the palace grounds, and after months of exploring, he had discovered a series of passages hidden inside the walls. Dexion had learnt while traversing the many unused corridors that they shortened the journey wherever he went. He mapped the sections and uncovered an extraordinary pattern. He could go anywhere undetected and materialise at various locations in and around the palace complex. There was a tunnel that led to where the High Priestess was detained, but he did not risk going there during the day as the healer was a constant presence, as were the guards.

Now the situation was different. He had the Moly and needed to see her.

When he arrived in the kitchen, he offered to help, knowing from experience the head cook would give him an ample serving of food and treats to take while he completed chores. He chopped wood, milked the goats that grazed beyond the kitchen and fetched eggs the geese laid. After he finished his duties, arms laden with meat, bread, milk and figs, he dashed away, dissolving into a narrow passageway.

The pup was still where he'd left the animal earlier, asleep on the bed. He yelped when Dexion entered the room.

'Shh ... you will get us into trouble. Here you go.'

Dexion placed a cup of warm goat's milk and raw meat on the floor. He set the pup in front of the food and smiled with fondness as he devoured the meat in a single gulp. It reminded him of the years surviving day to day on the street in Hippo Regius, with very little or nothing to eat before Master Evandros had entered his life. He, too, was lame. Not in the same physical sense as the wolf, but the murder of his parents and the man responsible for their deaths had scarred him and given him the ability of prophecy.

He pursed his lips. The gods had been quiet, but they had sent him the pup. *Or did they? Do you have a role to play in this quest?*

'You need a name. What shall we call you?' he asked, scratching the pup behind the ears. He clicked his fingers. 'I know! Lykeios, after the great god Helios, for the wolf is a sacred animal of his.' He picked up the pup. 'Let me see what is wrong with your paw, Lykeios.' He examined the damaged limb. 'We splint your leg for support, and in time it will grow stronger. What do you think?' Lykeios wagged his tail and yipped. Dexion grinned. 'Well, then, that is what we shall do.'

He left the pup in his chamber to go to the stables and complete the remainder of his tasks. He still had to serve food and wine to all those who gathered in the megaron. After dark, when everyone had eaten and retired to their rooms, that was when he would visit the High Priestess.

~

'Come here, Lykeios. We're going to see the High Priestess.' He came to the end of a passageway and pressed his back against the wall. He waited a moment, then poked his head around the corner.

'Looks like it is clear,' he murmured to Lykeios.

He scooted in the direction of the building housing the High Priestess, hiding in the wall's shadow before sidling along to the door.

'High Priestess?' He pushed the door ajar. 'High Priestess ...'

'Dexion? Come in quickly.'

He slipped through the gap and closed the door, plunging the room into gloominess.

'I am so pleased to see you, Dexion,' she said, sitting up. 'What have you there?'

He scratched the pup's belly. 'I found him on the mountain. The mother had left him behind because of his bad paw.'

He brought the pup closer to the High Priestess, who contemplated the wolf's serene composure.

'I believe the gods put him there for me to discover.'

'Yes,' the High Priestess agreed. 'There is something he must do.' She tore her gaze away from his penetrating and knowing grey-blue eyes. 'Were you able to locate the Moly?'

He nodded. 'I did and brought back as much as I could carry. They are in my room.'

'Well done, Dexion,' she said.

He beamed.

'I need you to create an elixir from the roots and give it to my brothers, and the other men. To make it, you require a pot, a tripod, a cheesecloth and an earthenware jug. Are you able to get those?' she asked.

'Yes.'

'First, clean the roots—there must be no dirt on them. Next, put them in the pot to boil. Cover the roots with water—not too much or it will dilute the concoction and the antidote won't work. Once the roots are soft, mash them until the mixture thickens and let it cool. Collect the mix into the cheesecloth and make a small ball, then squeeze the liquid into the jug. A clear-like substance should emerge. Squeeze the mixture until there is nothing left. Wash your hands when you finish. I don't want you to become ill from the potion. At mealtime, add a few drops in a cup of wine.'

Dexion's mouth went dry.

The High Priestess grabbed his arm. 'You can do this. After all, you are Mother's son.'

He swallowed, stroked the pup's head and tried to quell his racing heart. With more confidence than he felt, he responded, 'Best I get started.'

It took several days for Dexion to collect the equipment to make the potion. He and the pup used one of the forgotten passages he had discovered, and he set up a tripod and pot before lighting a fire. It was going to take a while for the water to boil.

He sat leaning against the wall, the pup crawling onto his lap. The dancing flames were mesmerising, and his eyes fluttered, head bobbing. He fought to keep them open.

The sharp yelping of the pup startled Dexion into wakefulness. 'Wha …?'

The excitable pup yapped at the bubbling pot. Dexion scrambled to his feet and hurried over. He gagged and covered his nose.

'Gods … that is revolting.' He screwed up his nose, darting away from the pungent fumes. 'How in the name of the gods am I supposed to mash it with that stink?'

He doused the fire with sand, keeping his distance from the fragrant odour.

'I'll wait until it's cooled. Perhaps it won't smell so bad.'

An hour later, he was mashing the remnants of the bulbs. At first, it thickened into a milky substance as he ground the mix into a pulp. He spooned the contents into the cheesecloth and tied the ends, then squeezed the bag, moving his hands from the top to the bottom, like milking a goat. Clear liquid dribbled into the jug. He kept pressing until the contents were dry. A slow smile spread across his face when he saw the quantity he had made. All he had to do was administer the antidote.

CHAPTER 14

Dexion stood behind the Atlantean, his gaze flitting from the queen to her guards. He shifted from one foot to the other, drumming his fingers against his thigh, while in his other hot and sweaty hand, he clutched a small bottle. His friend swung round to him.

'Are you unwell, Dexion? Your face is pasty.'

He gulped, his heart clamouring. 'I ... I ... am fine, Master Evandros.'

'Are you sure?' His friend eyeballed him. 'You don't look well. Perhaps I should call for the healer.' He half rose from his chair.

'*No!*' Dexion panicked, tongue sticking to the roof of his mouth.

Queen Antioche and others nearby swung their heads at them.

'I apologise, Master Evandros. I am not sick,' he blurted.

'Hmm ... tell me straight away if you feel ill, and I will ask for the healer.' The Atlantean narrowed his eyes at him.

'Of course, Master Evandros.' The words rushed out of his mouth.

His friend scrutinised his face a few seconds longer, and then he leaned towards the queen to converse. Dexion wiped his sweaty brow and swallowed.

It won't be the healer I'll be seeing, he thought, *more like the dungeons if the queen finds out what I am about to do.*

The servers entered the megaron, carrying bronze trays laden with aromatic food. Like a well-coordinated dance, they split into two lines and placed the plates onto low tables in front of the diners. Soon after, the wine bearers emerged. While the fare and general chatter distracted the women and men, Dexion tried to pluck off the stopper on the bottle, his hands shaking non-stop. He couldn't get a grip on the lid. He gritted his teeth, seized the stopper and wrested it off, and managed to tip a few drops into a cup without spilling any. Dexion clutched the mug and waited for the wine bearer, trying to regulate his breathing. He waited, attempting to control his nervousness as the red liquid was poured into the cup, followed by water, diluting the violet liquid.

Biting his lip to quell the butterflies in his stomach, he passed the drink to the Atlantean. He wasn't sure what to expect or how long before the elixir would take effect. All he could do was wait until the feast gathered momentum and the revellers got raucous. Soon the Amazons and men would move into pairs or threes and retire to different parts of the palace.

As a witness to the events in the royal household, he had noticed that when a woman became impregnated, she no longer attended the dinners and another female took her place. That was when he worked out that his friends and the Argonauts were used by the Amazons for breeding. Somewhat bemused, he did notice the men were not distressed by the ongoing ministrations of the women and were cheerful yet oblivious participants.

Dexion observed Phameas, Leander, Hektor and Homer as they reclined with a bevy of attentive females next to a pillar close to the hearth. Leander had his head stretched back, the cordlike muscles in his neck sticking out, his mouth open while a scantily clad woman fed him dried figs. Another female sat on Hektor's lap. They were feeding each other, kissing after each mouthful. Homer was lounging with his head on the lap of his female companion; his wax tablet, secured by a cord and looped around his belt, was within hand's reach. She was stroking his face. His eyes were closed and he was wearing a satisfied smile. Phameas, his Phoenician friend, sat between two women, his arms around each, kissing them, going back and forth without pausing for a breath.

This was the time when he normally left, but tonight he needed to stay to make sure the Moly worked. His stomach tightened as Master Evandros continued to eat, drink and chat with the queen. *It's not working,* he thought, disappointed. *Did I allow too much water and wine in the cup?*

'Evandros!' The queen bolted to her feet.

The Atlantean's head lolled from side to side before slumping forward and knocking the table over.

Dexion's eyes widened as his friend lay sprawled on the floor, unmoving. The queen leapt to his side, seized his face in her hands and wiped his clammy forehead.

'Evandros,' she said, her voice catching. 'What is it? Are you ill?'

He stood gaping, unable to move. *I have killed Master Evandros!*

The man's eyes rolled, and his breathing grew shallow.

'Evandros! Can you hear me?' the queen almost shouted, the lines around her mouth taut.

The big man convulsed, forcing the queen to let go. He thrashed about, limbs hitting and knocking over tables. Food and platters were tossed into the air and smashed onto the ground.

'Get me the healer!'

The spasms stopped, and he went still. After a long few minutes, he opened his eyes.

The queen embraced him, a hand on his chest, her face close to his. 'Evandros …'

He blinked up at her. 'My head is swimming and I feel hot.'

Queen Antioche pressed her damp cheek against his. 'I thought I had lost you.'

'I need to go outside.' The Atlantean clasped his forehead, hand shaking.

'Of course. I will help you.' The queen eased him upright.

'Whoa.' He swayed from side to side. Queen Antioche held him, her arms tightening around his waist.

With the queen's support, the tall, muscular man rose to his feet.

'Dexion, can you bring the jug with water?' He towered over the queen, and the two made a slow exit, the queen's guards marching at their heels.

'Yes, Master Evandros.'

Dexion grabbed the items and scampered outside to where his friend was propped against the stone blocks of the propylaeum, the queen clinging to his side.

'Perhaps you should sit down,' she said.

'That is a good idea.'

She led him to the marble bench. Dexion thrust the cup he had filled with water at him.

'Yes, water.'

The Atlantean gulped it down and held the vessel out to Dexion, who refilled it.

'Antioche, go back inside. I'll be alright here.'

She shook her head, her honey-blonde hair whipping from side to side. 'I will stay here with you.'

'There's no need—I am feeling better, and besides, Dexion is here and he'll get you if I require help, won't you?'

'Yes, Master Evandros,' he said, his heart clamouring.

'Go back inside and make sure you eat. It's important for you to keep well for our child,' the Atlantean added with a wan smile.

'But ...'

He took her hand and pulled her to him. 'Go. I will be fine.' He kissed her hard and long. 'The fresh air is helping. I'll stay outside until the light-headedness passes.'

Queen Antioche searched his face. 'Are you certain?'

'Does the sun rise every day?' He gave her another kiss.

'Very well.' She straightened and whipped around to Dexion, her grey eyes hardening. 'You do not leave his side, unless it is to get the healer.'

'Yes, Queen Antioche,' he acknowledged, lowering his gaze to the ground.

The queen left, accompanied by her guards, and cast a long look at her consort, the Atlantean giving her a brief wave. Dexion gulped as she scowled at him.

'I can't remember the last time I felt this ill,' said his friend, rubbing his forehead. 'I feel queasy, my mouth is dry, my limbs ache and I have a terrible headache.'

'Would you like the queen to come back?' he asked.

'No, though I might lie down.'

Dexion stood aside as the tall man stretched out on the stone bench, his feet touching the ground.

'Shall I get the healer for you?'

'I just want to shut my eyes and hope the pain in my head goes away.'

'As you wish, Master Evandros.'

He placed the jug on the ground and sat, arms wrapped around his legs. He leaned his forehead against his knees and berated himself for harming the one person whom he regarded as a father.

Dexion woke with a start; someone was calling his name. He must have dozed off. He rubbed his eyes.

A slow smile then crept across his face. 'Master Evandros?' he whispered.

'We have a lot to discuss,' said Evan. 'Give me the SparkNotes on what's happened.'

'SparkNotes?' he asked, confused.

'Tell me what's going on, but be quick. The queen may send her guards out to check on me.'

'Of course, Master Evandros.' He grinned, relieved to see his friend back to normal. He explained what had happened since their arrival and about the incarceration of the High Priestess, the visit from the Messenger God and how to make a remedy for the memory loss draught. Silence enveloped them when Dexion finished. The man, whose past and future were woven together from his unique parentage, lowered his head, clasping his nape with his hands.

'And I am going to be a father,' he added. 'What a mess.' He ran his fingers through his hair. 'There's not much I can do about that.' Evan took Dexion by the shoulders. 'It is important we give the others the antidote, rescue the High Priestess, fix the ship and get the hell out of here. When we go back into the megaron, behave as if nothing has happened and give Homer, Phameas, Leander and Hektor the remedy. We will attend to Jason and his crew after they have revived.' He stood and rubbed his forehead with a fist. 'The past months must have been dreadful for you, being alone and with our memories altered.' He gave Dexion a hug.

When they entered the megaron, the din was like a tumultuous wave slamming into his senses. Dexion took note of how the queen's face lit up when she saw the Atlantean. With his friend's go-ahead, he weaved his way to the four men, who acknowledged him with cheer. He smiled at them and poured water into their cups, adding a few drops of the antidote at the same time. He then hurried to the Atlantean's side to wait.

Thirty minutes later, Phameas was the first to leave the megaron, his gait as uncoordinated as a new foal's attempt to stand. Homer followed, catching up with the Phoenician, and assisted him outside. Hektor's head fell forward and hit the stone floor. He jerked upright, blinked glassy-eyed, and cast an eye around the room with a blank expression Leander said something to him, and the two men left.

Dexion hovered by the shoulder of his friend, who gave an imperceptible nod. With jug in hand, he slipped out into the murky shadows of the courtyard. Outside, he saw Leander doubled over and heaving. Homer, with his hands on hips, face tilted skywards, was sucking deep breaths and hiccupping at the same time. Hektor clung to a column, as if to draw strength from the sturdy structure, and Phameas lay curled against the wall, hugging his knees to himself and shivering.

'By the gods, I have not felt this awful since ... well ... I cannot bring to mind such a time ...' Hektor clutched his stomach.

'This is worse than when I fell and hit the ground face first the day the earth shook,' Leander said, white and drawn.

A film of perspiration covered Homer's brow and cheeks, his hair damp. He lifted a palsied hand to his face, wiping away the drops of sweat from his forehead.

'How can one feel hot and cold in same instant?' Phameas moaned and pulled his knees tighter to his chest.

CHAPTER 15

Evan stared at the fire, not noticing the dancing flames as his mind raced from one thought to the next, trying to piece together events, from what he now recollected to the recent discussions with Dexion. It was a weird sensation having the memories flood into his brain. He could recall each moment as vividly as a cinematic film, yet it felt surreal, as if it had happened to someone else and he was seeing the action unfold. It was like a voyeuristic panorama, except he was the lead character, a feebleminded protagonist. And then there was the woman sitting on his left: the queen of the Amazons.

'What a friggin' mess,' he muttered to himself and squeezed his eyes shut.

'Evandros, your companions have not come back. Is it possible they are afflicted with the same malady as you?' Antioche asked him.

'Huh?' He blinked at her.

The queen placed a hand against his brow. Evan jerked back from her touch. Her hand hovered between them as she gazed at him in concern.

'Shall I send out my guards to find out what has happened to your friends?'

He checked to see where his companions sat night after night with their coterie of female admirers and lovers.

'No, I'll go. I don't want your warriors to be offended if they have been sick,' he replied.

'I should call for the healer,' Antioche said.

'There's no need.' Evan stood. 'If it is like what I experienced, they will recover, and the fresh air is healthier for them than any remedy. I will bring water with me. It eased my headache and queasiness after drinking several cups.'

He collected a jug and cups and left the megaron, crossing over to where his companions gathered far from the main entrance. Dexion beamed at him.

'Here, have some water. Believe me, you'll feel better after having a drink,' he said, passing out the cups.

He waited while they drank, the pallor on their faces almost back to normal. Evan inspected each one of his companions' faces, keeping an eye out for telltale signs of recollection.

Minutes passed. Then more time went by.

'Master Evandros, I don't think ...' began Dexion.

'Just a little while longer ...' They waited and waited, and then he nodded. 'Ah huh ... there it is.'

Homer slid onto the ground, his mouth pulled into a thin line, and covered his face with his hands.

Leander's face paled. 'Gods! What have I done? How can I ever be with her now? I am an affront to the gods and to the woman I love.'

Hektor slumped against the column, his head hanging low between his shoulders. 'Dear Mother, forgive us.' His voice came out strangled.

Phameas faced Evan and Dexion, aggrieved by how dejected the others looked and felt. 'We cannot blame ourselves for what happened. We must accept that it did and move beyond our actions.'

'I don't believe I am able,' said Leander, miserable. 'How can I expect forgiveness from Alexina?'

'I am sure, in time, the High Priestess will forgive you,' replied Evan, 'but first we need to plan what we are going to do and quick, or the queen will send out her guards.'

'What happened to us?' asked Phameas.

'They gave us a powerful potion that affected our memories,' he replied.

'The morning after the feast, when we were on the beach, I asked you why we were here, and you answered we were on a quest for the gods,' Leander said. 'That's when it started, wasn't it?'

Evan nodded. 'Yes, I recall how you were affected after the dinner with the Amazons.'

'Why would the queen do this?' Phameas asked.

'This is an island of women; what do they need to continue the race of their people?' He paused, waiting for the realisation to sink in. 'Well?'

Homer pointed to himself and the others.

'Yes, just all the men.'

'They gave Jason and his crew this elixir?' Hektor asked in a low voice, his head still hanging.

'Yes, they were drugged too.' Evan crossed his arms against his chest.

'And what of the High Priestess?' asked Leander. 'Where is she?'

'Dexion can answer your question.' He invited him to speak.

'The High Priestess is in a room and being given a potion to keep her asleep, but the healer has been feeding her and she is now much stronger,' answered Dexion. 'The High Priestess requested the healer to allow me to visit. I discovered a secret passage to see her whenever I wanted without being caught by the guards.'

'Why do we now remember everything?' asked Phameas.

'The Messenger God visited the High Priestess and told her about a flower that grows on the mountain and how to make an elixir. The High Priestess explained it to me.' Dexion bit his lip, his face crumbling and resembling the young boy he was. 'I was so scared. I couldn't hear the gods' voices and I didn't know what to do or how to help you remember.' His eyes watered.

'You are extraordinary and brave,' said Evan, squatting and gathering the youth into his arms. 'You endangered your life for us, and that is something I won't forget.'

'What do we do now?' asked Phameas. 'We can't return to the megaron; the queen will know we are no longer under a spell.'

'That's exactly what we're going to do,' he said, 'and give the potion to Jason and his crew. We repair the *Argo*, sail to Krete and finish this quest.' He held out a hand. 'Dexion, hand over the bottle. You and Leander are going to rescue the High Priestess.'

Leander wrung his hands as he backed away. 'No. I am not fit to be in her presence. I cannot ... I ...' The lines around his mouth were intense and drawn.

'She'll want to see you,' he said, 'and, yes, she'll be hurt and angry at you. There's nothing you can do but be open and honest, and tell her you love her. And give her time to heal.'

'I cannot,' Leander protested, staring down at his feet, his voice almost inaudible.

Evan grasped his shoulders. 'You must. It's like having a thorn stuck in your foot. If you don't remove it, it burrows under the skin and becomes infected and makes you ill. It is best to remove the thorn straight away—it will be painful, but in the long term, it is better.'

Leander's eyes glistened with unshed tears. 'My heart is aching. I fear it may break.'

'I know,' he said in a soft voice. 'That too heals.'

Leander grimaced and nodded.

'What about the guards?' asked Hektor, speaking out only for the second time since being revived. 'They are armed, we are not.'

'We don't need weapons,' he replied, striding towards the megaron, clutching the bottle.

CHAPTER 16

Before they entered the megaron, Homer tapped Evan on the shoulder, scribbled on his wax tablet and showed it to him.

What are you going to do?

'Do?' he repeated.

Homer nodded.

'I will do nothing, but I have something to say.' He planted a palm against the mammoth bronze-coated doors.

Homer grabbed his arm.

'What?'

You—Homer scrawled—*me, Phameas, Hektor and Leander have lain with these women and impregnated them. And while the queen has duped us, she and her Amazons do not deserve our wrath or our enmity.*

He noted his half-brother's grim body language, and then he raised a questioning brow at Phameas and Hektor.

'Homer is right,' Phameas agreed.

'But the queen kept us drugged and captive for months!' he argued. 'Doesn't that anger you?'

'At first it did,' answered Phameas. 'However, it wasn't unpleasant. What man doesn't enjoy the attentions of beautiful women? In all honesty, I'd rather be entrapped by a colony of females than impaled by a sword.' He poked Evan in the arm. 'And you would too. Besides, a leader needs to protect their people and the queen cannot be faulted or accused for taking such action.'

'The High Priestess may disagree,' Hektor muttered, averting his eyes.

The High Priestess will be the first to affirm what happened was fated, and no good comes from punishing them. What is important from here onwards is that we complete the errand the gods have tasked us with and stop the Dark Master, wrote Homer.

Evan rubbed his brow. He was angry at the queen's actions, infuriated at her for duping and manipulating him and furious at himself for his stupidity. On the flip side, there was a part of him that admired her intelligence, her sense of humour, her strength, and her vulnerability, which evoked a feeling he had never experienced before.

'Fine, I will be polite and reasonable,' he said through clenched teeth.

He pushed the door open. The aroma of cooked food and the scent of heated bodies hit him like a hot cloudburst on a stormy summer's day. The queen caught sight of him as he stepped across the threshold; her face brightened for a momentary second, and then her smile faltered. He held her gaze, his eyes as hard as granite. She stood as he strode towards her, his companions flanking him on either side. Her guards sprang forward, lances pointed at them. Her handmaidens leapt to their feet and put themselves in front of their queen. The laughter and banter in the room died bit by bit, akin to blowing out the candles one by one, the Argonauts and Amazons staring.

Evan brooded as he regarded the queen and handed the bottle to Phameas. 'You and Homer give this to Jason and his men. Just a few drops in each cup of water.'

They marched off, leaving him and Hektor with the queen.

'Do you recall our conversation when I said our arrival here was not an accident?' he asked her.

'Yes, I remember,' she replied in a firm voice.

'Was it Eris or Kronos who brought us here?'

'The Goddess of Discord visited me here in this room and told me there was a ship full of men who would arrive soon and I didn't need to worry about the demise of the Amazons.'

'And?'

'That it would be preferable to keep you from leaving our island.' The queen held herself tall.

'By plying us with a concoction to make us forget?'

She nodded.

'And if you hadn't detained us?'

Antioche paused. 'She'd destroy every citizen, including our children.'

His eyes darkened. He clenched and unclenched his hands.

'I was only ...' she began, imploring him.

'You did what any ruler would have done, given the uncertain and dangerous ultimatum,' said a voice.

They spun around. Evan sucked in a harsh gasp.

'Dear Mother Goddess,' rasped Hektor, shocked, his face paling.

The queen went rigid and pursed her lips.

Leander strode forward carrying the High Priestess, his heated glare pinning the queen. Dexion trotted alongside, and puffing behind them was the healer.

'I am sorry, my queen, they arrived out of the darkness and forced their way into the room,' she said in a breathless voice.

'We must leave,' said the High Priestess, looking small and wan in Leander's muscled embrace. 'You have delayed us long enough. Your people's future is secured; now you shall make amends and provide equipment and timber to rebuild our ship.'

'I ordered my merchants to purchase various items essential to repair your ship when you arrived. Timber, rope, tar, linen and hammers are stored in a room next to the stables,' said Antioche.

'Have these goods transported to the beach without delay.' The High Priestess' ice-blue eyes crystallised.

The queen stiffened, her chest rising, and lifted her chin, her golden hair swaying. 'My warriors will see to it.'

'Leander, take me to the *Argo*,' said the High Priestess.

Leander pivoted.

'Wait!' the queen called out. At the High Priestess' consent, Leander swung back around. 'It is too dark and dangerous to walk to the beach at this hour. There are obstacles you are not familiar with, and you may be injured in the journey. It would be prudent to wait until morning.'

'Then we will remain here in the megaron. You and your Amazons depart this instant.'

The queen bristled. She and the High Priestess eyeballed each other, a stormy winter's grey versus the glare of a blue icecap. No one dared to speak or move.

'This is my home,' Antioche said in a quiet and even tone, 'and I am its queen. You may be a powerful high priestess possessing the ability to kill with magic; however, the gods brought you here, for a purpose of which they did not intend for you to be a part. That is not of my doing, except that keeping you sedated was the safest way to save you. The Goddess of Discord ordered your death, and this was the most felicitous way to keep you from dying.'

The Amazons stood, and without a command from their sovereign leader, they filed out of the room. When the last woman exited, Antioche walked over to Evan, her personal guards behind her. She placed a hand on his chest.

'I will care for our daughter,' she said, kissing him on the cheek, 'and tell her of her father's bravery and extraordinary feats.'

He blinked, his mind slow to respond. The soft touch and taste of her lips and the scent of her perfume lingered after she stepped away and departed. His heart did a strange lurch, followed by an odd thudding beat. To shake off the feeling, he rounded on Leander, whose pained bearing protruded like a thorn in a bear's paw, but he was not as distressed as the High Priestess. Evan took her from Leander's awkward embrace without a word, and she buried her face in his neck.

Evan left the megaron and sat on the stone bench where he had lain hours earlier after Dexion had given him the antidote. He cradled her in his arms and rocked her back and forth, alarmed by how he could feel her bones through the fabric of her gown. The High Priestess' tears ran down his neck and soaked his khiton. He shut his eyes and swallowed. Her anguish and heartache made him aware that regardless of her status and remoteness, she was still vulnerable.

'I know words mean little right now,' he said, 'but the pain and hurt you are experiencing will pass. Give yourself time to heal, and allow yourself to feel angry, but don't let the feeling consume you, for it will make you bitter.'

'Much like how you felt after Sibyl's death? For what the gods instructed me to do?' she asked, words muffled.

He slowed and resumed the gentle rocking. 'Yes.' What else could he say? That he wasn't really married to the woman called Sibyl, and it was his Atlantean doppelganger who was her husband? No, best to lie and let her believe that was the reason for his belligerent behaviour. Thinking about the other Evandros, Evan wondered what Zeus had done with him after wresting him from his life in the twenty-first century. Was he living his life back on Atlantis, or was he secreted in some unknown location? Zeus had told Evan that Evandros couldn't complete the quest as he did not have the requisite and innate skills or knowledge that he, Evan, had. Alexina began to speak, and Evan pushed his thoughts to the side to focus on what she was saying.

'She was not my choice,' she said, hiccupping, fresh tears running down her cheeks. 'I loved Sibyl as a sister, and for the happiness she brought you. I pleaded with the gods to sacrifice another, but they would not relent.'

He clamped his lips tight and worked hard to squelch the burning anger rising from the pit of his stomach.

'I do not blame you, or hold you responsible for Sibyl's death,' he said, embittered. 'The fault lies with the gods, for they are the ones who precipitated her death and sent us on this folly of a quest.'

'Evandros, the gods hear all and shall punish you for your words.'

He shrugged. 'They need me—they need all of us to do what they can't. If they harm me, the expedition is over.'

'I cannot protect you if you continue to defy them, Evandros,' she said.

'Alexina, if they kill me, then so be it. However, I will ask one thing of you.'

She lifted her head up at him, her eyes red and face blotchy. 'And what would that be?'

He gave her a crooked smile. 'When your heart has healed, open it back to Leander. He is a good man and loves you.'

She lowered her head, the teardrops splattering on her lap, marking spots on her gown.

'I want to make sure you are taken care of when I am gone,' he added. 'He is the man for you.'

'Evandros, you cannot know you will die,' she said, lips trembling.

'It's already happened once, and almost a second time. I am coming to terms with the fact that I won't return home.' He gazed up at the inky night sky, the stars twinkling like little beacons. 'But I'll make sure you and the others do, if I can defeat the Minotaur.'

'Evandros—'

'End of discussion,' he said, cutting her off. 'This conversation stays between me and you. Do I have your word?'

She hesitated. 'What of Dexion, Phameas and your half-brother, Homer? They have been loyal friends and deserve to be told.'

He averted his face and cleared his throat before he spoke. 'I'll tell them when I feel it is the right time to do so.'

A heavy silence descended upon them, a confidant to both of their hurts and secrets.

She laid a hand against his cheek. 'Do not leave it too long, for it will be much harder to say the words.'

He nodded and swallowed. She brushed away the dampness from his cheeks.

After a few moments, when he felt more at ease, he asked, 'Are you ready to go back inside?'

The High Priestess drew in a deep breath and nodded.

He stood. 'We really need to get you some food. You are too thin.'

CHAPTER 17

A res paced back and forth, bridling and snorting like an untamed horse. He whirled around, cape twirling, and stomped across to where Zeus sat on his black marble throne.

'Are you happy Eris and Kronos orchestrated this diversion to prevent our children from finding Mother's last object and restoring our power?' Ares narrowed his eyes and gritted his teeth at Zeus when he did not respond, and swivelled on his heel to appeal to his immortal siblings. 'We should have intervened sooner. The queen has detained them for long enough!' Ares' voice boomed in the celestial throne room, his words reverberating. 'Did we not agree to aid our children when they were in peril?'

'They did not look threatened or harmed,' said Hades, his mouth quirking.

'From the scenes we've witnessed, they gave the impression of enjoying their incarceration and being willing participants,' added Demeter.

'They did not know what they were doing! The queen,' Ares spat, 'gave them a potion to dull their memories!'

'Hermes called on the High Priestess with instructions for a remedy, which the boy Dexion administered to Evandros and the others,' said Athene.

'What of the High Priestess, who is incapacitated and too weakened to use her power?' Ares flung his arms in the air with contempt.

'She communicated her wishes to the healer and had the boy find the flower and create the concoction,' replied Athene, sniffing in defence.

Ares laughed with derision. 'And do we see them leaving the island? No! They are still there. Again I ask, why are we not assisting our offspring?'

'I instructed Zeus to leave Evandros and his companions to the mercy of the queen and her Amazons.'

The God of War wheeled around, caught unawares by the arrival of the newcomer. 'Mother!' He bowed low, cowering before the ancient goddess.

The Titaness stood in the centre of the throne room and the younger gods lowered their heads to her. Zeus and Hera rose to their feet and greeted her.

'As disagreeable as Ares can be, his question is pertinent,' said Zeus. 'The more Evandros is delayed, the greater the chance Kronos and Eris have to discover the last piece.'

'Ares' dispute has no bearing on the quest; Evandros' success is destined, and the rightful path will be restored,' she said.

Zeus' brow knitted.

'What do you mean?' asked Hera, mystified. 'Rightful path? I don't understand. Are we not preventing our downfall by appointing the mortals to recover the sacred objects and, in doing so, thwart the old Titan from accomplishing his detestable scheme?'

'You are,' replied the Mother Goddess, 'yet this intervention was never to transpire.' The Titaness' voice hardened when she next spoke. 'Not for another five hundred years.'

The King of the Gods narrowed his eyes. 'If I did nothing, we ceased to exist long before the birth of this Messiah!'

'Perhaps. However, by interfering and using Evandros as a tool to circumvent fate, you have escalated a course of events that cannot be rectified.' She redirected her penetrating scrutiny onto Apollo. 'Is the Oracle still silent?'

The God of Prophecy and Music rolled his tongue over his lips, avoiding the heated views his Family cast his way. He swallowed before answering. 'She has not been receiving any of my predictions.'

'The boy Dexion hasn't been responding to our messages either,' said Demeter.

'What does this mean?' asked Aphrodite, sidling closer to Hephaistos.

'Kronos has projected a cloud over our mouthpiece and shrouded their minds from us,' Athene snapped at the cowering Aphrodite.

'He has the power to do so,' agreed the Mother Goddess, 'though I believe there is another explanation precipitating their inability to hear you.'

'What else could it be other than Kronos' machinations?' asked Ares, eyes glowing red.

The Titaness clasped her hands behind her back and eyeballed each of her offspring. 'Do you recall the reason you no longer dwell amongst the mortals?'

'Our interaction caused dissension and the destruction of our children, and rebuilding the world has taken several thousands of years,' replied Poseidon. 'We vowed never to interfere with our progeny, even if they strayed from our ministrations.'

'But we have not interfered!' Hera's face clouded. 'We prevailed upon our offspring to prevent our demise.'

'While imperilling their lives,' said the Mother Goddess. 'To forestall your annihilation, they acted as you instructed them. The Atlanteans should never have been involved. Their path lay elsewhere and not entwined with yours.'

'How is that possible?' asked Hera, jutting out her jaw. 'They are our children. They owe their lives to us, for their world would not exist without our cohabitation.'

'As much as I don't always agree with Hera, she is correct,' said

Poseidon. 'The children of Atlantis are ours, and they comply with our demands.'

'You,' said the goddess, eyeing each one, 'have failed to identify the ramifications of what you have generated. Did not the destruction of Troy and Priam's people enlighten you as to your actions when you positioned your children—Akhilleus, Hektor, Odysseus, Paris, Aiax, Cassandra, Aeneas—to do your bidding? What of them now?'

'Aeneas and Odysseus survived, as did Cassandra—for a short time,' Apollo said, crossing his arms against his chest and tossing back his head.

'Yes, but what happened to their descendants?' She waited for a moment, allowing them to contemplate her words, and then resumed speaking. 'Evandros and his companions had a different path, a life that you have since altered. Your introduction of the Atlanteans into this time has caused an obstacle between you and the mortals, and fractured your communication with them.'

'What has Evandros done?' Hera demanded, her cheeks flushing and eyes dilating.

'Evandros has done nothing,' said the goddess, her voice colder than the Arctic, 'and you will not punish him.'

Hera shrank back, as did those standing next to her.

'Evandros has surpassed what I expected him to do, and you will not approach or harm him.' The aura surrounding the Mother Goddess changed from a cool white to a blood red. 'Zeus, honour his wishes, whatever he decides.'

Zeus bowed his head. 'I shall grant him his wish.'

'In addition, you are to ensure Evandros, my High Priestess and their companions leave the island with no further obstacles,' she ordered. 'The channel between the Oracle and the boy Dexion should clear upon their departure.' A golden light enveloped her. 'I suggest you move with expediency.' The gilded glow hovered over them. 'Do not fail me.' And then, like a shooting star, the Mother Goddess departed.

'What was the path of the Atlanteans Mother spoke of?' Hera asked Zeus.

'Their death,' he replied.

'And what is it now?' Poseidon asked in suspicion.

Zeus tugged at his ear, hesitating, lifting his face to the celestial ceiling of the throne room, the colours and patterns changing with the mood of the gods.

'Zeus, what is their fate?' Hestia asked with urgency.

'They will become immortal and rule in our stead.'

Zeus sat back down on his marble seat, ignoring their shouts and demands for an answer.

'If you knew this was to happen, why use the Atlanteans?' asked Hades.

Zeus rapped his fingers on the armrest of his throne and waited until the immortals fell silent. 'The lines of fate never run true,' he finally replied. 'The Atlanteans' future cannot be ascertained, for a decision may change the path, and Evandros was the only one who could stop our termination.'

'How confident are you the Atlanteans will not replace our sovereignty and be worshipped by our mortals in our stead?' Ares retorted.

'Evandros is the reason I am certain.' Zeus stroked the head of his eagle and said no more.

CHAPTER 18

E van and his companions left the megaron early the next day, except for Leander, who remained behind with Jason and the Argonauts. They hadn't recovered from the antidote and were still slumbering. The golden-haired Atlantean offered to stay until Jason and his men woke and returned to the beach with them. Homer carried the High Priestess, emancipated after her long captivity, her delicate condition a stark contrast against his burly chest and herculean arms.

Evan didn't encourage small talk; he was trying to work out why he felt hollow and confused. He wondered if it was the aftereffects of the drug. He noted that Phameas, Homer and Hektor exhibited listlessness, their eyes dull and faces haggard. They had been under the influence of the potion for five months. The effects of the drug grew weaker over time and as they developed a tolerance, requiring the healer to increase their daily dosage.

They trudged along the sandy path, each one of them creating a long furrow with every step as they marched over the dunes. The faint reddish tinge on the horizon gave birth to the rising

sun, the myriad of colours a painter's palette dream. As Evan
crested the ridge, the *Argo* came into view, sitting askew on the
shore, a solitary and abandoned effigy. He reeled as her painted
blue eyes stared at him in reproach, if that was possible; that was
the impression he got from the abandoned ship.

'She's upset at us for neglecting and forgetting about her,' he
said to Phameas. 'See the jagged mast and torn mainsail? And it
looks like she has been crying.'

Her weathered hull and the lilt of the ship struck Evan as being
worn and tired. The black tar between the wooden planks left
streaks of tears, a macabre caricature of a weeping woman with
mascara running down her cheeks.

'I do not believe she will sail again,' said Hektor.

Phameas walked along the hull, from prow to stern, stopping
every few paces to inspect the seams between the planks of wood.
He rounded the stern and moved out of sight. A few minutes later,
he stepped around the bow.

'She is strong and sturdy. We repair her mast and make a new
sail, reset the seams with fresh tar, and she is seaworthy once
more,' he said.

'One minor issue,' said Evan, knocking on the neglected ship's
hull. 'It's going to take time, and now we are reliant on the queen
to deliver the materials she had ordered to fix the *Argo*. Can we
expect the queen to supply us with the items?'

'The gods will provide us with what we need,' said Hektor.

'Just like they helped us leave the island,' he snarled. 'We
cannot rely on them for any assistance.'

'It was Hermes who presented the cure,' Hektor said.

'No, he didn't. He gave clues of the location to the one person
who was bedridden. It was the High Priestess who convinced the
healer to sneak Dexion in to see her, and she later explained how
to create the antidote.' Evan thrust a finger at him. 'If the gods

were going to act, they should have interceded straight away, and we'd have resumed our voyage earlier.'

'They could not do that,' said the High Priestess.

'Why not?' he asked.

'Mother visited soon after I woke. She told me we were here for a purpose.'

'For what reason?' he probed, hands on hips.

'She did not tell me,' replied the High Priestess, averting her eyes.

'That doesn't make sense,' he said. 'They tell us to trek across the Mediterranean for these relics and then detour to an island far from Krete that has no bearing on our task?' He crossed his arms. 'It is illogical.'

'We do not question the actions of the gods or their decisions,' she said. 'We are their servants and must do as they decree.'

'I don't like it,' he grumbled. 'There is always a hidden agenda with them.'

'That is the way of the gods. We must plan for the journey to Krete and locate the last of the sacred objects,' she said. 'Homer, please set me down here.'

Evan put a hand on his head, glancing around the empty beach. 'We can't do much until we get supplies.'

'The queen will provide the essential materials.' She sat, legs drawn at a forty-five-degree angle, and wrapped her arms about them, interlinking her fingers.

'Here come the others!' Dexion said, pointing.

Stumbling over the sand dunes were a miserable group of men —heads drooping as if weighed down by anvils, shoulders slumped, dragging their feet in the sand, leaving behind deep grooves. Jason, his familiar gait more sluggish than usual, trudged alongside Leander, who led the way.

Evan bit his lip, drawing blood.

'What in the name of the gods?' said Hektor, gobsmacked.

One sailor staggered and stumbled, crashing into the man in front of him. Like a set of dominoes, the Argonauts smashed into one another, precipitating a chain reaction until all were down. Evan pressed a fist against his lips. The corners of Homer's mouth twitched. Phameas roared with laughter as a few of the men struggled to stand and free themselves of the melee. Evan guffawed a few times until he couldn't withhold his laughter. Phameas clutched his stomach and doubled over. Jason stumbled and tried to stay upright, but someone behind him slammed into his shoulders and he fell face first. Hektor walked away, muttering under his breath. The last person standing was Leander, who avoided being toppled. He twisted left, then right, in bewilderment at the moaning crewmen, unable to move.

'What is wrong with them?' asked the High Priestess, baffled.

Evan bent over, clutching his stomach, and tried to control the hysterical laughter. He inhaled with a snort and started laughing again at the vision of the overturned individuals, limbs fumbling in the air like discarded marionettes.

'I'm not sure,' he said between guffaws. 'It may be the residual effects of the potion combined with the antidote.'

She stood with her hands on her hips as tears streamed down Evan's face and viewed the squirming mass of bodies. 'I still don't see what is so funny.'

Phameas howled, tears dripping, and collapsed onto his knees. Homer laughed and clasped his stomach. Dexion wore a slight smile. The High Priestess shook her head and rolled her eyes.

It took a while before Evan, Phameas and Homer regained control and went to assist Leander with untangling Jason and his crew. He chuckled at Jason, who gave him a sour look.

'Some help you were,' the captain of the *Argo* said with a sniff.

'We gave you and your men the antidote to restore your memories.' He smiled.

'I am not referring to the elixir,' Jason fired back.

'I guess not.' He bit his tongue to keep from laughing out loud.

Jason grimaced at him. 'How is she, the *Argo*?' he asked, walking around him to the weather-beaten ship.

Evan fell into step with the sailor. 'Phameas examined her from stern to prow and said she was seaworthy; the sail needs repairing, and the mast replaced.'

Jason placed a palm against the ship's hull. 'I am sorry to have neglected you, my beautiful girl. We will fix you and make you as sturdy as the day we first set sail.' He leaned his head against the sun-bleached planks. 'We should never have left you.' Jason beckoned his crew. The men encircled the *Argo*, laying a hand against her warm body, and whispered their own apologies to her. 'Now, Argonauts, we must make her proud of us again. We clear the sand from the deck and hold, remove the broken mast, tend to the sail and check the ropes, removing the ones that have perished and putting aside others that need replacing,' Jason rumbled at the sailors. 'By the gods, move!'

The men scurried about, dodging each other as they complied with their captain's orders. Evan was about to board the ship when Phameas reached over and tapped him on the shoulder.

'Evandros.'

He took in the stony expression on his friend's face and wheeled round to see what was happening. He swore. A mounted cohort of the queen's warriors trotted towards them, the black plumes on their bronze helmets swaying with the movement of their horses. To the rear of the regiment, moving like encumbered turtles, were two pairs of horses, each hauling a wagon, the wheels biting into the sand. The men stopped working and watched the encroaching entourage in silence.

The air bristled, the ozone sweet and pungent, similar to at the onset of a heavy shower of rain. Homer carried the High Priestess to the fore of the simmering group. Evan's breath and pulse raced as he recognised the familiar colours of the queen's bodyguards. He tried to temper his indignation, telling himself Antioche had done what all leaders do when presented with favourable opportunities. He joined his sister and half-brother with reluctance.

The lead warrior removed her helmet and dismounted with ease. She said to him, 'The queen sends provisions for your voyage.' When he did not respond, she added, 'The queen wants to know if you need any other items and, if so, asks you to prepare a list of what you require and she will arrange further deliveries.'

Phameas and Leander examined the contents of the wagons.

'There is enough food and drink to last many moons and the journey to Krete,' Phameas said to him and went to the next wagon. 'And here are the promised materials to repair the ship.'

Leander concurred. 'More than what King Mentor and Councilman Neleos provided together.'

He remained close-lipped.

'Please thank Queen Antioche for the supplies,' said the High Priestess. She nodded at Phameas and Leander. The two men reached into the first wagon and each grabbed a basket of fresh food and carried it over to the makeshift shelter. At Jason's cue, the Argonauts helped unload pithoi filled with wine and water, baskets of bread and more earthenware vases stuffed with olives, fish and meat and then emptied the contents from the second wagon. The carts emptied, the drivers, with a quick expert flick of the reins, had the horses about-faced and trotting back towards the palace. Half the retinue of the soldiers followed; the others remained with their commander.

'Queen Antioche also sends this gift and hopes it is useful in a time of need.' She held out the wrapped object to Evan. He did not move. She marched across and thrust the item at him, forcing him to take it, then spun on her heel and, with an agility that made the men gasp, mounted her horse and wheeled it around. She and her warriors departed at a fast canter and withdrew over the sandy mounds.

'What do you suppose the queen gave you?' asked Phameas, gazing at the unusual shape and length of the gift.

'It's a bow,' said Leander without hesitation.

He flung it at Leander. 'I don't want it. It's yours.'

Leander held up his hands. 'I already have a serviceable bow, given to me by Divine Poseidon.'

'Dexion, it's yours.' He held it out to him. The boy backed away and squeezed between Homer and Hektor, clasping his hands behind his back.

'You should unwrap it,' said Phameas. 'It may change your mind, and if not, sell it when we reach a port.'

Evan pursed his lips. He undid the rope and the cloth wrapping fell to the ground.

Jason whistled. 'The queen has given you a gift of great worth. I have never seen an Amazonian bow or quiver up close before. This is the work of a skilled craftsman.'

The artisan had crafted the bow from the limb of an ash tree, pliable yet strong, while they had made the quiver from hardened animal skin, leathered and embossed with brass. The etchings had a myriad of hunting scenes, and the images came across so lifelike the animals appeared to be fleeing from their hunters. The quiver was filled with black arrows, the fletching taken from peacock feathers. Hidden within was a belt.

Evan was taken aback.

'What is it?' asked Phameas.

'It's … it's … nothing,' he said in a hoarse voice, goggling at the leather strap.

Leander ran his hand over the bow. 'This has great shooting range. I can feel its power and age.'

'She has offered you a gift from her family,' the High Priestess said, her voice soft.

Jason gawked at the belt. 'This is most unusual, for no person has ever seen the girdle of an Amazonian queen. This,' he emphasised, patting the golden belt, 'is given by the queen to her daughter when she is about to die. It is an object of power for the Amazons. Without it, the queen's reign may end. I have never known a queen of the Amazons to give away her girdle, and certainly not to a man.'

He tried to make sense of why the queen would gift him such a precious heirloom.

'Why did she give it to Evandros?' Phameas asked, voicing Evan's own question.

'Perhaps the queen hopes he shall return and give it back to her.' Jason raised a brow at him. 'I know of one other man who was granted the Amazonian queen's girdle, and that was Herakles when he petitioned for Hippolyta as part of his ninth labour assigned by King Eurystheus. The interaction did not please Divine Hera, and she disguised herself as an Amazon and told the female warriors Herakles intended to kidnap their queen. The Amazons attacked, and a battle followed where Herakles killed Hippolyta, believing she had betrayed him, and thereafter he sailed away.'

Phameas raised a brow. 'Evandros, not even a great warrior can deny a woman—not one that is a queen and wields weapons as skilfully as you do.'

'Not happening,' he said in a quiet voice, then repeated, 'not happening.'

CHAPTER 19

A month after leaving the palace, and having repaired the *Argo* with long-awaited materials, they were ready to set sail. Evan assisted the High Priestess in embarking the ship, noting the healthy glow of her skin and the extra weight she had gained from regular eating. He then sloshed through the surf and joined Phameas at the prow with the others, waiting for Jason's order to push the ship into the water. They had spent the last few days stowing foodstuffs in the ship's hold along with additional ropes, oars and an extra sail.

'Best to be prepared,' Jason said to him as the crew loaded other stock requisitioned from the queen.

Jason stood sure-footed at the helm, grasping the steering oars, holding them aloft. With him were the High Priestess and Dexion, the sea breeze teasing the tendrils of Alexina's hair. Prior to boarding, the Argonaut had offered a libation to Poseidon, the Sea God, requesting safe passage to Krete. Evan had resisted the urge to tell him it was a waste of time, that the gods were fickle and no number of offerings would garner any favour or keep them out of danger. Instead, he'd kept his mouth shut and his opinion to himself; besides, Antioche's gifts troubled him. Why give him valuable family heirlooms that she would have passed on to her daughter? It made little sense. Perhaps it was her way of apologising for their incarceration. He sighed, vexed by rationalising her actions, which brought him farther from a logical and sane answer.

'All hands to the hull!' Jason bellowed.

The Argonauts took up position around the prow, the bronze beak glistening under the sun's rays and the repainted bright blue eyes on either side scowling in sullen defiance, daring the island to prevent their departure. A silent warning to whomever and whatever that the *Argo* and her crew and passengers were under her protection. Evan placed his hands against the smooth black wooden hull and smiled lopsidedly at Phameas.

'This brings back memories of my first experience doing this, and of when we met,' he said.

Phameas laughed. 'And do you remember what happened afterwards?'

'That I do, my friend,' he replied with a crooked grin. 'And being mocked by the crew when I fell into the water.'

'Now push!'

He dipped his head low between his shoulders, his feet digging into the wet sand, the cool crystalline sea splashing against his calves. He gritted his teeth and shoved at the immovable hulk.

'Again!' yelled Jason.

He felt slight movement as the *Argo* shifted from its sandy cushioned bed.

'Again!'

The *Argo* moved out of his reach and he sloshed forward as she slipped further into the deeper waters of the bay. The Argonauts shouted and cheered, rushing to climb aboard.

'Come along, Evandros!' Phameas urged, sploshing over to the shallow steps carved into the rostrum.

He was the last to clamber aboard, and when Jason saw him, he called out, 'Argonauts, oars in!'

Within minutes, Jason piloted the *Argo* away from the island, adjusted the steering oars and set a course for the depths of the glittering Aegean Sea. Evan stood at the bow and stared at the solitary figure sitting atop a horse on the highest point on the beach. He rubbed his chest as a dull ache increased. With every stroke, the person grew smaller until he could not see them, and the pain intensified. He waited until the Isle of Hephaistos receded into the distance and became a mere speck on the horizon, knowing she was still there on the hilltop and wouldn't leave until they were out of view.

He clenched the wooden railing until the veins on his hands and arms protruded like thick cords of rope. She had somehow infiltrated his thoughts and abducted his feelings, and despite what she had done, he could not dismiss her as a passing liaison. He started at the light touch on his back and saw the High Priestess and Homer, concern on their faces.

'How long have you been standing there?' he asked, relinquishing his hold on the beam.

'You miss her,' she said, searching his face.

He flung a hand in the island's direction, lip curling. 'No more than I miss being drugged and used as a baby-making machine.'

'Liar,' she whispered. He clenched his jaw.

You cannot blame yourself for what happened, wrote Homer.

'No, but I don't like being taken for a fool,' he said, punching his thigh. 'I failed to rescue you in time to prevent that worthless king of Kyrene from having his henchmen destroy your vocal cords, and now you have to write on the tablet to communicate. And I failed to safeguard you as I promised the Mother Goddess and you almost died at the hands of the queen.'

'You could not control either situation and I don't believe the queen intended to dupe you. She was protecting her people. As a scholar, you know leaders use situations to their advantage whenever the opportunity presents itself in order to ensure the security of their home. Queen Antioche was addressing the needs of her people—otherwise, they cease to exist,' she said. 'It does not differ from our quest to keep our families alive by preventing the Dark Master from destroying the gods.'

'Why do you believe the Amazons are dying?' he asked, disquieted.

'The healer told me.'

'She shared that with you, just like that?'

'No, but she grew to trust me, and as I couldn't walk or go anywhere without assistance, the healer confided in me,' she replied.

'Regardless of the reason, it doesn't mean a person should take advantage of another, whatever their predicament,' he said, jawline hardening.

She laid a hand over his. 'That is true, and Queen Antioche is not blameless—she did conspire to keep us under an enchantment.' She stepped closer. 'Yet you must forgive her, as I must Leander. Their actions arose from the ignoble Goddess of Discord, who intended to hinder our progress.'

He grimaced. 'There is a difference between what Leander did and the queen's actions and decisions.' He clasped her hand in his. 'Leander, like all these men, did not know what he was doing and being coerced to do. The queen ordered her healer to create the potion and administer it. I cannot forgive such behaviour. Leander was heartbroken when he realised what he had done, even though it was not his fault. He won't absolve himself of his infidelities. You must do that for him.' He lowered his head to hers. 'He is worthy of you, and you of him.'

Tears welled in her eyes. Homer nodded and gave her a one-armed hug.

'There you have it, your brothers approve,' he said.

She wiped her eyes with the palms of her hands.

Homer scribbled onto his tablet and then poked Evan in the chest, not too far from his heart, and then whacked him. Evan made a face at him, rubbing his torso and head.

'Homer is correct,' she said, reading the Linear script, eyes still watery. 'You must bear no malice towards the queen, for she too was beguiled, and when a goddess of Eris' repute makes a tantalising offer, no mortal would be able to refuse her. Even though you will not see her again, you need to forgive Queen Antioche.'

Evan averted his face, taking a keen interest in the vast azure seascape. He pointed. 'Dolphins!'

'Evandros,' the High Priestess said in a sharp tone. 'She is carrying your child.'

Homer disapproved, crossing his arms against his barrel-like chest.

Evan winced. It was as if Homer had punched him in the gut. He then straightened and steeled himself. 'When we have recovered the last object, I will return home. Alone.'

She opened her mouth and hesitated at the icy glint in his eyes. 'Homer, can you assist me to the cabin so I may rest awhile?'

Homer held out his arm, which she clutched, and with slow, even steps they walked away. The vein in Evan's forehead throbbed, and he rubbed at the dull ache forming at the base of his skull. *A child.* He grabbed the railing once again and gazed at the waves on the sea.

'Zeus, you had better honour your promise to me and send me back to my home in the twenty-first century,' he snarled.

∽

'**M**ast up!' Jason hollered.

Four Argonauts stowed their oars and dashed to hoist the sail. Two of them undid the ropes, ready to guide the rigging, while the other two pulled on the halyards to raise the sail.

'Ah, smell that! It is wonderful to be back on the sea,' Jason said with a broad grin. 'How could I have ever forgotten all of this?'

'Easily, with the aid of drugs,' Evan said, lip curling.

'What the queen did was dishonourable. However, there is not one Argonaut who is distressed or upset by the encounters,' Jason said in a light tone.

'That is not the point,' he bristled. 'What she did was wrong.'

'Perhaps and perhaps not. I must plan our route to Krete and you need a strategy for our arrival.' Jason checked on the new mainsail. It billowed, capturing the sea breeze, and he adjusted the steering oars.

Evan worked his jaw back and forth, waging an internal debate that stoked the impassioned embers within his gut. Jason was right: he had to focus his energy on the upcoming battle with Minotaur—if it existed—and not what had happened with the Amazons or with Antioche. He must forget her and move on.

'Do you have a route in mind?' he asked.

'There is an age-old route the Achaeans and their allies used when they fought the Trojans,' Jason replied. 'The ancient mariners plotted the safest course sailing by constructing a series of devices on various islands.'

'Can you describe these devices?' he asked, interest piqued, his ire ebbing.

Jason pointed to the sun. 'A great beacon from almighty Helios points to an island.'

Evan chewed on his bottom lip. 'Is it a signal of sorts?'

Jason nodded. 'It lights up the sky and flashes as lightning does.'

'Have you seen one?'

'Yes, there were a number of islands with these objects as we journeyed to Colchis.' Jason readjusted the steering oars before turning to Evan with a concerned look. 'What are the possibilities the Cyclopes will learn of our escape and try to intercept us again?'

'I'd say the odds are high,' Evan replied in a distracted voice. 'Do you know more about these people who built the contraptions?'

Jason clasped his chin and tapped a finger against his lips. 'Not a lot, except they came from the east, beyond the Pillars of Herakles, and were masters at plotting routes using the stars. They traded goods and developed alliances with other peoples they met.'

'Do you know how old they are?'

Jason shook his head. 'No one knows how old the devices are. What we can say for certain is that, whoever constructed them, the beacons are centuries old and were on the islands long before the great war between the Achaeans and Trojans.'

'Do you know what happened to them, these mariners?'

'Only what I told you. The one piece of evidence of their existence is the beacons.'

'Extraordinary,' he said. 'Will any of the islands around here have one?'

'Some do—I intend to use them for our journey to Krete,' Jason answered.

Evan shielded his eyes, scanning the horizon. 'How do you know which island has one?'

'It emits light at a particular hour during the day and I steer the ship in that direction. What is even better, the signal will point us to the next island that has a device.' Jason pointed to the sky. 'If we keep ahead of the sun, we should see a flare or beam on the horizon. Besides, I don't want to be out on the sea come nightfall.'

'Do all captains use these apparatuses to guide them?'

'Those who sail these waters would—legends of the ancient mariners and their creations have been told since the time when gods lived amongst humans.'

CHAPTER 20

'What is it? Ever since you've brought me here, I've had no contact with any immortals except for yourself and your minder,' Melaina said, thrusting a thumb at the larger-than-usual crow perched on an overhead branch of an ancient gnarly oak tree. Its golden eyes traced her every movement. The young goddess was relaxing on the grassy ledge of an enormous lagoon, her feet dangling in the cool water. 'Do you bring tidings of the world outside? What of my father, Kronos—has he noticed my absence?'

There was no reply. Melaina diverted her attention from the pool and frowned when her captor did not respond.

'Well, are you here to tell me I can leave?'

The God of Music and Prophecy sighed. 'Must we do this? Each time I come, you ask me the same question. You know the answer, so why ask?'

Melaina shrugged and swung round facing the lake. 'It amuses me to see you vexed.' She plucked at the grass at her side. 'There was no need for you to imprison me. I was not endangering your precious quest, nor was I harming anyone.'

'What you were doing was much more perilous,' Apollo said,

narrowing his eyes. 'Your infatuation and interference with the mortal Evandros put them all in danger. If we had allowed you to continue to meddle, it would have clouded his judgement and therefore impaired his reasoning. No, Father Zeus' pronouncement in removing your influence and machinations on the mortal was correct.'

Melaina pouted and flicked her hair, thrusting her breasts upwards. 'You cannot blame me for the effects of my allure.'

Apollo sneered. 'You continue to lust after a mere mortal, even after he tried to kill you.'

'It was a misunderstanding. I needed time to explain my motives,' she objected.

'Your designs on him were obvious,' Apollo retorted. 'The High Priestess had misgivings since your first appearance. How did you propose to convince her otherwise?'

Melaina jumped to her feet, her eyes flashing. 'If you and the other gods had not interfered, you would have seen my true intentions. However, you whisked me away before I could complete my task.' Her chest was heaving as she jutted her chin at Apollo. 'My father, Kronos, sent me to help them and guide Evandros to find the sacred relics.'

'Did Kronos reveal his entire plan to you? Did he explain why he allowed you to get involved?' Apollo became weary of her tirade, and of her accusations that he had orchestrated her capture. 'Do you believe he would reward you for helping to retrieve Mother's objects? You are as naïve as you are insignificant to him. If your father succeeds, he intends to banish you along with us.'

'He promised me the sanctity of Mount Olympos,' she said, stomping her feet.

Apollo laughed. 'Our home won't exist if Kronos wins. You mean nothing to him; this earth has more value than you. He gave you false platitudes so you would ingratiate yourself with the insignificant mortal.'

Melaina balled her hands. 'You are no different.' She sashayed towards him until she could smell his sweet musky scent and feel the heat of his body. 'You show up here on the pretence of disclosing important *information, but that's not why you visit. I know how much you covet me, and that is why you frequent often.'*

She smirked at the telltale bulge beneath his short khiton.

'Now what of Evandros? Has he arrived at Krete?' she asked, tilting her head up at him with a smug smile.

Apollo sneered. 'I've come with tidings. Evandros, his companions and the Argonauts along with their captain were shipwrecked on the Isle of Hephaistos, captured by the Amazon queen and retained as consorts.' He smirked at the crestfallen expression on her face. 'To my knowledge, all the men enjoyed their incarceration by the Amazons, and the queen was rather enamoured by Evandros. She kept him as her sole companion for the duration of their bondage.'

Melaina stilled, and her face numbed.

'I am happy to announce they have escaped because of the canny intelligence of my seer, Dexion.' Apollo beamed. 'Evandros and his companions are journeying towards the Isle of Minos.' The God of Music and Prophecy pivoted, took a few steps, paused and swivelled back. 'Thought you should know ... the Amazon queen carries Evandros' seed.'

Apollo tossed his long golden locks and sneered at her with disdain, then walked away as Melaina collapsed into a heap on the grass. She screamed. Her inconsolable and wounded wails echoed across the Utopian landscape, her howls of vengeance snuffed out as he restored the seal to the paradisaical prison.

CHAPTER 21

E van bolted upright.

'What is it?' He swung his head to the right and back, sweeping across the deck of the ship and out to the flat planes of the sea.

He had fallen asleep while his companions discussed the location of the last artefact and the Minotaur, having tuned out when the conversation had digressed to how to fight King Minos' mythical creature, not wanting to acknowledge his part in the inevitable duel or the possibility of his demise. He hoped that by the time they found the statuette, he'd be sitting on his comfy lounge where he belonged, watching television. He also had an unsettling dream of Antioche, who smiled at him, and then her face transformed into the rage-contorted face of Melaina. Her hands were outstretched, flinging balls of crimson flames at him. He woke as the fire flickered at his limbs, about to consume him.

Phameas' eyes widened and he clambered to his feet. 'By Baal, what is that?'

'Do you see it? That light shimmering in the distance?' Jason said with excitement. 'That is our destination.'

Evan joined Phameas, shading his eyes against the glare of the sun on the water. The mesmerising effect of the flickering glow on the horizon against the clear blue sky was hypnotising.

'Well, I'll be a monkey's uncle,' he murmured. 'What did they build to create such a powerful reflection?'

'Monkey? What monkey?' Phameas searched the surrounds, perplexed.

'It's a turn of phrase,' Evan replied, distracted.

'Oh ... I don't understand when you say strange things,' his friend said.

'Sorry.'

'And you must be more attentive. The others may hear you.' Phameas punched him.

'Ouch!' He rubbed his arm. 'You have a good right jab. And you're right, Phameas. I'll be more discreet.'

'Yes. For a smart man you can be stupid.' Phameas tapped his forehead as he spoke, glowering at him.

'Understood.'

'You really need to stop and think before—'

'Phameas, I get it, you don't have to go on about it,' he grumbled.

The Phoenician scratched his bearded chin, eyes darting and avoiding Evan's face. 'Ah ... good ...' He cleared his throat. 'If the gods continue with this wind, we should be within sight of land by mid-afternoon.'

'That may give us enough daylight to investigate those reflective emitters,' Evan said, appraising the glimmering light in the distance.

'What is so important about them? And why do you want to spend an afternoon finding the object?'

'I'd like to see what they are and how they work, who made them and why they built them on particular islands. There's been no mention of these machines during my years of education—it's possible no one has discovered the emitters.' He gesticulated to Phameas, excited. 'It is possible your ancestors built these. Wouldn't you like to know if they did?'

'If my people made these machines, it would be a great story to tell of their incredible achievements.'

'I hear a "but" coming.'

'These islands are far from home and I cannot see how or why my forebears would build them.' Phameas scratched his bearded chin, dubious.

'The Phoenicians sailed tremendous distances, much further than historians thought,' Evan said. 'We cannot discount the probability that they built these structures.'

'If my people constructed such objects, there would be some record or knowledge passed from person to person.'

'Unless they forgot the information over time,' said Evan.

J ason piloted the ship into a cove.

'Sail down! Oars out! Prepare for beach landing!'

A few Argonauts sprang from their seats and had the mainsail down within minutes. Evan, Phameas and Leander hastened from the prow to the bow, securing loose items, stowing supplies and extra equipment below the gangway. Homer took care of the High Priestess and Dexion, making sure they were both tied to the railing with leather straps. Hektor shifted the heavy ornamented box containing the labrys and secured it against the wooden truss behind Jason.

Evan clutched the rail and bit his lip at the fast-approaching shoreline. He placed his feet apart and leaned forward, waiting for the inevitable jolt that came when the hull of the ship contacted the beach. He scrunched his eyes shut as the wooden hull scratched against the sandbank.

'Oomph!' He rubbed his stomach, wincing at Phameas and Leander. 'At least we landed with no mishap.'

Phameas chortled and slapped him on the back. 'Excellent landing, Captain!' he shouted.

Jason raised a hand and beamed in acknowledgement.

Evan slung the shield over his shoulder, strapped on his sword and picked up his bag before clambering down the footholds in the ship's beak. Grey stones of various sizes blanketed the beach. He squatted, the water lapping at his heels, and selected a stone, the clean, polished surface reminding him of the short visit to Nice, France. Here, just as on the shores in France, the constant ebb and flow of the sea smoothened the pebbles, nature's emery board.

'Ahoy there, Evandros! Incoming!' bellowed one of the Argonauts.

One by one, sailors tossed overboard heavy ropes, gathered by the crew, who had jumped ashore. He hurried to help to drag the ship onto the beach and anchor the *Argo* for the night.

'Is there a reason we landed here and not at the township?' asked Hektor, pointing to a well-populated village.

Built on the slopes of a hill surrounding the akropolis was a large building that resembled the Temple of Athene in Athens. Grey smoke eddied from the rooftops of the houses that smothered the sanctuary and shrouded the town in a dirty cloud. The distance was far enough to dissuade the most curious from investigating, yet still visible to report unusual activity.

'Yes, there is,' replied Jason. 'Port taxes, and as I don't have cargo to sell, there is no need to pay the harbour master to moor the *Argo*.'

'You have been here before,' Hektor said.

'Many times. It is a popular stopover for many of us sailors.' Jason addressed Evan, who was scoping out the island. 'If you are seeking the device, it is that way.' He pointed west, in the opposite direction of the town, and where the land undulated at regular intervals, the formation reminding Evan of the curves of a female body. 'Can you see the glittering light in the distance?'

He shielded his eyes and nodded. 'That is further than I expected. How long will it take to walk there?'

Jason tilted his head to the side and put his hands on his hips as he studied the refracting beams on the horizon. 'Two to three hours, I'd say. You should get back before nightfall if you leave now.' The Argonaut gave him a lopsided grin. 'Be sure to bring plenty of water and food.'

'Right ...' *How important is it to locate this object?* He mused. Was it going to help in their search for the Mother Goddess' statuette? No, it wouldn't, but it excited him to discover a technology that hadn't been unearthed by archaeologists or written about by historians and that he could claim as his own—just like Howard Carter had done when he'd unearthed Tutankhamun's tomb, though Evan wouldn't need to replaster the wall as Carter had done when he'd lied to authorities about his magnificent discovery.

Jason had sauntered over his men, who were setting up camp on the beach.

'Shall I get us water and food?' Phameas asked, breaking his contemplative mood.

'Yes, that would be great, Phameas,' he replied. 'We should ask if anyone else would like to join us.'

'Homer will come, as will Dexion. Hektor, I expect, will stay behind. Leander is as skittish as a seagull and will take any opportunity to get as far away from the High Priestess as he can.'

'I have a feeling you are right, my friend.'

They wandered to where Homer and Leander were busy setting up a tent for the High Priestess, while Dexion, his pup scampering by his side, carried colourful rugs and cushions—a gift from Queen Antioche—and distributed them under the canopy. Hektor assisted the High Priestess to the tent and under his other arm carried a three-legged table. He set it down and then helped the High Priestess to recline onto the cushions. Dexion placed a platter of fruit on the table and within her reach.

'Phameas and I are going to locate the flashing emitter,' he said.

'I'll come with you,' said Leander, as quick as a cobra striking.

Phameas gave Evan a knowing smile.

Homer indicated he would accompany them.

'I will remain with the High Priestess,' said Hektor.

'What do you hope to learn if you find this object?' she asked, rearranging the cushions.

'How they made it and what material they used, and I may work out who built them,' he answered. 'We need to leave now so we can return before sunset.' He then addressed Phameas, Homer and Leander. 'Bring your weapons. Never know what or who is out there.'

CHAPTER 22

Before they left the beach, Evan approached the makeshift tent.

'Dexion, are you coming?' he asked.

The boy shrugged and nodded at the wolf that lay curled by his feet.

'I do not want to leave Lykeios behind.' The pup pricked up its ears and lifted its head at Dexion's voice.

'Lykeios, is it?' Evan squatted and scratched the animal's head. 'I am sure Lykeios can walk. Bring a bag in case he gets tired.'

Dexion jumped up and raced out from under the canopy. 'Come on, Lykeios!'

The pup scampered after him, mouth open and tongue hanging out.

'We should be back before the sun sets,' Evan said to the High Priestess and Hektor. 'What is it?' he asked, squirming at her intense gaze at him.

'Do you intend to bring Dexion and Phameas to Atlantis?' she asked.

He floundered, taken aback by the question. 'I ... I ... hadn't thought that far ahead. It's possible Phameas may want to return home.'

She nodded. 'Yes, that is so, but Dexion doesn't have a family.'

'That is correct.' He pinched the bridge of his nose. 'Is there a reason you mention this now?'

'Dexion has developed an attachment to you and sees you as a father. You hold his fate in your hands.'

He took note of how Dexion and the pup interacted with Phameas, Homer and Leander. 'I guess we have formed a bond since we met in Hippo Regius.' He stood, eyes dilating. 'In that case, if something happens to me, he is to stay with Phameas, and I want a guarantee from you and the gods that they will not be left behind or destitute.'

Her head jerked back. 'Evandros ...'

His black eyes bored into hers. 'Promise me you will take care of them.'

She bit her bottom lip. 'Yes ... I'll see to it.'

He eyeballed Hektor. 'Phameas and Dexion need not know of this agreement, is that understood?'

Hektor turned up his nose in contempt. 'What would be the purpose of telling them of your impending demise? It would not serve them well, nor would it aid in our quest to find Mother's sacred object.'

'Hektor!' she gasped, outraged. 'You are speaking to my brother!'

'My apologies, High Priestess.' The Atlantean lowered his head. 'My tongue often runs of its own accord. I did not mean to offend you, but I speak the truth. It is crucial we stop the Dark Master from locating Mother's precious item and using it against the gods, and destroying our home and our people, no matter the sacrifice.'

'I congratulate you for an insincere apology, Hektor, but you are right,' he said. 'We must succeed, even at the cost of my life.'

'Evandros ...' the High Priestess began.

'The others are waiting for me.'

Evan ducked under the overhanging cover and strode towards his friends. He composed himself and redirected his thoughts to the cool, clean sheets of his twenty-first-century bed linen, the glorious shower stocked with various shampoos and gels, and the luxurious towels. *That is what I am looking forward to.* By the time he reached his companions, he was calmer and his mind clearer.

'Come along, the day isn't getting younger.'

The path snaked across the undulating land, the climb subtle as the incline graduated to the highest peak on the island. Evan halted on the crest. His woolly mane whipped about his face and the hem of his khiton flapped against his legs. He cursed as strands of hair flew into his mouth, not impressed by how long it had grown during their incarceration by the female warriors— vital months that could have seen him back in the twenty-first century sooner.

Homer tapped Evan on the shoulder, pointed and wrote on his tablet. *That looks like a temple.*

Evan peered across, noting the familiar structure with pediment and columns. 'It does appear to be one.'

They continued along the path, the flickering glare coming from the same location as the temple.

'I wonder which god the temple is dedicated to?' asked Leander when they arrived.

'It doesn't show signs of recent use,' Phameas answered, leaning over the altar. Evan joined him, noting the accumulation of fine white ash, and moved on.

The sanctuary backed onto the cliff, and parts of the surrounding walls that protected the temple had crumbled. In other sections, portions of the wall lay strewn on both sides, as if pushed by opposing teams of invaders. Evan approached the building, which struck him as being untouched. The paint on the columns, tympanum and metopes had faded, but he could still see the remnants of the original vibrant colours that had once adorned the fixtures.

'Not so sure that they abandoned it,' he said and pointed. 'There are remains of ash in the altar.'

Homer walked up to the large wooden doors of the temple and tried to push them open. He put his shoulder against the weather-beaten timber, the hue bleached by the sun and from the gusty winds that whistled and buffeted them. Evan tapped his half-brother on the arm.

'It's not essential we go inside. The machine will be outside,' he said, 'otherwise it could not be seen by sailors and used for navigating.'

'Do you know what this object looks like?' asked Leander.

'No idea, but shouldn't be too hard to miss—not if we saw the flare from the sea.'

'We've walked a long way to find this ... whatever it is. It had better be some magical instrument, Evandros, for if not, you are paying for the most expensive wine I can purchase at our next port.' Phameas flung his arms in the air.

'I can't know for certain. It could be anything from a large mirror to a pit with a fire burning day and night,' he replied. 'Besides, you owe me wine for beating you in three successive games of Senet.'

'Baal knows you cheated in all the games.' Phameas smirked at him and then lifted his face to sniff the air. 'If there's smoke, I can't smell it, though with this wind it wouldn't be safe to leave an unattended fire pit.'

Evan poked a finger in the ashes in the altar. 'Cold.' He stood. 'Let's search the grounds. It has to be close, it's what Jason used to navigate to this island.'

Dexion's pup bounded ahead and took off around the rear of

the sanctuary. The faint sound of sharp, short, high-pitched yelps struggled over the clamorous wind.

'Lykeios!' The Sicilian boy took off.

'Dexion! Wait!' Evan sprinted after him, the pounding of feet resounding behind him as his companions followed. Seconds later, he skidded to a stop. 'Oh, my good God!'

'Great Baal!' Phameas' mouth hung open.

'Only the gods can create such machines,' said Leander, staring.

Homer planted a hand on his head, eyes wide in awe.

Dexion clutched his wriggling pup, standing ten metres away from the wall of the temple and beneath the largest round mirror Evan had ever seen, the diameter twenty metres. The mirror curved like a shallow bowl. The once-glossy bronze surface facing the sea was smooth and the bottom of the dish blackened, as if scorched by fire. An enormous tripod held it propped at a forty-five-degree angle, the legs as thick as a man's thigh and four times the length. He approached it, sidling from one side, then the other, noting the different positions of the poles, similar to the legs of a three-legged table and fixed to the convex surface of the reflector.

'It must weigh a ton,' he said. 'It would have taken a lot of men and oxen to move this into place.'

'Ahoy, Evandros, come here.' Phameas beckoned him over animatedly. Homer and Leander joined them, and they studied the bedrock. The Phoenician knelt and brushed aside the soil to reveal a groove that encircled the entire contraption. Evan crouched next to his friend and cleared the metal hoops.

'Homer, what do you make of it?' he asked.

The large Atlantean walked around to the other side and removed the dirt from the base, uncovering more metal hoops.

He gaped at them in amazement. *This is a moving platform. They harnessed bulls or oxen to the legs of the tripods to turn the mirror in either direction, depending on the sun's location.* Homer pointed to the tripod and mirror. *See, there are smaller hoops attached to the underside.*

Evan's face brightened. 'These metal hoops move the mirror up or down and to the left or right!' He stepped under where the three legs crossed each other beneath the mirror. 'This is ingenious. Could it be they are some communication system?' He calculated how the animals moved the device and estimated how the projection of sunlight beamed across the sea to another mirror.

'Did Jason mention that several islands had these reflective emitters?' asked Leander.

He nodded, eyes shining. 'Yes, which suggests islands of a certain distance had these communicators erected and citizens taught how to use them. It is possible they were also used to transmit information and messages to other islanders.' He asked Phameas, 'Have you seen anything like this as a sailor?'

'No, I would remember such an impressive object,' Phameas replied. 'I hadn't heard about these devices until Jason mentioned them.'

Evan ran a hand along the curvature of the oversized bronze bowl.

'It is old, much older than Jason may believe,' said Leander, tapping on the pitting on the legs of the tripod, 'and not used in a long time, seeing the amount of bird droppings spread across the top and around the base.'

'Jason thought a race of mariners built them,' Phameas said.

'I don't think seafarers constructed these,' said Evan, examining the apparatus. 'The people who designed the devices intended to use them to communicate across vast distances. Imagine this: marauders are going from island to island, destroying townships, killing men, raping women and pillaging.

This machine'—he rapped his knuckles on the object—'could relay warnings and signal for help within minutes.'

They would need to know what codes to use so they all understand each other, Homer wrote.

'Yes.' Evan nodded. 'I expect a select group of individuals was chosen; they maintained the mirrors and knew a combination of signals to relay. The fact that it is here, behind a temple, suggests it would have been priests or priestesses who lived here, and appointed guardians of these machines.'

'That is logical,' Leander admitted. 'A pity Hektor isn't here. He could tell us more on the construction process of the machine.'

'The design is straightforward, no real secrets about the way they built it,' said Evan, pulling out his writing pad and charcoal. 'What I'd like to know more about was how they used it and for what purpose.' With quick, decisive strokes, he sketched the enormous apparatus, moving around it step by step. Dexion put the squirming pup down and trailed behind him, the wolf accompanying them.

'How old do you think the mirrors are?' he asked Evan.

He paused from his drawing and studied the reflector. 'I couldn't say, maybe over a thousand years old. It would take a lot of oil and polishing to get these working again.'

'What material is it made from?' asked Leander. He knocked on the metal, the sound similar to a bell tolling.

He ran a hand over the smooth surface. 'It would be a mix of bronze and tin, an alloy called speculum. Whoever built this and the others, if they still exist, they were master engineers. To make something of this magnitude and with an understanding of the sun's movements, they had to be intelligent. I haven't seen the level of sophistication of this machinery anywhere else in our travels.'

Homer nodded and asked, *Could it be Atlantean?*

'I am not sure,' he replied. 'It is possible. We lost most

technology and knowledge from ancient Atlantis after its destruction, except for what the survivors remembered and rebuilt.'

'Best we return,' said Phameas, eyeing the changing colour on the horizon.

'Another ten minutes and I am finished,' he said, returning to his drawings. He muttered to himself, engrossed in getting the dimensions. Not wanting to leave any detail out, he did not notice the drop in temperature.

'What is happening?' Leander clasped his bow in a tight grip, his other hand poised to pluck an arrow from his quiver.

'Huh?' Evan blinked, still preoccupied by the device.

'Look!' Dexion pointed at the sky.

'What the heck?' He gaped at a flock of birds suspended mid-flight.

'By Baal, only the gods can stop birds from flying,' Phameas said, stunned.

'Listen,' he said.

'To what?' asked Phameas.

'Exactly. There's no wind, and it was blowing a gale.'

'Master Evandros, come here! You must see this!' Dexion was crouching and staring at the ground.

'This is too weird,' he said. A spider had stopped mid-step on a blade of grass, and a line of industrious ants had come to a halt.

'What is goi ...' Leander's voice faded and he sagged onto the ground, just as a gossamer fabric flutters to the floor.

One by one, the others succumbed and flopped onto the earth.

'Oh my God.' Evan dropped his book and charcoal, darted to Dexion and checked his pulse. Then he leaned across to Phameas, then Homer and Leander. His fingers trembled as he moved from one to the other, unable to feel their heartbeats. He picked up Lykeios, and the pup lay limp, the head flopping backwards. 'What is going on?'

'Do not fear, Evandros, for they are still alive.'

'And who the heck are you?' His pulse raced and he narrowed his eyes at the cowled figure who stood close to the temple wall.

The newcomer clasped his hands, hidden within the folds of his sleeves. His manner relaxed and affable.

'You know who I am,' he replied in an amused tone.

He cradled the pup closer. His heart skipped a beat. *Shit, shit, shit, shit.* His eyes flickered to his unconscious companions. *They won't be much help, idiot.*

Kronos examined the temple behind him. 'An impressive structure, is it not? Such trivial materials, and ones the younger gods are fighting to retain. Yet they use mortals to do what they cannot.' Evan squirmed under his intense scrutiny, and though the heavy cowl concealed his face, strength and dominance oozed from his presence. 'You know, as I do, that their time has ended. Their loyal vassals are no longer happy with their displays of arrogance and their disdainful behaviours. Mortals require reassurance that their lives are worthy and recognition for their devotions. They do not want to live in fear if they cannot adhere to the younger gods' whims and tenets.' Kronos' voice grew more urgent. 'I can offer mortals an existence far greater than what Zeus and the others have provided. I bring hope and new beginnings for all—including yourself and your companions— who will benefit from the seed I have sown. With the fruit of my own blood, I alone can preserve the souls of humans.'

Evan stroked the head of the inert animal in his arms and then considered his insensate friends.

'How do you intend to save humankind?' he asked, stalling for time. 'You haven't inspired a great deal of confidence by harming my friends right now.'

'If I wanted to kill your companions or you, you would be dead. You display unique intelligence for a mortal, which is why I am here,' Kronos replied.

'Gee, thanks for the compliment.'

Kronos clasped his hands behind his back and nodded at the temple. 'I have seen the nefarious treatment of your fellow humans by Zeus and the other Olympians. The younger gods flaunted their disregard of the mortals on many occasions and often on a whim. Together, we can offer the humans of this world and generations to come a life of value and importance. With the extraordinary gifts of your people—the Atlanteans—they can achieve remarkable feats and create a world where all live in harmony, worshipping the one true god.'

'The gods punished the Atlanteans for their superiority and knowledge, and for their disdain and domineering behaviour, by annihilating them. What if that were to happen again? Do you have a plan in place for that?' Evan asked.

Kronos tilted his head to the side. 'Do you not have confidence in your fellow Atlanteans?'

He shrugged. 'People have a way of disappointing you and are not always trustworthy. It is human nature.'

'And therefore, the one I have chosen will be free from such wretched behaviour, remain true to himself and offer humans a unique doctrine that is noble and honourable, unlike the false promises of Zeus and his siblings. I vow in their stead an alternative leader, a different god, who can provide hope and is a teacher of the virtuous. He is wise, nurturing, forgiving and understanding of human frailties, and as the Messiah, he will restore devotion to those blinded by the capricious tricks played by the lesser gods.'

Evan fought hard within himself not to blurt out the horrid machinations that had followed the birth and subsequent death of Jesus. But if he were to disclose such information, would it prevent the rise of brutal slayings of innocent people who chose not to follow the teachings of Christ? And what of those who extolled the word of God and hid behind sacramental vestments while seizing power and money and destroying the lives of those who did not succumb to their 'righteous' beliefs? He had studied the historical ascent of Christianity and other religions, and those who carried out dreadful acts of war while spouting the virtues of their faiths and condemning those who did not.

'I cannot decide on behalf of the Atlanteans. I must inform the Elders. What is it you are proposing?'

'The dominion of this earth,' replied Kronos. 'The path to creating a new world order under one almighty deity will be fraught with danger and countless enemies. If you stand with me, we shall vanquish those who oppose us and construct a realm of our design, one beneficial to our purpose and master plan. We can, once and for all, destroy the tyranny of the Olympian gods, restore order throughout the world and together ensure that the message of the Messiah is heard and preserved for eternity. The Atlanteans, as rulers, will spread the word of the Messiah and establish a new kingdom as supreme beings. No other race of humans shall be your equal.'

Evan nodded and was careful in his response. 'A fair proposal. How much autonomy would we have? Are we free to reign as complete rulers without interference, or is your intention to establish a set of doctrines we follow and impart to the others?' He thought of Moses and how God imparted a series of commandments for humans to live by and faithfully follow. *Would there be a Moses if Kronos loses? Or would the Atlanteans replace Moses and God give them the edicts instead? And if Kronos wins and brings forth the birth of Jesus centuries earlier, as Zeus claims was the Titan's intention, does that mean the timeline of the world will be brought forward?* Evan needed time to ruminate on the possibilities and problems associated with what Zeus and the other gods wanted and Kronos' ultimate objective.

Kronos smiled. 'Now I understand why Zeus selected you to lead. You are indeed more intelligent than your mortal companions.' The Titan paused. 'The Atlanteans will be granted autonomy to rule as desired, but there is one caveat: in return, the Atlanteans will spread the conditions and rule of my word.'

'Ah huh.' *Yep, Moses is out, then.* 'As I stated earlier, I can take your proposal to the Elders when I return to Atlantis.'

'Do you know why the Olympian gods obliterated your ancestral home?' the Titan asked.

Evan shook his head.

'Zeus and his brothers Poseidon and Hades knew that the Atlanteans would be the catalyst of change, and of their demise.' Kronos' voice rose. 'You and your fellow Atlanteans can still fulfil your ancestors' wishes and found a mighty empire, once I eradicate the Olympian gods.'

Evan cleared his throat and asked, 'What do you gain from this allegiance?'

'Recognition as the Almighty Father of the Messiah, and Supreme God of all worshippers.'

Evan laid the pup next to Dexion. 'I cannot decide on behalf of the Atlantean Eld—'

'Has Zeus promised you that the Atlanteans will live if you find the sacred objects?' Kronos asked.

'He did.'

'Do you trust him to honour his word?'

'Can I trust you?' Evan shot back. 'You ate your offspring.'

'I regret my actions,' Kronos admitted, 'and I have learnt from my decision, and from the disastrous ramifications. This is why I am installing a new god, a benevolent figure to compensate for my mistakes and for crimes I've committed against my children. Your life, your companions, and the Atlanteans, I assure you, will remain free from harm.'

Evan was torn. He knew what the future held with the birth of the new god, and yet he did not want to see his half-brother

Homer and his family, nor Atlantis, destroyed. *Frick, what a friggin' mess Zeus has put me in!*

'What say you, Evandros of Atlantis? Will you join me and the new Messiah?'

'I will see you on the Isle of Krete,' Evan said, straightening his shoulders. He checked over the inert bodies of his companions to avoid looking at the Titan, not wanting to acknowledge his presence.

CHAPTER 23

E van blinked; his hair whipped about his face. He saw birds resume their flight, following the current of the strong wind as if undisturbed by the unique occurrence. One by one, his companions stirred, glancing around and at him, bewildered.

'What happened?' asked Leander, getting to his feet.

'Kronos.'

'The Dark Master was here?' asked Phameas, dumbstruck.

'In the flesh,' he replied.

What did he want? Homer asked, a deep frown etched across his forehead.

'He demands—'

'Wait!' interrupted Leander. 'Should we not postpone discussion until we're protected by the white light of the High Priestess?'

Evan evaded Homer's scrutiny and tried not to squirm.

'The Dark Master wants revenge,' said Dexion, 'and he means to destroy Mother.'

'I am aware of his intentions,' he said.

'Stop. We do not discuss this further,' Leander said, 'until we return to the beach where the others are waiting, and if the High Priestess is strong enough, we will learn of Evandros' encounter with the Dark Master.'

Evan raised an eyebrow at Leander's assertive tone.

'Such an important conversation needs to include everyone.' The golden-haired Atlantean stood taller.

'I don't disagree, Leander,' he said, 'we just don't want to broadcast it to everybody by alerting them to the unconventional visit.'

'Oh …' Leander's face crumpled. 'I didn't mean to … I wasn't aware I … I am sorry.'

'Never mind, Leander. The shock of my unexpected visitor didn't help,' he said. 'It makes people say things and react without first considering the power of our words.' He squeezed the other man's shoulder. 'Let's return to the others.'

'I am sorry, Evandros,' he said, trudging behind.

'It will work out, you'll see.'

Homer patted Leander on the shoulder and gave a reassuring smile.

They arrived back at the beach in time to see the sun set, the orange, yellow and red glow of the sky merging with the sea. Further along, mirroring the copper-coloured sunset, were campfires where hours earlier they had left the High Priestess, Hektor and the Argonauts.

Phameas sniffed the air. 'Ahh … roasting fish.' He rubbed his stomach and quickened his pace. 'All that walking has made me hungry.'

'You have arrived in time for dinner,' Jason called out as they neared. 'We've caught a good haul of fish, thanks to Divine Poseidon.'

'That's perfect, Phameas here is famished.' Evan grinned. He nodded at the others. 'And so are we.' He set his sword and shield on the sand and dropped his bag alongside. Jason handed him a well-cooked fish, the skin burnt to a crisp. He peeled away the layer to reveal the white-fleshed and succulent meat. He popped a piece into his mouth. 'Delicious,' he said between chewing.

'Did you find the emitter?' asked the High Priestess.

'Oh yes,' answered Phameas. 'Biggest contraption I've ever seen on land. Must have taken giants to build and move it.'

'It was impressive.' Evan went on to describe the features of the contraption.

'Who do you think made it?' Hektor asked.

'A good question, to which I don't have an answer, except they were skilled engineers with an exceptional knowledge of the sun's movement,' he replied. 'It is old. I estimate they built it over a thousand years ago.' He took the book from his bag and flicked through the pages until he came to his drawings and notations on the artefact.

'That is quite the device,' Jason commented as he stooped to examine Evan's illustrations. 'I've never seen one, but there are more scattered on different islands.'

'A shame we will never know who designed and constructed them,' Evan said, passing the book to the High Priestess.

'What else happened?' she asked, flipping the pages and scrutinising the drawings. She peered up at them when no one answered.

'We had a visitor,' he said, exhaling through his nose.

'More like an uninvited guest who came to see Evandros,' Phameas said with a mouthful of fish. 'He put the rest of us to sleep.'

She placed the book on her lap, the cover closing with a snap. 'Was it whom I suspect?'

He sighed. 'Kronos.'

The muscles in her face tightened. Jason sucked in a sharp breath.

'What did he want?' Hektor asked, his tone accusatory.

Evan was about to respond when she held up a hand. Her eyes flashed a warning. A blur of white descended over them as they sat around the campfire and then shimmered into nothingness.

'What did he speak of?' she asked.

'His offer was compelling,' he replied. 'The central theme of his proposal was an alliance between the Atlanteans and himself, and his new, yet-to-be-born son.'

'Son?' she questioned.

He nodded. 'Kronos will sire the new god, a Messiah of the people, and he aims to rule through his heir.'

'Moloch!'

'By the gods, this is monstrous,' said Hektor, appalled. 'Does Divine Zeus or any of the gods know of his plans?'

'Zeus knows, which is why we are here,' Evan replied.

'We must tell them of the Dark Master's visit!' Hektor made to stand. The High Priestess grasped his hand.

'First, we learn what the Dark Master revealed to Evandros; then we decide what to do. Now sit down, or you will break the protective shield,' she told him.

Hektor sat back with a thump, his face turning a mottled red.

She let go of his hand and asked Evan, 'What of the alliance he mentioned?'

'He wants the Atlanteans to join him and give him the sacred relics, spread the word of the birth of the Messiah and the hope he brings to humankind. In return for protecting his offspring, Atlantis will become an empire, rulers of a new world order. Kronos also promised to protect Atlantis and Atlanteans from any who seek to destroy our home.'

'Divine Poseidon had made that same pledge when he addressed us on Atlantis,' Hektor blurted.

'Hush, Hektor,' she said, patting his forearm, 'we were all there.'

'Is the Titan's oath trustworthy?' asked Jason.

'Kronos expressed the same of Zeus,' Evan replied.

'Divine Zeus is honourable! All the gods are They are our immortal parents,' Leander said, imploring the others to concur.

The High Priestess reached over to him and squeezed his hand. 'Leander, no one disagrees. It's a matter of what advantage we can take from this unique offer.'

'Oh … I hadn't thought of that,' he said. Leander then noticed her hand on his. The High Priestess flushed and she yanked her hand away.

Did you agree to help him? Homer asked, holding his tablet out at him.

'Not in so many words,' Evan answered.

'What did you say?' she asked.

'I said I'd see him on Krete.'

'You agreed to assist the Dark Master!' Hektor roared.

'I did not accede to anything.' He gave the burly Atlantean a withering look.

'You just stated you'd see the Titan in Krete,' Hektor argued.

'Yes, but I did not say I'd give him the objects or cooperate.' Evan crossed his arms against his chest. 'The intention was to ensure Kronos and his band of troublemakers leave us alone, so we arrive in Krete without further interruptions. The Titan is pompous and confident in believing we would agree to his terms, and basically heard what he wanted to hear.'

'That is dangerous, Evandros,' said the High Priestess, forehead wrinkling. 'There's no way of knowing how the Dark Master will react when he learns you do not plan to give him Mother's sacred objects.'

He shrugged, ignoring the chill seeping into his bones. 'This entire trip has been fraught with peril. What is one more to add to the growing list?'

'Deceiving an immortal never ends well, and misleading a

Titan, one filled with ire and revenge, is foolhardy,' she said, disturbed. 'I must confer with Mother.'

'Why did the Dark Master speak to Evandros and not one of us?' Leander asked.

'He is Divine Zeus' son,' said Dexion, 'and Mother's chosen protector.'

'What?' Evan blinked. 'I don't quite understand. What do you mean "Mother's chosen protector"?'

'Protecting the High Priestess is one part of your task; the other is to find and safeguard the sacred items.'

'No,' he growled. 'My job was to recover the relics, and that is it, nothing more. If Zeus and Mother renege on their word, I will give the objects to Kronos.' He swung to the High Priestess, jaw tight. 'Remove the white light. *Now.*'

The shimmering dome of the shield dissipated mere seconds before he stood. He stomped away, leaving gouged impressions in the sand.

'That's it! I've had enough of this ridiculous game you are playing!' he shouted at the sky. 'I am sure these unnecessary interludes must entertain you, but I am not laughing. No one is. You put us here for your own personal gain, yet you've not suffered or faced tragedy! You haven't even bothered to help when we needed it. What is the point, huh? You swoop in when it suits you, and then nothing for months! You are all a bunch of selfish arseholes! It's no surprise people no longer venerate your kind. You lost them because of your arrogance and pretentiousness. Jesus gave them what they—'

Evan catapulted backwards and thudded into the dune, his backside buried into the hill. He grunted and wriggled his legs and arms, puffing, beads of perspiration forming on his forehead. He sensed a presence and stopped.

'I wondered how long it would take to get your attention.' Evan jiggled his limbs and body until he fell forward, panting. He stood and brushed off the sand, facing Zeus, who clutched his lightning bolt, his eyes flashing and his jawline clenched tight. 'Send me home—I am done with this idiotic mission of yours. Bring back the other Evandros. He can finish the job.'

'No.'

He plonked himself on the ground and crossed his arms. 'Well, then, you lose. I am not moving.'

'You will do as instructed or you, your companions and the Atlanteans die.'

He shrugged. 'No matter. I know what happens, and it doesn't include you, your Family, or the Atlanteans. It never did.'

Zeus pursed his lips and then spoke. 'What of your unborn child and Antioche? Do you not want to see them live?'

He dropped his gaze to the shoreline. 'I am not meant to be here to begin with, and what happened shouldn't have transpired. That is on you.' He thrust his chin at Zeus. 'Send me home.'

'Evandros, we have tasked you with a considerable burden.'

Evan bolted to his feet. 'Mother Goddess.'

'Mother.' Zeus bowed his head.

The Mother Goddess took his hand. 'You have excelled where many would have failed, including the one—your namesake—who slumbers in the realm of Mount Olympos under the watchful presence of the Charites, the three Graces. You are my creation and that of your Divine Father, powerful, discerning and a leader we required to fulfil ancient prophecy. When Evandros was born, we thought we had made him comparable to Akhilleus in his temperament and capable of accomplishing the quest. However, he was incomplete.'

'Incomplete? What do you mean? That he was inadequate for

the job?' He caught the shared communiqué between the two immortals. 'Well, tell me.'

'Evandros lacks courage and resourcefulness, and while he is erudite, his inability to be cogent and assertive would have seen him fail and die.'

Evan rapped his fingers against his thigh. 'What you are saying is that you both, and I don't want to know the details of how'—he grimaced at the thought—'created me as a replica of my doppelganger, and that is as far as the similarity goes—and then you added extra characteristics to function the way you wanted me to behave to win the fight against Kronos?'

'Evandros' deficiencies are too great,' said Zeus.

'Why didn't you just add those qualities you desired into him?' he asked. 'That would have made more sense as he is from this time and place.'

'His imperfections did not manifest until he became a youth,' Zeus answered. 'We considered killing him, but the High Priestess was fond of her brother, and as she is pivotal to our success, we refrained from ending his life. Instead, we forged you.'

Evan clasped the back of his neck, flummoxed by Zeus' callous explanation. He cleared his throat. 'If Evandros was already— what, thirteen, fourteen years old when you made that discovery, how can we be the same age if you produced me afterwards? And how did I know how to use weapons to fight?'

The Mother Goddess smiled. 'We engineered your conception here, and it was Zeus' suggestion to have you raised far from this time. We infused you with the various gifts from the immortals, and your ability to wield a weapon is as innate as that of Ares.'

'So my mother and father aren't my parents.' He sank to the ground.

'They are. Your mother gave birth to you and a small part of their essence lives in you. However, your lineage and blood are ours. You are one of the Family.'

'Is that why I don't have any of Evandros' memories of growing up here? If I am born of this time, why can't I remember anything from this period, apart from what I studied and learnt in the future?' he asked, bewildered.

'We decided it was prudent that you not have any reminders of this time in order for you to grow up unencumbered in the future and not be confused by seemingly odd recollections that you could not explain,' said Zeus.

'It was also an advantage that you were fully immersed in living and participating in a futuristic world without being hindered by reminiscences and ties to the past,' added the Mother Goddess. 'If we had enabled you to retain Evandros' experiences, then Kronos would have learnt of your existence and we could not allow that to happen.'

'That's cold-blooded.'

'It was necessary to guarantee you grew up without influences of the past.'

'Well, that is not true.' Evan looked at them. 'I am your creation, which explains my career as an architect who specialises in constructions from the ancient past, as Mr. Zeus Pantokratora here can attest, and who hired my company to "fix a structural problem" at the "Family home". Then there is my affinity for the sea and love of swimming; how easy it was for me to learn multiple languages, of which I know five and read Linear A, an indecipherable language in the future. I have an eidetic memory, which at first I thought was a gift, but now, I'm not so sure. My interest in the ancient world, this period of time and dating back five thousand years in this region, was not by chance. My life and education were predetermined by you.'

'There was always the possibility some of the residual effects from our lifeblood would manifest in you. And it worked better than we expected,' said Zeus.

'How wonderful for you.' Evan pointed at them. 'I am a man out of time, with no real connection to the past, present or future.'

He surveyed the almost invisible shoreline, darkness setting, and cast a gaze across to the campfire that lit up the *Argo* and the figures reclining within the warm glow of the golden halo. 'Pandora wasn't enough. You had to make a male version. The current chaos and the yet-untold horrors of the future didn't forewarn you of the incumbent complications?'

'We fabricated Pandora to teach mortals a lesson in humility. We designed you to destroy Kronos and prevent our extinction.'

'And in doing so, change the history of the world to one that is amenable to you.'

Zeus stiffened. 'Would you prefer a life of instability, where slaughtering people for their beliefs that oppose the new order is encouraged, or one where mortals live with the freedom of choice and are not hunted and killed for worshipping the gods?'

Evan faced them, taking in the icy glare from Zeus, then the Mother Goddess' more considered appraisal. 'He is a Titan—how am I supposed to even maim him?'

'You'll find a way.' Zeus stabbed him in the forehead with a finger. 'It is all in here, and we will be there to end his despotic ways.'

'What if he slays me first?'

'We all die.'

CHAPTER 24

They set sail as soon as the sun rose the following morning. The Argonauts plunged the oars into the surf once it was deep enough to row, and Jason piloted the ship out of the cove. Evan sat with Phameas and Dexion, trying to figure a way to contend with Kronos and come to terms with what Zeus and the Mother Goddess had disclosed the previous night. He bit the inside of his cheek and drew blood, brow furrowed as he pondered the rich Mediterranean blue of the sea, not noticing the fine sprays of water as the prow ploughed through the ripples of waves.

He understood their reasoning for creating him and using him as their weapon, though they hadn't explained why Evandros had been secreted away on Mount Olympos. Could the two of them not coexist in the same time frame, which was why he was here now and Evandros wasn't? What of himself in the twenty-first century? Was he alive or comatose somewhere, just like Evandros slumbering away on Mount Olympos? Why Zeus and the other gods wanted to prevent the birth of Jesus made sense. They simply didn't want to give up their position as gods of humanity and their particular domains. They saw Jesus as a threat to their existence, and following his death, their power waned as more people converted to Christianity. Possession of Mother's artefacts would prevent Kronos from succeeding and becoming ruling god. Was Kronos the same god of the Judaic, Christian and Islamic faiths?

God gave His prophets Abraham, Moses, Jesus and Muhammad a list of rules that formed their holy scriptures, and He was both benevolent and compassionate. Kronos was an elder god, pre-dating the younger gods, the Olympians, by thousands of years. The Titans were belligerent and vengeful, and their warlike nature and Kronos' fear of being usurped had seen to their downfall. Could Kronos be looking to make amends by bringing forth a new god, with Judaism the first of his creations?

The sea breeze did little to relieve the confusion and unease, his mind tumbling from one scenario to another before coming to the calculated visage on the Mother Goddess' face that Zeus had not seen. What did she want from him? And why weren't they rescued from the island? Was the diversion to trick Kronos? He squeezed his knee, the flesh pinching beneath his fingers. *No, no, no. There's something else going on, but what is it?* He pursed his lips and brooded. They had planned all along for him to complete this task his ineffectual "brother" couldn't perform. Conceived without recourse, like Frankenstein, a commodity to fulfil a task. He swore. Not much he could do about it but come up with a solution that could work, but how to execute it?

'Evandros, have you considered that your Divine Father and the Mother Goddess are aware of the Dark Master's intention to coerce you onto his side?' Phameas asked.

He pondered the cloudless sky, blue and sunny, and marvelled not for the first time at the clear and pristine atmosphere.

'The gods see and hear all, and they are all-knowing,' the Phoenician continued, unperturbed by his lack of response. 'I believe they expected the Dark Master to approach you with an offer that would entice even the most loyal servant to accept. By Baal's beard, I'll wager they want you to do it. I can envisage how it will happen. You retrieve the sacred object from the Minotaur's lair after a lengthy and gruelling combat, emerge bloodied but still able to walk, with a bit of help from me and Homer, of course. The Minotaur was not an easy foe—an angry beast, most likely hungry—and there's a good chance you're injured.

'With the last sacred object in your possession, mind, you are smart enough not to touch it, as you know what will happen if you do! You take the precious item to the High Priestess, who, shocked by your poor condition, is glad you smote the terrible monster. She is ready to receive the object, but you refuse and insist you continue with her to the tree sacred to the Mother Goddess. The High Priestess, displeased by your suggestion, tries to dissuade you, saying the location is a secret and they allow no man into the forest. You shrug and give her an ultimatum: you accompany her, or you toss the sacred piece into sea.'

Evan's mouth twitched at his friend's outlandish story, and he lowered his head to avoid laughing out loud, grateful for the distraction.

Phameas kept speaking. 'The High Priestess allows you to travel with her, realising there is no point in arguing. You see, she realises what will come to pass once she reunites the items …'

Evan's head catapulted upright and he eyeballed his friend. 'Of course! She knew all along.'

The Phoenician blinked. 'Huh? What—'

'You just said it, she knows what will happen.' He observed the High Priestess as she spoke to Jason. He'd always felt her aloofness had a touch of duplicity, that of her status and duty of a High

Priestess and her role as an Elder of Atlantis, a position that encumbered her with the power of authority. Evan sensed she was hiding the truth from them, even from her fellow Atlanteans. The question was why, and what might that truth be? In time, he'd work it out, but he knew without a doubt that the objects were integral to her scheming.

'Dexion, have you felt any deception from the High Priestess?' he asked.

The boy sat next to the men in silence, his wolf pup lying contented on his lap. He stiffened, his hands stilled, and his face went slack. Lykeios yelped, but Dexion did not respond. He sat motionless and facing straight ahead, as if something or someone had captured his attention.

'Dexion?' Evan waved a hand in front of his eyes, but he did not react. Lykeios kept barking.

'This does not bode well,' said Phameas. 'Is he in a trance?'

'Not sure.'

'Do you think a god has taken hold of his mind, or whatever it is they do to seers?'

'I don't know.' His gut twisted. *Did I ask a question I shouldn't have?*

Lykeios' fur stood on end. He barked at the sudden gust of wind and sprang forward to protect Dexion. The pup snapped at the air, growling, teeth bared. Evan searched the clear sky and then the horizon, but he saw nothing. Homer and the High Priestess started towards them. The peculiar squall propelled them backward, Alexina clinging to the wooden beam. Homer grimaced and tried to press forward. His feet skidded on the planks, the breeze preventing him from advancing further.

'What is happening?' Leander shouted.

Evan shrugged and lifted his hands, palms facing upwards, baffled.

'Evandros!' Phameas lurched headlong, catching Dexion as he tumbled sideways.

The wind eased. There was a thud. Evan saw Homer lying spread-eagle and face-down on the deck. Leander and Hektor helped him to his feet.

Evan hovered over an unconscious Dexion, whose face was as white as a bed sheet.

'Dexion?' He touched his forehead and shook his head, troubled.

'What is it?' Phameas mimicked him. 'I don't understand. He isn't cold. Is that odd?'

'Very.' He took Dexion's hand and placed two fingers over his pulse.

'Why are you doing that?'

'I am checking his heartbeat,' he replied.

'His heart isn't in his wrist, it is there.' Phameas pointed at Dexion's chest.

'I know, I am calculating his heart rate.' He sat back on his haunches and put Dexion's arm down. 'His pulse is good and strong.' He dragged a hand over his mouth and chin. 'He appears to be fine.'

'Except he's not awake.'

'What happened to Dexion?' the High Priestess asked, kneeling beside them and examining Dexion.

'I don't know.' Evan scratched his head.

'We were talking and then Dexion went rigid,' Phameas said.

'He didn't respond or move when we spoke to him,' he said, 'and now he's unconscious.'

'Where did the squall come from?' asked Leander.

And why did it stop us from assisting Dexion? Homer scribbled.

'I've no idea,' Evan replied, bemused.

'It did not harm Dexion or either of you,' she said. 'I can only surmise it did not intend to hurt anyone or the ship.'

'Then why is Dexion unresponsive?' Hektor asked.

'The one person who is able to answer your question cannot.' The High Priestess placed a hand over Dexion's heart and closed her eyes. After a few minutes, she sat back on her heels. 'He is resting and will return after he has recovered.'

'Is that what he told you?' asked Evan, arching an eyebrow.

'No, it is what I have sensed from him. It did not injure him, though his essence is wearied.'

'Do you know why?' He examined Dexion's relaxed features.

'Whatever he experienced drained his psyche, and he needs to replenish his energy.'

'Did you learn what happened to him?' asked Leander.

She shook her head.

'We then wait until he wakes,' Evan said, 'when he is capable of telling us what caused him to collapse.'

Lykeios licked Dexion's cheek, and when there was no reaction, he stretched out alongside the boy, muzzle between his paws, light grey-blue eyes on Dexion's face.

'We have the best protector to guard him,' said Phameas.

D exion's dark brown eyes flashed open and he stared at the inky night sky. Disorientated, he drew in a heavy breath, his mind awash with images and orders. A lone bright star shone in the pitch-black realm of the goddess Nyx. Her celestial presence, both ominous and reassuring, cloaked his wakened state from his closest friends. A tear rolled from the corner of his eye and down the side of his temple, splashing onto the deck. Mother had been explicit in her instructions, and though he had pleaded with her to change the course of destiny, she had refused.

'It must be this way,' she had told him.

Mother had then taken him in her arms and whispered further

directives. He hadn't wanted to return to consciousness and would do anything to avoid lying to his friends. It would have been preferable to die, but Mother had charged him with an obligation he could not refuse. Two lives now depended on him, and it would be his responsibility to ensure he protected them, no matter the cost to himself or the others.

CHAPTER 25

Evan and Phameas did not leave Dexion's side. The boy's complexion had gone back to his natural bronze colouring, and Evan itched to wake him, wanting to know what had happened. It took considerable willpower not to shake him awake. Lykeios lifted his head and snuffed. Dexion stretched, rolled onto his back and rubbed his eyes. Evan drew up his knees, and Phameas sat cross-legged as they waited. Dexion yawned, blinked and propped himself up on an elbow. He smiled as Lykeios licked his face.

Evan passed him a cup with watered-down wine, and Phameas gave him dried fruit and a piece of hard bread. He took them without a word. Dexion set the cup aside when he finished eating and drinking.

'How are you feeling?' asked Evan.

'Better now,' he said.

'Do you remember what happened?'

Dexion hesitated and then nodded.

'Have you experienced anything like that before?'

'Yes, twice,' he replied in a quiet voice and lowered his head.

'When my parents and I were captured by marauders to our island. The second time was when they were killed by the man who bought us as slaves. They tried to prevent him from using me for his pleasure. Then I slit his throat after one night and ran as far away as possible, and lived on the streets of Hippo Regius until you arrived.'

Phameas muttered, beseeching Baal, his face darkening.

Evan gave the boy a hug.

'This was different,' Dexion said, pulling away.

'How?' he asked.

'After the images, Mother came.'

'Did she mention anything we should know about the High Priestess or provide information that will help us?'

'Mother has instructed the High Priestess in what she must do.'

'I sense there is more. What else did she speak of?' asked Phameas in a flat tone.

'That Master Evandros has to go with the High Priestess to the sacred tree and reunite the Great Mother with her divine objects.'

'By Baal, my tale was told in jest and to lighten Evandros' mood.' Phameas was flabbergasted.

'Maybe you are a prophet,' Evan joked, giving him a weak smile. 'You dreamt of being surrounded by beautiful women, which were the Amazons, and now this story of yours is affirmed by the Mother Goddess.'

Phameas ran a hand through his curly sable hair. 'I have as much foresight as you do.' He snorted. 'You will have a difficult time convincing the High Priestess you are to go with her to the tree to restore the sacred icons with your goddess.'

'Now that is a prophetic statement.' He studied the High Priestess, who was sitting with Hektor, Homer and Leander. 'It doesn't matter what she wants, the Mother Goddess has made her intentions clear.' He turned to face Dexion, whose mournful expression gave him pause. 'It will work out, Dexion,' he said. *Either Zeus makes good on his vow, or I'll give Kronos the objects.*

With skilful hands, Jason and his crew guided the *Argo* into a picturesque bay where two moles jutted out from the land. The rocky structures protected the harbour and beaches from the waves and provided a haven for ships during stormy weather. Phameas helped to furl the mainsail while the oarsmen rowed towards the shore with steady and smooth strokes. The crystal-blue water gave way to a white-and-grey foam and a looming coastline. Jason issued orders to stow the oars. Evan braced himself for the dry landing, clutching the pup with an arm, and checked Dexion was secure in his harness. The beach loomed closer. He closed his eyes as the helm scraped the shoreline and lurched backwards as the ship grounded to a crunching halt.

The *Argo* was not the only vessel in the harbour; five other ships lined up alongside, so close a person could jump from one to the other. The crew leapt ashore, shouting familiar greetings to the assembled sailors. The men hugged and clapped each other on the back. Their carefree laughter and shouts of joy reminded Evan of being at a football match. He let Lykeios leap from his arms and helped Dexion out of his harness.

'Quite the gathering,' he said to Jason, joining the captain to toss anchors into the water and beach to secure the ship.

Jason straightened, hands on hips, in a buoyant mood engendered by the loud greetings and laughter between the Argonauts and the other sailors.

'This is a popular location for many crews. The locals are amiable and hospitable to all who dock here. See there.' He pointed. Evan turned to look. 'Here come the villagers, bringing a variety of goods to sell, and there will be lots of revelry and music.

My men enjoy coming to this island, and we always visit whenever we are in the vicinity.'

The citizens set stalls up on the beach with fruit and vegetables, warm bread, wine and trinkets available for purchase. The scent of spicy food and noise reminded him of the first experience he'd had ashore, arriving in Hippo Regius after being dumped by Zeus amid a shipwreck. It was a culture shock, Evan not being used to the chaos of the markets and the myriad of odours, from unwashed bodies and cloying cooking smells to the dung from animals, that permeated the air. It had taken him a while to adjust to the calamitous sounds, the people, the lack of fresh water to drink and to wash—though he had taken every opportunity to bathe, even if it was a swim in the sea, to feel a semblance of cleanliness.

The atmosphere was festive and everyone was in good spirits. He straggled along with his companions, munching on a fig. However, his mind was on their impending arrival on Krete and the completion of the mission. *If I die here, what is to become of me in the twenty-first century?* It was a concept he didn't really want to consider. After all, this was an elaborate dream. *Or is it?*

'Do you still intend to return to your home after you recover the relics?' Phameas asked him. They had found a quiet spot on the beach, away from the throng of locals and new arrivals, and were eating bowls of stew.

Evan paused, chewing, and then swallowed. 'Yes, if Zeus and Mother keep their word.'

And if they do not? Homer asked.

He reflected on his conversation with the immortals and finally said, 'I have to wait until this is over to find out.'

CHAPTER 26

T he Goddess of Discord stood on the balcony, pondering, not for the first time, the Atlanteans' escape from the Amazons. Should she send the Cyclopes to prevent their arrival on Krete? No, better to wait and see what Kronos has orchestrated and Zeus' countermeasures. She had witnessed Hermes call on the High Priestess during her incarceration. Eris smirked. The queen had shown remarkable cunning and willingness to detain the witless males and prevent them from leaving. Mortal men were guileless when they encountered the affections and temptations of women.

It had angered Kronos to learn that the Atlanteans' memories had been restored and that they had departed from the island. She smouldered at how he had ranted and raged, blaming her for allowing them to get away and not deterring Zeus and his apathetic siblings from liberating their champions. He'd then dismissed her, saying he no longer needed her, and if she meddled any further, he would send her back to Tartaros.

She rapped her fingertips on the stone surface of the balustrade. A large she-serpent, with the upper body of a woman and the lower half of a snake, slithered across the cold inky-black marble floor and joined her on the balcony.

'Ekhidna, you have come home,' she said, glancing at the reptilian creature, who reared upright. 'You have been away for quite a while. I trust you were fruitful.'

'The task you set was difficult. Few know of the Titan's plan, and those who once sided with him refused to speak for fear of his wrath.'

The goddess sniffed. 'Did you persuade them into changing their minds?'

Ekhidna gave a nod and licked her lips; the tip of her forked tongue fluttered and sibilated.

Eris smiled, her eyes gleaming. 'What did you discover?'

'Kronos intends to be the father of a new immortal and has chosen the High Priestess to carry his spawn,' replied the serpent. 'She, alone, has the power to possess the objects, and as a loyal servant of the Mother Goddess, any child she produces will inherit her gifts.'

'And that is why Kronos has selected her.' She scrutinised the serpent's emotionless face. 'What else have you uncovered?'

Ekhidna swayed from side to side. 'During the great Titanic war, the gods injured Kronos. He was maimed and disfigured, and Zeus imprisoned him and the other Titans in the bowels of Tartaros. Those who knew him heard him vow vengeance on numerous occasions.'

'Yes, yes ... I know of the Titan's desire to oust the Olympian gods,' Eris said, rolling her eyes. 'It was all he spoke about, and how he intended to inflict the same pain on Zeus as he had endured through the millennia.'

'Of course, Mistress.' Ekhidna bowed her head. 'As sire of the Messiah, the Titan will become supreme deity and father to all mortals. It is Kronos' plan to establish, through his son, an immortal kingdom where he rules as the sole veritable god to all living beings in this world.'

'What ...?' Eris was stunned. 'He seeks dominion of all?'

The serpent swayed from side to side, eyes blinking as the goddess raged.

'He deceived me! The false platitudes and promise to rule Olympos to entice me to do his bidding!' She pounded a hand on the balustrade. 'How dare he! How dare he think to manipulate me! Me, the Goddess of Discord!' Her heart-shaped face and milk complexion darkened and grew malevolent. 'What does he know of vengeance? He shall pay for his deceit.'

She soared into the air and flew out over the sea.

'What are you doing here?' Zeus sprang from the dais and bounded across the throne room to the golden doors.

'How did she get past our hounds?' Ares stormed behind Zeus, pulling his sword from its sheath.

'How dare you come here!' Hera's eyes blazed as she rocketed to her feet.

The Olympians surrounded the intruder, the barrage and waves of hostility roiling like a surging volcanic eruption. Eris clasped her hands and waited in bemused silence. The tirade faded to a dull murmur, similar to a mainsail falling slack on the death of the sea breeze.

'I am here to offer you an alliance,' she said to Zeus.

The King of Gods and Men took a momentary pause and studied her face for signs of deception.

Ares' lip curled.

'You? An ally? We do not need your help, nor do we want it.' Hera's voice dripped with contempt.

'I know the truth of Kronos' plan,' she added.

Zeus crossed his arms against his chest. 'Why should we listen to you, after the havoc you have engendered?'

'You have no reason to,' Eris answered, unperturbed, 'except the information I harbour may change the outcome of your ... our plight.'

Athene laughed with derision. 'There is no "our". You sided with the

Dark Master. Now you request an alliance for your benefit and sole interest.'

'But of course, why else would I solicit a union with you?' Eris smiled.

'You know Kronos cannot win and you want to join us to avoid being sent back to Tartaros,' Aphrodite answered, eyes flashing with loathing.

The Goddess of Discord tutted. 'My dear sister, Kronos has curried favour with your champion, Evandros. And from what I have noticed, your Atlantean hero wasn't thrilled at being manipulated by his father. Kronos' enticing and profitable offer, as I believe it is, may be difficult for a mortal, even one of divine parentage, to refuse.'

'Zeus, how did you not know of the meeting between Kronos and your son?' Poseidon lashed out at his brother.

'There is nothing to worry about. Besides, there have been no further delays.' Zeus flicked a hand at the goddess. 'From what I saw, Evandros and his companions are settled in for the evening.' He lowered his tone at Poseidon. 'Each of us was to keep under observation our children. How did you not see this encounter?'

'We have other realms to manage, and Evandros is your son and your responsibility. You insisted he is the one to prevail against Kronos,' Poseidon said, baring his teeth.

'And he shall,' said Zeus.

Poseidon reflected for a moment, studying his face. 'You knew Kronos would approach Evandros and tempt him with a proposition.'

'Yes, and so did Mother.' Zeus ignored the Sea God's outraged sputtering and asked Eris, 'What is it you want?'

'In exchange for my wealth of information, I want your word that, once the war with Kronos is over, you will allow me and my companions to remain free,' she replied.

'How can we trust her? She was quick to join Kronos after his assurances of false power and untold gifts. This could be part of their scheme, to lull us into complacency so that we fall into their hands and lose everything,' Hades said.

'My brother speaks the truth. How can we trust you?' asked Zeus. 'What morsel of knowledge do you have that I don't already know? Your offer is worthless.'

'Then why would I come here, and alone?' she asked, arching her brows. 'Why would I risk my life by entering your dominion?' She took a step towards the King of the Gods. 'Kronos has a plan that even I find deplorable, and with or without your help, I intend to stop him from succeeding.'

CHAPTER 27

E van sat at the wooden railing of the ship, his legs dangling over the side, his feet showered by the spray of the water. He leaned his head against the frame and stared across the expanse but did not take in the unspoiled panorama of the sea. He contemplated Homer's question regarding what he'd do if Zeus or the Mother Goddess reneged on their agreement. What Kronos proffered was a conundrum. And why did the Titan speak to him, and not one of the others? Evan sensed there was more behind the self-assured approach by the Titan, and that bothered him. The old god had no doubt strategised and plotted while incarcerated in Tartaros, a place of nothingness, with ample time to wallow in hatred and deliberate how to exact retribution. Such a bleak and forbidding environment had to warp his reasoning, immortal or not. Resourceful and canny, Kronos was certain to emerge as the victor.

'The wily old bastard is hiding something, but what?' he muttered to himself.

If he gave Kronos the objects, could he secure the lives of his companions? If Kronos agreed to his terms, history as he knew it would remain the same. Or would it? The survival of the Atlanteans could change the balance and power structure between the rise of civilisations. There was a possible alternative—give the icons to the Mother Goddess and she would once again become the supreme deity. Under her nurturing and guidance, the world would be calmer, more harmonious and less violent than one ruled by an unforgiving God whose harsh retribution was swift and final.

Evan tapped his head against the rail. He longed to wake up in his comfortable twenty-first-century home and laugh at the incredulous dream he had experienced. His head sank below his shoulders as if weighed down by an anchor, and he sighed. This fantastical scenario reminded him of a book he had read as a kid, where the main character and his friends had gotten caught up in a computer game and couldn't leave before completing each level and then reaching the end.

'If this is how it must be played, then let's get this game over with.' His musings were interrupted by the sound of Phameas' and Dexion's raised and excited voices as they played Senet. If anything positive came out of this bizarre dream or whatever it was, he has made terrific friends, real or imagined. A face flashed before him. Why would the Amazon queen come to mind? And why now? He felt a quiver in his stomach and shook it off. *Too weird.* He stood and joined his companions. 'Who's winning?'

'Not me, that is certain!' Phameas laughed.

The *Argo* glided swiftly, Jason trying to make up for the time they'd lost while cloistered on the Isle of Hephaistos. He piloted the ship with ease, and it responded to his light touch on the helm as if it were an extra limb. They stopped each night on an island, a tactic that, Jason explained, did not risk the wrath of the Sea God or that of the Titan.

'I know why you are sailing from island to island, Jason, but at this rate we'll never reach Krete,' Evan said one morning as they were leaving the security of a cove.

'It may be slower and more arduous, and I know I promised to take you to Krete, but I will not further endanger my men or my ship,' he said with grim determination.

'I understand your reasoning, I really do. However, we left the Isle of Hephaistos over four weeks ago,' he said. 'We should have arrived by now.'

'And you will.' Jason bellowed orders to raise the mast. 'Another week or two at most.'

'I don't mean to sound ungrateful. It has been a long journey and I am ready to go home.'

'I appreciate your frustration, Evandros. The gods have tasked you with an onerous burden, and they will reward you for saving their lives and all of humanity.'

He sniffed. 'We'll see. When was the last time you visited Krete?'

'It has been some years,' the captain replied. 'Why do you ask?'

'The eruption on Thira impacted the island and I wondered if people have resettled in the same locales they inhabited prior to the destruction.'

Jason scratched his head. 'I will be anchoring into what was once the port of Amnissos, which is now just an inlet. The houses and buildings are no longer in existence. There are small villages further inland, one of them called Amnissos. They adopted the port's name and are some ten to twenty stades away from the bay.'

'I see.' He leaned against the railing and cast an eye across the azure sea. 'Thank you, Jason. I'm glad we met. Even if Zeus arranged for you and your crew to be here, it has been an honour getting to know you. I'll never forget your generosity and friendship.' He gave Jason a small, tight smile and left him at the helm to join Phameas, Dexion and Homer.

Two weeks later, Evan was slumbering when Homer shook him; he whacked his hand aside.

'Go away.' He felt a finger poke him in the ribs. 'Leave me alone!'

'Evandros!' Phameas tipped a jug of water over his head and torso.

He sputtered and bolted upright. 'What the blazes ... what's the matter? Are we under attack?'

His friend chortled. Homer gave him a wide grin.

'Look.' Phameas pointed.

He got onto a knee to get a better view. 'About time,' he said, standing.

On the horizon, glittering under the brilliance of the sun, was the outline of land. Evan stood at the prow, grasping the railing, circumspection growing with every nautical mile the *Argo* sailed closer to the land mass. His stomach clenched, and the vein at his temple throbbed. He clasped his bearded jaw, mouth dry at the sight of the encroaching islets that dotted around the pinnacle of the peninsula. When he'd last visited Krete, he had come by plane. The shoreline showed the ravages of the cataclysmic volcanic eruption that had torn apart the island of Thira, leaving its unique shape and famous caldera.

The original coastline was underwater, though parts of it yielded the punishing evidence of how far inland the sea had reached, and of the devastating damage of the tsunami. The pitted cliff face looked as though someone had taken a massive mallet and pounded at the escarpment. Evan drew in a ragged breath.

His mission was almost at an end and he would soon discover the outcome of his part in this crazy dream.

Phameas and Dexion flanked him at the bow. Homer, Leander, the High Priestess and Hektor joined them.

'Jason is navigating the *Argo* towards an old port called Amnissos,' Evan said. 'He suggested that someone there can give us directions to Knossos, where King Minos built the labyrinth and locked the Minotaur inside.'

His trip to the Palace of Knossos in the future had been memorable, the impressive structure set in a nondescript location twenty minutes away from the modern capital of Heraklion. It was a major tourist attraction, which received over ten thousand visitors each month, and where there were a smattering of shops and cafes situated opposite the historical site. He had stayed for hours, studying and drawing the light wells, staircases and earthquake-proof walls; the palace was an engineering masterpiece. He had walked around the ruins, staggered by the size and breadth of the buildings and of the various levels that contributed to the myth of the labyrinth.

Jason steered the *Argo* along the northern coastline, bypassing a harbour where a small settlement nestled within its protective embrace. Opposite was a large island, which he piloted towards.

'This cove is not a suitable location to disembark,' said Hektor. 'The currents would cause the ship to overturn!'

'Hektor, I have made this journey many times. Do not fret,' said Jason.

A rocky precipice loomed, and just as the *Argo* cruised straight for the unforgiving landform, Jason adjusted the steering oars, navigating the strong currents until the ship faced the mainland. Ahead was a river that split the plain in two and flowed into the sea. Jason set course for the mouth of the estuary, where there were a few beached ships moored. On the plateau of a tabletop hill was a settlement.

Homer scribbled something on his wax tablet and showed it to Evan. *Is it possible that this is the motherland of our ancestors?*

'I'm not sure,' he replied. 'It's too far to see the buildings, though it is probable that the Palace of Knossos was where the Atlanteans came from. We'll know more after we ask the inhabitants.'

'Knossos was home to our people,' said the High Priestess.

'And Thira?' Leander asked. 'We cannot discount the circular features of the island.'

The High Priestess stood poised, the sea breeze toying with tendrils of her hair, concentrating on the ever-encroaching shoreline. 'The two islands were the nexus of Atlantis,' she answered. 'The seat of Krete and its rulers was its political and economic centre. Thira and many of the surrounding isles were trading centres and under Atlantean rule.'

'Did other Atlanteans survive besides our ancestors?' Leander asked, excited.

'Where are they? Why have they not made themselves known to us?' Hektor asked her.

'They did not survive the great deluge,' she replied without inflection. To Evan's ears, she sounded like an automaton, similar to the recorded voices one heard when ringing the telecommunications and insurance companies or banks. 'Not all the islands were occupied—they were not fit for living on or for farming—however, they were important ports for the Atlantean fleet.'

How is it we were not told of this? wrote Homer, the Linear script carved into the wax.

'Our ancestors believed such knowledge was no longer essential, and they wished to avoid the possibility of us repeating the transgressions of our predecessors, which caused the gods to punish them for their hubris,' she replied.

'How do you know that was what the ancestors intended?'

Evan couldn't help asking, not convinced she was telling the entire truth.

She fixed her icy blue gaze on him. 'Our forebears housed the sacred texts in the Temple of the Mother Goddess, where the High Priestess and a few select priestesses were privy to them, and allowed to read and study the texts.'

'Was Sibyl one of the appointed few?'

She didn't answer.

'That explains why the gods selected her as a sacrificial pawn,' he said in reproach.

Homer patted his shoulder, and Phameas gave him a rueful grimace.

'No one else will die for this fool's errand,' he said, eyes clouding. He flashed a warning finger at her. 'And I don't want you to spout how the "gods hear and see all". What are they going to do? Kill me? They won't, not until I've finished the job.'

'Your insolence and disrespect of the gods will incur your death,' said Hektor.

He shrugged. 'We will all die someday.'

CHAPTER 28

J ason stood next to Evan, a few metres from where the *Argo* lay beached, the ebb and flow of the tide washing their feet. Behind them, the Argonauts were busy securing the ship while Homer and Hektor assisted the High Priestess in disembarking. Leander, Phameas and Dexion busied themselves with setting up a tent for her.

'"Out in the dark blue sea there lies a land called Kretos, a rich and lovely land, washed by the waves on every side, densely peopled and boasting ninety cities ... one of the ninety towns is a great city called Knossos, and there, for nine years, King Minos ruled and enjoyed the friendship of almighty Zeus",' Evan recited as he took in the view of the hilltops beyond the estuary. Jason gave him a sidelong glance. 'A famous poet recited the history of a major war between the Hellenes and Trojans and then recounted the story of Odysseus, king of Ithaka, who on his journey home landed here.'

The captain scratched behind his ear. 'This is where the nymphs raised your father, brought here by his Mother Rhea, to protect him from being eaten by Kronos.' He gave Evan a crooked smile. 'Now, the old Titan is seeking to destroy his son in his birthplace. Odd times.'

He wandered along the beach, Jason moving with him.

'King Minos was also Zeus' offspring, and renowned as a scrupulous lawgiver, fair and just, except for when he angered Poseidon. Now that is a story.'

'Not surprising. The immortals are notorious for their retaliation and retribution. There's a line from a play by Euripides: "The gods visit the sins of the fathers upon the children",' Evan quoted. 'It should be "the gods inflict their sins upon unsuspecting mortals".'

Jason stopped mid-step and gaped at him.

'What is it?' He scoured the landscape and clasped the hilt of his sword, ready to pull it from the scabbard.

'The sins of the father.' Jason slapped his forehead. 'Great gods, don't you understand?'

'Not sure what you mean.' He shrugged, hand raised in the air, palm facing upwards.

'Ouranos, Kronos, Zeus, King Minos and now you—you are the bearer of the sins.'

'What?' He gave a half-suppressed laugh and relinquished his hold on the hilt. 'Rubbish. The only sin committed was by me, for listening to Zeus and trusting him to honour his promise. Let's not discuss this matter any further and point me towards that village you mentioned.'

'I suggest we leave for Amnissos, which is west of here over that ridge, for directions to King Minos' palace,' said Evan. They arrived back at the ship and where the others milled outside the High Priestess' tent. He took in their weary faces. 'We don't all have to go. Besides, we'd move faster if just a few of us go.'

'We started this journey together, we continue the mission with everyone,' said the High Priestess, eyes glinting.

'As you wish.'

He led the way, striding towards the mouth of the estuary, and then deviated west, keeping the sea on the right-hand side. They walked in silence for a good twenty minutes when, before long, nestled in the foothills, rooftops of buildings loomed.

'I expected it to be further away,' Leander said, surprised, 'like other towns and cities we've travelled to.'

'Jason said destructive waves decimated the original port town King Minos' fleet used when the volcano on Thira erupted,' he said. 'The survivors rebuilt the township of Amnissos inland and on higher ground. I suppose they decided the current location was far enough from the sea yet close enough for fishing and to receive goods from neighbouring civilisations.'

'A sound decision. The townspeople can escape if threatened by invaders or another deluge,' said Hektor.

'Nothing and no one is safe from a tsunami,' said Evan.

'I believe we will find descendants from the great flood.' The High Priestess clasped her hands at her back.

'Tsunami? I don't recognise that word,' Hektor accused.

'Tsunamis are tidal waves caused by undersea earthquakes,' he explained.

'Hmm ... how do you know this? I am certain our Elders are not acquainted with this word,' the Atlantean argued and glanced at the High Priestess for affirmation.

'Evandros, as one of Atlantis' preeminent scholars, has access to texts which we are not privy to,' Leander intervened.

'It is not a term the Elders are conversant with,' she said.

Hektor shot him an unpleasant smile.

Phameas adjusted his hat. 'My people know of such waves as Evandros described, and we honour Yamm, God of the Sea, and sacrifice to Baal for safe passage. Entire ships and lands have been swallowed in the wake of these fearsome waves, which is why we deem it essential to appease the gods.'

Dogs started barking as they approached the outskirts of the village, curbing further conversation.

'Dexion, you'd better keep Lykeios close.' Evan pointed, spotting the convergence of canines scampering towards the entrance of the town.

'Yes, Master Evandros. Come, Lykeios.' Dexion slapped his thigh, and the wolf padded to his side.

The group passed through a gateway, and the barking grew sharper. A few of the braver canines rushed at them, growling. Lykeios bared his teeth but did not bark. Dexion placed a hand on his head while Leander moved to the pack of hounds and murmured at them. They stopped snarling, sat back on their haunches and panted at Leander, tongues hanging out of their mouths.

'That is impressive.' Evan gawked at the mangy dogs clustered around Leander, licking his hands. 'Can you do the same thing with humans?'

People emerged from buildings, a trickle at first, and then groups formed, standing in the middle of the street. They whispered to each other and gestured at them.

Leander sighed. 'The technique only works on animals.'

The High Priestess moved to the fore and the murmur of voices grew louder. There was noise and commotion coming from the rear of the crowd, and the people parted like an inverted V. A man and woman paraded towards them, the female dressed in a bell-shaped skirt and open blouse, her breasts exposed, while the male wore a bright-coloured loincloth and was bare-chested.

'Gods.' Leander's mouth fell open.

'Great Mother.' The High Priestess' eyes widened.

'I am Rusa, Elder of Amnissos,' said the male.

'And I am Kitane, Priestess of Maia,' said the female.

Homer prodded Evan and nodded in the townspeople's direction.

'That is really annoying, Homer,' Evan mouthed. The big man grinned lopsided at him and clasped Alexina's elbow, and they moved to address the couple. 'I am Evandros, and this is our High Priestess of the Mother Goddess, Maia.'

There was excited chatter and movement from the residents as they gawked.

'These are our companions: Homer, Leander, Hektor, Phameas and Dexion, and his wolf, Lykeios. We seek directions to the palace of King Minos.'

'The palace no longer stands,' said Rusa. 'Why do you wish to travel there?'

'We have journeyed from Atlantis at the behest of the gods,' the High Priestess answered. 'We must reach the palace to complete our quest.'

Rusa's lips parted and Kitane trembled. They leaned towards each other, heads almost touching, and spoke in low tones, glancing from Evan to his companions.

'What is the matter with them?' he asked, confused.

The High Priestess tilted her head to the side and studied the pair. 'I believe our arrival was expected.'

'How is that possible?' he asked.

'The gods.'

'We have waited many years for this day to come,' Kitane said, eyes shining, 'for our sisters and brothers to return home.'

A great roar and cheers drowned out her last words, and before either could respond, the villagers bounded forward, hands reached out to touch them. Their faces shone with joy and adoration as they pressed against them, eager to get close. With the throng hemming them in, it was difficult to move or hear their questions. Evan glanced over at Dexion and Phameas, bewildered and overwhelmed by the enthusiastic and joyous crowd. The warm welcome and the animated reaction from the citizens reminded him of their arrival in Messenia.

CHAPTER 29

R usa raised a hand, spun one way, then the other and said in a loud voice, 'People!' Those nearest him flinched; a few covered their ears. 'Citizens of Amnissos! I understand your excitement at seeing our sister and brothers, and your desire to be with them.' The crowd quietened and waited, the air electric and crackling in anticipation. 'Kitane and I must take our visitors and recount the time of our rebirth. Tomorrow, we will hold a feast in honour of our guests' long-awaited return and offer gifts to Divine Maia and sacrifice a bull to the god Poseidon. Until then, I ask you to grant us leave with our friends.'

The people bowed and smiled at them, and as they had arrived, they departed, walking along the main street, veering left and right for their homes without complaint or voicing disappointment.

'Please, come,' said Kitane, 'we have much to share with you.'

Rusa indicated towards the centre of town. Kitane touched the High Priestess' arm and motioned in the same direction as the townspeople had departed. Alexina accompanied her, and Evan and the others followed, with Rusa walking between Leander and

Homer. Rusa was not a short man compared to other individuals they'd encountered on their travels, but he was still a head shorter than Leander. He and the golden-haired Atlantean struck up a conversation, the former waving his hand from one side of the township to the other, referring to particular sites, effusive and proud in his description of the town. Leander listened and nodded, interjecting with a question that elicited further detail from an excited Rusa.

Kitane led them to a two-storey rectangular house with a flat roof, its style reminiscent of the homes constructed in Carthage. The entrance was on the second level, to which Kitane scaled a staircase. Evan drank in the design, his eyes feasting on how the entry to the dwelling might serve as a balcony with a nice outdoor settee. Two large wooden doors reminded him in their width and height of the church his grandmother had dragged him along to as a child. On either side of the door were windows, each fixed with wooden slats that created a three-pane window.

They plodded after Kitane, filing one by one into the house. For Evan, this was like taking a kid into a toy store. He didn't know where to look first. To the right, an oversized horizontal support buttressing vertical planks, the thickness matching. A metre above the beam was a plastered wall painted in bright colourful scenes filled with animals—wild dogs and wolves running along a riverbank, chasing ducks and geese—surrounded by an idyllic vista. The main wall had a vibrant scene of women collecting saffron in a field. Rich hues of crimson, gold and sapphire burst into life against the ochre background, interspersed with flying birds.

In the corner was a three-legged wooden stand, the meticulous carving bespoke of a craftsmanship that only a few gifted artisans could attain. On the left was a kitchen, as much as he could label it, for in the corner was a hearth filled with coals, and sitting atop were two three-legged terracotta pots, one bigger than the other.

Under the window were a table and two stools, and in the centre of the room was a kline with cushions. Rusa grabbed the stools and placed them near the couch. Evan scrutinised the design on the paved floor. Large interlocking circles, the circumference painted in white, contrasted against the terracotta colouring.

'Please sit. I am afraid there aren't enough seats for everyone, but I have woollen rugs.' The priestess approached a wooden facade and pulled open a panel to reveal a closet. Evan followed, fascinated by the unique storage unit, his eyes noting the construction of the wall and how the builders had integrated the cupboard. She took a step back and bumped into him. 'Oh ... I didn't see you there.'

He stuck out his arms. 'I'll carry those for you.'

Her face was radiant. 'Thank you.' She handed him the yellow-and-blue rugs and closed the cupboard door.

He wished he could study the structure of the house. A quick inspection would give him insight into the construction. The beams ran in half-metre lengths across the ceiling, adding strength to the building, and between the doorways, two horizontal planks supported the architrave and hid the ingenious cupboards. There was ample natural light provided by the row of windows on the opposite wall, serving as conduits for fresh air and views of the farmlands.

He spread the rugs on the floor and sat with Dexion, who nursed Lykeios. Phameas sat on his left. Homer and Leander sat on the other rug. Rusa scurried forward carrying a three-legged table and set it next to the High Priestess and put a jug on it. He poured wine into earthenware cups and handed them out. Kitane sat on a stool facing the High Priestess, who reposed on the kline with Hektor. Rusa sat on the other stool.

'Which of the gods spoke of our coming?' asked the High Priestess.

'We believe it was Poseidon,' Rusa answered.

'Did he not come to see you?' Hektor asked in disbelief.

Rusa straightened, his posture not dissimilar to the statues of Egyptian pharaohs, his eyes widening. 'Divine Poseidon, show up here?' He shook his head. 'Oh no, the mighty Sea God informed us of your return through the entrails of a bull we sacrificed in his honour.'

'How did your ancestors survive the terrible devastation? According to our historical annals, the water swallowed those who did not escape on boats,' said the High Priestess. 'Though Evandros knows the history of our people best and has studied their accounts.'

Evan had a mouthful of wine and started coughing when she mentioned his name. He cleared his throat. 'The documents state nothing about those who remained behind or what happened to them, although it alludes to the probability that any survivors from the catastrophe were remote.' He caught Homer's disapproving shake of the head and rushed on. 'Ahem ... can you tell us what took place after the flood?'

Kitane nodded. 'The deluge destroyed the noble house of Minos, and the other sacred centres, from Zakros in the east through to Phaistos in the south, and out west to Aptera. Many perished, swept away as the great waves washed across the land. Those who evaded the devastation moved inland, and some of the fortunate survivors escaped into the mountains, seeking refuge in the peaks. These were our ancestors, who rebuilt our town. They lived in peace for several years, until an invading force of marauders, Hellenes from a city called Mykenae, raided and razed our cities. Those who were not killed in the invasion fled to the hilltops once again and built homes in the highest locations to avoid further attacks.'

'But your ancestors decided to come back here? Why? Weren't you concerned about being invaded again?' asked Leander.

'Decades had passed and our forefathers yearned to be near

the sea once more. They had never forgotten the stories and the glory of those who once lived here,' replied Rusa. 'They wanted to restore what they had lost.'

'And did they?' Hektor asked.

Rusa clasped his hands before replying to Hektor. 'We are too few, and after the invasion, people were too frightened to leave the mountains, and many remained there.'

'No one rebuilt the cities after the raiders departed?' Hektor questioned, disgusted.

'The palaces were beyond repair, and as Rusa said, our numbers are small. It was essential to rehabilitate the fields for growing crops and providing grazing pastures for our animals,' answered Kitane. 'Our population cannot sustain the municipalities of long ago, and even to this day, a minority of our people occupy farming regions.'

'Of course. I cannot imagine the terrible ravages you and your forebears had experienced,' said the High Priestess, 'and you have accomplished much.'

'How did your ancestors avoid death from the towering waves that swept across this earth?' asked Rusa.

'The High Priestess had received a portent that a wall of water which blanketed the sky would flood the land of Minos and its sister, the island of Atlantis,' she replied. 'The High Priestess approached the king with her visions and he denounced her presage, forbidding her from announcing the prophecy of the gods to the citizens. He exiled her to Aptera. However, she and her priestesses found another way to reveal what they knew. Our ancestors believed the High Priestess and her priestesses, and they prepared for departure. In the days before the deluge and with the help of Divine Poseidon, they navigated their course to the Great Ocean and built a new Atlantis.' She took a sip of wine. 'The gods and our forebears agreed that we were to live in seclusion and peace for eternity. As recompense, we, the descendants, continued to thrive and flourish and secured Atlantis from further wrath of the gods.'

'What did this agreement between the gods and your ascendants include?' asked Kitane.

'We designed our laws to prevent the recurrence of the transgressions exhibited by the ancients. The gods stipulated we remain isolated and not communicate with other civilisations to let them know of our existence. The rules guide our way of life and remind us what will befall our people if we are to anger the gods again,' she answered.

'Every Atlantean child learns of the danger of the ancestors' misdeeds that led to the destruction of our ancestral home,' Hektor said. 'We do not want to repeat the folly of their avarice and disrespect the gods.'

Kitane and Rusa recoiled at the heat in Hektor's tone and sought a reaction from the High Priestess, whose face remained impassive. Evan studied the wall frieze while Leander pretended to be fascinated by the decorations on the floor and Homer closed his eyes. Phameas' eyes were ping-ponging everywhere, avoiding the four who were seated. Dexion sat composed and unruffled by the growing tension, his pup snoozing on his lap.

'But you have come home,' said Kitane, breaking the uneasy atmosphere, 'to prevent the downfall of the gods.'

'When were you told of our quest and our pending arrival?' asked the High Priestess.

'Divine Poseidon revealed that your arrival would coincide with the rise of the spring equinox,' Rusa replied.

'That's about two months after we left the Isle of Hephaistos,' said Evan. The High Priestess nodded.

'What can we do to help you?' Kitane asked.

'We require a guide to take us to the Palace of Minos,' she answered.

Kitane nodded at Rusa. 'Bring the boy Nereos.'

Rusa took off without a word.

'There is nothing of the palace but ruins. What is it you seek?' the priestess asked.

'An object in the labyrinth,' replied Evan.

Kitane was startled. 'You are referring to the story of King Theseus and the battle with the Minotaur.'

'Yes.' Evan shifted on his backside, easing the numbness from sitting on the hard floor.

'I am not sure there is a labyrinth,' she said, 'but there is a maze of caves that goes beneath the foundation of the palace.'

'Do you know if there is a way into the caves?' he asked.

'Young Nereos will tell you. He found an entry to the cavern, though I cannot say where it leads.' Kitane glanced over at the entrance just as Rusa and the youth showed up in the doorway. 'Here is Nereos, he can explain what you need to know.' She beckoned him in. 'Come, come.'

The dark-haired, lean adolescent fidgeted, his eyes flicking from one face to the next like a fly buzzing from spot to spot.

'What do you know about the caves?' Evan asked.

The teenager licked his lips. 'Ah ... my grandfather used to tell me stories about an extraordinary race who once lived at Knossos. I wanted to see it for myself and explore the palace. I went many times and found a cave.'

'Do you remember where it is?'

Nereos nodded, biting his thumbnail.

'Excellent,' Evan said, standing. He managed to avoid groaning out loud from sitting on the floor for too long. 'You come and visit us at the beach tomorrow morning, give us directions to the palace and the location of the cave.'

Dexion, Phameas, Leander and Homer clambered to their feet, stretching and rubbing their backsides.

Nereos' neck craned upwards, following their stature, his mouth falling open.

'We'll see you at daybreak, Nereos,' he said with an amiable smile. 'We must head back to the beach, or Jason and the Argonauts will come searching for us.'

The High Priestess agreed and stood. 'Thank you for your hospitality, Priestess Kitane.'

'May Gaia safeguard you,' said Kitane, rising to her feet, 'and may you be successful in the quest of the gods.'

CHAPTER 30

Jason and the Argonauts had readied a blazing campfire, a welcoming beacon, not too far from the High Priestess' tent. As they neared, Evan smelt roast pork wafting on the gentle sea breeze. His mouth watered, and his stomach rumbled. The last substantial meal he had eaten was on the previous island, where the villagers had sold hot food. Since then, it had been nothing but hard, stale cardboard-tasting bread, withered fruit and olives and diluted wine. It surprised him he was functioning at all with the meagre diet they'd consumed.

Later in the evening, he reclined on his side, eyelids drooping from the glow and heat of the fire, his appetite sated.

'Have you heard of the tale of King Minos, his queen and the Minotaur?' asked Jason.

An Argonaut grinned. 'It will send shivers down your spine and back up again.'

'Never anger a god,' another warned.

'Or dishonour them.' There were a series of nods from the crew.

'Is this the same story you told us about Theseus and the Minotaur?' Leander asked Evan.

'It's a part of the same legend. The passage I told you was about how Theseus offered to be one of the nine youths who travelled to Krete and sacrificed to the Minotaur. Which, if you recall, happened every year for nine years in retribution for Theseus killing King Minos' son while he was in Athens competing in the Panathenaic Games. The tale Jason is referring to goes back to the beginning and tells how the Minotaur was created.' Evan encouraged Jason and raised his cup to him. 'Let's hear the story.'

One of the Argonauts urged, 'Go on, Jason, tell them.'

'Yes, Jason, tell them about Minos' hubris,' another encouraged.

'It's been a long time since you've told a story,' said Orpheos.

Jason nodded, downed a mouthful of wine and began in a soulful voice. 'The king made a terrible mistake, and it would haunt him until his death. The God of the Sea presented Minos with a gift, a magnificent white bull, when he requested to become supreme ruler of Krete, and in return for the god bestowing him the kingdom, he promised to sacrifice the animal to Divine Poseidon. When he saw it, the king thought the bull too perfect to kill and instead ordered his herdsman to relocate the animal to a meadow with his other stock and slaughtered another instead. Poseidon was not pleased.' He paused, eyeing his captive audience. 'For Minos' wrongdoing, the god cast a spell over his wife, Pasiphae, inducing her to fall in love with the beast.'

'Great Mother!' Hektor said, repelled.

Homer's eyes widened. Phameas choked on his drink. Dexion cocked his head to the side, unperturbed by their reactions. The lines around the High Priestess' eyes grew more prominent.

'Why would he do such a thing? Did he not realise it's not

possible to conceal one's actions from the gods?' Leander asked, shaking his head.

'Foolhardy and futile,' added Hektor in reproach.

'It does not end there,' said Jason with a twinkle in his eye.

'Moloch! What other calamity can happen to this king and queen?' asked Phameas, aghast.

The captain rewarded him with a crooked smile. 'The queen, so enamoured by the bull, had Daidalos build her a wooden cow, into which she climbed. With Queen Pasiphae inside, they rolled the heifer out into the field where King Minos' prized bull was grazing.' The High Priestess' face paled. Evan surmised she guessed what was going to happen next in the story. 'From this ... union, she conceived the Minotaur, half-human and half-creature. King Minos was furious and instructed Daidalos to construct a labyrinth to confine the monster.'

Evan almost burst out laughing seeing his companions' gobsmacked reactions and chugged back mouthfuls of wine to hide his amusement.

Quite a story, scrawled Homer, stunned.

'And true.' Jason poured more alcohol into his cup.

'Does anyone know the shape or length of the labyrinth?' Evan asked as mortified silence descended over the group.

The Argonaut tugged an earlobe. 'Many people claim to have seen it and there are various descriptions, but none that are reliable enough to accept or use as a guide.'

Nereos arrived the next morning as the sun peeked over the rim of the horizon, the faint orange, yellow and ochre hues pushing away the dusky embers of the night sky. He hovered on the fringe of the campsite, shifting from one foot to the other.

'Dexion, why don't you rescue Nereos from his anxious wait,' said Evan, stoking the fire, 'and have him join us for breakfast.'

'He looks green around the gills,' Phameas commented lightly as he popped a morsel of roasted fish into his mouth.

Dexion raced towards the youth, his pup scampering alongside.

'Hmm ... he does present as if he's going to be sick,' Leander agreed.

'Perhaps a good slug of wine will give his cheeks a bit of colour,' said Jason.

'As long as he can provide us with the information we require to find the cave, what does it matter how he feels?' said Hektor, crossing his arms against his chest.

Hektor, sometimes your lack of social graces offends the gods, scrawled Homer in disapproval. *You remember the importance of offering xenia and of guest-friendship?*

Hektor cheeks reddened and he bristled at Homer, spinning around to sit in stony silence, his back to the others.

The High Priestess exited her tent and sat between Homer and Phameas. She raised a brow at Hektor's bearing but did not comment. Homer passed her a drink and a plate with figs, a piece of flatbread and cooked fish. On their leaving Amnissos, Kitane and Rusa had insisted they have fresh produce, an assortment of vegetables and a basketful of bread baked earlier that day. It was a welcomed relief after the diet of dried fruit, cured meat and rock-hard bread.

'Welcome, Nereos!' said a sunny Leander, dispelling the aura of hostility. 'Come, sit and have something to eat.' Leander patted the space next to him.

'Th ... tha ... thank y ... y ... you,' the youth said, flushing. 'I h ... h ... have ea ... eaten.'

Jason thrust a cup at him. 'Then a little wine, to help warm the blood.'

Nereos sat with a thump, accepted the cup and downed the liquid in a gulp.

The High Priestess peered at him, eyeing Nereos from head to toe, his ruddy cheeks deepening under her steady gaze.

'Nereos ...'

The adolescent's head jerked and twitched as he swung to face Evan, who tried to set him at ease with an affable smile.

'How many times have you been to the palace?' he asked.

Nereos swallowed, his Adam's apple bobbing in his throat. Jason refilled his cup. 'Ah ...'

Evan rubbed Lykeios' head. The pup panted and licked his hand. 'Dexion's wolf, Lykeios, has a bad paw. He can't walk on it, yet he is determined. He runs and likes to play chase with Dexion, isn't that right?'

Dexion beamed with pride and nodded. Lykeios, as if on cue, rose and hopped over to Nereos and rubbed his nose against the youth's face. Nereos smiled and laughed as the wolf licked him from the chin to the hairline. He scratched behind the pup's ears.

'How often have you been to the palace?' Evan repeated.

'Quite a lot,' replied Nereos, relaxed and grinning, rubbing Lykeios' belly.

'Is there a track or route that goes to the palace?' he asked.

'There is an ancient road that leads straight to the old buildings,' answered the youth. He pointed north-east of the beach. 'There is a trail over the hill that intersects the ancient road about four stades inland.'

'Is it passable?' asked Leander.

Nereos nodded. 'Villagers and those who reside nearby mine the loose stone blocks and use them to repair sections of the road.'

'What of the palace? Is it a sound structure?' asked Hektor.

'No.' His tone saddened. 'Portions of the masonry are unstable and it is hazardous to enter. There are countless rooms under rubble, and spacious areas where you see tall pillars, some of which are still standing, though a lot are broken and lay splintered, strewn across the ground. There are stairwells, but debris blocks most of them.' His eyes shimmered with wonder. 'It must have been a majestic place to live. The frescoes are charming and full of life.'

'What do you know about the people who once lived there?' Alexina asked, leaning towards him.

'A little from what my grandfather told me, from what he learnt from his grandfather. He described the wonders of their luxuries, comforts that sounded too fantastical to be true. My grandfather said they had hot and cold running water, and toilets! He explained how the artisans and engineers were renowned and coveted by other civilisations. Their skills even reached the ears of kings from Egypt.' Nereos' eyes sparkled as he spoke.

Hektor nodded.

'You know of these marvels?' the teenager asked him.

'Of course, we too have hot and cold running water, and toilets and water mills that power our granaries,' replied Hektor.

Nereos goggled at Hektor.

'What details can you provide about this cavern you discovered?' the High Priestess asked.

He swung his head to her. 'Ah ... the entrance to the cave is located beyond the central court, and you go to the southernmost point, where there is a standalone structure. It may have been a stable or storeroom. That is where access to the cave is situated. It is difficult to get there or find, and lots of ruined sections of the building impede your approach, but it is the only way to get there.'

'Thank you, Nereos, that is helpful,' she said, smiling at him, concluding the conversation.

Evan then stood, the others following in his lead.

'I can lead you to the road,' Nereos said to Evan and Alexina, scrambling to his feet.

'The information you have provided is more than enough,' she said, 'and what we are to encounter is perilous.'

'But if I accompany you, it will be quicker and I can guide you through the safest parts of the site,' he implored with an eager face.

'We cannot guarantee your safety.' Hektor loomed over the youth. Nereos shrank back and sought out Leander, pleading, who patted him on the shoulder and gave an apologetic shake of the head.

CHAPTER 31

'What is our course of action?' Leander asked.
'It would be advisable to explore the ruins before attempting to enter the cave,' replied Phameas. 'Only a fool would confront this Minotaur without knowing escape routes and familiarising himself with the structure of the building.'

Homer nodded. *Phameas is correct, we search the palace first and identify obstacles that may impede our progress.*

'And draw schematics of the site to arrange for unforeseen situations,' added Hektor.

'No,' said Evan, jutting out his jaw. 'After all the setbacks we've had, we find the statuette, return it to its rightful location and leave for home.'

'Phameas' advice is sensible and perceptive,' said the High Priestess. 'Evandros, we proceed with caution. We do not want to further risk lives. And as you have stated, we've faced many delays, and it is essential we use the time to prepare and be ready to confront any threats the Dark Master and Goddess of Discord present.'

Evan tapped a finger against his thigh. 'I disagree. No amount of preparation and planning will make a difference in fighting a mythical monster or contending with gods. To succeed and return home, we retrieve the icon and let the gods do their part. It is their fight.'

'And in the process the Minotaur will kill you!' Phameas' cheeks grew mottled and he jabbed a finger at Evan. 'Are you in a hurry to die, Evandros? With all your cleverness, this has to be the most stupid suggestion you have made, and I will not accompany you to your execution.' The Phoenician pivoted on his heel and stormed away.

'Phameas! You know I am right!' He started after his friend. 'Phameas!'

'Master Evandros.' Evan came to a stop at the tone of Dexion's voice. The boy sniffed and wiped his nose with the back of his hand. Evan's heart twisted, and he knelt down. Dexion rushed at him and almost bowled him over, arms wrapped around his neck. Evan swallowed a lump in his throat and patted Dexion on the back.

'I know what is going to happen,' he whispered. 'I suspected my journey ends here, and this is how I return home.' To make light of the situation, he continued, 'See, now I have the gift of prophecy.'

Dexion's tears drenched Evan's shoulder. 'You must do as Phameas says.'

Evan pursed his lips, noting the gloomy countenance on Homer, Leander and Alexina's faces. Hektor remained aloof and stood apart from them.

Homer stuck out his tablet. Evan read the Linear script.

'Fine, we'll explore the palace and search for the cave,' he said, resigned.

Dexion sniffed and nodded. Lykeios mewled at them. Evan reached out and stroked the wolf's head.

'All right, let's go,' he said, 'or we'll lose what's left of the daylight to search the site.' He stood and ruffled Dexion's hair. 'Get your gear.' Dexion shadowed his every move, and Lykeios scooted after them.

He hoisted the aegis over his shoulder and then strapped on the sword, tucked between his left shoulder and shield. He collected the knapsack, complete with water bag and writing tablet. Within ten minutes, he was leading his companions away from the campsite, following the tributary and heading over the hill until they came to the intersection where the ancient road and the shepherd's path joined. Phameas walked alongside him in stony silence, while Homer ignored them and kept walking. Dexion was perkier, his step light and his face freer of the earlier emotional outburst. Lykeios, tongue hanging from his mouth, trotted alongside, while the High Priestess, Leander and Hektor trekked behind them.

No one spoke, which Evan preferred, still annoyed at the delay in searching for Mother Goddess' statuette.

CHAPTER 32

'Tomorrow we leave early and begin searching for the icon!' said Evan, flinging his writing pad into his knapsack. 'We have ample material and detailed sketches to fill a book. We have squandered too much time surveying the area and buildings.'

'I concur,' said Hektor with a nod. 'We've explored the palace and made contingencies for perils. We now finish what the gods appointed us to accomplish.'

'Thank you!' he said, throwing his arms in the air. 'Let's return to the campsite and organise supplies for our trip back here.'

'Evandros, I understand your haste in locating the sacred object,' said the High Priestess, 'I, too, wish for a resolution. However, no matter our urgent desire to complete the errand of the gods, it is for them and our people that we must succeed, for if we do not, what we have endured since leaving Atlantis is for nought.'

'I know that, but no amount of overseeing and surveying the conditions and layout of the site can prevent the inevitable,' he said, frustrated. 'Whatever the outcome, and just like pulling out a tooth, best done quick to avoid lingering pain.'

She raised a brow at him. 'Tomorrow, then.' She rounded on her heel and set off for the road back to the beach. Hektor lumbered behind.

'I don't believe a rotten tooth compares to battling the Minotaur or a Titan.' Phameas scratched his head.

'An interesting comparison,' Leander acknowledged with a slight smile. 'The High Priestess concurs with your eloquent description.'

Homer slapped him on the back of the head.

'What was that for?' He rubbed his skull.

For being smart-mouthed. She is our sister; you remember that.

'Yes, well, we need to get this over with,' he said. 'Besides, we'd exhausted every part of the palace, what we could access. There wasn't any more to discover or draw that we haven't seen.'

'We did not check the central court and beyond,' Leander said. 'Perhaps it may be reasonable to investigate the area—'

'We are not wasting another day mapping or climbing over ruins! Nereos' descriptions are extensive enough to locate the cave's entrance.' He kicked at a loose stone on the paved road.

'Ah, yes, except we did not find a safe passage to the central court,' Leander pointed out.

'Given what we saw today, I am confident we will.' He came to a stop as they crested the hill, drawn to the strange gathering on the shoreline. 'What is going on?'

'What are they staring at?' Leander shielded his eyes against the sun's glare.

'There's one main reason to keep a lookout on the horizon, unless there are beautiful mermaids frolicking in the water. That would get my attention'—Phameas pointed—'or an approaching vessel.'

Evan quickened his pace, Dexion running to keep up with him. Phameas, whose stride was shorter, hastened his pace to match Evan's gait, while the two Atlanteans had no issues keeping up.

Jason and his crew had amassed by the bow of the *Argo*, staring across the expanse of the azure sea. He beckoned them. The urgency on his face was enough for Evan to walk faster.

'What is it? Have Kronos and Eris ordered their oversized giants to come for us again? Or is it a harpy?' He examined the sky, scouting for the large-winged monster.

Jason's brow was knitted, and he pointed. 'Can you see that dark shadow in the distance?'

Evan shaded his eyes against the glare of the sun on the water. 'What do you think it is?'

'Trouble.'

'Is it a ship?' asked Leander.

Phameas answered, 'From the shape and movement, I'd say so.'

'Phameas is right. If it were a harpy or some other creature, it would be considerably higher in the sky,' Jason added.

'How long before the ship reaches here?' the High Priestess asked.

'If the captain is sharp and resourceful, he will anchor at sea and delay until morning, when it is safer to manoeuvre around the atoll to evade being shipwrecked,' he replied. 'Or if he keeps sailing, they will dock late in the evening.'

'A wise captain would remain offshore, far from being capsized by winds and waves, yet within sheltered distance to sail inland if needed,' Phameas concluded.

'Let us hope the captain is canny,' she said, 'and makes same the astute judgement you suggested.'

Hektor pulled out his axe. 'I advise we make provision for a defence. We do not know if they are hostile or friends.'

Homer nodded, his face bleak.

'Perhaps it would be best if the High Priestess and Dexion stay in the village,' Leander said.

The High Priestess crossed her arms, ice-blue eyes glittering. 'I will wait here.'

'Leander makes a good point,' Evan said. 'If there is a skirmish, it will be tough to shield you and the objects.'

'I can protect myself,' she said, face hardening and her jaw tightening.

'Yes, you can.' He shuddered at the memory of the crimson light she'd radiated when they had encountered the Mykenaean warriors on their way to Corinth. He would never forget their horrific screams as the flaming light sheared and seared their limbs, and their terrible deaths. 'Leander, odds are we need the High Priestess. She has the power of the items and can use the red light.' To avoid being pinned by the High Priestess' frosty glare, he swung around to Jason and asked, 'What's your strategy for defence?'

'A few of my slingers will remain on the ship with Leander, whose gift with the bow and arrow adds extra power.' He pointed to the mouth of the estuary. 'About eight Argonauts will stand guard there, and the rest secrete by the cliff face.'

'Our defence is too thin.' Hektor frowned in disapproval. 'We will not withstand an attack.'

'My tactic is to show force, not to engage in battle,' said Jason, 'and with the luck of the gods, discourage them from coming ashore.'

'It is possible the captain is seeking safe harbour and has no intention of fighting,' said Evan. 'Regardless, I'll be with your men at the river's edge.'

'As will I,' added Phameas.

Homer rapped at his chest.

'Me and Lykeios too,' said Dexion, his pup yelping in accordance.

～

E van squatted by the entrance to the High Priestess' makeshift tent. 'Leander worries about the consequences of the icons you hold and of using them to protect us. He understands, as I do, the burden you carried after the altercation with Memnon's soldiers. You should be angry at me for saying you need protection, not at Leander.'

Her eyes glinted with indignation. 'The reasoning behind the words is not in contention. It is their meaning and their implication.'

He lowered his head. 'I know, and I am sorry to have offended you. You are right to be angry, and I am annoyed by my stupidity.' He regarded her, shamefaced. 'Whatever transpires, it is your ability to harness the objects that will reinforce our defence.'

She mellowed. 'Evandros, what is it? Are you privy to information that I am not aware of?' She examined his face.

He averted his face towards the setting sun. The hues of yellow, orange and red were spectacular, but he could not appreciate the stunning display. 'No. Zeus has been quieter than usual. I am uncertain if that is a positive sign or not. We need to be alert and speak out if we see something that is not the norm.' He clutched a handful of the sand and let it trickle. She caught his hand, stilling him.

'What aren't you telling me?' she asked.

He tilted his head at her. 'Vigilance is important.'

'Evandros …'

'We need to keep the fires small,' he said, standing. 'We don't want to signal our whereabouts to the crew on the ship.'

He strode away and joined Phameas, Homer, Dexion and the pup at the convergence of the river and sea. He almost laughed out loud. The scene reminded him of a western movie when a posse of good guys and bad guys faced each other before shooting it out. His mirth faded as fast as the dying sunlight. He watched the darkening shape on the water, the size increasing as it sailed closer.

'You'd think the pilot would stop to anchor at sea,' he said.

Thirty minutes passed. The markings on the mast would have been visible, but in the fading light, it was difficult to see.

'Something is happening,' said Phameas, striding closer to the water's edge. Evan walked with him and scoured the advancing twilight, trying to catch sight of what his friend could see. 'They are stopping!' Phameas clapped his hands. 'I can hear the anchors being thrown over the side.'

'We have a shrewd captain,' he said, the knot in his gut loosening. 'Now we wait until morning to find out who it is and what they want.'

CHAPTER 33

E van dozed in snatches of fitful naps, plagued by strange dreams of harpies, monsters and sword-bearing female warriors. He roused to wakefulness as a glimmer of sunlight edged its progress from its eastern slumber, heralding a fresh day. Tinges of pink faded as the sun bridged the perimeter of the horizon and spread across the sky. He rubbed his palms together and stamped his feet to get the blood circulating, and tried to dispel the unsettling disquiet of his turbulent thoughts. He kept track of the incoming ship with mixed feelings, eager for a distraction, in spite of the possible problems this new arrival might entail. Evan and Homer saw figures bustling to and fro across the deck. Within minutes, oars plunged into the sea and the ship cruised towards the coastline.

'The captain is piloting the ship towards our location,' said Phameas, coming alongside them.

The mainsail was hoisted and flapped in the wind until it billowed, smoothing out the image. Puzzled, Evan wondered why the Argonauts became agitated and raised a brow at Jason. The

Argonaut dragged a hand over his mouth and chin, his complexion pale as a lily. Evan's gut constricted as if someone had squeezed his intestines.

'That is an Amazonian ship,' Jason remarked, his tone flat.

'What?' Evan blinked at him.

The vibration of breathing became heavy and resonated, like shouting into an abyssal cave.

'The ship is Amazonian.'

'How …? What …?' he stuttered as thoughts tumbled in his mind, similar to laundry in a dryer. He didn't notice the others, who arrived a step behind Jason.

'It cannot be …' Leander's expression grew haunted.

The Argonaut dragged a hand down his chin. 'The sail has the crest of the Amazons—a female warrior holding a bow and arrow.'

'Could the vessel belong to another colony of Amazons?' asked Hektor.

'I don't think so. I thought Herakles had killed them all until we shipwrecked on their island,' Jason replied. 'It is possible other Amazons survived and settled somewhere else, but …'

Goosebumps popped along the length of Evan's arms and legs. 'No. Antioche told me their ancestors were the remaining few who escaped and avoided capture. After they fled from Herakles, the Amazons migrated further east along the Black Sea and established a new settlement in Taurica. They lived there for decades in peace until tribal warriors from neighbouring areas invaded, claimed their land and forced them to leave.'

'Why has the queen come here?' asked Phameas, hands on hips.

'The queen wishes to talk with Master Evandros,' Dexion replied.

They appraised Dexion with unspoken curiosity and then turned to Evan.

'Don't ask me! How can I know why she wants to speak to me? There is no reason for her to come. Not after what she did.' He flung an arm at the fast-approaching ship.

'You don't expect the queen is here to take us back into captivity?' asked Leander, clasping his bow tight, knuckles whitening. 'She only let us leave because Dexion provided us with the antidote and Evandros threatened her.'

'No ...' Dexion's eyes had a faraway look. 'She has something for Master Evandros.'

'Other than fathering her child, what else did you do?' Phameas' eyes twinkled, the corners of his mouth quirking.

'Nothing! She has no reason to be here. I made it clear I didn't want anything further to do with her or the Amazons.'

'Hmm ... I daresay she had other plans,' said Phameas, stifling laughter. 'She has followed you here, and it must be important, or why would she travel so far from home?'

'We will find out soon enough.' Jason nodded at the ship. 'In about an hour—sooner, judging by the speed it is coasting. I suggest we remain armed until we learn of their intentions.'

'The queen does not wish to engage in a battle,' said Dexion.

'Thank the gods.' Leander's tanned skin returned to its normal shade.

Why do you think she is here? Homer wrote.

Evan shrugged. 'I have no idea, Homer. It makes little sense to come so far from home just to talk to me. How many different ways can I tell her I want nothing more to do with her and that what she did was wrong? What more is there to say?'

This doesn't feel right, Homer said, concerned.

'I agree—whatever it is, it can't be good,' Phameas said, the jocularity gone from his face and voice.

'I should inform the High Priestess,' Hektor said.

Evan sighed. 'Why don't you go do that, Hektor? I'm not happy about this either, but there's no point speculating until the ship makes landfall.'

The High Priestess stood alongside Evan, tracking the Amazonian ship as it sailed into the cove. He rapped his fingers against his thigh, his stomach fluttering like he had caged butterflies inside. He couldn't figure out why he was anxious about the pending arrival. Granted, they had not parted on the most amicable terms, but it hadn't been disagreeable. In fact, the queen, realising the situation was no longer under her control, hadn't prevented them from leaving. He bit his bottom lip. *Unless Eris has put an idea in her head to claim revenge, or the crazy goddess has concocted trouble and she needs our assistance*, he thought. *Nah, she's an Amazon. There's nothing she couldn't handle herself.* The High Priestess reached out and stilled his fingers. He swivelled around to her.

'Whatever the reason the queen has come, I am certain she doesn't intend to cause further distress,' she said.

'How can you know what her plans are, after what she did to us? Aren't you upset by what she did to you? I'm still angry at her for colluding with Eris and holding us captive. If Dexion hadn't gotten the elixir, you might have died.'

'I do not believe she would have allowed that to happen. Her primary objective was to reinvigorate her people with offspring, at which she succeeded.' Her ice-blue eyes bored into his. Evan's cheeks warmed, and he took a sudden keen interest in the sand and the colour of the granules.

He cleared his throat. 'In our defence, we didn't realise what we were doing ...' His face grew hotter. 'What I mean is, we knew what to do ... it ...' He coughed. 'What I'm saying is, we didn't know the queen had us drugged.'

'I am cognisant of what transpired, Evandros, and how you could not counter her actions,' she said, turning to the advancing sleek black-hulled ship.

He slumped with relief. Her intense scrutiny and the penetrating sense of her seeing through him had almost had him blurt out everything about himself—his real self, not this persona he had to portray. He started as a voice shouted and resonated across the blue water. He noted the swift manoeuvre of the oars pulled from the water by the rowers. There was a flurry of activity on deck. His breathing quickened as he recognised the military colours of the queen's personal warriors.

'At least there aren't many soldiers on board,' said Jason.

Evan jumped, startled. He'd been so engrossed by the impending arrival that he hadn't noticed the others assembling.

'The crew is trained to engage in combat,' said Hektor.

'Yes, that is so, Hektor,' Jason acknowledged with a nod and then pointed. 'Have you noticed they did not arm the men?'

A quiver ran down his spine. *Stop, you dimwit, there is nothing she can do to you. Not anymore, so get over it, you pathetic weed.*

'Oh ...' Jason's mouth fell ajar.

'To my reckoning, there are at least thirty warriors on board and that's not including the queen's personal retinue,' said Phameas, raising a brow at Jason. His eyes widened, the white stark against the tanned complexion of his skin. 'Great Baal-Hamon! How long have we been absent from the isle of the Amazons?'

'About fifty days have passed,' replied Leander. 'Why do you a ... ah ...'

Everyone gawked at the queen and then whirled to Evan. He rubbed his eyes and took another look. The queen stood at the prow, her pregnant stature conspicuous and apparent.

'That is not probable,' he said in a hoarse voice, the colour draining from his face.

'The gods have blessed you with the Great Baal-Hamon's fertility bounty,' said Phameas, pounding him on the shoulder.

'It is as if she is carrying two babies,' said the High Priestess.

'Wha ...?' His legs trembled, and he hyperventilated. Homer caught him, his limbs folding. 'Oh ... Jesus ...' He sank to the ground and gasped. 'I can't breathe ...'

The High Priestess knelt beside him and placed an arm around his shoulders. 'Breathe in and breathe out,' she said in a soothing voice. He heaved. She kept repeating the words until he felt the tightness in his chest ease. He lifted his head and winced, hearing the distorted echo of crunching sand, the noise amplified by his agitated mind. Sand sprayed like a wave, and the prow plunged deeper into the shore and wedged the ship. The vessel wobbled as it nested and then stilled. The crew responded and scooted across the deck, throwing anchors overboard. Several men jumped into the water and stood with vigilance by the bow.

Homer helped him upright and seized his elbow in a firm grip. He swayed. Homer tightened his hold, and Leander stood on his left and held him by the upper arm. The Argonauts gathered behind, not wanting to miss out on seeing the royal guard disembark. The sound of the water lapping against the sand and the seagulls squawking filled the numb silence. The warriors did an about-turn, standing in silence for their queen to emerge onto the prow.

Soon, her familiar honey-blonde tresses, which hung loose about her shoulders, teased by the sea breeze, came into view. Assisted by the captain, she strode to the wooden railing and stepped onto the first notch of the ship's beak. The men, posted on either side of the red-painted beak, did not take their eyes off the queen as she negotiated each step with agility and grace. With one hand on her pregnant stomach and the other at her side, she reached the shore with ease, the water ebbing and flowing over her bared feet. She frowned in concern at the ashen and unsteady Evan and walked over, her guards in tow.

'Has Evandros taken ill?' she asked. 'I saw him collapse.'

'Your … um … the state of your condition surprised him,' replied the High Priestess, taking the lead. 'As it did all of us.'

Antioche patted her girth, beaming with joy. 'As it did my physician and me when the change occurred.'

'What brings you here, Queen Antioche?' she asked.

Antioche's gaze flickered towards Evan. He felt better but washed out, much like the effects following a severe tension headache. He couldn't stop staring at her. She was radiant and more stunning than he remembered. The colour of her hair was darker and more golden under the sunlight. He noted her guarded eyes but was too paralysed to speak. She then turned to the High Priestess.

'I've come at the request of Divine Zeus,' she said.

He spluttered and his eyes flashed with disgust, feeling the warmth of the blood returning to his face.

She started at his reaction.

'Why are you really here?' asked Leander. 'Have you come to drug us and take us away?'

'No …'

'Then what brings you here?' Hektor asked, arms crossed against his chest.

'I want to help you in your quest,' she answered, speaking directly to Evan. 'I have brought with me thirty soldiers to assist in your search and to fight the Minotaur.'

'Jason and his men will aid us in our venture into the labyrinth,' said the High Priestess.

The queen nodded. 'I understand. I also have gifts from the gods, which I shall present to Evandros in three days' time, at the birth of the new moon.'

'Why not give them to him now?' asked Hektor. 'Then you can depart.'

'Divine Hephaistos instructed me to deliver them to Evandros when the moon is new,' she answered, 'and not before.' She wheeled around on her heel and strode away to converse with her captain.

'Now what do we do?' asked Leander.

'We wait for the new moon,' replied the High Priestess.

CHAPTER 34

The crew of Queen Antioche's ship set up a camp on the beach, four smaller tents with two flanking a large round tent, with quick efficiency. To distract himself from the furore of activity and thinking about Antioche's mysterious arrival, Evan studied the drawings he'd made of the ruins during their explorations of the site. Nereos' descriptions had been useful and helped to identify locations of the rooms, in addition to his knowledge from touring the site in the twenty-first century. His brow creased when a shadow blocked his light.

'Where is Dexion?' he asked as Phameas and Homer sat next to him.

His half-brother pointed. He smiled, watching Dexion run, zigzagging along the shore with the pup chasing him.

'Somewhat of a surprise, Queen Antioche arriving.' Phameas nodded at the Amazon camp.

Why do you think she came instead of sending a trusted warrior? Homer's pen flew across the wax tablet as he etched out his concerns. *I know when my wife was expecting our children, she found it difficult to walk and became weary more often. Such a long journey, even one for a woman of her standing and exemplary training, would be arduous.*

He avoided peeking over at the campsite. 'Who knows why she came?'

'Well, it's easy to work out why she is here.' Phameas gave him a sly grin. 'The issue is, what does she hope to happen?'

'I am not interested, whatever her motives. You both know I'm returning home as soon as we recover the last object.' He pounded his heels into the sand. 'Both the Mother Goddess and Zeus agreed to send me home.'

The queen's arrival has caused you distress. Homer raised his brows at him.

'And her body in such a significant state ... well, everyone saw how you reacted.'

'Let's not belabour the point.' He crossed his arms against his chest. 'How far along she is in her pregnancy surprised me, that's all, and I did not expect to encounter her ever again after we left the island.'

How do you feel now that you've seen her?

He hesitated. 'I don't know. My mind has been consumed with the next stage of the quest, the impending battle with the Minotaur and getting home. Encountering Antioche again was not what I expected or anticipated. Not here and right now.'

Liar.

He ignored Homer.

'And now that she is here?'

'It does not change what we are required to do,' he said. 'What's important is to finish this business and get everyone home.'

Phameas nodded. 'Agreed.'

'There is something I'd like you to do for me.' He gazed at Dexion and the wolf frolicking in the surf. 'Would you take care of Dexion in my absence? He has no family, and after I am gone, he'll be alone, and I don't want him orphaned again.'

'Yes,' answered Phameas straight away. 'I shall care for him, Evandros, as if he were of my own blood.'

'Thank you, Phameas.' He fell silent and then added, 'If, by chance, I die here, I'd like my body sent back to the twenty-first century. Would you make sure the Mother Goddess and Zeus do this? I know this is asking a lot, but I'd be grateful if you did this for me.'

Phameas' eyes welled. Homer's jaw clamped tight. They nodded.

Evan tugged his ear and bent his head to study his toes, clearing his throat. 'Thank you.'

He mused, recalling when he had first met Zeus, the strange dreams and periodic loss of time. Preoccupied with his melancholy thoughts, he failed to hear the clomp of sand crunching underfoot.

'Evandros.' Phameas prodded him with an elbow. 'One of the queen's guards has arrived.'

Evan looked up at the statuesque Amazon.

'The queen wishes to speak with you,' she said.

He peered behind the warrior. 'Where is she?'

The Amazon stiffened. 'She is in her tent.'

'I am sure she is,' he muttered and handed his book and charcoal to Phameas. 'Lead the way.'

He felt the weight of Phameas' and Homer's gazes on his back as he trudged behind the Amazon. There would be lots of questions when he returned later—of that he was certain. If another had been summoned, he'd behave in the same manner, wanting to learn what the meeting was about. Two royal soldiers guarded the entrance, their faces unsmiling and attentive. He recognised them as the same warriors who'd remained outside Antioche's chambers. They would have heard what transpired behind the doors. He felt his cheeks go warm at the thought and hoped his face wasn't red. To detract from his embarrassment, he studied the structure of the shelter. It was circular, about eight metres in diameter and three metres high, the material made from cured leather.

His escort gave the guards a quick flick of her fingers, and they pulled aside the heavy leather flap for her to enter. He trailed after the warrior into the dim interior of the enclosure. He paused for a minute to allow his eyesight to adjust to the feeble light. Two of the four braziers were lit. Luxurious deep-russet-coloured rugs covered the expanse of the enclosure, and sheer fabrics lined the walls, adding a majestic touch. To his left stood a tripod with a large bowl filled with water; on his right were a table and a setting for two, cups and a jug, and wooden chairs. A fur-lined bed featured in the centre, topped with a myriad of cushions in various shades of purple and red.

'Evandros, I am pleased you came.'

He swivelled about when Antioche emerged from behind a makeshift wall at the head of the bed. She had changed and was wearing a full-length saffron khiton, making her skin more golden. She moved to a flaming brazier, the fiery glow accentuating her curves.

'I … um …' His throat seized and he had to cough. 'I … ah … don't, didn't think you gave me much of a choice.'

'It was not an order to come,' she said, voice hurt. 'If you wish to go, you may.'

He grimaced and swore at himself for being an arse. 'I apologise, I did not intend to be impolite.' He rubbed his temple. 'Why did you ask me here?'

Antioche walked to a table and sat. She poured rich ruby liquid into the cups and held one out to him. He eyed the bowl and then her.

'It is wine, this I affirm by Artemis' virtue,' she said.

He took the proffered cup, sat down and waited for her to speak.

'When Divine Hephaistos and Artemis came with their gifts and instructions from Zeus to come to Krete, they mentioned something most peculiar.' Her grey eyes held his ice-blue ones.

'What was that?'

'You are not from this world, and time is against you.'

His heart battered against his ribcage and then raced as if he were fleeing from an unseen malevolent being.

Her forehead crinkled. 'What did they mean?'

He took a swig, gulping down the wine. 'They are referring to Atlantis and its isolation for over a thousand years. As to the meaning of their second message, it may mean Kronos is here and …'

'And?' she prompted.

'He has discovered the final item.' He set the kylix down, head cocked to the side. 'What I can't work out is why did they send you, a pregnant woman, so far from home with "gifts", and then make us hang around for three days to present them to me?' He straightened. 'It makes no sense. Throughout this entire mission, the gods have been adamant about the urgency of finding the sacred items and reuniting them with the Mother Goddess. Now we have to wait?' He tapped the surface of the table with his middle finger. 'It is not logical to sit here for three days until it is a new moon. There must be a reason for the delay.' His brow furrowed. 'Did they provide further information or a clue?'

'Only that it was important you receive these gifts before you confront the Minotaur or you will fail.'

'I have the labrys the Mother Goddess instructed us to find, the one weapon that can kill the Minotaur. No, they are hatching some other plan.' Evan hunched forward, elbows pressing into knees, hands clasped. 'And why you? They could have brought the items to me, as they did when Skylla attacked our ship. Poseidon and Ares repaired the *Argo* and replaced the lost weapons.' He stood and paced. 'They want you here, but why?' He paused mid-step. 'Dexion will know what the gods are up to.' He swung around.

'Wait, Evandros.'

He stopped. Antioche moved to stand. Her face paled and she bit her lip, sinking back down. She doubled over, clutching her belly. Beads of perspiration dotted her forehead. He rushed to her side.

'What is it? Do you want me to call the physician?'

She squeezed his hand, panting, and shook her head. 'No … it … it will … pass.'

'I should get your doctor.'

'No, please stay with me.' Her head dropped lower as she panted and then inhaled in a long, steadying breath. He put his arm around her, not sure what to do. She rested her forehead on his shoulder, her ragged breathing easing. Minutes passed, the colour on her face returning to her normal complexion.

'What happened?' he asked. 'How often are these spasms occurring?'

She gave a shaky laugh and wiped her brow, fingers trembling. 'The baby is quite active and strong.'

'You were just three months into the pregnancy at the time of our departure. What are you now? Seven, eight, nine months? Almost ready to give birth.' Evan sat back down and waited for her to respond.

She nodded, tucking an errant strand of hair behind an ear.

'How is it possible? Did something unusual happen after we departed? Other than Hephaistos and Artemis paying a visit.'

She reached for a cup. Her hand was shaking, the contents splashing over the rim. He reached across to steady her clasp on the drinking vessel.

'I had a strange visitation while bathing in the sea. A large, beautiful and majestic swan flew from the sky and landed on the water next to me. It was curious the way it sat and stared at me, as if it was examining my psyche—and there was something else. A little odd peculiarity.'

Evan cocked his head. 'What was that?'

'Like it wanted to kiss me.'

He tensed. 'I am sensing there is more to this chance meeting?'

Her mouth quirked. 'It caressed my breasts.'

His eyes widened. 'It did what?'

'It nuzzled my nipples, much like a lover does.'

He grasped his jaw and squeezed. 'Then what did the oversize bird do?'

'It shimmered and a blue light surrounded it, and afterwards I felt a palm stroke my stomach.'

'If I could kill him, I would.'

'Who?'

'The friggin' swan was Zeus.' He launched to his feet. 'He'll have to explain what he did to you and why.'

'Evandros, stop.' She struggled to her feet. 'Are you saying the King of the Gods visited me?'

'It sounds as though he did. The swan is one of his animal familiars.'

He took a step to leave, but Antioche clutched his wrist, preventing him from going.

'If it was Divine Zeus, he sought me for a reason. Gods need not explain their actions to us; their purpose has greater meaning and we defer to their supremacy.'

'It's not their divine right to accost every person they choose or desire.' The colour of his pupils darkened. 'He took advantage of you and that is unacceptable.'

Her head tilted. 'Why? He is a god and we are their servants. It is how we honour them.'

'No. They must earn our respect before being honoured, and I have seen no virtues in the gods that warrant our worship of them.' He attempted to extract himself from her clasp, but she refused to let go. 'Zeus owes me an explanation.'

'Why?'

'He does nothing without some self-serving design, and I don't trust his motives.'

She held his hand against her breast. Evan's heart flipped in his chest. The heat of her body radiated and awakened every nerve in his body, and the scent of her perfume reminded him of the many intimate moments they had shared. He clenched his jaw.

'If Divine Zeus has a plan that involves me, then I am grateful he has chosen me.' She cupped his face. He felt as if he was drowning in the grey pools of her eyes.

He bit his lip, trying to snap out of the mesmerising effect she was having on him. 'He shouldn't have touched you.'

'Why?' she asked in a soft voice.

He struggled. His internal voice was telling him to be cold and analytical, yet his body was capitulating, a sensory overload at her proximity that he was finding difficult to ignore.

She touched his lips with her fingers. His breathing quickened. He embraced her, drawing her closer to him, her belly pressing against his stomach. Her pupils dilated and her lips parted. He pressed his mouth against hers, to which she responded with equal fervour. She clasped his nape, grasping his hair as their kiss deepened. He thrust his tongue into her mouth, wrapping his arms about her waist. He pulled his mouth from hers, their breaths mingling, picked her up and carried her to the bed.

CHAPTER 35

Roused into wakefulness, it took Evan a little while to clear his mind from the shroud of fogginess. He blinked. The gloominess of the interior made him rub his eyes, trying to identify shapes. He lay there disorientated by the unfamiliar surrounds until he brushed his hand against the silky pelt of fur and realised where he was. He scrunched his eyes shut and gave an inward groan. *You are so weak. She flutters her silvery eyes at you and you abandon all sensibility.* Her warm, curvaceous body tucked into his, awakened every cell of his being. She was an enigma, astute and stunning, yet with a vulnerability. The compulsion to protect her was strong, and he had never felt that about anybody, except for his family. To confuse matters further, she was pregnant with his child. He touched her belly, her smooth skin taut under his callused palm. His hand bounced.

'Oh, wow.'

Antioche placed a hand over his. He gazed at her in wonder, and she smiled, her face soft and tender.

'That was some kick.'

'Sometimes you can see the baby's foot.'

His heart constricted and he swallowed hard. 'You know I have to leave.'

Her smile dissolved. 'I know,' she whispered, tears forming.

He clambered out of bed, bent to pick up his khiton and threw it on. He left without another word. The flap dropped behind him, and he hesitated, the brightness of the morning sun a stark contrast to the heaviness and hollowness that affected him. *I get it now, Atlas' burden of carrying the Earth on his shoulders.* Just like the onus of responsibility to complete the mission and leaving Antioche. It left a hollow pit in his stomach. He ran his fingers through his hair.

'What an effing mess. Zeus, you owe me an explanation, and you'd better show yourself!'

He stormed away, his footprints leaving hollowed depressions in the sand, clenching and shaking out his hands over and over.

Antioche stifled a sob and ran a palm over where Evandros had lain, her fingertips tingling from his warmth and the remnants of his scent overwhelming her. She buried her face in the fur-lined covers and cried until she could weep no more.

Outside, the sound of voices filtered into the tent. She struggled upright, weary from the emotional tumult, not much different to riding a wild horse, bucking and neighing in a never-ending struggle for capitulation. Except, she didn't want Evandros to cede; she wanted him to be hers of his own free will. Never had she had a lover, male or female, who had captivated her in such a manner. He was unusual; his speech, mannerisms and education surpassed the wisest individuals with whom she conferred.

'The queen is unavailable.'

'I am going to speak with her.'

The majestic Atlantean marched in, hesitated and skimmed

the interior as if blind. Antioche didn't care how bedraggled she looked as she climbed out of the bed and did not bother to hide her nakedness. She gathered her saffron khiton from the floor, wiped her wet cheeks and dabbed at the hot blotches on them. Antioche gave the other woman a cursory nod.

'My brother has the remarkable ability to affect those around him and draw them to him like honey to a bear.' The High Priestess waited while she slipped on her clothes. 'Yet to those who oppose or confront him, he is implacable and merciless.'

'I would not describe him as such. Even when he learnt of my deception and imprisonment of you all, he did not retaliate,' she said, waddling to the small table and easing herself down onto a chair. 'He's too refined and tender.'

Her visitor reflected. 'That is true of him. He also has a dark side, a characteristic that is intimidating.'

'I would not have expected that of you, afraid of your brother. You are one of the strongest women I have encountered. Your inner strength is formidable.' Antioche called for a guard and ordered her to bring more wine, fruit and cheese. She then added, 'I witnessed a glimmer of Evandros' menace, but it was over in moments. Divine Zeus visited while I bathed and that angered him, though I do not understand what the great god did to upset him.'

The High Priestess perched opposite her. 'What exactly happened?'

She reiterated what she had told Evandros and his reaction.

'I see.' The High Priestess' eyes brightened. 'That explains your current state.'

Antioche agreed. 'My physician was at a loss to explain how my pregnancy advanced within a matter of months. When Evandros explained who it was, I then realised the import of what happened. He intends to ask Divine Zeus what he did.'

'Yes, that does not surprise me.' The High Priestess scrutinised her. 'Why do you think Divine Zeus hastened your gestation?'

A chill shot down Antioche's spine, as if a spectre had brushed against her skin. As she was about to reply, an Amazon entered, carrying a dish laden with fresh fruit and goat's cheese, set it on the table and withdrew without uttering a word. She plucked a grape from the platter and rolled it between her thumb and fingers. 'To coerce Evandros into doing something he does not wish to do.' She examined the High Priestess. She had not seen the similarity between sister and brother before, but she noticed it now. Their mouths and nose were the same, as was their steely countenance.

'I believe that too. The relationship between Evandros and his divine sire is stormy, which is not what it had been in the past, and not prior to our departure from Atlantis.'

'What do you mean?'

'As a child and during our youth, Evandros never argued nor dared to confront his family or friends, and in particular, not his Divine Father. Evandros changed after the shipwreck. He is not the sibling I adored and grew up with.' The High Priestess paused and intently scrutinised her. 'Throughout the months you spent with him, was there anything he said that you thought was odd or surprising?'

Antioche popped the grape into her mouth and chewed as she regarded the statuesque woman opposite her. 'I am not sure what you are asking. He is unlike any man I've taken as a lover, and each day was an adventure. How he thought first before speaking or answering a question, and the judicious manner in which he conversed, I found exhilarating and wonderful.'

'Did he discuss matters or beliefs in your time together that struck you as foreign or perplexing? Perhaps unfamiliar?'

'High Priestess, are you suggesting Evandros is an impostor?'

she asked. 'If that is so, what evidence do you have to suggest he is not your brother?'

The High Priestess did not respond straight away and then said, 'I've felt there was something different about his demeanour. The gentle side of him was non-existent when he stormed the palace in Kyrene to rescue us. The brother I grew up with was mild, almost timid, and had an aversion to using weapons, despite being an accomplished swordsman. It was as if he had undergone a transformation. He is the epitome of a scholar. The breadth of his mastery and intelligence is unsurpassed, even greater than I have witnessed. It is his volatile nature, which he never exhibited before departing Atlantis, that is unlike him.'

'Have you considered that Evandros' genuine strengths have emerged since journeying from your home? In order to succeed, he learnt to harden himself and be a skilled fighter to prevent you and the others from being killed.'

'Is that what he told you?' asked the High Priestess. 'He has disclosed much to you.'

'It is what he did not say,' she replied. 'Evandros' perception of how to address emissaries, their solicitations, his understanding of political matters indicate he is educated, and he enjoys reading and learning. His inherent capabilities, and the result of his experiences, are what you have seen. It transformed him to overcome each challenge he has faced. You and the others would not be here today if he had not.' Antioche broke off a bit of hard cheese and ate it with a grape. 'Perhaps it is these characteristics in his behaviour that you do not approve. He is no longer the spineless and meek individual you knew or commandeered, and as you are not familiar with this attribute, it scares you.'

The High Priestess countered, 'He does not frighten me.'

She arched her brows. 'Yes, he does. You cannot control him, and that strikes you with fear. He is no longer the pliable sibling.'

The High Priestess averted her face. 'Does this aspect of him not distress you?' she asked after a period of silence.

She nodded. 'It does, but not the same as you.'

'How so?'

'I am queen of the Amazons, and as those before me, we consider no man an equal. They are a commodity to provide seed to increase our race. A ruler is a fierce leader, a soldier never dominated by any person and less so by a man. I am loath to admit, and my forebears would execute me for confessing, but I would permit Evandros to rule alongside me.' Her face softened as she spoke.

'You have fallen in love with him.'

'I believe I have.'

'Is this why you have travelled here, to declare your love for Evandros?'

'I came at the behest of the gods. They permitted no other from my home to take my place. I am to present Evandros with the gifts they have bestowed on me two days hence. I still offer my warriors to aid you in the fight against the Minotaur.'

'That is not possible. He is to engage the Minotaur and no other can assist him.'

'It will kill him!'

'That is conceivable.' The High Priestess nodded. 'He has the sacred labrys, a weapon made to destroy the Minotaur.'

'How powerful is the weapon?' the queen asked, the lines around her eyes and mouth tightening.

'As powerful as Evandros.'

CHAPTER 36

Evan joined the others by the campfire after his swim in the sea. Hektor was roasting the morning's catch on a makeshift wooden spit. Homer passed him a cup of watered-down wine. Phameas sent him a surreptitious glance as he sat, eyes full of intrigue and unspoken questions. He gave a bowl to Hektor and smiled at Dexion, ruffling his hair. The boy rewarded him with a warm grin. The wolf nosed his shoulder, wanting his attention too. He rubbed Lykeios' belly for a few minutes, smiling as the pup rumbled in contentment. He took the bowl from Hektor and tucked into the food.

'When did Nereos say he was coming?' he asked after swallowing.

'He should be here in the next half hour,' replied Leander. 'He mentioned he had a few errands to finish beforehand.'

'Good. There are a few details I want to confirm with him before we set out for the ruins.'

'We then kill the Minotaur and retrieve Mother's sacred icon,' Hektor added, tossing a log onto the fire.

'I don't expect it is going to be that easy.' He put aside the dish.

Homer thrust his tablet under Evan's nose. After a quick scan of the tight and chiselled script, he replied, 'Yes, the Minotaur won't be hiding either. He'll start hunting as soon as we enter the cave.'

'How large do you think the cave might be?' asked Phameas. 'Wide enough for two or three people to walk abreast? Or narrow, where we proceed in a single file?'

'Great questions, Phameas, ones Nereos can answer when he arrives.' He drew up his knees and clasped his arms around them.

'If we are to wait for the boy, we should continue your practice with the labrys,' said Hektor, hovering over him.

'That is an excellent idea.' His friend elbowed him in the ribs before he could stand up.

'Evandros.' Phameas poked him harder.

'Ouch! What the heck is ...?' He rubbed his ribcage, annoyed, and then noticed everyone's reaction. He twisted around. 'Oh ... I didn't expect to see that.'

'What do you think it means?' asked Leander, unsettled.

'We'll soon find out.'

Evan stood, the other men following his lead as the High Priestess and the queen headed their way, the Amazon royal guard marching behind them.

'I have invited Queen Antioche to participate in our discussion this morning,' the High Priestess said. 'With her formidable skills and prowess as a warrior, her perspective on how we approach the lair of the Minotaur is welcomed. In addition, I have agreed to her offer of her warriors' military presence, which is an added advantage if we happen to be attacked or require protection.'

Evan wanted to curse the High Priestess for placing him in an unmanageable situation. He bit the inside of his cheek, drawing blood. His instinct told him that whatever happened from here, no matter the decision, he would pay in some way. From the inscrutable expression on the High Priestess' face, it was clear to him there was no changing her decision. Dexion rocked on his heels, the only one not surprised by their joint presence.

'I ...' He wavered, taken aback by the faces goggling at him. 'The queen's input is respected and I value her proficiency as a warrior and leader.'

The High Priestess nodded in approval, and the men made room for them to sit. He helped Antioche ease herself down on the sand and sat next to her.

'What assistance can my warriors and I provide you?' asked Antioche.

'We require protection to ward off any assaults while we are recovering Mother's precious possession, and your soldiers can guard us while we are searching the cave. Given prior incursions, it is inevitable that the Dark Master and the Goddess of Discord plan to use their minions to steal the sacred icons from our possession,' the High Priestess answered.

'I disagree,' Evan interjected. 'Kronos wants to possess the objects. He won't accept an intermediary to take them, not at this end stage. Besides, he doesn't trust anyone else to retrieve them or take them from us.'

'Evandros' comment is valid.' Leander sat cross-legged, tapping his chin with a finger. 'Since the beginning, it has been the Dark Master who wanted Mother's sacred objects. The Goddess of Discord and her beasts were distractions to impede our efforts to find them.'

'The Dark Master is clever. He has manoeuvred us and the goddess into doing his bidding,' said Hektor. 'With the last sacred item yet to be discovered, all he needs to do is sit back, wait and seize the icons when we have all of them.'

'Hektor is right,' Evan agreed. 'He has been patient, and he has been planning this for centuries. We cannot make mistakes, not now at our final juncture.'

Or be careless, noted Homer.

'Not after what we have endured.' Phameas stabbed a finger at the ground. 'I intend to fight the Dark Master and anyone who tries to steal the objects.'

'As do I,' said Leander.

'And I.' Hektor nodded.

'Me too,' Dexion said, chest puffing out.

'The Argonauts and I intend to join you,' said Jason, unsmiling.

Homer thumped his chest with a fist.

'We need to be prepared to defend ourselves.' The High Priestess addressed the Amazonian queen. 'You and your Amazons secure the perimeter of the palace to avert an attack.'

'No.' Evan's jaw was set.

Everyone gawped at him, surprised.

'No to defending ourselves, or no to leveraging the defensive clout of the queen and her warriors on our passage to the palace?' asked the High Priestess.

'Queen Antioche is close to giving birth,' he answered. 'The risk is too great for her to travel and be in combat. She remains here with her physician and personal guards.'

Antioche gaped at him, her cheeks reddening and her eyes narrowing. 'Evandros, I have been a soldier since a child and borne arms since my mother presented me with my first bow and arrow.'

'I am not questioning your prowess as a fighter, which is insurmountable,' he said. 'You are about to have a baby, and being in a tense situation may induce delivery. It is not wise, nor is it safe for you or the baby. Your soldiers are capable of following our orders.'

'I concur with Evandros.' Hektor sniffed. 'We cannot have the queen's warriors distracted by the onset of her birthing when they need to be on alert.'

Phameas then spoke. 'I've been in many battles, and distracted soldiers are the difference between life and death.' The Phoenician shrugged an apology at the indignant Amazon and cleared his throat, murmured some unintelligible sound and swivelled his head in the opposite direction.

Evan dared not meet Antioche's gaze. Her seething anger and heat emanated from her body like the stoked embers of a bushfire. He wished for the uncomfortable mood to end soon or, better yet, perhaps he could sink into the sand to avoid further hostility. He swallowed, a trickle of sweat dribbling down the side of his face, and pressed on. 'Antioche, it is best your commander lead your warriors while you remain here.'

There was an awkward silence. He took a sudden interest in the grains of sand, avoiding direct eye contact with Antioche and everyone else.

'As you wish. The commander of my Amazons will take my place and escort you,' she said in a frosty tone.

'Good morn to everyone!' said a cheery voice.

They spun around, seeing Nereos approach them.

'Hello, Nereos!' Leander called back in relief. 'You have arrived at the perfect moment. We have further matters to discuss regarding the cave.'

Phameas leaned into Evan and whispered in his ear. 'I do not envy you, Evandros. Your woman is bristling like a charging bull.'

He winced. 'I wish the earth would swallow me now.'

CHAPTER 37

'Oi! Zeus! Are you out there? We need to talk!' Evan marched back and forth near the mouth of the estuary, far from earshot of the campsite. He kicked at the sand and tramped the ground in his wake, causing a small wave of granules underfoot. 'You coward! You owe me an explanation. It's immoral how you take liberties, raping young, innocent females, and then to molest a pregnant woman! The lawmakers in my century would throw you in jail for sexually assaulting women, men and children! If I could, I'd string you up by your—'

'That is enough, Evandros.'

'No, it is not.' His blood bubbled and broiled. 'What the hell were you doing, pretending to be a swan and fondling Antioche while she was swimming? Have you no respect at all for women?'

'Ah … I see.' The King of the Gods rocked on his heels. 'Your affection for the Amazon is the reason for your unsavoury accusations.'

'That is not what this is about,' he growled. 'That was no casual visit. You made a deliberate choice to seek out Antioche and violate her. There is no good reason for abusing women, and you'd better explain what you did.' He simmered and grew still, the distinction between the pupils and irises in his eyes no longer visible. The immortal remained impassive and clasped his hands behind his back. 'Right, I'll broker an arrangement with Kronos, and then it's your problem to negotiate with the consequences of your choices. You and the rest of your Family can go get—'

'Evandros, you do not know of the demands made or how difficult it is to keep the other immortals from wanting to slay you, saying you are unfit to lead and cannot succeed.'

'You chose me.' He jabbed a finger at Zeus. 'I did not want to be here, I don't belong here. I am here because of you. Now, tell me what you did to her!'

'It was necessary to check the health of your progeny and that of the mother.'

'Why was that so important, and why now?' Evan crossed his arms against his chest. 'Antioche would have had the baby in due course, but after your interference, she is going to give birth much sooner. Why did you precipitate the baby's development?'

'Mother thought you may wish to witness the birth of your offspring before returning home, and I agreed.'

'Why on earth you'd think that would be okay? You've endangered Antioche and the baby by forcing her to sail here when she should be home, preparing for the birth.'

'Did it not gladden your heart to see the queen again?' asked Zeus. 'After all, you lingered in her tent for the night.'

His cheeks warmed. 'No, that is not good enough. You are avoiding my questions.'

'It is imperative that I ensure my bloodline continues, and as you are my direct descendant, it was crucial to eliminate any probable imperfections.'

'Are you suggesting Antioche, queen of the Amazons, has defects?' He was incredulous. 'Her heritage is one of the most illustrious in human history.'

'The combination of our immortal blood and the lineage of the Amazons is a powerful union,' said Zeus. 'It is important for our descendants to remain strong and critical that our bloodline continue through the ages. For this reason, it is your duty, and that of your sister and the Atlanteans, to procreate and strengthen our connection and immortality within the human race.'

He staggered. 'Wha ... I did not expect to hear that. The search for Mother's icons was a ruse. The real objective was using us to propagate the planet with demigods.'

'No, finding Mother's sacred items is fundamental to our plan. They are crucial in preventing the Titan from installing his own progeny in our stead. However, if you fail, your liaison with the Amazon and the resultant child secure our Family's divine inheritance, allowing us to return as supreme divinities.' A blue halo engulfed Zeus' body.

'It was your intention from the beginning to reintroduce the Atlanteans, let civilisations know they exist, to pave the way for a full migration where they reassert their power in this region. You and the Family had used them for breeding and creating demigods.' He jerked his thumb at his companions chatting by the fire. 'Brilliant strategy. Either way, you win.'

'Kronos' ultimate downfall is paramount in order for the Family's pre-eminence and worship to continue and be upheld by our faithful followers.' Zeus' head twitched. 'This conversation is over.'

'Wait! If we succeed, how much of my life and the history I grew up with will be different when I return home?'

'Change is a component of the outcome we designed,' the god stated. 'The influence of the individual they called Jesus ceases to exist and subsequent manifestations of His teachings are obsolete.'

'You are afraid of Him.' Evan's eyes widened.

'No, He is like you, a mortal with power, yet able to die. No, it is Kronos we stop, and his ambition to be the sole immortal of our domain.'

'If we lose, he attains his goal.'

'If that does occur, as the Titan spreads his power through his Messiah, we populate the world with our bloodline. When our descendants have grown in number, we conquer Kronos' stranglehold on mortals, and our Family's sovereignty is re-established. That is when we vanquish his seed and rid the realm of his treachery.' The aura surrounding Zeus changed to red.

'I won't be alive to witness that, if it happens.'

Zeus arched a brow, his lips thinning. 'As my son, you are gifted with longevity. That is the reward of divine blood.'

'Huh?' Evan was stunned, a thousand questions flitting through his mind. 'But didn't you state that my mortality is the same as Jesus'?' was all he could manage to ask.

'Yes.' Zeus nodded. 'Though you do not age at the same rate as the others of your kind. Time does not affect gods or their children, even those of mixed parentage, as it does the lesser races of beings.'

'Do you mean Antioche, Phameas and Dexion age faster and die before me? And our child, too?' he asked.

'That is correct.'

'You have to alter their physiology to be the same as mine.'

'Your companions are to continue with their lives as usual.'

'But you are capable of making it happen. Yes?'

'No, Evandros.'

'Why not?'

'Their bodies cannot sustain the cellular changes of ageing, and they may succumb to unforeseen complications.' Zeus stated.

'Then I'd like Dexion and Phameas to return to the twenty-first century with me.'

'What of your queen and the infant? Do you not wish for them to accompany you?' asked Zeus.

Evan squirmed. He was conflicted. A part of him wanted to say yes, but Antioche was bound by her duty and position as queen. 'She'll choose to stay with her people.'

'I shall consider your request.'

And then the King of Gods and Men was gone.

CHAPTER 38

'You should see her,' suggested Phameas, 'and accept those gifts.'

'Why don't you go and I'll wait here?' Evan said to his friend.

Phameas hooted with laughter. 'Nope, she's your woman, and even if Baal-Hamon were to flay me, I wouldn't go. A warrior knows when to fight and when the battle is lost. The queen understands, even if she will not admit defeat. Were she to accompany us, you would worry about her and your unborn child, and that isn't good—it could get you killed.'

'Thanks, Phameas, you are a bouquet of flowers.'

'What? Flowers?' Phameas' face scrunched up in confusion. 'Your gods want you to retrieve the last item so we can finish this quest. Now is not the occasion to concern yourself with the emotions or ramifications of abandoning the queen.'

'You're a harsh man, Phameas.'

Phameas gave him a nudge. 'Go to your woman. This may be the one situation where she allows you to be right.'

'She is not my woman.' He lowered his brows at Phameas.

His friend laughed. 'You are mistaken, my friend. She is, and you are her man.'

'Phameas … you have it all wrong.'

'I see, and that is why you stayed with her the entire night a few evenings ago.' Phameas smirked at him. 'I am sure you spent the night talking.'

'It was a moment of weakness.'

'Are you sure? I've seen the way you look at her when she goes for her swim.' Phameas covered his heart with his hands. 'She has you here.'

He swallowed hard. 'It's not that way at all. And you know I'm returning home when this is over.'

His friend's sunny outlook dimmed. 'Then it is even more important for you to make amends with her.'

'I wish you and Dexion could come with me.'

He shrugged. 'I wouldn't know what to do in your world, and there are too many strange contraptions and flying machines in the air where birds are supposed to be, not people. It's best I remain here. Do not worry about me and Dexion—we intend to share many adventures.'

Evan clasped his shoulder, words not forthcoming.

Phameas cleared his throat. 'Make peace with her.'

His hand dropped to his side. 'You are a good friend, and I'll never forget what you've done for me.' Head lowered, he plodded across the beach to Antioche's tent. 'I'd like to see the queen.' He towered over the warriors standing by the entrance.

The sentries ignored him, their faces as hard as agate.

'I'm unable to complete this mission without the gifts Poseidon and Artemis gave her. We cannot afford to fail, not after what we've struggled and fought for to get here. Let me through.'

The Amazons did not react and remained stock-still, as if their features were carved from marble.

'For goodness' sake, this is—'

There was a scream.

'Antioche!' He dashed into the tent before the guards reacted.

The squalls of agony grew louder. He stumbled over the thick bear rug. Antioche was on the bed, clutching her stomach and curled in a foetal position.

'Antioche!' He paled. 'Oh … shit.' He doubled back, running into the guards. 'Get the physician! Your queen is about to give birth!'

They gaped at the queen writhing in pain.

'*Go!*'

They wheeled about, their armour clinking, and fled the tent.

'The healer is on her way.' He knelt by the bed and wiped her brow.

She peeked at him with feverish eyes and then clenched them tight, letting out a screech.

He flinched.

'Dear Goddess, it hurts. I didn't expect it to feel as if my insides were being ripped apart.' She gritted her teeth and clutched her stomach.

'With the next contraction, take a deep breath and exhale,' he said, placing his hands over hers. She gripped his hand.

Her back arched, and she was breathing fast.

He winced as his fingers became an angry red.

'This … is one of … the gifts.'

'Pardon?'

'The gods revealed …' Antioche drew in a sharp breath and exhaled. 'One gift … is our child.' Tendrils of her hair clung to her damp forehead, her body drenched in perspiration. 'I did not believe them. How could I …?' She sucked in a breath, crushing his fingers. 'I was not full term.' She exhaled shakily. 'Yet here I am, and our baby is about to be born.'

'Jesus …' Evan muttered in a strained tone. 'What bastards.'

'Evandros ...' She tensed and grunted as another wave of spasms seized her body.

'What is it?' he asked, grimacing as she wrung his hand, fingers now purple.

'The second gift ... a bow and a quiver full of arrows for the boy.' She indicated behind him, where her armour and weapons hung on a wooden T-piece stand. 'There, in the leather sack. It is important he learn how to use it before you encounter the Minotaur.' She moaned. 'Give it to him.'

'I'll leave after you've delivered the baby.'

'The God of the Sea and the Huntress insisted the boy receive the weapon on this day.'

He baulked, bewildered by their actions and reasoning to give such a weapon to Dexion.

'Evandros.' She panted through gritted teeth. 'You *must* give them to him! Now!'

'I'll be back.' He approached her gleaming golden armour in quick, long strides and took the concealed items. He hesitated, torn between staying and going, as Antioche clenched the bedcovers, her knuckles white. She let out a long guttural scream, and he scooted out of the tent and staggered, careering into the side of the tent. The brightness of the sun rendered him blind.

'Evandros!' Phameas and Homer hurried over. 'What's happened?'

'The queen has gone into labour.' They gawped at him. 'Antioche is going to have the baby.'

'Now? Here?' Phameas gaped at him.

'She told me the baby is the first of the two gifts.'

'Moloch!'

'Where is Dexion?'

'He's teaching his wolf how to sit and follow,' Phameas replied, dazed.

'I need Leander. Where is he?'

Homer pointed at the *Argo*.

'Why? What is going on?' asked Phameas as they ran to keep up with him.

'The other gift is for Dexion. Leander!' He spotted the fair-headed Atlantean sitting in the ship's shadow, checking the tension on his bow.

'Yes, Evandros?'

'You need to teach Dexion how to shoot with a bow and arrow before we leave for the palace.'

'Of course.'

'Good.' He did an about-turn, sidestepped Homer and Phameas and dashed around the prow of the ship. 'Dexion!'

The boy stopped what he was doing and ran over.

'These are for you.' He thrust the leather bundle at him. 'Leander will instruct you on how to use them.'

Dexion untied the bindings to reveal a finely wrought ebony double-concave bow with a string made from sinew. The god Hephaistos had etched the exterior of the quiver in gold and silver, portraying fleeing deer, boars, bears and birds.

Leander reached for the bow and balanced it on the flat of his palm. 'It is a magnificent piece and well weighted,' he said and gave the bow to Dexion.

'I need to get back to Antioche.'

'What is the matter, Evandros?' Leander asked. 'Has something happened?'

'She is about to have the baby,' he shouted, sprinting to the rotund tent.

Evan flung the flap aside and burst inside. He blinked several times, sightless for a few seconds. Two warriors held Antioche upright. With her were the High Priestess and the physician. They gawked at him.

'Out! I forbid you to be here!' the older woman bawled at him as she stood in front of the naked queen.

'I'm here to help.' He took a step.

'Help? What help can you provide? Leave—the queen alone must deliver the baby.'

'I am not going anywhere.' He stuck out his chin. 'The infant is also mine and I intend to stay for the birth.'

'You cannot—'

'Phoebe, I want ... Evandros ... to stay.'

'But, my queen, it's not appropriate for him to be here when you give birth to your baby.'

'The physician is correct,' the High Priestess concurred.

'Evandros ... stays.'

The healer made a face as Evan knelt by Antioche's side and took her hand. The High Priestess was stunned, and he challenged her to object with an arched brow.

'We need bladders filled with hot water.' The physician gestured at the warriors. 'Lower the queen onto the birthing stool.' She gave Evan a flinty and heated glare. 'You hold her from the rear.'

He scooted behind Antioche and embraced her. She leaned against him, her body and face sheathed in perspiration, and rested her head in the nook of his shoulder.

'Place those bladders on the queen's stomach.' The healer lowered herself to the floor and nodded in satisfaction. 'Breathe in, and out. Again. Breathe in, and out,' the woman kept repeating, and she bent lower to peer between the queen's legs. 'Not quite time yet. Keep breathing in and out.'

Evan breathed along with Antioche, holding her tight. 'You are doing great, Antioche.'

The healer took an additional peek. 'Push! Again! Keep breathing.'

Antioche's face contorted as she pushed.

The wail of a newborn flooded the interior of the shelter.

'A girl!' The physician beamed, holding the newborn up to the queen.

Antioche moaned, her cheeks blotchy and red.

Evan relaxed and smiled as the physician laid the wailing baby on the bed and returned between Antioche's legs for the afterbirth. Puzzled at the delay, the older woman squatted and poked a finger inside the queen's vagina. She brushed her brow with the back of her bloodied hand.

'What is wrong?' Antioche asked, wearied.

'The gods have blessed you. There is a second daughter.'

'What …?' Evan blinked.

The queen shook her head. 'No …'

'Yes, another baby, and you must push.'

'I cannot. I am too tired.'

'I know you are, Antioche,' he said. 'You are queen of the Amazons, fearless and brave. We have a beautiful girl, and a second one is ready to be born.' He kissed her cheek and gave her a smile of encouragement. 'You can do this.'

She bit her bottom lip and closed her eyes, then she drew in a breath and exhaled. Inhaled another lungful of air and pushed. She screamed and slumped into Evan's arms. When nobody spoke, he tensed and did his best to be calm and at ease.

'What is it? What is wrong with our baby?' Antioche sat upright, wincing.

Then the baby howled. She flopped back into his arms and smiled. 'I want to hold my babies.'

The physician and the High Priestess exchanged a look.

'What is it?' she asked them.

'Is there something wrong with the baby?' His heart felt as if someone had squeezed it.

'No … it's …' The healer was not happy.

'Is she defective?' Antioche asked in a worried tone.

The physician hoisted the infant and pointed at the appendage. 'You could say there is a defect … it's not a girl.'

Evan laughed. 'Is that all? There's nothing else the matter with the baby?'

The older woman grouched. 'It's a boy!'

'I am not sure how you determine the gender of a newborn, but there is always a fifty percent chance it could be a male or a female baby.'

'You don't understand. Having a baby girl is far more essential to our race. Boys, or any males, do not have a place in our society.' The physician curled up her nose as she thrust the baby boy into the High Priestess' arms as if he were a serpent.

'What do you do with baby boys?' he asked, alarmed by the woman's reaction.

'We re—'

'Enough! I am tired, I wish to bathe, and most of all, I demand you hand my babies to me.' Antioche struggled to sit upright on the stool. Evan assisted her. 'Call my attendants. I want my bath, right away!' she ordered her bodyguards, who did a quick about-turn and marched out. She held out her hands to the High Priestess, who placed the newborn baby boy into her arms. 'And my daughter.' The High Priestess moved to the bed, picked up the sleeping babe and gave her to her mother. Antioche kissed each on the forehead and gazed at the twins in wonder. One nestling near her breast encountered her nipple and opened their mouth.

'Leave us,' she whispered.

'My queen, you require assistance in bathing and preparing undergarments for the bleeding.' The physician gave Evan a dirty look; he stood defiant and stuck out his chin at her. She continued, 'The wet nurses are waiting outside, ready to enter and feed the children.'

'I intend to nurse my little ones,' she stated. 'Summon my

attendants to help me bathe and prepare the garments I require.' Her gaze hardened, eyeing the physician. 'Evandros is to remain with me and our babies until they attend to me.'

The physician pursed her lips and, with a grunt, rose to her feet. 'Send an attendant if you need my aid.' She packed her gear and left without a word.

The High Priestess placed a hand on the babies' foreheads and a light blue glow emanated from her palms. 'The love and the protection of the Mother Goddess is with you from this day of your birth and throughout your lives until the day on which you depart this world.' She smiled at the twins, acknowledged the parents and left.

Evan placed a wrap around Antioche's shoulders. She smiled at him and then at the two small faces nestled against her breasts. He sat next to her, putting an arm around her.

'You are an amazing woman, Antioche,' he said in admiration. He kissed her. She responded, her mouth opening under his. A while later and with reluctance, he lifted his mouth from hers and asked, 'As to this little fellow, what's your decision?'

'I plan to raise our son with our daughter,' she replied, 'and tell them every day about their extraordinary father, who was on a quest of the gods to save them from being destroyed by the Dark Master.'

His throat constricted. Antioche lowered her face, teardrops falling and splattering onto the babies' swaddling.

'Queen Antioche, we are here to fill the bath,' announced a timid voice.

She nodded.

'I'll leave so you and the babies can rest.' He dithered. 'Would you like me to stay and help you?'

'My attendants can assist me.'

Why was he reluctant to leave? 'I'll visit later.'

'It is best if you do not.' She averted her face. 'I have come as instructed and presented you with the gifts as the gods instructed. Now you need to complete what you came to do.'

'Antioche ...'

'Evandros ... it must be this way.' Her lips quivered.

His stomach ached as if someone had punched him. 'I understand.'

He stood, unable to decipher the intensity of emotions that barraged him like the wild winds of a cyclone. With a final look at her bowed head and the twins, he walked towards the exit. He shut his eyes and wavered mid-step at her weeping. It took all of his self-control and resolve to keep from returning to her side. He pushed aside the flap and let it drop behind him.

CHAPTER 39

E van stood on the water's edge, the waves lapping over his feet, covering them with sand. The preceding day's events kept repeating in his mind, like a bad soapy not worth viewing, yet you couldn't help wanting to know what happens next. His mother watched the daytime soapies while she did the ironing. She claimed it was mindless drivel and helped her finish the pile of clothing quicker. Thinking about his mum made him sad, as did thinking of his father, yet when he reflected on the situation with Antioche and the newborn babies, he was conflicted. He knew his feelings for her were more intense than he'd felt in past relationships, and now there were the twins.

'Damn it! They knew all along!' He voiced a few choice expletives and sought out Dexion. He was honing his skills with the weapon under the attentive and patient tutelage of Leander. The Sicilian boy lowered the bow and the arrow and whirled around to him. *You should've warned me, Dexion, prepared me for the possibility of this complicated conundrum.* Dexion smiled as if he'd heard Evan's thoughts and then resumed shooting at the makeshift target.

He stomped over to his gear and shouted, 'Get your weapons, we're leaving!'

He strapped on his armament and stooped to unlatch the wooden chest, removing the oversized labrys, the double-headed axe they had found in the cave on Thira. He slammed shut the lid and thundered over to where Jason and the Argonauts assembled, their mood tense and bleak. Phameas and Homer jogged to join them, and as Hektor and the High Priestess approached, the Amazon warriors marched behind in a two-line formation. Leander and Dexion trotted over, Lykeios loping alongside.

'Anybody who wishes to remain here may do so. No one here will think less of your decision nor judge you. Our journey hasn't been smooth, oft-times dangerous, and we've lost people close to us.' He eyeballed the assembled group. No one turned away from his intense gaze. 'If you decide to accompany us, be prepared to face immortal beings and to be killed.'

The atmosphere was still and hushed.

'On arrival at the ruins, we'—he pointed at Phameas, Dexion, Homer, the High Priestess, Leander and Hektor—'cross the central court that leads to the cave. Jason, split your men, some to come with us, the others to stay to guard the ship and campsite. Commander,' he instructed the Amazon, 'you and your warriors guard the entry and exit points of the palace. Stop anyone who comes or tries to access the grounds, no matter who it is.'

The commander nodded.

'Let's move.'

'Evandros, before leaving, we must offer a libation to the Mother Goddess and ask for her protection,' said the High Priestess.

His companions agreed.

He sighed. 'Fine. I guess we need all the advantage we can garner.'

An Argonaut dashed to the supply of food and drinks.

'Where is the queen?' Leander asked. 'I thought she would be here.'

His jaw tensed. 'She just gave birth, best she and the babies rest.'

The sailor soon came back, preventing further questions, and handed the jug of wine and cup to the High Priestess. They encircled her, shoulder to shoulder. She lifted the bowl and a blue nimbus surrounded them.

'Mother Goddess, we dedicate this libation to you and to Divine Zeus and humbly ask for the safe return of all those who are here and for your protection during battle.' She poured a little of the ruby liquid onto the ground, took a sip and passed it to Evan. The ritual reminded him of the occasions on which he'd attended mass and the priest had drunk from the chalice, and then the parishioners would drink from the cup at communion if they wished. *Here's another ritual the Christians adopted*, he thought wryly. He downed a mouthful of the bitter liquid and handed it to Phameas. The cup went from person to person until everyone had a drink.

He then led the way, setting off towards Amnissos. After a few stades, he peeked over at the campsite and saw Antioche standing in the tent's entryway, both infants in her arms. Phameas patted him on the back.

'Do not worry—think of the reward your woman gives you on your return.'

'Phameas, stop calling her my woman. Antioche does not belong to me.' He scowled in annoyance.

'Ah huh. So you say.' The Phoenician grinned at him and ducked as Evan's hand shot out.

'Next time, I won't miss.'

Phameas laughed as they trekked along. They made a large force, in particular the Amazons, formidable and an intimidating sight in their armour that glittered like gold under the sun. When they reached the peak of the hill, Evan cast a casual peek at the beach, his line of sight picking out the large tent. He noted a dark form in the entrance and his gut twisted. He set his jaw and marched on, berating himself for the sense of loss he felt and resolving to concentrate on the deed ahead, lest he be killed in the process.

At the forked road, he merged to the left on the same track they had taken days earlier. He knew it as the Royal Highway, so dubbed by the archaeologist Sir Arthur Evans during excavations in the early nineteenth century. The road to Amnissos, parts of which had washed away during the volcanic eruption on the nearby island of Thira and the ensuing tsunami that had devastated the coastline of Krete; it had once been a thriving port village, receiving goods from all over the known world.

'Is there any certainty of a labyrinth at Knossos?' his friend asked him. 'It might have been an elaborate ploy by the ancient king to manipulate people and keep control of his dominion.'

'That's what all rulers did and continue to do.' Evan shrugged. 'What's the matter, Phameas?'

'What if there is no labyrinth, and it's somewhere else?'

'The labyrinth is there.' He saw the concern on Phameas' face. 'I know it is. Besides, we've travelled too long and too far, and I am not jeopardising this next stage on a probability. The Minotaur and the chamber of tunnels are there, waiting.'

The Phoenician's long curls jiggled. 'The gods of my homeland are powerful, and I shall request Baal to safeguard you.'

'And everyone else.'

He clasped his bearded chin and nodded. After a little while, he asked, 'Why is this place so valuable to your people?'

'It was where the king lived and was regarded as supreme ruler over other kings, and from here they enforced laws. The Palace of Knossos was also the largest and the most magnificent of buildings. There were many other palaces, from the west to the east of Krete, and though not as big as Knossos, they were marvels of engineering.'

'A pity the great flood destroyed them,' Leander commented, overhearing their conversation.

'We will restore the palaces to their original acclaim and importance,' the High Priestess declared.

'Is that what the Elders decided?' Leander asked.

'Yes. We migrate to our homeland, reclaim the region, and reconnect with the world to rebuild relationships with neighbouring provinces.'

'That is not what the Divine Gods agreed to,' said Leander, unsure. 'It is wrong to go against their instructions. They will punish us if we do.'

'Our ancestors did not abide by the tenets of our gods and it was their hubris that brought their demise.' She quickened her pace. 'It is our duty to continue and honour the laws established by Divine Zeus and the gods, and in return, they reward us for our diligence and reverence.'

'What of the agreement between Zeus and the gods that we return to Atlantis after completing their errand?' Evan asked. 'Not that I care, but I know Zeus won't be pleased if no one goes back home.'

'We intend to go home as promised. We then plan our journey to resettle the land of our ancestors,' the High Priestess replied. 'This is where we belong.'

CHAPTER 40

Melaina weaved between the trees, running her fingertips along the smooth trunks as she passed by. The air was neither warm nor cold, and the sky was a pristine blue where fluffy white clouds seemed to hover overhead. She sighed, plopped down on the banks of the lagoon and plucked at the grass. The surface of the water was like a mirror, glassy and smooth. She lay on her side and propped her head up on one hand, moving the other back and forth over the grass, the blades tickling her palm. Her gaze kept going back to the glossy surface of the lagoon. A smile crept along her face and she jumped up, flung off her khiton and dove into the water.

Her laughter echoed across the lagoon as she splashed and whooped, twisting one way and then the other, causing ripples and mini waves. She was breathing heavily when she came to a stop, her breasts rising and falling above the waterline. Melaina glanced up at the sun peeking behind the clouds and gave a little wave. Within seconds, she heard a splash behind her and was showered with a light sprinkle of water. She grinned.

'I thought you might be around watching me,' she said, standing taller and turning.

Apollo's eyes dilated, and his chest rose and fell in quick succession.

'I sensed you were always nearby as I bathed and wondered when you would appear.' She fluttered her eyelashes at him and thrust her breasts higher. She put her hands on her hips and tilted her head to the side.

Apollo raised a brow at her but didn't move. He then glanced over at his raven as it circled overhead, squawking. Melaina gaped, her arms falling to her sides as Apollo turned his back on her and waded onto dry land.

'Get out and get changed,' he ordered. 'Your ploy of seducing me won't work. Do you think I was going to fall for such a cheap trick? Pathetic. That's what you are. You are not even worthy of being an immortal and bring shame to our kind.'

Melaina sniffed and tossed her head, her long black tresses swaying across her shoulders. She gave him an icy glare and sashayed out of the water, taking her time, until her naked body was in full view. She stepped onto the grass and let the water drip onto the ground, then swung her back to her captor and bent over to pick up her gown. She beamed, hearing the sharp intake of breath behind her. Melaina fussed with the material of her khiton, flipping it one way and then the other.

Apollo began to laugh. 'I must give Evandros his due. He didn't want you, and flaunting your body at me is not working. Poor Melaina. Unwanted and cast off by a mere mortal and all immortals.' He continued to chortle, his laughter fading as he ascended into the sky.

Melaina screamed until she was hoarse and tore her dress to shreds. When she calmed down, she channelled her thoughts to the one individual who had caused her pain and placed her in this prison.

Evandros.

She could hardly hear the rustle of the trees or the water lapping against the levee as she plotted. She would hide Evandros in a location where no immortal could find him, not even his clever father, Zeus. There she would torment him by first slaying his bitch Amazon in front of him and tossing his offspring into the pond to drown. Then she would tie him to the ground, whip his flesh until he bled and ride him like a horse. Her breathing quickened at the thought of feeling him inside her, in her mind's eye watching the rapture on Evandros' face as she had sex with him. No, she wouldn't kill him immediately.

Melaina felt the air change around her. She needed to find a way out. She had searched the entire realm without luck. As she glanced up at the sky, she noted a dark speck and thought it was Apollo's raven. She was about to dismiss it but realised it hadn't moved. She clapped her hands with glee and leapt into the air, then flew towards the odd blot in the otherwise blue sky.

CHAPTER 41

The High Priestess' announcement sat heavy, like a dank and dismal cloud, on all except for Hektor, who beamed and walked with a bounce in his step. Evan recalled the interaction in the throne room on Atlantis, forced by Zeus to watch as Poseidon instructed his alter ego and the other Atlanteans to find the sacred relics of the Mother Goddess. What had transpired after the meeting between Alexina and the Elders he had not seen, but did Zeus and the other gods know what they had discussed? He was certain they did, and Zeus and his Family were waiting until the complete restoration of the icons. If they were successful in preventing the birth of the Messiah and destroying Kronos, there'd be no reason for the Olympian gods to deny the Atlanteans' desire to reoccupy the region. He understood their motivation and their desire to return to their ancestral birthplace —it was what he'd sought since being dumped amid a shipwreck almost a year earlier. Whatever the outcome, he did not expect to witness the event.

The road straightened and in the not-too-far distance, he saw the misshapen outline of buildings on the rocky outcrop, a welcome distraction from his musings. From his vantage, he saw how various structures were constructed on terraces, and the way in which the force of the earthquake had exposed the colonnaded rooms. Lykeios darted ahead. They approached the site from the west, the road sloping upwards, the incline unnoticeable until Evan swivelled around, impressed by the sophistication of the construction and the view of the valley below.

'By the gods!' Jason stumbled and came to a stop.

'Great and almighty Zeus!'

The Argonauts staggered to a halt, eyes wide and mouths hanging open. The disciplined Amazons did not react or voice their surprise, but the amazement on their faces was evident. Lykeios sat on his haunches and barked.

'Only the likes of immortals could build such magnificence,' Jason said in awe.

The tapered columns, some buried and broken, had retained their vibrant red colour, topped by pillow-like capitals, and the plinths painted in black. Parts of the colonnaded stoa stood tall and proud, and beyond the pillars, large quantities of debris and earth carpeted the central court that had once held the bull-leaping events. Evan could almost hear the crowds as they lined the vast rectangular space, cheering as the master gamekeeper herded in a bull.

'Our forebears engineered and constructed this place and the other palaces,' the High Priestess told them, ascending the broad steps. At the top, she whirled around, arms out wide, eyes shining.

'Did you see this level of construction on Thira?' Jason asked, stupefied.

Evan shook his head. 'There was nothing except hills and foliage.'

'Here we stand, on the threshold of our ancient forebears. Their splendour and power still resonate.' Hektor marched onto the first step, his face all aglow as he smiled with pride up at the High Priestess.

She beamed at him and clambered the remaining steps to the forecourt, the layer of plaster almost gone. Remnants of colour hinted at the vibrancy of life and richness of the celebrated palace.

'The Choros,' she whispered in wonder, staring at the floor. 'It is here.'

Leander scampered up the stairs and paused at her side in amazement. 'How did we not see it before?'

'There was too much debris covering the expanse,' she replied.

'The strong winds from the last few days stirred the dirt and rubble,' said Hektor.

'Or something or someone cleared the course,' said Evan, 'making sure we saw it.'

The Dark Master? asked Homer, scanning the grounds.

'He is not here,' answered Dexion.

'More like someone who is working with him,' Evan said, pointing skywards.

'The Goddess of Discord.' The High Priestess' lips tightened.

'There's no one else who can remove the amount of timber, rocks and large blocks of stone that spread over this area. Not even a windy day could clear away what was here. It is too convenient.' Evan, hands on his hips, studied the painted floor. 'They want us to go this way.'

'Then we shall.' She waved a hand at the immense concourse.

The Phoenician asked, 'What is a Choros?'

'It is where our predecessors performed sacred dances to honour the ancestors in recognition of those who died, venerate the living by showing gratitude to the Mother Goddess and demonstrate how we vow to nurture life.' She crossed the main court. 'There are patterns on the floor we follow—a tribute to the past, present and future.' She wandered, criss-crossing from one side to the other, taking in the faded sequence. 'It is all here.' She glowed, exhilarated. 'Come along.'

They cut across the court, ignoring the flight of stairs that led to paved grounds. Evan recalled from his trip to the ancient ruins that it had once been a theatre facing south. They came to another staircase, and at the bottom the path diverted, one part leading west, which was blocked, and the other to the northern entrance. The detour took them in the opposite direction from the theatre, and they followed the length of the wall. The walkway reminded him of the road they had travelled from Corinth to Lechaion, one of the two ports that served the Greek city.

'The layout is like home, yet it is not.' Leander scrutinised the ruins.

'Our ancestors replicated several features,' Hektor noted.

'Look!' Leander said, animated. 'This wall backs onto the lustral room.'

The doorway had caved in, barring them from entering. Homer and Evan clambered over the collapsed blocks and wooden beams to see if there was a way inside.

'High Priestess, would the lustral room have held the same function as how we use it?' Hektor asked.

'No. In the time of the ancients, visitors who wanted to see the king first came here for purification. We use the room to confer with the Mother Goddess.'

'Be careful,' said Evan as he navigated the wreckage near the portico. 'Parts of the roof have collapsed and we have to walk around.'

'I wonder what happened here?' Leander stepped to the other side, spying damage.

Homer and Phameas moved closer. 'There must have been a fire,' Phameas answered. 'See here.' He pointed to the scorch marks on the upper section of the wall where timber frames had once stood. 'There was no chance to stop the fire from spreading.'

'I would say the fire was ignited deliberately given the condition of the stone and sections of the timber,' Hektor said, unimpressed.

'Who would have done such a thing?' asked Leander, running a hand over the blackened wall.

'Nereos mentioned that a race of warriors invaded many decades later in the deluge's wake,' replied the High Priestess.

'The Mykenaeans,' said Jason. 'They were establishing control throughout the region and raiding neighbouring rivals.'

'In times of disasters and war, it's what marauders do to dominate and gain supremacy,' said Evan. He beckoned the commander of the Amazons. 'We need a contingent of warriors to stay here to prevent any unwanted guests from following us and another detachment back at the central court.'

She nodded, and without her saying a word, ten of her soldiers peeled back and stood in formation, hands resting on the hilt of their swords.

He picked his way through the debris, weaving and dodging fallen beams that lay strewn, intersecting the wide corridor, slowing their progress. Lykeios, sure-footed with three legs, moved much faster and progressed forwards, waited for them to catch up and then took off again.

'If we could move as quick as Lykeios, we'd be further ahead,' Phameas said, grimacing and swearing as his foot slipped between misshapen stone blocks.

'There's too many of us to proceed faster,' Evan said, helping the High Priestess over the rubble.

Lykeios scampered into a gap.

'Where did he go?' asked Jason.

'There is a corridor ahead,' answered the High Priestess. 'He may have gone in that direction.'

No sooner had she finished speaking than the wolf bounded back and barked.

'We cannot go that way,' said Dexion.

'How do you know?' asked Hektor. He shoved his way to the front and started through the doorway.

'If it was safe, Lykeios would wait for us. Instead, he came back,' replied Dexion.

'Where to from here?' Leander asked.

Evan checked his drawings.

'The east wing,' replied Hektor.

'It's too circuitous and will take too long to get to the cave,' said the High Priestess.

Evan indicated upwards. 'We go via the upper floor.'

'It's not stable,' said Hektor.

'The alternative is to go back to where we started and find another way through the west court, except from our earlier explorations of that region, the damage there is much worse,' he said.

'We continue from here. Lykeios will lead us.' The High Priestess nodded at Dexion.

'Lykeios, go! Find a pathway through the palace.' Dexion gave his wolf a gentle rub behind the ears.

The wolf did a swift turn and scampered back from where they had come. It took them less than twenty minutes to enter the pillared hall and pass through a corridor adjacent to the one they had entered. Much quicker than going back the way they had come and losing over an hour's worth of climbing and walking.

Evan visualised the architecture and layout of the Minoan site he had studied while at university. This route would take them to the storerooms. He did a mental head shake, annoyed and angry that his interest in ancient history and architecture had been preordained by the machinations of Zeus and the Mother Goddess. It hadn't been his decision. Then did that mean his life and the choices he made were a lie, as fictitious as a character in a book or movie?

He stumbled.

'Careful, Evandros,' called out Phameas. 'Best we catch up with Lykeios.'

Evan nodded and dismissed the ill-boding thoughts rather than be injured before the confrontation with the Minotaur.

CHAPTER 42

E van scrambled over broken stone and fractured wooden beams, breathless as he hastened to keep up with Lykeios. He shifted rubble to fit through the narrow aperture Lykeios had entered earlier and slid down the other side, swearing when he abraded his hands trying to slow down. He gave a cursory glance at the magazine of rooms that housed six-foot-tall pithoi, once filled with prized olive oil, wine, dried fruits, wheat, barley and surplus food for times when the harvest was poor. Evan remembered his first time seeing the size of the urns in the Heraklion Museum, and later being impressed by his visit to the ruins, where fragile pithoi were left in situ.

He trailed Lykeios, the wolf trotting along the corridor flanking the storeroom. The way ahead was clear, spared from the devastation that had laid waste to the connecting rooms. On his left, a line of pillars facing east lay collapsed and fragmented, providing an unobstructed view of the central court. The pediments were all that remained, with the edges of the paved walkway jagged.

Leander stopped next to the extensive damage.

'Such a disappointment,' said Hektor, 'to discover such devastation.'

'You can imagine how magnificent it was,' Leander said. 'See the frescoes? The colour is still intact.'

The composition was painted on the north-facing wall, extending from the floor to ceiling, bordered with eight rows of thick lines in blue and orange, followed by a row of crescents in shades of brown, yellow, red and green. It split the scene into four panels illustrating crocus gatherers. The sequence began with women going to the fields gathering saffron, returning to the palace and transforming the precious collection into powder. From his research, Evan had learnt the stamen was prized by many ancient civilisations, used for dyeing fabric, as a paint mixture, in cooking and for ceremonial rites.

'With the restoration of the palaces and our return, we will once again become a link between our people and other civilisations.' Confidence was in Alexina's voice and stature, and Evan had no doubt she believed what she stated.

'It could take years to rebuild,' said Hektor, hesitant. 'Much of the building is beyond repair.'

'You are here to determine what can be restored and what needs rebuilding,' she said. 'As master engineer, you will oversee the reconstruction of each palatial site, and Homer, as our water master, reinstates the drainage system and water supplies.'

Does this mean Hektor and I won't be travelling home? asked Homer.

'The Elders expect our return. They and the Senate are in the process of selecting Atlanteans to accompany us when we resettle our ancestral home.' The steely determination on her face was one that he had not seen before.

'Will our families come with us?' Hektor asked.

She nodded. 'Yes, those families appointed by Atlantis' leaders.'

'This was the plan from the start, wasn't it?' Evan asked. 'To repatriate Krete? I am curious, did you and the leaders intend to go ahead with resettlement if we weren't tasked to find the objects by Zeus?'

'This is our home, and through reunification we intend to share our knowledge with other civilisations and resume ties with those with whom we once traded.' She jutted out her chin. 'The sacred objects are our destiny and have led us back to our rightful birthplace.' With that, she changed direction and followed Lykeios.

'If the ancestors created our buildings based on these designs, this corridor ends and goes into a room,' said Leander, trailing after her.

Evan was manoeuvring to the front when he caught up with her.

Lykeios began barking.

'That is just great.' He swore, hands on hips.

Sections of the ceiling blocked the passage. Thick beams as wide as a man's thigh and over six feet long lay strewn over fragments of stone, big and small. A breeze ruffled his hair. There was a gaping hole in the ceiling and he had a clear view of the cloudless blue sky.

'We won't be continuing in this direction.' He swivelled about. 'I remember seeing a doorway back a few metres. Let's return from where we came and see if there's a way through to the southern entrance.'

'Lykeios!' called Dexion and pointed.

The wolf backtracked, and as Evan was about to follow, he glimpsed something glitter amongst the rubble. He stooped to pick it up and brushed the dirt away.

'Oh my, that is beautiful. High Priestess, you should see this.' He held out his hand to her, the object small in his large callused palm. Her lips parted.

'What did you find?' asked Phameas.

'A ring.'

She reached out and plucked the golden jewel from his palm. 'Not just any ring,' she said, awed. 'It was a ring worn by the High Priestess during the sacred dance to the Mother Goddess. See here?' She pointed to the main figure. 'That is Mother, and these are her priestesses dancing. They are in a field with flowers, and on the grass surrounding the goddess are serpents.' She drew in a shaky breath. 'This is the Dance of Renewal. Priestesses of the Mother performed the dance when flowers were in bloom and snakes vibrant with life. Our ancestors had forgotten about the ritual.'

'How could our forebears forget such an important dance?' asked Hektor. 'Was it not a part of the tenets?'

'When the ancients escaped the great deluge, we lost much and the knowledge of many dances died with the priestesses and the priests of Poseidon.' She slipped the ring on her finger, her face radiant. 'This is a significant find, and it is our duty to reclaim the Choros of both the renewal and rebirth for all Atlanteans.'

'I haven't heard of the Choros of Rebirth,' Leander said.

'It is when a life is sacrificed and makes way for another to be reborn.'

Evan felt a chill run up his spine. 'When was the last Dance of Rebirth performed?'

Her face closed over and her demeanour changed. 'Nine days before we departed Atlantis.'

He went still. 'Prior to that?'

She did not reply.

A deathlike silence fell over the group. He walked away.

'What of the dances we perform now?' asked Leander, breaking the tension. 'Are they not the same?'

'Not all. Our predecessors did not want to risk the wrath of the gods and kept those that inspired a harmonious existence as well as creating new ones.'

Like the bull-leaping and the Dance of Thanks, Homer added.

'They celebrate life and regeneration and honour the gods for their benevolence.' Leander shifted from one foot to the other.

She nodded. 'The ancients believed these dances appeased the immortals, and they have for thousands of years. We have lived in peace and accomplished more than what our forebears did.'

'If these ancient rituals are no longer performed, why was the Dance of Rebirth kept and not the others?' Evan asked, arms crossed against his chest.

'It had not been commemorated in many years and the dance steps were believed to be long forgotten,' she replied, 'until the very first High Priestess of the new Atlantis, on her death, conveyed the dance to her successor, and from that time on, the secret was passed from successor to successor.'

'What did the high priestesses of the past tell you when you were alone in the cave on Thira?' He narrowed his eyes at her. 'How many of the clandestine rites did the ancients think too dangerous to conduct?'

Her eyes flashed, and her cheeks reddened. 'What transpired between myself and the ancient priestesses is sacred.'

'Of course, until there's another innocent sacrificed.'

'Evandros, you know as I do, the gods are not forgiving and must be obeyed. Neither you nor I am exempt from their decisions.'

'Your logic is flawed. The gods fear losing their supremacy and worshippers, which is why we are here, to retain their control. They need us, we do not need them, and this they know. Their power is waning, and it is a matter of time before they become extinct, expunged from the unhealthy and one-sided relationship they have with humans.' He took a step towards her, and she shrank back, sucking in a breath. 'Shall we continue?'

CHAPTER 43

E van didn't wait to see her reaction. He wanted to find the statuette and leave. After inspecting both directions, instead of heading up the passageway, he went to the right and scaled a staircase, moving larger pieces of rock and timber aside to clear the path.

'Bugger,' he cursed. Large blocks of stone obstructed their approach to the second floor. The wooden double doors had tumbled from their hinges and lay inwards. He was about to turn back when Lykeios gave a sharp yelp. He saw the wolf perched on a mound, the gap wide enough for a person to squeeze through.

'Is that safe, boy?' he asked.

Lykeios barked, swung around and continued onward.

'What do you think, Evandros?' asked Phameas. 'Is it secure?'

'One way to find out,' he replied and clambered up the slight incline, shifted the bigger pieces aside and wriggled through the hole.

He popped up from over the heap of rubble and smiled at them. 'Lykeios has found an exit. We must move and now. I'm not sure how stable this mass of rubble will remain. Best we get out before the mound collapses and the roof caves in.'

Phameas and Dexion went through first, followed by Homer and the High Priestess, then Leander and Hektor, after which Jason and a few of his selected Argonauts scaled the mound and the remaining Amazons climbed through. Just as the warriors slid to the floor, the pile of debris trembled.

'Move!' Evan yanked Dexion out of the way, made sure Phameas was nearby, and sprinted, hoisting Dexion onto his shoulder and jumping over a damaged wall. He ran until he felt they were far enough from the dangerous site, then lowered Dexion to the ground and bent over breathless, locks of hair clinging to his forehead.

'Are you okay?' he asked Dexion between gasps.

The boy nodded, clutching Lykeios.

'Did everyone get away?' he asked, wiping his brow.

Jason and his men were wheezing and coughing up spittle. The Amazons stumbled out from the cloud of dust, covered from head to toe. He did a quick head count. 'We are missing people.' He rushed back, ready to leap over the wall, when a heavy hand wrenched him backwards. A deafening boom came from inside. Plumes of grit the colour of dirty grey clouds exploded akin to a pyroclastic flow. Evan choked as he inhaled particles of dirt and dust and clasped a hand over his mouth. Screams echoed, shrieking for help. Crumbling walls and timber cracking drowned out their shrills.

'No!' He tried to escape from the shackles of his captor, but big, powerful hands held him back. 'Let go of me!'

A grim-faced Homer clutched tighter, his hands as sturdy and unrelenting as manacles, as he struggled to get free.

'You ... bastard ... let go!'

Then it was quiet.

He slumped to the ground, collapsing against Homer's legs.

'I could have saved them,' he said, voice catching. He swallowed a lump in his throat and repeated in a hoarse voice. 'I could have saved them.'

Homer growled at him.

'How do you know? I could have reached them.'

Homer bared his teeth at Evan.

'You would have been killed, if Homer had not stopped you,' said Phameas, spitting and waving his arms back at the building. His tanned face was covered in a light film of dust. 'We had to escape, or we would be dead too.'

'We must continue,' the High Priestess said.

Evan's jaw tightened. 'Do you not feel any sorrow for those who have just died?'

'All lives are important, and those who've lost theirs will be rewarded, and we acknowledge their sacrifice by retrieving Mother's sacred object and ensuring that our gods remain supreme.'

'What a cold and inhumane woman you are. There are no accolades for suffering and dying a horrible death.' He hurled back at her.

Leander put a hand on his shoulder. 'The High Priestess is correct. We keep going or lose our battle against the Dark Master.'

He wrenched away from Leander's clasp. 'And what if more of our people die?'

'We cannot change the path, for it is fate,' he replied.

'That is bull—'

'The Divine Gods have the power to alter our destiny,' said Jason, cheerless. 'I've lost two good, loyal men. Do you remember when the harpy killed young Leon crossing the Corinthian Gulf? Every person and creature dies. When is a matter for the gods. We'—Jason pointed at everyone—'honour them with tributes and continue living. That is what we mortals do.'

Evan held his tongue. No matter what he stated and regardless of the soundness of his argument, they would disagree. His companions did not know the future, and if they did, it wouldn't change their perception of Zeus and his merry band of immortals. Whatever happened here and now, he believed, would not affect the ascension of the Messiah. If it was predestined, as his companions kept reminding him, then the birth of a new god was inevitable.

He lifted his face to the sky and visualised his home, his place of work, the untouched coastline where he swam and his parents. That was where he belonged. Not here.

'Dexion, where is Lykeios?'

'He's waiting over there.'

He spotted the animal sitting by a doorway. Lykeios rose at his approach, barked and entered the murky interior. Evan paused on the threshold and waited until his eyesight adjusted to the dimness. He lagged after the sure-footed wolf as it trotted the length of the corridor before breezing through a narrow entryway, then another before scarpering out of sight.

'Where did Lykeios get to?' asked Phameas.

There was a bark.

'He is outside.' Evan wrestled his body through the ingress and caught sight of Lykeios at the foot of the incline. His foot slipped into a hole and he fell on his butt. 'Shit!'

'Master Evandros!'

'Are you all right?' Phameas grabbed his elbow and helped him to his feet.

He grimaced and rubbed his backside. 'I'm fine. I didn't realise how dilapidated the steps were.' He started up the road, joined by Phameas and Dexion. On their right were the southern propylaea that opened to a columned staircase and a walkway which led to the entry of verdant grounds, filled with debris and overgrown plant life.

'That is the description Nereos gave of the location of the cave.' Hektor started moving in the opposite direction.

'I wonder if they used the building for stabling horses, donkeys and bullocks? The structure is the same as the one we use at home,' said Leander. 'If so, the location of the labyrinth is ingenious.'

'Why so?' asked Evan.

'It is possible King Minos intended to conceal the location where animals were housed and, in doing so, hide the Minotaur behind a menagerie of beasts. Clever and strategic.'

'I daresay King Minos ordered Daidalos to build the labyrinth to make sure the Minotaur was secure, never released, and to his perverted way of thinking, the stable was where the Minotaur belonged, confined in a prison that had no easy exit.'

'It does not matter the king's reasoning—we are here for the sacred object.' The High Priestess walked over the stone structure.

'I do not have a good feeling about this,' said Phameas, trudging behind.

CHAPTER 44

The air was still as they descended the slope. The mood was as taut as a string on a bow, and yet, there was a feeling of expectancy. Evan stretched his neck from side to side, trying to ease the tension. Whatever happened would determine whether he went home—if he survived the battle with the Minotaur. He resisted the urge to turn around and run back to the beach. Lykeios brushed against his leg. He glanced down, immediately comforted by the animal's presence. Did the wolf sense his need for compassionate understanding? He almost face-palmed his forehead, berating himself. How could any person understand the mind of an animal, even one with intelligence?

Hektor ducked under the door frame and one by one they entered the building. Evan lingered behind, taking in the clear sky and the fragrance of orange blossoms, and then shuffled in after them.

'Do you suppose the Dark Master and Goddess of Discord are here?' asked Phameas, whispering.

Evan's heart raced the further they forged into the shelter. 'If they are here, they'll reveal their presence soon enough.'

'That is not a very comforting answer,' the Phoenician said.

'We are entering the Minotaur's domain.' He peered into the nebulous interior. 'Nothing about this is comforting.'

'Has anyone seen the entrance to the cave?' Hektor asked, striding forth, his head turning one way and then the other.

'It cannot be too difficult to find if young Nereos stumbled across it,' Leander replied, joining him in the search.

'It may not be obvious,' Evan said, moving left, 'or someone would have found the cave sooner.'

Perhaps it has an enchantment and blocks us from seeing it, said Homer.

'Then how did Nereos find it?' Hektor spat out in derision.

'Right place, right time,' Evan replied in a half-joking tone.

'The gods guided Nereos in unearthing the cave,' said the High Priestess, 'and provided us an opportunity to meet him so that he could tell us where to find it.'

'As they cannot aid us, they use other instruments, and people like Nereos, to convey their message,' Leander added.

She nodded.

'Then where is the cave?' Phameas asked, palms facing upwards.

'It is here.' She ventured to the other side.

Lykeios barked.

'Master Evandros, Lykeios has discovered the cave.' Dexion squatted with his arm about the wolf's neck, preventing the animal from venturing into the dark void.

Evan joined them. 'We need torches.'

Ten minutes later, the group trekked a short length into the tunnel, Evan's torch illuminating the craggy walls and the pitted, cavernous ceiling. Granules of sand crunched underfoot, the floor smoothened from people traversing inside thousands of years earlier. The skin and hair on his arms prickled, the myth of Theseus and the Minotaur and the unlucky chosen Athenian maidens and youths, who paraded along the same pathway towards their death, coming to mind. Here they were, wandering into the depths of King Minos' labyrinth, willing sacrificial victims for the mythical creature. He hefted the double-headed axe, hoping the blades were sharp enough to at least maim the beast.

'Evandros, tell me about the labyrinth,' Phameas asked in a tight voice, his eyes flicking from side to side.

'King Minos commissioned a brilliant inventor and engineer, Daidalos, to construct a maze to imprison the Minotaur,' he replied.

'How is it this creature has not escaped? There are no guards or devices to prevent it from leaving,' asked his friend.

He shrugged. 'Who knows? Perhaps, as Homer suggested, the network of tunnels is enchanted, or there's a spell to stop the Minotaur from getting out. Or maybe it doesn't exist.'

Phameas stopped walking, staring at him in astonishment, waving an arm. 'Have you taken leave of your senses? This whole area reeks with ill-boding and death, can't you feel it?'

'I am trying not to,' Evan replied, his senses tingling with disquiet.

'The walls are bleeding.' Leander recoiled.

Evan moved the torch closer and felt as if a fist squeezed his heart. Fine lines of crimson liquid trailed down the cavern's wall. He reached out to touch rock face but stalled, his hand millimetres away from the surface. He shivered as he touched the stone. It was cold and the liquid a mere few degrees warmer. They clustered around him as he examined his blood-red-tipped fingers. He sniffed at it and rubbed the fluid, feeling the grit under his fingertips.

'It's not blood, it's ochre. A mix of oxygen and water has formed iron oxide and leached through the rock,' he said, relieved.

'Where is the water coming from?' asked Leander.

'There must be a subterranean stream.' Evan wiped his fingers on his khiton. 'Let's keep going, we don't want to keep our host waiting.'

'This is not the time to be making light of our situation, Evandros,' the High Priestess admonished with a small shake of her head.

'No, but you're not the one who's facing the Minotaur.'

Her face softened. 'You are correct, though I cannot imagine how frivolous statements would set your mind at ease.'

'It helps to distract me from the impending confrontation.'

'You should concentrate on how to kill the Minotaur,' Hektor spat at him.

'Of course, why didn't I consider that?' He rolled his eyes. Homer tapped him on the shoulder. 'No, Homer. I have to confront the Minotaur, it's how we get the last icon. Neither you nor anybody else can go in my stead or help.'

'I disagree,' said Leander. 'From the outset, we've all contributed to the search, faced obstacles that we have overcome. Together, we will combat the Minotaur and retrieve the sacred object.'

'What Leander says makes sense,' said Phameas. 'We draw its attention, keep it occupied while you fight.'

'The Mother Goddess' instructions were clear. I'm to combat the Minotaur, no one else.' He confirmed with the High Priestess. 'Isn't that so?'

'Yes,' she agreed. 'However, she did not mention help wasn't possible. Leander's suggestion is excellent and does not defy Mother's orders.'

'Not so sure about that.' Evan ran his fingers through his hair. 'We've gotten this far—to go against the Mother Goddess' directive may be our undoing.'

'We should heed Evandros' caution,' Hektor said. 'If we do not follow Mother's instructions, what we have done thus far will be for nought.'

'And if it kills Evandros, we lose everything and Mother's object will never be retrieved,' Leander argued.

'While Evandros fights the Minotaur, we search the surrounding area for the sacred item,' said Hektor in a cool, flat tone.

Leander gawked at him in disbelief. Homer scowled at Hektor, tock Evan by the elbow and pulled him away. Phameas and Dexion followed the two men, Lykeios trotting at their heels. Leander set off without another word and caught up with the others. Jason and his men did not hesitate and streamed behind.

Evan heard Hektor say to the High Priestess, 'You know I speak the truth.'

'Come along, Hektor.'

CHAPTER 45

'Evandros and his companions have entered the labyrinth,' announced Athene, striding over the expansive marble floor of the throne room. She waited by the base of the steps of the dais where the king and queen of the immortals sat, relaxed and sipping ambrosia from their golden kylix. 'Shall I maintain surveillance on how they progress, Divine Father?'

'What of the Amazonian queen? Her arrival and the birth of Evandros' babies have caused uncertainty for your champion,' asked Poseidon.

Zeus' face hardened. 'Evandros is doing as I've tasked him. Success is near. Once the High Priestess has set the sacred icons in their rightful place, our existence is assured forever more and we live on for eternity.'

Poseidon twirled his silver trident, gazing at the King of the Gods. 'Was it necessary to make him wait three days for the gifts? The sacred objects would now be in our possession, our supremacy restored and the Atlanteans on their way home.'

'It was essential for Evandros to be present until the infants were born.' Zeus' eyes became flinty.

Hera laid a hand on her husband's arm, restraining him from rising.

'Dear Poseidon, the most important factor is knowing Evandros is inside the labyrinth, and close to finding the last object. Success is near and we continue ruling as destined.'

'What of the Minotaur? What if Evandros cannot defeat it?' asked Apollo. 'It is of divine blood, and difficult to kill.'

Zeus bolted to his feet, shaking off his wife's hand. 'Evandros is of immortal blood! His triumphs are due to his heroic deeds, demonstrating astuteness and adroitness against all calamities. It is to us to defend him from further harm. Victory is within our reach.' He levelled his lightning bolt at Apollo. 'Is that troublesome Melaina secured?'

'Of course,' Apollo replied, offended. 'It is impossible for her to escape from the dominion in which I have imprisoned her. I alone know of its location and how to unlock the seals that confine her.' Zeus' gaze bored into the youthful god's eyes, the air tingling with his power. 'I assure you, Divine Father, she cannot flee.'

The King of the Gods did not comment, instead turned to instruct the other gods in his court. 'Athene, Artemis and Hermes, attend to my son and his companions and warn me immediately of any discordance. Hera, Hestia and Demeter, shield the mortals at the beach, and'—he pointed at Poseidon, Hephaistos, Hades, Ares and Apollo—'we will guard the Isle of Minos. When the old Titan arrives, we defend our champions until the icons are under the care of Mother's High Priestess, and we depose him into Tartaros forever.'

'What of Eris? Do we tell her of our plans?' asked Demeter.

'She is not trustworthy. She has gone to great lengths to thwart the Atlanteans from reaching Minos' island,' Athene stated.

'Eris is my concern,' Zeus said, 'and I alone accept responsibility for any action she takes.'

'What do we do to impede Kronos from approaching?' Hades asked. 'Though I venture he is already sitting and waiting nearby.'

'We shield the land and are alerted as soon as he attempts to break through.' Zeus' broad, muscular chest strained against the silvery khiton. 'He is not there, not yet, but soon will present himself.'

'What makes you certain the old fool is not hiding and ready to strike?' The God of War sniffed.

'Mother has not arrived. I expect him to set foot on the island when the High Priestess has the sacred statues in her guardianship.'

'And we intercept and seal him into Tartaros,' Poseidon said, clutching his trident.

Zeus nodded.

'If Mother doesn't show up, perhaps Kronos won't steal the precious vessels, and we have won,' Hestia commented in a hopeful tone.

'Kronos intends to bring forth this new god and become the sovereign deity of all mortals. Mother's absence will not discourage him from wresting Mother's creations from our reach and using them.' Zeus was blunt. 'Are we of one accord?'

'We defeated the Titans before and can do so again,' said Hades. He clicked his fingers and Kerberos came galloping through the doors. His clawed feet skidded on the smooth floor and he slid to a stop at his master's side. The three-headed dog snarled, revealing sharp fangs.

Ares smirked. 'And it is one old Titan that we are fighting.'

'We should not underestimate Kronos,' said Artemis. 'A foe such as he is unpredictable and cunning. We must prepare for any deceptive measures he uses.'

'Agreed. He is formidable, and determined to conquer us.' Zeus thrust a hand at the celestial roof of the chamber, fingers outstretched and taut. It shimmered, a gold-white light flickered and a bolt of lightning lit up the ceiling. 'The last and final act is ours. Together with the reunification of Mother, the serpent and labrys, we assert our domination over the world.'

The King of the Gods and Men stormed across the glittering floor, his khiton billowing and hair flowing, and vaulted into his golden chariot. The immortal steeds bolted, a flash of lightning streaking across the cloudless sky.

CHAPTER 46

The harshness of the deafening quietness competed with that of Evan's heart, which pounded against his ribcage. His mouth was as parched as the sun-scorched lands of the Australian outback, and no amount of water kept his tongue moist. He felt a trickle of sweat run down from his temple, along the side of his jaw, and dampen his already drenched and sticky khiton. He gripped the handle of the cumbersome weapon, not wanting it to slip from his damp palms. Why did it have to be him? Zeus could have chosen his doppelganger, who understood this world and lived in it, to do this. *Is this real? Am I really in a labyrinth beneath the Palace of Knossos?* He veered left at the end of the passage and proceeded further into the labyrinth, taking care not to make too much noise. Each change of direction drew them farther beneath the bowels of the palace. The tunnels felt as though they were getting lengthier than the previous junction as they delved deeper with each step.

Perhaps twenty minutes later, though he couldn't be certain how long they had been walking, he called for a stop. The obscurity of the continuous and everlasting passage was worse than traversing the interminable deserts of Egypt. At least there, they had been outdoors and breathed fresh air. Here, within the confines and the mustiness of the labyrinth, the air was oppressive. He drank a mouthful from his water container, throat constricting as he gulped and sputtered. He squatted, leaning against the uneven surface, the cold stone cooling his overheated body. Dexion and Phameas joined him, concern imprinted on their faces.

'The question of mortality makes a person deliberate their life's choices and achievements when confronted with the inevitability of being slain,' Hektor said.

'You must not think of death, or have doubts,' said his friend, glaring at the broad-shouldered Atlantean. 'You can defeat this beast you call Minotaur. I have seen you battle against those soldiers in Kyrene—one man against ten, fifteen men—and you prevailed. You fought the soul eaters, killed two of the creatures. And what of the sea monster at Thira? You are brave, a hero and a skilled fighter.'

'Except when a raider stabbed me and I died during the fight against the brigands who pursued Theodoros.'

'You had slain many of the bandits, and your goddess restored you to life.' Phameas nudged him. 'I have seen no other person do what you have done, nor any who is as skilful as you are with the sword and shield.'

'Your fear and lack of courage enable the monster to crush you,' said Hektor. 'And for your ineptitude, we shall fail and our families be doomed.'

Evan hurtled into Hektor, pinning him against the wall, his forearm pressed against his throat. The Atlantean gasped and attempted to inhale, his face turning purple. He punched Evan, the gesture limp and as ineffectual as a swat. His complexion grew mottled and darker.

'Evandros!'

Homer and Leander soared at them and grappled to pry his arm from Hektor's throat. His pupils and irises were fathomless. The Atlantean's head lolled to the side.

'Master Evandros, stop!' Dexion tugged his khiton.

The High Priestess moved alongside of the limp Hektor, who was fast fading from consciousness. 'Evandros.' She touched his cheek and repeated his name.

His eyes were pitch black, and as endless as the space beyond the Earth.

'Release Hektor. He is of no consequence. It is essential to remember who you are to live for.' She stroked his arm. 'Antioche and your baby daughter and son await your return. That is what you are fighting for, your children to learn who their father is and of his deeds.'

He blinked, the words penetrating, and eased his grip. He then realised Hektor was unconscious and his arm slipped to his side. Hektor crumpled to the floor like a discarded marionette and did not move.

Leander hurried to aid him. 'He still breathes,' he said.

'Come, Evandros, let us sit for a moment.' She seized his hand and led him away from the group.

Jason and his men pressed up against the wall as the High Priestess and Evan walked past. She encouraged him to sit with a gentle tug and spoke in an even, quiet voice, his head lowered. When she finished, he nodded, rose to his feet and helped her up.

'We resume our quest to locate Mother's icon,' she said.

'Hektor hasn't awakened,' said Leander.

'We will stay with him,' said Jason. He said to Evan, 'I thought no one could move as fast as Akhilleus, who had the gift of the gods. He was a formidable warrior and just as mercurial. A combination I did not expect to witness until I met you.' He stepped closer to him. 'Slay the Minotaur and find the icon.'

He acknowledged Jason with a slight nod, picked up his

discarded torch and, with the High Priestess at his side, resumed walking.

'Evandros?' Jason held out his hand. 'Leave the torch. Phameas, Leander and Homer have theirs and you'll need both hands to use your weapons.'

He took scarce notice of the fluttering flare, his mind whirling from his fugue and what the High Priestess had mentioned. Evan passed the torch to Jason and, with the guiding light carried by the others, set off into the nexus of the elaborate maze.

The tunnels rerouted at junctions, so many times that he lost count. He slowed his pace, nose crinkling and ears prickling. There was a faint brushing sound, similar to rubbing material together.

'What is it?' asked Phameas, wielding his sword. Evan put a finger to his lips and shifted into a fighter's stance, labrys at the ready.

Homer strode ahead.

'Wait, Homer!' he hissed.

Homer halted, turned around and gave him a thumbs-up. He recommenced walking when, from out of the darkness, he was hurled aside. He smashed into the wall and lay unmoving, his weapon clattering to the ground.

'Homer!'

A loud bellow resonated, the walls vibrating, Evan's ears rang, the effects lingering much like after leaving a rock concert. Lykeios started barking, fangs bared and hackles raised.

'Jesus, Mary and Joseph!' A chill swept through him from his scalp through to his toes, as if someone had thrown a bucket of ice over him.

'Great Moloch!' The Phoenician's breathing became rapid, his sword jiggling up and down in his hand.

Leander paled, stepped in front of the High Priestess and aimed an arrow at the encroaching shadow.

'Dear Mother.' She pressed her fingers against her mouth.

The Minotaur hovered on the edge of the circle of light, his muscular torso, arms and legs distinguishable as a man's. Golden eyes leered at them from a white bull's head. Long, curved sharp horns jutted out from above his ears, and his tail swished back and forth. He bellowed again, displaying his ruby-red tongue and maw of stained teeth.

'Well, then, Theseus didn't kill him after all,' Evan quipped with a weak laugh, sweat beading on his forehead.

The Minotaur roared at the mention of Theseus and charged.

'Shit!'

He swung the axe, the air whistling as he missed.

'Get back!'

'We can help!' Leander aimed an arrow at the Minotaur.

'There is no room!' Evan pivoted, slashing at the Minotaur, trying to force him backwards.

He circled in the opposite direction. The Minotaur moved with him. The muscles in Evan's forearms stuck out like thick, ropy cords and his biceps bulged, hefting the oversized labrys. The beast's head lowered, his shoulders hunched, and his ears perked. He pawed the ground, one foot first and then the other, his long tail flicking from side to side, faster and faster. Evan's mouth went dry. The Minotaur feinted one way, snorted and charged, hurtling at him from the opposite direction. Evan sidestepped and wielded the axe as if he were about to chop wood. The Minotaur dodged the trajectory, skipping backwards. The double-bladed weapon hit the stone floor, sparks flying.

He thrust the blade at his foe, trying to pin him against the wall. The Minotaur captured the weapon and wrenched it, causing Evan to falter. Evan, gritting his teeth, clung to the handle and anchored his stance. His sandalled feet skidded on the cavernous floor. The tendons in his neck, chest and arms protruded as he grappled to prevent the beast from wresting the labrys from his grasp. The Minotaur bellowed in pain. Evan fell on his backside, the axe flung over his head and clanging against the rock face, his spine scraping against the wall. The Minotaur rushed headlong at him.

'Get out of there!' Leander shouted.

He bounded upright, levelling the labrys at the Minotaur. He lowered his weapon, staring. The tip of a blade stuck out from his stomach.

'Kill it, Evandros!' Phameas yelled. 'It is injured.'

The Minotaur swung around and struck Homer. His body arced through the air and landed with a loud thud. He lay sprawled, struggling to rise.

'Now, Evandros!' the High Priestess screamed.

He hesitated.

'Evandros! What are you waiting for?'

He held the axe aloft, poised to strike, but then he paused. Blood streamed in rivulets from the Minotaur's gut down his legs and pooled at his feet.

'We've come for the figurine of the Mother Goddess,' he said. 'Allow us to pass and find the statuette and we'll leave you in peace. We'll withdraw from your home without further needless conflict.'

The beast laboured and whistled as he inhaled and exhaled.

'What are you doing, Evandros?' whispered the High Priestess, the tone of her voice uneasy and strained. 'It cannot understand what we are saying.'

'Kronos promised humans.' He spoke as if he had a hearing impairment, the words not clear yet their meaning audible.

Evan shivered, goosebumps peppering his arms. The High Priestess blanched and hastened nearer to Leander.

'Moloch!' he heard Phameas exclaim.

'Gods.' Leander cringed.

Lykeios growled, teeth bared and poised to attack. Dexion's olive complexion had an unhealthy sheen.

Evan turned a deaf ear to the exclamations of his companions and tried to read the bull's face for a glimmer of emotion. He swallowed. 'Kronos has been here to see you?'

The Minotaur did not reply.

'Did he say what he wanted?'

Evan's tongue was dry, the sound of his blood pumping so loud he almost didn't hear the question Leander asked.

'A statue.'

'Did you give it to him?'

The Minotaur's gaze skimmed from Evan to his travelling companions, one by one, and he licked his maw.

Evan changed position, blocking the beast's view. 'You are Asterios. Would you prefer to be called by your name?'

The Minotaur bared his yellowed teeth.

'I am Evandros, and my father, so goes the claim, is Zeus.' He took another step, his knuckles white as he gripped the handle.

His head sank to shoulder height, eyes glowing as Evan inched forward. The Minotaur tracked his movements, a predator stalking its victim.

Evan's heart skipped and somersaulted and then thudded. 'Perhaps we can work together ... permit us to take the icon, and I'll remove the sword and treat your wound.'

'Hungry.'

'Did anybody bring food—dried meat, bread, anything?' he asked, not daring to take his eyes away from the menacing being.

'I may have something,' Leander answered. Evan heard him rummage through his bag.

'I have bread.' Phameas sidled up close, thrust the stale bread at him and scooted backwards to re-join the others.

Evan extended the morsel of food to the Minotaur. His snout

rippled as he breathed in and then lowed, sending shivers down Evan's spine.

'Something else, anyone? Leander?' He tossed the offering aside, his hand trembling.

'I might have food it may like.' Leander slipped up to him, withdrew a sliver of meat and lobbed it to the Minotaur. The desiccated piece hit the beast on the stomach and fell at his feet. He sniffed, picked up the meat and after inspection threw it away.

'Hungry,' the Minotaur repeated.

'We've no food.' He tensed, hands quavering. The labrys almost slipped from his sweaty palms; he tightened his grip on the handle. The atmosphere in the shadowy confines of the maze thickened.

He bellowed.

Evan winced, ears ringing.

'Evandros!'

The Minotaur, nostrils flared, flew at him, his speed surprising in spite of the injury and the weapon in his gut.

Evan whipped around, the sharpened blades grazing the flesh on his broad, bristly torso. He shifted his weight and switched the blade across its chest again, missing his snout by mere millimetres. The Minotaur roared. The second cut was deeper. Enraged, the Minotaur rammed into Evan and fell on top of him, forcing the axe to slip from his grasp and become trapped between their bodies. The Minotaur's rancid breath made him retch and swing his face to the side. His hot, wet exhalations left drops of moisture on Evan's neck; the Minotaur's teeth nipped at his skin. The tip of the blade lacerated Evan's clothing and nicked his ribcage.

Flashes of images from Evan's arrival flickered through his memory, from being dumped among the debris of a shipwreck, later rescued by a merchant captain on a Phoenician ship, befriending Phameas and later Dexion, seeing Carthage and visiting the library, rescuing the Atlanteans, finding the golden serpent, the expedition to Pylos, jumping over a charging boar, the dazzling power of the High Priestess as she'd saved them from the king of Mykenae and his crazy daughter, Princess Adrasteia, meeting Jason at Corinth, going to Delphi to meet the Oracle, then trekking to Athens, meeting Plato, being capsized by the sea monster Skylla and finally being shipwrecked and enslaved on an island governed by Amazons. Then there came the birth of his children with Antioche, the queen of the Amazons.

Evan gazed at the bullish face and a sense of calm came over him. He shoved against his attacker's husky trunk and thrust him away. His eyes widened and he dodged a punch. He grabbed the Minotaur's wrist and delivered an uppercut to his jaw. The Minotaur grunted but didn't falter, instead pulling Evan, who used the momentum to slide behind the creature to drive the blade deeper into its body.

The Minotaur howled.

Evan twisted the sword.

Bovine shrieks echoed through the tunnels. Evan's ears rang, but he ignored the din, levering the blade upwards. The Minotaur elbowed Evan in the stomach. Evan gasped, winded. The injured creature seized the blade. Evan blinked, sweat dripping into his eyes, as he fought to regain control of the sword. He tugged, wresting the sword from the Minotaur's ironclad hold, and plunged the blade downwards.

The beast dropped to his knees, his head bent, and struggled to breathe.

Evan stood over the Minotaur. He lifted his head. Blood dripped from his mouth, teeth coated in deep vermilion fluid. He nodded at Evan.

'I am sorry.'

CHAPTER 47

Dark crimson fluid spread from the Minotaur's neck. His head lay a few feet from the body, his golden eyes fixed wide open on Evan, the colour fading. He lowered the axe. Blood smeared the double-headed blade and sprayed across his khiton, resembling a blood splatter at a crime scene. Evan felt numb, and disheartened.

'Moloch, Evandros, you killed the creature!' Phameas bounced up next to him.

'I don't understand,' he said, saddened. 'I offered him a chance to live, and he chose to attack.'

The Phoenician gestured at the Minotaur. 'What does it matter? We can now retrieve the sacred item without further danger.'

Evan squatted, seeking information from the slain Minotaur. 'This is wrong. Why was he here and not protecting his lair?'

'The Minotaur prevented our advancing into its lair,' Leander replied, slipping the unused arrows into his quiver.

'No, something is amiss.'

'This is not the time to ponder, Evandros. You accomplished

what Mother required of you,' the High Priestess said. She skirted the Minotaur's body, Leander following her.

'Hold a minute!' They waited for him to continue speaking. 'This doesn't feel right.'

Leander flicked a sidewards glance at her.

She appraised the dark passage ahead. 'I do not sense there is anything wrong.'

'That concerns me. This is too easy, the confrontation with the Minotaur.'

Phameas spluttered. 'Easy? If Homer had not struck it from behind, you would be dead.' He eyed the Minotaur warily, waiting for him to get up as he had done before. 'I am going to see if Homer has awoken and check his injuries.' Phameas sidestepped the slain Minotaur and scurried over to where the big man had fallen.

'That's my point.' Evan eyeballed her. 'It was if the Minotaur sacrificed himself.' He placed a hand on Dexion's shoulder. 'Why have Dexion here, who has the gift of foresight, given to him by the gods? I wouldn't have allowed him to join us—it's too dangerous—yet they insisted he come along.' He studied the young boy. 'Are you receiving any messages from our immortal patrons?'

Dexion's mouth pursed. 'I cannot hear them.'

'When Dexion can't detect their messages, it means they cannot determine our whereabouts.'

'They know we are here,' said Leander.

'Yes, that is true'—he nodded—'but they can't hear or find out what we are doing, and that leads me to my second concern. A more powerful deity has cast some spell to deflect their capacity to identify our position.'

'You believe the Dark Master is here.' She tensed.

'He's been here and given the Minotaur an ultimatum: either defend or prepare for serious ramifications. I got a sense he didn't want to fight but had no choice. The attacks were half-hearted.'

Leander rounded on him in surprise. 'It intended to kill you!'

'I'm not convinced that was what he wanted to do.'

'If that is so, where is the Dark Master?' the High Priestess asked. 'Why is he not here?'

'He is waiting and biding his time, aiming to take the icons once we have them,' he replied.

'It is possible the Dark Master is somewhere awaiting our emergence from the cave,' she said, 'and for that we are prepared. The reunification of the sacred relics and Mother will see to our victory.'

'Somehow, I don't believe it is as simple as you suggest.'

'The Divine Gods chose us. They knew we would succeed.' She drew herself taller, her power as the Mother Goddess' mouthpiece and conduit radiating from her stature.

He rubbed his cheek. 'I wouldn't count those chickens just yet. We're still to recover the object.'

'What have chickens to do with the Mother Goddess?' Leander asked, bewildered.

'It's a saying meaning not to be too hasty in expecting an idea to go as planned before it has happened. Best to be prepared for any surprises.'

'Ah … that is wise.' Leander nodded.

'What do you expect the Dark Master will do?' asked Phameas, crouched by Homer's side.

'Anything, everything. He wants the objects and intends to use whatever advantages to achieve his goal, no matter what.'

'The Olympians can stop the Dark Master,' said the High Priestess, confidence oozing with every word.

'Are you not listening? Kronos is a Titan, and he is holding a grudge, not to mention he is powerful. With that combination, he will not allow them to stop him. It won't be that easy,' Evan argued. 'He has thought about revenge for a long time and intends to win.'

'The immortals shall triumph and Mother's sanctity be restored,' she said with a haughty shake of her head. 'And their sovereignty complete.'

'What if the Mother Goddess became the sole deity?' He held her gaze. Her lips parted. 'You cannot tell me you haven't thought about it.' He waved the blooded blade at her. 'Why have us divert to Thira to retrieve this weapon, if not to use it to guarantee her reign?'

'You dare disrespect Mother!' The High Priestess' nostrils flared. 'Her intentions are to reinstate the Divine Gods' dynasty, and the double-headed labrys was for you to slay the Minotaur.'

He gave her a wry smile. 'I have great respect for the Mother Goddess. However, you haven't been forthcoming with your intentions. Whatever you have plotted, I recommend you revise it, or someone you care for may get hurt or killed.' He lowered his head at her, his nose millimetres from hers. 'Do you wish to see the Mother Goddess as the divine ruler of humans and gods?' He softened his voice further. 'If so, do as I say before dear old Dad, the Family and Kronos work out what we are doing.' His ice-blue irises glinted when she gave an imperceptible nod. He rounded to the others. 'There is a possibility Kronos has laid more traps. The first was coercing the Minotaur into fighting. We must be vigilant for what comes next.' He paused. 'Are we good?'

Phameas nodded. 'I am with you all the way, Evandros.'

Dexion clasped his bow and arrows in his hands. 'I am ready, Master Evandros.'

'We will vanquish the Dark Master, Evandros.' Leander thrust his bow at the dark corridor.

Evan drew in a deep breath. 'Let's finish this.'

'What of Homer?' Phameas asked.

'How is he?'

Phameas shook his head. 'I cannot wake him.'

The large man lay still and unmoving. Evan propped the axe against the wall and crouched, giving his half-brother a good shake.

'Homer? Can you hear me?' He felt for his pulse, which beat strong and consistent. He shook him again, with more vigour. Homer did not stir. He reached for his water container, popped the stopper and poured the cool liquid over his half-brother's face.

'What are you doing?' the High Priestess asked, alarmed.

Homer groaned, his eyelids fluttering.

'Trying to rouse him.' He tipped more on his half-brother's face. 'Hey there, Homer, good to see you awake.'

Homer blinked and moaned. He touched his skull, grimaced in pain and tried to move.

'Steady—you could've broken a bone. Let me help you.' He tucked an arm around Homer's back and eased him upright. Homer sucked in a painful breath. Evan braced him next to the axe. 'I suspect you have a few broken ribs. It would be best if you stayed here while we continue the search for the object.'

Homer grunted, shoved Evan aside and gasped, his face whitening.

'Homer'—Evan stilled him with a hand on his shoulder—'if you come, you may further injure yourself. Besides, we need you to guard our backs in case someone or some monster ventures this way.' He gave Phameas an urgent look of plea.

The Phoenician nodded. 'Dexion and I will stay here too and stop anyone who comes.'

Evan stepped over to the dead Minotaur, pulled out the sword and handed it to Homer. 'Rest up.' Before leaving, he said to Phameas, 'Remember the bullroarer? Use it, if you need to.' He grabbed the axe and set off at a fast pace.

They sped through the passages, turning right or left at the junctions. The gloomy interior was fathomless and reminded

Evan of the caves he'd explored in Margaret River and of the incredible stalagmites and stalactites, formed from mineral deposits after thousands and thousands of years of water dripping through the cave ceiling onto the floor. How he wished he could be there, with friends, venturing through the Crystal Caves. *Soon, Evan, you'll return home. Just this one more job and it's over.*

Their breathing filled the cavernous route, pronounced with each step taken, no one seeking to break the silence. He felt like he was walking a tightrope, the line sagging as they moved closer to the centre of the labyrinth, expecting the inevitable recoil when someone fell. His khiton clung to his torso, the coarseness of the linen accentuated by its dampness. He scoured ahead, searching for an object or anything that looked out of place. What that could be, he didn't know, but he was confident he'd recognise it straight away. After a few left and right turns, the hair on his nape stood on end. He stopped.

'What is it, Evandros?' Leander whispered, peering into the void. He cocked an arrow, arm tense and bracing to draw on the string of the bow.

He pivoted, ears prickling, and listened.

'Evandros ...'

'Shhh ...' His vision strained against the obscurity. 'We're not alone.' His neck tensed, and a small vein pulsed at his temple. He lifted the blade in readiness and held his breath, listening. His stomach fluttered at the brushing sound, followed by the sound of a heavy item that was being dragged. 'What the hell is that?'

'Evandros, can you see what it is?' Leander asked, arrow primed.

'No,' he answered, 'but it's close.'

'Great Mother!' The High Priestess recoiled, covering her mouth.

'What the frick is that?' Evan almost dropped the axe.

Leander stood stoic, his jawline hardening as he took aim.

'I come bearing news from my mistress,' it said. 'Which of you is Evandros?'

Evan's blood froze. The creature had a woman's face and torso and the tail of a serpent, bigger than the photos of the largest python that proliferated on social media networks and the Internet.

'I am.' His voice sounded odd to him, as if he had spoken underwater.

The serpent swung towards him, its hypnotic green lenses pinning him. 'I am Ekhidna. My mistress has assigned me to protect you from Divine Kronos.'

He blinked. 'Wha …?'

'Who is your mistress?' the High Priestess asked, shrinking as the she-dragon swivelled in her direction.

'The goddess Eris.'

'No! She has done nothing but cause problems since the start of our journey. What is she up to? Why are you really here?'

'My goddess has dispatched me to help.'

'That is preposterous!' His eyes changed colour. 'Why now?'

'My goddess does not explain why, only that I am to assure your safety.'

'This is bullshit! Your goddess just doesn't change sides—not after seeking to block our progress at every opportunity. She has a motive.' He shoved the axe in its face. The serpent did not react. 'Slither back to where you and Eris are hiding and tell her we don't need her help or yours, and that Tartaros awaits her return.'

'I cannot.' Ekhidna swayed. 'She ordered me to remain with you, and I do not go against the wishes of the goddess Eris.'

His eyes glittered. 'I do not have time for games.' The beat of his heart steadied and his stance stilled. 'Leave or return to your mistress in pieces.'

Ekhidna tucked a strand of her long brown curly hair behind her ear. The human action gave him a momentary pause until she drew herself upright, undulating from side to side, and towered over them. 'My mistress predicted you would react in such a manner, and she proposes that when you meet Divine Kronos a second time, you heed the whereabouts of the Amazon queen and your offspring.'

Evan froze. 'Is that a threat?' He gripped the haft of his axe, the veins in his arms protruding. Darkness swirled within his eyes with the onset of a tempestuous maelstrom.

'No, a warning,' she replied. Ekhidna swung away and slithered down the passageway, receding into the coal-black depths.

He peered into the obscurity, ears straining at the sound of nothingness, body geared to spring as a lion attacks its prey at the slightest movement.

'I have to return to the beach,' he said, wheeling about on his heels.

The High Priestess reached out to take his arm. 'No. We retrieve the statuette and leave for the sacred tree.'

'Did you not understand what that snake said?' he roared. 'Antioche and the babies are not safe. I have to protect them.'

She narrowed her eyes at him. 'We must continue. If we do not, it does not matter if the Dark Master kills the queen and your children, for we shall be deceased too.'

He clenched his jaw, the fire in his blood searing a trail through his veins.

'Goddamn it!' He hacked at the wall, sparks flying, ignoring the jolts running up his arms from the repetitious impact. He kept smashing the walls, oblivious to his companions.

After a long time, he slowed and then stopped, chest heaving, his hair drenched and dripping from the ends as if doused from a morning shower. Without saying a word, he stalked off into the chthonic bowels of the Minotaur's lair.

CHAPTER 48

Evan held a torch aloft in one hand and the blood-smeared labrys in the other, careering along, his sole intent to find the idol and return to the beach. With the Minotaur slain, Kronos was now the major obstacle, and while Evan didn't know what to expect from the old Titan, he knew it would be difficult. The offer of protection extended by Eris' minion also surprised him. *What did she want?* He scoured the dim passage, scrutinising the walls and floor for a clue of the whereabouts of the icon, like they had discovered in the cave on Thira.

He continued at a rapid pace akin to an Olympian race walker. He slowed and covered his mouth and nose. 'Gods, that is rank!'

The passageway opened into a large domed space, similar to the beehive tomb the Mykenaeans had built for their kings and buried with their life's possessions and weapons. He blanched and dry-retched, his gut roiling at the stench. The labrys slipped from his hand and clanged as it hit the cavernous floor.

'Dear Mother.' The High Priestess stumbled. He caught her.

'By the gods,' Leander said, aghast. 'How ... what ...?'

'The stories were true,' he said, voice hoarse. 'How is that possible?'

He could not tear his eyes from the macabre mound. A pile of human bones towered over them and skimmed the roof of the cavern. From the collection, it was difficult to determine how many youths and maidens had been sent to their deaths over the thousands of years.

'So many ...' Leander rubbed his brow. 'How long ...?' And then he fell silent, brooding over the grisly mound.

The High Priestess tucked a strand of hair behind an ear, hand trembling. 'We'—she sucked in a breath—'need to explore the tomb for the sacred idol.' She lowered her bag to the ground.

'You do not mean we have to ...' The Atlantean contemplated the assemblage of discarded ribs, limbs, shoulder blades, thighs, vertebrae in dismay.

'Let's search the perimeter,' Evan said. 'The statue may be hidden in a niche or a cavity in the wall.'

'Yes, that is much more plausible.' Leander moved away from the pile, staying close to the wall.

'I'll join you,' said the High Priestess, rushing to his side.

'I'll start in this direction, then.' Evan picked up the labrys and gagged. The foul odour of rotting flesh and offal hit him like a tidal wave. His mouth watered and he swallowed the rising bile. 'Bugger this.' He ripped part of the hem of his khiton, tied it about his nose and mouth and scooted in the opposite direction of the other two. He searched the surfaces and crevices, using the butt of the labrys to check the deeper niches so as to avoid touching the sacred figure if it was stored inside. It was then he noticed the arrangement of a separate pile of skulls resembling the shape of the lair. He loathed to venture closer, but instinct told him the Minotaur had created the macabre sculpture for a reason.

'I really don't want to touch those.'

The High Priestess and Leander rounded from the other direction. His shoulders sagged as he joined them.

'I think the figurine is in that.' He pointed.

Leander's face contorted in anguish. The High Priestess studied the collection, rubbing her hands up and down her thighs.

'Are you certain?' she asked.

He gave the pile of skulls another once-over. 'No, but the niches are empty, save for the odd dead animal, and I can't see anywhere else the Minotaur may have hidden the object.' He rubbed his brow. 'That pile is the most credible spot.'

Leander dragged a hand over his mouth and clasped his chin. 'It is the perfect hiding place.'

'No person would consider fossicking through that,' Evan said. 'Nobody in their right mind would go near it. It's conceivable the Minotaur buried the statuette under it. That's where I'd hide it.'

The High Priestess had an aggrieved expression on her face as she brooded over the skulls.

'Well, neither of us wishes to venture close or is willing to disturb them. Would you expect anyone to search through the skulls?' He flung an arm at the pile. Leander fidgeted with an arrow while the High Priestess pursed her lips. 'We're the only ones here—not even the almighty gods, Kronos or the Mother Goddess are in this place. Why do you suppose that is?'

'The High Priestess is the only person who can hold and use the sacred icons,' answered Leander.

'Says Zeus, but can you please explain how two Titans cannot possess them? The predecessors dedicated the statue to the Mother Goddess. She should be able to collect them, but why can't she? I understand why Zeus and the rest of the Family cannot extract the objects, for they may alert Kronos to their presence. But that's all moot now—he knows we're here, so what is the point of all this sneaking around? We're in a room filled with countless remnants of the victims who once had dreams and wishes.' He gestured.

The High Priestess opened her mouth.

'And don't tell me "the gods have decreed it so" and we must adhere to their command. This is the last item.' He thrust the labrys at the skeletons. 'Why isn't Kronos here to claim it?'

'Perhaps the Dark Master requires Mother to willingly hand the sacred objects to him,' said Leander.

Evan's eyes lit up. 'Now that makes sense. Brilliant, Leander. Why didn't I consider that?' He scratched behind his ear and pondered the cobblestoned floor, not noticing the design. 'Why does he need her to present him with the icons?' He squatted and pondered the pile.

Leander's brow creased in deep furrows. 'If the Mother Goddess gave the Titan the sacred pieces, it may be possible the curse of destruction is lifted and he can use them without being harmed.'

'A good answer, but why now?' He paced back and forth. 'There is more to this entire quest, other than Kronos being given Mother's icons. He is after something else.'

'He cannot have the High Priestess,' Leander declared, hands on hips.

'I agree, we cannot allow Kronos to capture her.' He tapped his fingers against his lips. 'There is more to the Titan's plan. If he can't abduct the High Priestess, then he would have to capture another woman, who is strong yet pliable, easy to train and prepare for his ultimate goal. The female would have to be young and naïve …' He paled. 'Oh, jeez … no, no, no …' He headed for the exit. 'I have to leave.'

'Evandros! What is it?' Leander called out after him.

'Kronos is after my daughter!'

'Evandros! You do not know that is the Dark Master's intention,' the High Priestess cried out. 'The way to stop him from succeeding is to find Mother's statue and present them at her sacred tree.'

'You continue to the tree and stop Kronos. I am going to protect my family.'

'You must remain here!' She clutched at his forearm, her fingers digging into his skin.

He took in her clawlike grasp on his forearm. 'Let go. Now.'

She dug her fingernails in. 'Mother instructed you to keep me safe.'

He whipped the blade under her throat.

'Evandros! Stop!' Leander clutched his wrist. 'If you kill the High Priestess, we lose everything, including your daughter.' Leander then pleaded with her. 'Evandros has done what the gods tasked him—let him leave to protect his family.'

She shook her head, drawing blood from the sharp edge of the axe. 'No, he is needed here!'

Evan shifted his grip on the handle.

'Evandros, wait!' Leander pleaded. 'High Priestess ... Alexina, he has more than fulfilled his duty. I will remain with you to find the statuette and we will both go to Mother's tree.' He prised her fingers from Evan's arm. 'Do it for me, for our future ...'

CHAPTER 49

The High Priestess' grip relaxed and Evan wrenched his arm away. He leaned in and spoke into her ear.

'If my family comes to harm, it will be on your conscience.'

He wheeled around and ran back through the labyrinth. The darkened passages did not slow him, nor did the numerous changes in direction. He sprinted, his feet pounding on the stone floor, beating out a rapid staccato. A dim light beckoned as he rounded the next bend. He heard the faint chink of metal. The light grew brighter, and he charged forward. The clanging of multiple weapons drawn echoed within the tunnel.

'Arms ready!'

His mind was muddied, but the voice sounded familiar. He shook off the confusion and ran on, his thoughts consumed with images of Kronos injuring Antioche and abducting their babies.

'Wait! It's Evandros!'

A part of his consciousness noted Phameas lowering his sword.

'What's happened? Have you discovered your goddess' likeness?'

He careened headlong. A memory clicked as a disembodied part of his self caught sight of Phameas hauling Dexion out of his path.

'Something is wrong.'

'Master Evandros! Stop!'

Evan blinked. Homer heaved upright to prop himself against the craggy surface and shuffled to the centre of the tunnel.

'Move out of there, Homer!' Phameas shouted. 'Evandros! Halt!'

Lykeios barked, fangs bared.

His pace faltered.

'Phameas?'

'Yes, I am here with Dexion and Homer and the pup Lykeios. Remember, we remained behind, to protect your injured brother?'

He slowed and stopped. Lykeios growled.

Phameas took a step but stopped, seeing the pitch-black shade clouding his vision, a telltale sign his friend's dark persona had taken hold.

'What has happened? Where are the others?' The Phoenician peeked around him.

'I must return to the beach,' he replied. Some of the colour in his irises emerged through the ebony mist.

'Why? Did you find the statuette?' Phameas sidled closer. 'Where are the others? Have they been injured?'

Dexion's face went slack. 'I sense the Dark Master is near, as is Mother.'

Evan darted over to him. 'Is Kronos with Antioche and the babies?'

His breathing was shallow. 'Noooo … but he requires something … someone …'

'I have to go.' Evan bolted forward, driving Phameas backwards.

Homer seized his shoulder, perspiration sheening across his forehead as he laboured to write. *Why must you return?*

'Kronos intends to kidnap my daughter.'

'What? How? Why?' Phameas asked, flummoxed.

'He seeks to use my daughter as the Messiah's mother.' He struggled to shrug off Homer's heavy manacle.

How do you know this? Homer wrote.

'It makes sense! Kronos requires a female descendant of Zeus and that would be my newborn daughter. This is how he gets revenge against Zeus and the other gods, by using the bloodline of the King of Gods and Men to create his offspring.'

'I thought he wanted to seize the High Priestess,' said Phameas. 'That's what you said when we found the labrys on Thira. Kronos intends to use the High Priestess as she is the human embodiment of the Mother Goddess, and the only person who can hold the objects. The child she conceives will inherit her ability to use the sacred icons.'

Evan's gaze clouded momentarily and then he shook his head. 'No, she was in the beginning, but not now … I must go.'

Homer squeezed the crook of his neck, and he winced.

Releasing his vice-like grip on Evan, Homer wrote on his tablet. *Are you certain the Titan is after your child? It may be a diversion, designed to distract you from finding the sacred statue.*

'No, he is after my baby girl. Leander and Alexina are searching for the statuette.'

Homer scoffed. *If I were the Dark Master, I would create a diversion to lure you away from protecting the High Priestess. She alone has the capability to touch the sacred icons.*

'No.' He tried to dodge his brother's strong hold, but Homer pulled him around until they were face to face. Evan struggled to extricate himself from Homer's clutches. 'No, he means to kidnap my child.' He grimaced as Homer's fingers dug deeper into his shoulder, pressing into the clavicle.

That is what I would have you believe. The big Atlantean rapped him on the forehead. *Are you listening to yourself? Can you hear what you are saying? What would you do if I said to you the Dark Master sought to take one of my children and not our sister, the High Priestess?*

He opened his mouth but uttered no words.

Homer nodded. *You are thinking with this*—he stabbed at Evan's heart—*and not with that.* He slapped him across the head and further wrote, *Having children makes you feel warm, protective and proud, but you are here to guard the High Priestess and the Mother's sacred icons, and we defend you, whatever arises.*

'Evandros, from the day my captain stopped to inspect the shipwreck and discovered you amongst the debris, I've always known you to be honest, pragmatic and rational. You are not a man to act in such haste and without logic. If you were the Titan, what would you do to ensure that the one person who can defend the High Priestess is no longer at her side?' Phameas eyeballed him.

The fog lifted and he cursed himself. 'I've been an idiot, haven't I?'

The Phoenician crossed his arms against his chest.

Homer gave an emphatic nod.

Phameas raised his brows at him. 'You allowed a woman and babies to muddle your brain.'

Return to the High Priestess. Homer pointed in the direction from which Evan had come before waving his tablet at him. *And beg for her forgiveness.*

'That should be fun. She'll never let me forget I abandoned her and Leander,' he stated.

Homer nodded again.

'You should sit down.' He noted the greyish tinge on his brother's face and guided him to the floor. 'I'll return as soon as I can. You need medical help.'

Homer waved him away and slumped against the wall,

drawing in shallow breaths and letting his tablet drop from his hand. Evan gnawed at the inside of his cheek, noting the fresh blood on his clothing.

'Find the sacred object. Leave me to attend to Homer's injury,' said Phameas, kneeling.

'Right.' Evan cringed. 'Best I get the scolding over and done with.' He spun around.

'The Titan wants an answer,' Dexion blurted. 'He is coming for you.'

Evan's pulse slowed, and he felt as if he were witnessing the scene from outside his body, and then his blood coursed through his veins as if the hounds of Hades were after him.

Phameas asked, 'What does he want from you?'

'The icons,' he replied, wiping his mouth with the back of his hand. 'Is he here now?'

'He is close. Divine Zeus and the others have surrounded the island, and he is waiting.'

'For what?' Phameas asked Evan.

'My guess is for the Mother Goddess to arrive,' he answered, 'and he'll make his move when she does.'

'The Dark Master cannot win if our High Priestess is successful.'

'Kronos is not here for a simple exchange or just to defeat the gods.'

'Then why do all this? Why inflict such pain and cause havoc if not to possess the items?' asked Phameas.

'Hatred drives him, and he aims to destroy the worship of the gods and Mother. In doing so, he eradicates them from existence and from everyone's consciousness, thus punishing them for deposing him and the other Titans from their reign. It is power Kronos desires, over every living creature and the human race, and to succeed, he creates a son who personifies goodness, sincerity, honour and charity, who speaks of benevolence and respect for one another. And as his father, Kronos reigns as Supreme God, unseen yet forbidding. Malevolence spreads through the actions of treacherous men who seek domination and authority by condemning innocent individuals to harsh punishment and death.' Evan pursed his lips. 'Humans are very good at killing, maiming, hurting and destroying, not caring about the impact of their actions on others. We've been doing this since the birth of humanity.'

'Then what is the purpose of this Messiah you speak of?' asked Phameas. 'If He is what you claim, then would it not be better for the world that He is born?'

Evan gave him a crooked smile. 'The Messiah was born, and the good intentions He preached disregarded and long forgotten after He died. There are wars, mayhem, terrorism, destruction of the environment, disasters on a scale that rival the great flood stories of Gilgamesh and the Deucalion. Whether or not Kronos' intention is well-meaning and he really wants to make amends for his actions, retribution is his main goal.'

CHAPTER 50

Evan arrived back at the lair, where he had abandoned the High Priestess and Leander. They swung around at the tramping of his footsteps, each gripping skulls. Leander's face lit up and he offered Evan a warm smile. The High Priestess sniffed at him, whirled back around and continued with the grisly task. Leander beckoned him over with a tilt of his head and moved aside for him. He set the labrys against the wall and prepared to dismantle the strange configuration of skulls. He shuddered, recoiling at the first touch, but after a while, he got used to the weirdness and the texture and concentrated on moving them from one place to the next.

They worked in silence, alone with their thoughts and the clink of bones as they built another pile. The base of the mound widened as the mass grew smaller, forcing them to spread further apart. Evan thought about why the Minotaur had separated the skulls from the skeletal frames of the bodies. It would have taken him a great deal of time to create a pyramid of skulls.

'Evandros, have you speculated as to the Minotaur's motive for hiding Mother's sacred statuette under the skulls?' asked Leander.

'The only conclusion I can draw is that he wanted us to find the statuette and hid it under the mound of skulls.'

'You are making the assumption that the creature could reason and rationalise,' the High Priestess countered. 'It did not demonstrate signs of intelligence when it attacked us—it was purely animalistic.'

'I disagree. The Minotaur was sentient. His actions were considered and he was strategic as we fought.' Evan set a skull on the growing pile. 'And you didn't see the look in his eyes just before I was about to behead him. He understood what was happening. The Minotaur created the macabre mound as a clue for us.'

'Then why did it fight you?' asked the High Priestess. 'It could have let us through and it still would be alive.'

'Perhaps he wanted to die,' said Leander. The High Priestess gave him an incredulous look.

Evan agreed. 'He's been alone in the labyrinth for a thousand years, maybe longer, and he didn't want to live any more.'

'And the only weapon that could kill him was the labrys Evandros used, one forged in Mother's cave on Thira,' concluded Leander.

'You are deducing that it knew about the labrys,' the High Priestess sniffed.

'I'd say the Minotaur knew about a weapon that could kill him but not the type,' said Evan.

The High Priestess gave them a lengthy look before turning her attention back to the skulls, and they resumed their gruesome task. A few hours later, his back ached at the constant bending and swinging from side to side. He placed his hands on his lower back and straightened. With an inward groan, he felt the vertebrae in his spine pop one by one, the satisfaction of stretching and standing upright easing the pain. He rotated one way and then the other a few times, then did some side stretches.

He halted mid-action, seeing the peculiar stares they flashed him, and resumed the sordid relocation.

The other stack got larger and yet they continued to work in silence, which he was happy to prolong. The glacial disapproval emanating from the High Priestess was as blatant as driving a sharp tool into large blocks of ice. He figured her unmistakable silent condemnation was better than the lashing of her words.

'Bugger,' he muttered to himself as he picked up a skull. *Why did it have to be me?* He removed a few more to reveal an object as long as his forearm wrapped in a dirty beige linen cloth. 'Double bugger.' In a louder voice, he said, 'I've found it.' He backed away and stepped between the original collection and the new stack, avoiding the stockpile of human bones and skulls.

'It's bigger than the figurine we have on Atlantis.' Leander stood shoulder to shoulder with the High Priestess as she unwrapped the dirty linen and held it aloft. The statuette, made from painted faience, had a full-length flounced skirt and an embroidered apron, with a belt that emphasised a narrow waist and an open bodice that left her voluptuous breasts exposed. Sculptured hands were outstretched but empty, as if waiting to receive a precious offering. Glossy sable hair crested above the buttocks, and crowning the head was an intricate diadem, interspersed with red and green gemstones.

'She is ...' Leander said, awed.

'Yes.' The High Priestess rotated the statuette in wonder. 'She is beautiful.'

Evan hefted the labrys from hand to hand, strode to the exit and back, then headed to the exit again, sighing out loud.

'Do stop pacing, Evandros,' she said. 'I am still vexed with you, and your impatience to leave will not improve my mood.'

'That is clear.' He tapped his foot on the ground. 'And while you are taking time to examine the icon, Zeus and the others have arrived and Kronos is approaching, waiting for the Mother Goddess to get here.'

She lowered her arms. 'When did you learn of this? Are you certain?'

'Does the sun rise in the east?' he asked. She narrowed her eyes at him. 'Dexion sensed their presence. You ask him when we catch up with them.'

'We should listen to Evandros,' said Leander.

'Just as we did earlier, when he spurned us without recourse?'

'I won't apologise.' He stiffened. 'Nor am I going to make excuses. It's your responsibility to take the icons to the tree.'

The High Priestess, with deliberate slowness, rewrapped the sculpture. She gave him a frosty glare. 'You will be accompanying me.'

'I did my part, now it's your turn to take over.'

A faint red glow emanated from her hands. 'You will do as Mother has instructed and escort me to her tree.'

Evan clenched a hand; the veins in his arm thickened. Leander stepped between them. 'Evandros, you did promise Mother to protect the High Priestess.'

'Fine. However, it does not change the fact that Kronos soon arrives, and he intends to steal the objects, no matter how or who tries to stop him,' he told her.

'You sound confident that the Dark Master shall win,' she said.

'Kronos has nothing to lose and everything to gain, and you,' he said, 'are part of the plan.'

'Have you changed your mind? You did not hesitate to desert us, spouting that your baby daughter was in danger and the Dark Master wanted her. Did you discover you were in error and had made an ill-considered decision?' She placed the statuette into her bag.

Evan clamped his teeth together before replying. 'You got me there, I was wrong. Now can we get out of here?' He headed out of the lair. 'If you want to continue arguing, save it for later ... if we survive.'

The trip back to where Phameas, Dexion and Homer waited for them did not take them long. Homer winced, trying to sit upright, and turned to the High Priestess, waiting for a response.

'We found it.' The High Priestess smiled and nodded at him.

Homer grunted in approval and readied himself to stand up.

'Don't you move,' warned Evan. 'Leander and I will help you.'

Evan and Leander hoisted Homer between them, and they lumbered through the labyrinth to where they had left Hektor with Jason and the Argonauts. Phameas took the lead, the flame of his beacon fluttering and casting lengthy shadows against the cavernous wall.

'Evandros! Is that you?' called out a voice. The clanging of swords swept over them.

'It's us, Jason!'

The arc of light brought them into view of Jason and his crew.

'Thank the gods.' His shoulders sagged, the point of his sword dipping to the floor. 'What of the Minotaur? Where is it?'

'Dead.' Evan checked the Argonauts clustered behind Jason. 'Where is Hektor?'

'I had men help him outside. He wasn't rousing and no amount of water had any effect, and I decided fresh air may be better for him.'

'Good idea.'

'Did you discover any treasure?' he asked, face brightening in hope.

'Not sure you would call it treasure,' replied Evan, glancing at Leander, who pursed his lips. 'There were a lot of bones ... human.'

'No sign of jewellery or gold, then?'

'We didn't search for any valuables,' he replied. 'If you and your men want to search the Minotaur's lair, it is yours.'

Jason grinned. 'Let's go, Argonauts.'

He grabbed the Argonaut's arm as he was about to walk past. 'Jason, you may need to ... shift things around. I hope you won't be too disappointed if you don't uncover a trove of jewels, gems or gold.' He then let go. 'Don't be too unsettled by what you see.'

CHAPTER 51

K ronos slowed his approach when Krete came into view. He halted and hovered, searching the skies and clouds, certain Zeus and the other immortals were nearby. A cloud drifted across his line of sight. He batted it away, sending it over the lands of Asia Minor, precipitation scattering the surface of the sea. He descended lower, the shimmering Mediterranean reflecting the rays of the sun, and ignored the dolphins frolicking below. Satisfied he was alone, he surged ahead, the island looming.

A bolt of lightning struck overhead.

His hair stood on end. He touched his scarred face, the painful memory of the fiery white flames of lightning bolts consuming his flesh as fresh as the day his mother, Gaia, had told him of a portent that one day, his own offspring would usurp his reign. After castrating his own father, Ouranos, Kronos had become King of the Titans and claimed as his wife Rhea, who had birthed three daughters and three sons, whom Kronos had consumed. It was Zeus, the youngest, who had duped him into drinking an elixir to regurgitate all of his children, due to the trickery of Gaia, who had hidden the newborn babe, Zeus, and instead offered him a rock wrapped in swaddling to swallow.

Kronos seethed and rounded to challenge his irreverent and impertinent progeny.

'That's as far as you go, Kronos.' Zeus held an incandescent flame of lightning aimed at him. 'You will desist.'

Poseidon flanked Zeus, clasping his trident, and Hades restrained his foaming three-headed pet, Kerberos, from attacking. Hephaistos with his iron hammer, Ares holding his sword and Apollo poised with his bow and arrow rounded on the Titan.

'Here we are again,' Kronos said, mouth quirking. 'Fighting over the dominion of this world.'

'On this occasion, you have no other Titans to aid you.' Zeus levelled the bolt of lightning at him.

Kronos clasped his fists behind his back, his insides coiled tight like a boa constrictor. 'I do not require assistance to oust you from this universe.'

Ares scoffed. 'You could not defeat us with the combined help of the Titans, and here you oppose us on your own. You are doomed to fail and you shall die.'

'For one who wages war, you are as incompetent as you are ineffectual. You blunder and bluster, waving your weapons, toothless in your courage. Leave the fighting to those who battle with ingenuity, such as the wise Athene, who does not depend on brawn to instil fear.'

Ares growled, bracing to spring at him. 'You dare ...'

Kronos smirked.

'Halt, Ares!' shouted Zeus.

Apollo loosed an arrow at the Titan, which he deflected with a casual wave of his hand.

'Apollo, of all the immortals, you are the most pathetic—enamoured by my feckless daughter, who could not even win the favour of a human and rendered you impotent.' He wagged a finger. 'Are you certain your little paradise still imprisons her?'

'I'd know if she escaped,' Apollo bleated, beseeching Zeus.

Kronos' head tilted to the side. 'As long as you are certain.'

Hephaistos twirled his sledgehammer.

'Poor Hephaistos, their treatment of you should anger you most of all —despised by your mother at childbirth and thrown away to perish. Shunned for your abhorrent features and deformity by the others, and in particular, by your bride, Aphrodite, who cheated and lay many times with Ares. You bring shame to the house of immortals for not punishing her and her deplorable lover.' Kronos tut-tutted.

Hephaistos bristled. The handle of the sledgehammer creaked under his clutches, his breathing laboured.

'Don't listen to him, Hephaistos,' said Hades.

'Words, empty words,' said Zeus, 'that is all you have.'

'Words are power, and I am keen to reunite with your heir, who is awaiting my arrival. When the sacred icons are in my possession, you and your Family,' Kronos hissed, 'cease to exist. When the mortals seek redemption and are poised for clemency, a new god benevolent and virtuous, shall rise and He will lead them, ardent followers of His brilliance and selflessness.'

Poseidon barked out laughing. 'Our subjects will never accept this god of yours.'

'There will be no new immortal.' Zeus' lip curled, his lightning bolt fiery and luminous.

'Ah ... you see, it is preordained. There is nothing you can do to stop the coming of the Messiah.'

Zeus roared and flew at the old god, hurling sheets of lightning. Poseidon followed, thrusting his trident into the air. Gusts of winds battered the shore and water; massive surges of waves propelled at him. From the other side, Hades tossed balls of fire.

Kronos cackled.

With a click of his fingers, a net dropped from the clouds above and ensnared the gods. Zeus tried to rip the netting with his fingers and Poseidon thrust his trident at the holes, but the mesh remained intact.

Ares wielded his sword, the lattice impenetrable against the sharp edges. Zeus threw a lightning bolt; it ricocheted. Hephaistos dove out of the way. Apollo leapt aside.

'Now to capture the rest of your Family,' Kronos jeered and fled.

CHAPTER 52

Half an hour later, they emerged from the labyrinth, stumbling into the stables, where they had started. Evan drew in a lungful of fresh air, trying to erase the stench of death, the scent of varying stages of decomposition leaving an unpleasant acrid taste in his mouth. The commander of the Amazons issued an order to her warriors to check the entry of the cave.

'Jason and his men are searching the lair,' he said. 'They'll return after they've completed their search. We'—he gestured at the High Priestess and himself—'must complete the mission. You'll accompany the others to the beach.'

'We're not going,' Phameas declared, hands on hips. 'We've voyaged too far to leave now, and seeing how easily you find trouble, you require our help. Besides, we'—he indicated himself, Dexion and Evan—'have journeyed too far together, and I promised to stay to the end. That was my oath to you, your gods and mine; I do not break my word.'

'Phameas, the Mother Goddess wants the High Priestess and me to finish the quest alone,' he said.

'That may be so. However, your goddess did not say we cannot accompany you to the sacred tree.' The Phoenician crossed his arms against his chest.

'You are playing with words, Phameas. She was quite clear about who was going.'

'It feels like a trap,' his friend argued.

Lykeios whimpered and brushed against Evan's legs.

'There is a way,' said the Amazon. 'You wait.'

'Wait for what?' asked Phameas.

'You cannot accompany the queen's consort and the High Priestess. However, if you bide your time and wait for the sun to move west, you can follow thereafter.'

'Consort! I am not anyone's consort!'

The commander ignored him, her indifference more vocal than a response.

'That is such bull—'

'That is a good idea.' Leander's face brightened.

'If we waited … say ten, fifteen minutes,' Phameas finished.

Leander nodded. 'That would give Evandros and the High Priestess a chance to gain favourable advantage.'

'Yes.' Phameas agreed, bouncing on his feet. 'I like the suggestion.'

'There is a flaw in your reasoning, as there is in the consort claim,' Evan opposed. 'Do you believe that the Mother Goddess and Kronos or Zeus are that naïve? They would have considered every option, including you trailing us.'

'Not at all. They are gods,' replied Phameas, 'but by my reckoning, they are more concerned about you and the High Priestess reaching the tree, the Dark Master and each other, rather than worrying about what we are doing.'

'There is logic in Phameas' argument,' said Leander. 'The gods have enough to occupy them, and our slight transgression is of little import.'

'Again, your assertion is misplaced. As you, the High Priestess and Hektor keep stating, the gods see and hear all.' He pointed at the sky. 'Do you intend to test them?'

Leander turned to the Phoenician and the High Priestess, seeking their support, but they remained silent.

'You know I am right.' Evan poked Leander in the chest. 'You would not cross your father, even if it was the proper course of action, and if you did, the consequences are too considerable to risk. It is best that you travel back with the others and ask Antioche's doctor to tend to Homer and Hektor's injuries.'

Phameas growled. 'Your gods may punish you, but they cannot discipline me—only my gods can. They allow my people to learn from our mistakes and make our own decisions. Though'—he wagged a finger at them—'when the situation is dire, they act, and you do not want to be in their path when they are angered.'

'No matter which of the gods you honour, neither of you, nor anyone else, is coming after us.' He hoisted the labrys over his shoulder and spoke to the Amazon. 'Escort them to camp.' He then set off at a brisk walk.

'Master Evandros!'

He didn't stop.

'Master Evandros! Wait!' Dexion called out. 'Take Lykeios.'

He halted and gave Dexion a remorseful shake of his head. 'No, he is your wolf.'

Dexion lower lip quavered. 'Lykeios must go with you, or you may not survive.'

His heart did a flip and lurch. 'Then that is to be my end.'

'No!' Dexion took his hand, preventing him from leaving. 'You must return, or Mother's vision is doomed.'

'What are you talking about?' He searched the boy's frantic face.

'If the Dark Master kills you, you cannot protect your children.'

His stomach writhed in anguish. 'The queen has her warriors to guard them.'

Dexion's eyes watered. 'They cannot fight an immortal—only you can.'

'And what if Kronos kills Lykeios while defending me?' Evan took a deep breath. 'No, we proceed alone, and between the two of us'—he nodded at the High Priestess—'we can defend ourselves.' He knelt and patted Lykeios between the ears. 'I need you to safeguard my family. Do you understand, Lykeios?' He held the wolf's pale blue eyes. 'Go to Antioche and the babies.'

Lykeios woofed and galloped away.

'Master Evandros ...'

He embraced the boy. 'It's alright. This is how I expected it to end.'

Dexion clung to him, tears flowing down his cheeks.

'You must take care of Phameas—you know how easily he gets distracted and forgets what he needs to do.' His throat constricted. Dexion nodded, snuffling. 'You are a good lad, and I am ever so grateful for your friendship.'

Phameas cleared his throat. 'When you come back, I want to hear what happened at the tree.'

'That is a promise.' Evan stood, nodded at Phameas, and then he gave Homer an affectionate smile. 'Whatever happens, Homer, return home to your family and care for them.' He then spoke to Leander. 'You are an honourable man and I'm certain the gods will reward you.' He gave a wink and Leander's cheeks reddened. 'Now, High Priestess, let's finish this business before the day is over.'

CHAPTER 53

The High Priestess took the lead and walked down the slope, heading for the ruined steps where Evan had tripped and fallen down hours earlier. She picked a path through the debris of what used to be a staircase. From the many artistic representations he was familiar with, the staircase led to a tiered colonnade and to the red-and-black pillars made famous by Sir Arthur Evans, an archaeologist of the nineteenth and early twentieth centuries. The discovery of the historic site and of a civilisation long forgotten except in mythology was monumental. Preoccupied by his musings, Evan stumbled into a ditch.

'Damn it!' He hopped about and swore, seeing blood seeping from his big toe.

She swung around as he squatted to brush away the dark crimson fluid. 'Are you hurt?'

He paused in his ministrations, pressed his lips together and took a deep breath. 'It's okay.' He tore the ragged edge of his khiton and wrapped it around his toe. He stood, ignoring the throbbing pain that surged from his toe and up his leg. She resumed walking.

He muttered under his breath and limped after her. They traversed the length of the north-western side of the palace, Evan careful to dodge jutting rocks and blocks of collapsed walls. He noted the damaged altars in the west court, where in his century only the bases remained. Further along was another altar. He pictured the historic site he had visited as a tourist and the numerous buildings that encompassed the area. It was vast, with sections not yet excavated.

'Are we walking towards the hills from the Royal Road?'

'Not quite. If the design of the palace is like at home, there ought to be a walkway leading into the valley, where we'll see a river. We follow the waterway to the mountains, and there we should find a dell—and at its centre is Mother's tree.'

'Are there markers or identifying features I need to be aware of while scouting?' He bypassed a fallen column. 'Odds are the trail is overgrown or buried.'

'You may be correct. However, Mother's instructions were explicit: we come in this direction if debris blocked the path to the sacred forest. There should be an image of her holding snakes etched into the stone pavement and pointing towards the water.'

'Should be easy enough to spot.' He gave the uneven terrain a once-over, ever watchful to avoid stubbing his toes again.

He stored the images he saw in his brain to draw later in his writing pad. There was plenty to keep him occupied for hours when he got back to the beach. From all that he had seen and experienced, his architectural company would be busy with reconstructing and recreating many of the designs that filled his mind. It could revolutionise architecture and the building industry.

'What are your plans after we complete the quest of the gods?' she asked.

'Huh ...?' He was slow to register the question. 'Oh, I don't believe I'll be here when this is over. My fate lies elsewhere.'

'Are you returning to the Isle of Hephaistos with Queen Antioche and her children?' Her tone was reproachful.

He stopped to analyse the surrounding area for the engraving. 'No ... that is not where I am supposed to go.'

'What do you mean? If you are not travelling with the queen, you will return to Atlantis.' The High Priestess huffed in annoyance at his vague answer.

'My destiny isn't there either.'

'Evandros.' She grabbed his backpack, forcing him to skid. 'You are speaking in riddles. Where are you going if not home?'

'My destination remains with Zeus and Mother, whatever they decide.'

'What did Divine Apollo's mouthpiece tell you? What is this fate you speak of, and what have Mother and Divine Zeus devised?'

'Pythia ... oh my good God.' He smacked his forehead. 'The signs were there this entire time, and she predicted it, and she told me. I am such an idiot!'

'What are you speaking of? What did who know? The Oracle?'

He got angry. 'I thought she meant someone else, but now I know who she referred to.' He lifted his face to the sky and shouted, 'It changes nothing! We have an arrangement and I expect you to honour it!' He stalked away, forcing the High Priestess to run.

'Evandros! What has happened? What arrangement, and with whom?'

He stopped so suddenly that she ran into his back. Evan didn't feel the impact of the collision; his eyes glinted, pupils dilating. 'I am doing my job in this onerous duty and you'—he pointed at her —'do what it takes to finish it.' He wheeled about and thundered away.

He fumed over being tricked and peeved at himself for failing to see how he was manipulated. To distract from his ratty thoughts, he retraced the individual stages, from arriving at the places he had visited and meeting the individuals encountered on his odyssey. His parents and friends would not believe a word of his experiences. Then a revelation came to him.

'Ah huh ... I see it all now. Tell me about the plans you and the Elders concocted?'

'What?'

'You and the other three Elders met before leaving Atlantis and discussed strategies for the conclusion of this mission.'

Her shoulders tensed. 'To converse outside the protection of the white light is perilous.'

'Fine, apply the white light.' He waited as she ensconced them in the protective aura. 'What did you contrive?'

'We spoke of the location of Mother's sacred icons and of celebrating our success.'

'Don't lie to me. There is no one here but you and me,' he said, eyes flashing. 'You have been withholding information since the start of this folly of a quest. What do you know and what can the icons do?' When she didn't respond, he went on.

'Fine, then, let me fill in the details of your meeting. After Sibyl's sacrifice, you discussed how the objects can be used once in your possession. Except for one minor yet important detail—the statuette of the Mother Goddess was a copy of the original. This you didn't know until my visit with Pythia. In spite of the setback, the intention was still to bring the objects back to Atlantis. That all changed with your visit with the Mother Goddess, who instructed you to reunite the items with her sacred tree on Krete.

'Together, the three items wield power, which is why Kronos wants them, and why the Elders devised a scheme to use them, announcing to the world you are here, strong, illustrious and ready to take pride of place as the ancestors had done. The systematic approach to letting other civilisations know about Atlantis and its citizens, who survived and are as potent as before, needs rigorous implementation and thorough consideration. As we experienced, there are communities that have not forgotten the tyrannical and imperialistic behaviours of the ancient Atlanteans.' He reflected. 'Mother put a stop to your schemes and ordered you to bring the objects here to connect with the land of their creation and prevent Kronos from succeeding. It is here they must remain for the power of the relics to work. Your plan was audacious. How were you intending to execute this plot without alerting the Mother Goddess or Zeus?'

'Divine Poseidon granted the Elders permission to rebuild on our ancestral lands if we located them.'

Evan guffawed. 'I bet he didn't share that morsel of information with Zeus or Mother.'

'He is our patron deity and we obey his commands,' she snapped, cheeks flushed.

'Yes, but her instructions ruined your dreams of subjugation,' he said.

'The sacred sculptures belong to the Atlanteans.' Her jaw tightened.

'They once did, but not anymore. I am curious as to the outcome of the reunification of Mother, the icons and the tree.'

'What do you mean?'

'There are three possible outcomes.' He held up his fingers. 'One, Kronos wins and we are dead. Two, the Titan doesn't succeed and Zeus and the Family and the Mother Goddess are victorious, and the worship of the gods remains. Or three, the Mother Goddess rules as supreme deity.'

'The restoration of Mother's worship is long-awaited.'

'Okay, then, we must survive this next stage of the quest and you have restored the objects at her tree to guarantee her succession as Supreme Goddess.' He wondered what the world would be like if the Mother Goddess became the overarching deity. No person persecuted or vilified for their beliefs, no crusades, wars or acts of terrorism in the name of God. *If only we can change human nature.*

CHAPTER 54

E van continued to ruminate on the probable succession of
the Mother Goddess as supreme deity. Zeus and the
Olympian gods were too fractious and selfish; the world needed a
benevolent immortal who unified all humans regardless of faith.

'Evandros! You walked past Mother's image.' The High
Priestess veered north-west.

He berated himself and sidestepped a shallow pit, catching up
with her within a few easy strides. They approached a line of
cypress trees, interspersed with pine and plane trees. Beyond the
forest was a stream. The skin on his arms tingled as they entered
the cool canopy of the woodland and he felt the change in
temperature. Or was it something else? He shrugged off the sense
of dread and inspected the dense forest. The thick cluster of
trunks added to his foreboding.

'What is it?' he asked when she stopped. They had been
walking for twenty minutes, following the waterway, the sacred
forest not yet in sight.

She gestured at the treetops.

'Not again.'

Birds had halted mid-flight and the leaves on the trees were motionless.

'What do you mean?'

'The same happened when Kronos paid me a visit during our investigation of the communication device, except you are awake. He rendered the others unconscious.' He studied the skyline, circling on the spot. 'I don't like this.'

'I am not sure who you were expecting, but is that how you greet an ally?'

They spun around.

'Eris!' The High Priestess' jaw tightened. 'Are you here to inflict another of your elixirs upon me?'

The Goddess of Discord chortled and floated over the river, Ekhidna slithering alongside her. 'My dear, if I was here to induce complications, I would have already done so.' She stepped onto the embankment, her khiton dry. 'I thought it was best to address you in person as you had refused Ekhidna's service.' She stroked the dark tendrils of the she-serpent.

'We don't need or want your help.' He jutted his chin at her. 'Your interference set our voyage back by months.'

'You should be grateful I intervened and not Kronos. If he had, you would be dead.' She cocked her head and eyeballed him. 'Apart from yourselves, the others are expendable.'

'Not to me.'

'What is it you want?' the High Priestess asked. 'Why are you here?'

'Kronos has … reneged on his promise to me, and I have learnt my plight lies with that of the other immortals.'

He barked out laughing. 'And you desire revenge now?'

Eris' golden eyes glittered. 'I prefer retribution. The Titan is under the assumption that we are still working together, and I am generating obstacles to thwart your success.'

'Your unexpected presence and flimsy explanation don't instil a great deal of confidence,' he said in a frosty tone.

'This is why I am here.' Eris sidled closer to the High Priestess. 'Do not attempt to deploy the objects against me. You will fail.' She studied him. 'He is wary of you, for you are most unusual, and he finds that puzzling. Kronos intends to execute you to get the icons, and I am here to ward off your demise.'

'Don't Zeus and the immortals plan to stop Kronos?' A chill slithered up his spine.

The goddess nodded. 'Yes, that is their intent. However, Kronos is wily and bitter. He means to destroy his children and neither you nor the High Priestess with her trinkets can stop him.' She plucked at an invisible strand of thread on her gown. 'No one except me.'

'What makes you certain you can defeat Kronos?' he asked.

'He does not enjoy the existence of my dear companions.' She stroked Ekhidna's hair. 'They repulse him and he intends to banish them when he wins, and I cannot permit that to happen.' She shifted her attention back to them. 'My pets were my only source of comfort during my time in Tartaros, and I intend to use my power to prevent them from being harmed or exiled.'

'Your motivation has zilch to do with the possibility of dying along with the other immortals.' His brow arched.

'Of course it does,' she snapped. 'I do not enjoy being threatened and no one, including the Titan, is ruining my destiny.'

'How do you propose to protect us?' asked Alexina.

'To preserve the current situation, I cannot remain with you. Instead, Ekhidna is here to escort you where you must go and back to the beach.'

'A sound but foolhardy tactic,' he said. Eris stiffened. 'Won't Kronos find out you've switched allegiances when he sees Ekhidna with us?'

She gave him a smug smile. 'No. The simplicity of this strategy is he thinks she has captured you and is surrendering you to him.'

'I am not convinced by this idea of yours, nor do I trust you.' Evan replied, his tone flinty.

The goddess sniffed. 'Why are mortals so distrustful?'

'Gee … could it be that you lot are narcissistic, egotistical, arrogant and malicious beings?'

'Evandros! You are speaking to a goddess.' The High Priestess was aghast.

'He is right,' said Eris, shrugging, 'and I am here for selfish reasons. If I wanted you dead, you would be, except I do not. Whether my desire to safeguard assures you does not matter. I guarantee you no harm.'

'Don't make promises you cannot keep.' Evan aimed the labrys at her. 'Nobody can make such claims.' He deliberated for a few moments. 'This alliance is on fragile ground, and if you or your pet break your word, I'll destroy you.'

CHAPTER 55

They pressed on along the low-flowing stream, Ekhidna trailing them, rocks smoothed by the endless passage of water currents. Evan stopped for a drink. The cool, crisp, clear liquid diminished the heat of his body as it coursed down his throat and into his gut. He peeked over at the High Priestess, who stood a few feet away, waiting.

'Best you have some too—could be our last.'

She tapped her foot on the ground. 'Then we should hurry to avoid that possibility.'

'It won't make a difference, I guess, whatever the outcome.' He stood. 'How far is the tree?'

'On that incline.' She pointed a hundred metres west of their current location.

'Lead on.'

She set off, their unconventional protector slithering beside them. Evan wrung his hands on the labrys, glancing one way and then the other.

'What is the matter?' she asked. 'Your head is flitting about like a bird.'

'Don't you feel that … weirdness?'

'Weirdness? I am not sensing anything unusual.'

'The nothingness is unnatural.' He indicated at the pines and holly oak trees, and at the shrubs and flowers festooned in white, yellow and pink dispersed as ground cover. 'Where are the bees, birds and animals? It is too quiet.'

She inspected the surrounds, hesitated and said in a muted tone, 'Our new companion could be the reason.'

'Possibly.' He scratched the back of his neck, trying to ignore the uncomfortable sensation that was rising within.

They deviated from the river and climbed westward, the ascent getting steeper. His ears twitched at the noiseless habitat. He didn't accept that Ekhidna's presence caused the eerie absence of animals and insects. It felt more preternatural. Not the same as when Kronos or the Goddess of Discord revealed themselves. He repositioned his grip on the handle of the axe. He could feel the weight of Alexina's gaze on him.

'Not much farther to go.' He took in the vista they were approaching. 'I don't see how we find Mother's tree. How do you recognise which one it is?'

'It will unveil itself when necessary.'

He came to a standstill. 'Is the tree there or not?'

'It is there,' she replied, not slowing, 'and it is expecting our arrival.'

Evan muttered under his breath and trotted after her. Ekhidna slithered ahead as they crested the hill.

'What does she know that we don't?' he asked, glimpsing the tail end of the she-serpent disappear into the shadows of the shrubs.

'They would not need us if Ekhidna knew where or how to find Mother's tree.'

'Good point. Are there markings on that boulder?' He started towards a large rock.

She joined him. 'There are faint etchings in the rock.'

He squatted and rubbed his fingers over it, feeling the semi-scoured depression on the hard surface. 'It's eroded and smoothed over from years of weathering. I haven't enough water to wet it to see the etching.'

'I recognise what it is,' she said. 'It's an image of Mother.'

He leaned closer. 'I'll take your word for it,' he said and straightened. 'Which path do we take?'

She checked from the boulder to the tree line of the woodlands. 'There is a canopy forming a passage between those trees.'

He gaped at the unique formation of plane trees as they grew in parallel lines, the upper limbs and leaves creating a shelter. 'I've seen nothing like it.'

Ekhidna slithered back alongside them as they walked towards the tunnel of trees.

'Halt!' The serpent sped across and blocked them from continuing.

'What's wrong?' He stepped in front of the High Priestess, holding the axe in readiness.

'It is the Titan—he is nearby.'

'Is he in the forest?' Evan searched the foliage ahead.

'No.'

'Where is he?'

'He is waiting for you to enter the realm of Gaia, and then he'll materialise.'

'I'm not surprised,' he said. 'What I can't work out is why you aren't allowing us to proceed.'

'My mistress instructs that you leave the labrys behind.'

'No. I'm not giving up this weapon.'

Ekhidna raised herself and towered over them, swaying from side to side. 'The Titan will not accept you are my mistress' captives.'

'It is possible Kronos already knows of Eris' deceit. If he is as powerful as your mistress and the other gods suggest, then this whole pretence is futile.' He scoffed.

'Perhaps the Dark Master does not see everything,' the High Priestess said, gazing at Ekhidna with a thoughtful expression. 'Consider how he called for the Goddess of Discord and her companions to interfere and never announced himself throughout our expedition.'

'He did present himself to me,' he said, sceptical of her reasoning.

'Yes, but only that single time.' Her eyes sparkled. 'Why didn't he make himself known when we travelled to Aegyptos, or when we reached Pylos?'

'The harpies attacked us in Egypt.' He paused and then added, 'And he sent Melaina when we landed at Pylos.'

'Yes! The Dark Master sent substitutes in his place. He needed them to learn of our progress.'

Evan pursed his lips. 'Kronos knew where we were, and that is how he could disrupt and hinder our search.'

'No, that is what he wants us to believe.' The passion in her voice grew. 'The Dark Master has a flaw; he uses and needs these individuals. They are his vessels to our world.'

'Not so sure about that. He is a Titan,' he said, 'and the old gods had significant powers. Do you know why the war between the Titans and Olympian gods lasted ten years? It was trickery and subterfuge that helped the younger gods win.'

'Not so. The Dark Master and the Titans lost because of their inability to react to the strategies Divine Zeus and the immortals used to combat them. The Titans' lack of ingenuity and innate skills to improvise doomed them, and they instead relied on their brutality and strength.' Her cheeks flushed in excitement. 'The Dark Master cannot and never could see and hear all. He does not possess the capability to do so. The Olympians harness significant power and are all-seeing and hearing.'

'Granted, the Titans used brawn and were ferocious, but we shouldn't underestimate Kronos. If Zeus had not had the help of the hundred-handed monster to challenge the Titans, the world today would be very different.' Evan nodded with certainty. 'No, the old god is much more treacherous than you realise, and it is unwise to speculate that he doesn't know what is happening right now. We need to be more cautious. I don't trust him. He is capable of devious actions.'

'I agree he is unscrupulous and no doubt would kill us to gain Mother's sacred objects, but he can only amass information by using others.'

'Then tell me, how did he find out we were on the island with the communication devices? We did not encounter any of Eris' "pets" after leaving the Isle of Hephaistos; in fact, our progress was free of disruptions,' Evan contended. 'He is clever and ruthless, and I expect he has had a plan since being incarcerated in Tartaros. He's had time to conceptualise, revise, work out every conceivable issue and devise a solution if a problem arose.' He hoisted the labrys onto his shoulder.

'I disagree. The Dark Master does not know everything we do.'

'Nor do our patrons. That is why you use the white light to shroud us,' he pointed out.

She started towards the dense forest. 'You are not willing to leave behind the labrys?'

'Ekhidna is escorting us, and despite my being well armed, that suggests that my two weapons are ineffective against a being with magical abilities.' He narrowed his eyes at the serpent. 'Just so you are aware, I killed the Minotaur with this.' And he brandished the labrys at her.

CHAPTER 56

E van and the High Priestess entered the forest, Ekhidna slithering at their heels. The density of the woods reminded him of the enclosed copse at Plato's Academia. It felt like ages ago that they had been in Athens, as if years had passed from the time they'd met the famous philosopher when in fact it had been seven months since they'd left the port of Piraeus. A great deal had happened since, following their departure from the Hellenic city and their belated arrival on Krete.

A twig snapped under his sandalled foot, the undergrowth crunching with each step. He was wary of their serpent sentinel, her large sinuous body ever present, and he did not doubt that despite her ponderous movement, she could strike fast, before anyone reacted. The leaves overhead rustled, the evergreen canopy swaying in the wind, beams of sunlight fighting to beat their way through. He stepped into the small patch of sunshine, the rays caressing his arms with their warmth and then receding as quick as they'd surfaced, blocked by the dense canopy. The temperature dipped, akin to the ebb and flow of the tide, a battle between sunshine and the screening of the trees.

A rich scent of loam and pine filled his lungs each time he inhaled. The myriad of sounds, smells and sights, accosted every cell in his body. On the single occasion when he'd returned to the twenty-first century, although briefly, the textures of his bedsheets, the fluffiness of the towels and the smell of cooking breakfast had been real as the woodlands. Not for the first time, he wondered if the human brain could conjure places, people and experiences in such explicit detail where it couldn't distinguish between reality and fiction. An extraordinary organ that was masterful, yet mysterious. A person could heal ailments with their mind, train their thoughts to transform and create new lives. Was that what his mind did? To what purpose, and why this era?

His "father," Zeus, had stated that they had redeployed him to the future to learn about the history of the world, and when thrust into his distant past, he was to prevent the birth and rise of the Messiah. Evan's recollection of this ancient period came from what he had learnt from books and education; and now he understood, after his confrontation with Zeus and the Mother Goddess, the ease with which he wielded a sword and brandished a shield. He flinched, remembering the sharpness of the blade piercing his ribcage during the brawl with the brigands. The gaping wound, feeling cold and hot, dark red blood, his blood, spilling onto the ground. He couldn't or wouldn't forget the feeling of losing consciousness as his life drained away.

Then there was the woman at his side, his sister. But his "real" younger sister had died young from cancer. She was nothing like the High Priestess, of whom he had no memory, nor did he remember the other Atlanteans, including his half-brother Homer. His thoughts moved to Antioche. Could he deny her existence, or that of his newborn babies?

'Evandros! Watch out for the tree!'

'Wha …' He stuttered to a stop, seeing the large oak that had fallen across the path. 'Right … thanks.'

'You need to be more attentive. We are nearing Mother's tree. An attack is imminent,' she warned him.

'I'll be more observant.' He approached the waist-high log. A silvery-green leafy plant with pale pink flowers sprouted along the span, entwined with ivy, the blackberries a stark contrast against the grey tree trunk. 'We have to climb over it.' He held out a hand. 'I'll help you ... if you wish.'

The High Priestess reached for his hand. The smooth softness of her skin contrasted his callused and weathered palm, epitomising the dichotomy of their relationship. He took stock of the height of the fallen tree and the khiton she was wearing.

'I am going to have to lift you.'

'I will jump over it.' She tugged her hand from his, folded the hem at her waist and secured it with the sash. She took a few paces and bolted towards the log, somersaulted and landed on the other side. She grinned at him, making her appear more youthful and carefree. He gawked at her. 'You forget, I was the champion bull-leaper for two years running.'

Ekhidna smirked and glided over the obstacle and waited with the High Priestess on the other side.

'Come, Evandros.' The High Priestess untied the sash, her khiton falling to its full length. She arched a brow at him. 'It will be nightfall before we return to the beach the way you delay.'

'Right.' He leapt over the log and they continued walking, following an old overgrown path that wove between saplings and ancient trees. Evan reached out to pat a trunk and the tips of his fingers tingled, the bark warm.

'The tree trunks are getting bigger the deeper we go.' He ran a hand over the thick and scaly bark of another. 'They are old. Check out that grand old masterpiece!' He pointed. 'It'll take five or more people holding hands to stand around it. I'm surprised the forest is still here.'

'This forest is sacrosanct to Mother, and it is forbidden to enter or chop down a tree.'

'For now that is true, but forests this dense won't last long, not with the constancy of development and the growing population. This will all be deforested and the timber used ...' He came to a standstill.

'Never! This is the most hallowed place on earth, and Mother allows none to enter the realm.' She stood with hands on hips. 'Not all may enter Mother's domain, only those who ... are you listening to me?'

'Is that the tree we're seeking?'

She beamed. 'Yes, that is her tree.' She scurried over.

'I've never seen trees do that.'

The trees were interlinked, forming nature's version of a plait. One was an oak, one an olive, and completing the triumvirate was a frankincense tree. The combined circumference would require twenty people to encircle it, perhaps more.

'Oh, there's the Lygos tree. The flowers have a medicinal use for women, and other matters,' she said. 'I shall harvest them. They will help Antioche in the days to come.'

He drew nearer, observing how the oak tree was at the centre with the others embracing it. 'Are they sentinels, protecting the oak?' he asked, reaching out, fingertips hovering within centimetres of the entangled trunks.

She rushed over, slapping his hand. 'Do not! Only the High Priestess may touch the sacred tree. I first must recite a welcome to Mother before I reconcile the divine objects.'

Evan eyed it with circumspection. 'What happens if I do? Will I vanish into the ether, writhe in pain, or is the prohibition more about scaring interlopers and villagers with the threat of death and damnation, a story fabricated to strike fear?' He examined how the limbs and leaves spread across each other to form a massive umbrella.

The root system of each tree intermingled, a marriage fed from the nurturing earth and energy from the sun, strengthening its union. 'With the rise of Christianity, the so-called righteous threatened the poor and most vulnerable in their societies with stories of a vengeful god to frighten them into submission and coercion, or be cast into the fire or water to die.' He stepped closer to the trees. 'Masses died, innocent folk, because of fanatical and corrupt individuals who distorted the message preached by the coming Messiah.' He bowed his head and placed his palms where the trunks intertwined.

'Evandros! Stop!'

A blue light filtered through his fingers and flowed up his arm, over his shoulder, and engulfed him. His skin throbbed. The corrugated lines of the trunk warmed his hands and pulsated as if it had a heartbeat.

Of course its heart beats, for it eats and breathes and lives, as do you, Evandros. Now let my daughter complete her duty. Kronos waits for her to open my womb, and that is when he will attack, when we are at our most vulnerable. Prevent him from entering.

Evan pulled away, the blue light gone. He said to the High Priestess in subdued reverence, 'She is here and so is Kronos.'

CHAPTER 57

The High Priestess remained as motionless as a statue. Evan stepped away from the tree and clicked his fingers in front of her face. At first, she did not respond. He called out to her, and she reacted.

'Did you hear me? Kronos is here.'

'How are you not harmed?' she asked, staring at him, stunned. 'No person lived after touching Mother's sacred tree.' She frowned and checked him over. 'Do you feel any pain?'

'Nope.' He then asked, 'What makes you sure that someone would be injured or die if they did? Have you seen it happen? Perhaps if it fell on somebody, then yes, they'd be crushed or killed.'

'No, I have not seen someone die from coming into contact with Mother's tree. They do not need to be told. We learn from childhood the danger of doing so. It is obvious you have forgotten that lesson,' she commented, pursing her lips.

He spread out his arms. 'Nothing happened. I am alive and breathing. Another story fabricated to prevent anyone from learning of its location—that is how deceptive and inaccurate information spreads. Create enough fear and it becomes superstition, and attached to the stories are the tragedies that befall a person if they refuse to comply.' He spoke to Ekhidna. 'Go ahead, touch it.'

The serpent, alarmed, shook her head and slunk away. 'I cannot—it is forbidden. Not even my mistress would cross paths with the Titaness.'

He rounded on the High Priestess in disgust. 'Alexina, perform whatever rituals you must, or we'll have company before you know it. Ekhidna, stand guard over there'—he pointed to the other side of the gnarled and conjoined trees—'and kill anyone who approaches.' Evan headed in the opposite direction and came to a standstill at the timbre of her voice, sonorous in the forest's tranquillity as she recited a litany.

'I call upon Gaia, the beautiful and fair, to rise. O Goddess, mother to all gods and mortals, who brings forth bountiful fruits and flowers, and anchors the eternal world in our own. Come, Great Earth Mother, hear the prayers of your children. We welcome your guidance and grace, for you are Gaia, Mother of All.'

She lifted her arms, took two steps forward, two to the side and two backwards, swung right and then left, all the while humming. Evan then realised she was dancing and that he was witnessing a long-forgotten ritual, lost throughout history. The High Priestess repeated the steps in reverse, the leaves rustling in unison. She increased the tempo of the dance steps, becoming frenzied, twirling one way and then the other. She then came to an abrupt stop, chest heaving, brow moist and wisps of damp hair clinging to the sides of her cheeks. He scoped out the forest and looked up at the treetops. All was still. She clapped her hands for two rapid beats, swayed from side to side, arms outstretched, and clapped again.

'Great Earth Mother, we await your awakening.'

He shifted from foot to foot, the quietude paralysing. The log wobbled and rocked.

'What the heck?' He felt the ground tremble.

The ground quaked, and a crash reverberated like cars colliding, transforming the forest into a demolition derby. The High Priestess pressed her hands against the tree trunk. Neon-white light broke through the seams between the sacred trees. He dropped the labrys to shield his eyes.

'Holy crap!'

He skipped to avoid the blade as it fell millimetres from slicing off his big toe, then lifted an arm as luminescent rays beamed from the core of the trees. Evan scrunched his eyes tight, but the incandescence penetrated his eyelids. Black spots filled his vision, and he stumbled, tripping over a fallen limb. He teetered on his feet, trying to regain his balance. The blindness faded, and he could detect the outline of shapes. He stooped to pick up the labrys and shuffled towards the gaping fissure.

'That is a womb?' He ogled. The trees had peeled away like the skin of a banana, the cavity beyond a dark yawning pit. 'Wait! Where are you going?' He reached out to her.

Evan blanched. Her eyes radiated the same whiteness that emanated from within the trees. 'You are to remain here.' She departed into the void.

'Sure ... I'll wait here and guard the area.' He kicked at the pebbles, scattering them in front of him, then swung the labrys back and forth like a pendulum. 'What now? Is there any reason for me to stay?' The momentum of the axe slowed, then increased with the speed of his thoughts. 'Nope. No incentive. I've plenty of ideas to keep me busy for the next ten years. That is where I belong, not here, chased by weird-arsed creatures and beings with an identity complex. No, I am done with all this nonsense.'

'What about Antioche and your babies?'

He whirled around, brandishing the double-headed axe. 'Who said that?' he asked Ekhidna. 'Did you say something?'

The she-serpent stared at him, bewildered. 'No, what would I say?'

He regarded her for a moment longer and then surveyed the bowels of the wooded dell. He started at the sound of a faint crackle and crunch of leaves and sticks. Evan pulled his sword from its scabbard and swung both weapons towards the sound.

'An honourable man would not leave his children fatherless.'

'Who's there?' he demanded, tramping over the gnarly roots.

There was an audible sigh of disapproval.

'Come out and show yourself.' From his periphery, he detected Ekhidna. 'There is someone here.' He pivoted and called out, 'I've no time for games.'

'I am not here to play games, dear Evandros, I am here to collect.'

His eyes narrowed. 'And here I thought you were stuck with Apollo.'

A form shimmered near the fallen log and solidified. 'He tricked me into his little realm, but I managed to escape.' Melaina sneered at Ekhidna and dismissed her with a loud sniff. 'Your choice of female companionship is questionable, and with a creature of such disreputable note. You disappoint me, Evandros.'

'I can only try.'

Melaina's face rippled with hatred.

'What do you want?' His ice-blue eyes matched his frosty tone.

'I've come to collect what I am owed.'

'Which is what?'

'*You.*' She flew through the open space, arms outstretched, screeching like a mad Ker, the fanged and taloned female spirits.

He sprang backwards, rolled his ankle and fell.

Ekhidna soared from behind, casting a shadow over him, and careened into the raging immortal like a missile. The serpent coiled her body around the goddess and squeezed. Melaina screamed and shouted, spittle spraying everywhere. Evan scrambled to his feet, wincing as he hobbled over to them.

'What can I do to help?' he asked Ekhidna.

'You pitiful mortal, you have no power over me!' she howled as Ekhidna's serpentine body constricted tighter.

'Ekhidna here is doing rather well without my help, but thought I should ask.' He squatted, his pupils dilating until they became inky. 'I have killed the Minotaur with this labrys, and I have no hesitation about using it again.'

'I am immortal, you cannot kill me!' she shrieked, struggling against the serpent's muscled body.

'Shall we put that theory to the test?' He stood, grasped the labrys with both hands and lifted it overhead.

Melaina screamed.

'Evandros, killing an immortal is not a straightforward task, not even for you, who have slain the Minotaur.'

'I wondered when you'd show yourself.'

'Let us converse, but first, lower your weapon.'

He scoffed. 'No.'

'How dare you answer no! To my father and the gods of gods!' Melaina shrilled, trying to loosen Ekhidna's binds.

'Desist, daughter,' Kronos ordered, giving her a disdainful sneer. 'I shall cast my offspring far from here if you instruct the creature to release her.'

'What's in it for me if I ask Ekhidna to let your daughter go?'

'I can promise your offspring and their mother will remain free from harm, and I will punish those who act against my commands.' Evan took note of how unsympathetic and callous the Titan was towards the entrapped goddess.

'I'll hold you to your word,' he said, lowering the axe. 'Ekhidna, release her.'

Melaina launched herself at him as soon as she was released.

Kronos, with a click of his fingers, launched the goddess into the air; she passed from sight into the horizon and in the direction of Egypt.

'Faaatherrrr!'

CHAPTER 58

'I should thank you, I guess,' Evan said, though it came out more as a question. 'I suppose you are here to collect as well.'

'Do you have the items?' Kronos asked. His golden irises glinted from within the shadowed cowl of his cape.

'No.' Evan hoisted the labrys onto his shoulder. 'The High Priestess is the only person who can wield the items, and I've seen what happens when a person tries to take possession.' He quailed. 'It's a dreadful way to die.'

The Titan peered behind him. 'Where is the High Priestess?'

'She left to commune with the Mother Goddess.'

Kronos' eyes blazed. 'Do not mention that treacherous scourge in my presence.'

Evan twirled the axe. 'Doesn't change the fact that the High Priestess isn't here and neither are the objects.'

'Have you decided on the offer I proposed?'

'It is a very tempting proposition.' He circled around Ekhidna to stand near the tree. 'And I gave it considerable thought.' He clasped his chin. 'I've a few questions.'

'What are they?'

'The Minotaur should have killed me but didn't,' he replied. 'It wasn't an easy fight, and he injured Homer. However, for the considerable strength and power he possessed, the Minotaur was reticent. I sense you had a part in this and am asking why.'

Kronos clasped his hands inside the folds of his cloak. 'I offered him the sacrifice of flesh.'

'That makes little sense, given that he is dead.'

'How many of your companions died before you entered the labyrinth and took the Minotaur's life?'

Evan clenched his hands. 'You orchestrated it to happen this way? To what end? Those people had lives, families.'

'It is necessary to cleanse the world of all ills, and those who died have contributed their lives for the betterment of an improved empire.'

Evan shuddered. 'I demand assurances for my companions— that they are given the same benefits you've granted me,' he said, 'and that you do not harm them and they live a comfortable existence. That includes Antioche and the twins.'

The Dark Master bowed his head, tapping his mouth with a scarred finger.

Evan stretched in the direction of the gaping hole and strained to hear voices or for a patter of feet. 'Why now?' He straightened, not hearing anything.

'What are you asking?'

'Why are you planning to overthrow Zeus and the other immortals and summoning a new god here and now, instead of, say, in the next few centuries?' He craned his neck, checking once again for movement inside the trinity of trees.

'What does it matter to you?' Kronos tensed. 'I need not explain myself to anyone, and certainly not to an inferior mortal.' He grunted when Evan bent to the side. 'What are you doing?'

'The muscles in my shoulders are tight from lugging this axe, and stretching helps.' He shifted the labrys, relieving the pressure.

'No, of course you don't need to tell me, a lesser mortal as you've stipulated, why. A word of caution: it is not fitting for the "father of the Messiah" to be disdainful of humans, or your surrogate worshippers will revolt. Best to reconsider the way you think of us, or the revolution will happen before your son's first birthday, and I know you don't want that to occur.'

Kronos bristled and rocked back and forth on his feet. 'As a chosen mortal, your purpose is not to challenge but to be obeisant, ensure the security of my offspring and spread the message of his teachings.'

'Hmmm ...' Evan clicked his tongue. 'I am not good at following orders. I make my own decisions based on what I've learnt rather than being told what to do. I am sure if you chatted with Zeus, he'd attest to how difficult I am.' He then slapped his forehead, eyes wide in mock horror. 'How senseless of me—you and Zeus are not on speaking terms.'

'You have opted to perish.'

'We all die, even you. Your time on earth is over.'

Kronos laughed. 'Do you expect Zeus and his contemptible siblings to come to your aid? I have shaped a net and trapped them over this island, and they cannot escape.'

'Clever,' Evan praised. 'Though I have not sided with Zeus either.' He beckoned Ekhidna with a finger while continuing to draw Kronos into an argument.

'You fool! You swore allegiance to that ... that ... deceitful Titaness! Her perfidious nature sentences you to death.'

'You've already mentioned that. How I see it, it matters not who I side with. My existence is in jeopardy no matter what I do, so I've cast my dice with the Mother Goddess.'

'You could have lived an eternity as a king, and you elected to forfeit riches and immortality in favour of a wretched female! You mortals are unworthy and deserve the calamities that come to pass to such miserable beings.'

'No reason to get personal, Kronos. We humans are resilient and resourceful, which is why when the time comes, you and your kind cease to influence what we say or do.' He caught Ekhidna's slight manoeuvre to the Titan's rear and nodded.

Kronos growled. 'Your impertinence is unacceptable ...'

'One of my better gifts'—he smiled—'and it's helped me throughout this laborious ordeal.' He examined the blade. 'My friend Ekhidna and I believe you should leave for your own safety, as we can't be accountable for the actions of Zeus and the Family. Who knows how they might react?'

'I entrapped them! Only I can release them from the net!' Kronos spat.

'I wouldn't be too cocky about that.' He signalled behind him.

Kronos twisted about and gawked. Zeus, Poseidon and Hades led Olympian gods into the clearing. 'What ... how ...?' He stopped. '*You* released them!'

Eris weaved through to the fore, positioning herself alongside Zeus. 'Yes. We'—she gestured at the younger gods—'have a common interest, and the terms are much more agreeable than in our former union.'

'You have made a fatal mistake,' he rumbled.

'I did, with you,' the Goddess of Discord replied in contempt.

Kronos lifted a scarred arm, and a flaming orb materialised above his palm. Evan dashed forward and leapt into the air, swinging the axe. Kronos howled, flinging his head back, clutching his limb. A dark yellow fluid gushed from the stumps of his fingers, the severed digits twitching at his feet. He roared and struck Evan, the blow catapulting him backwards. Evan hit the trunks with a heavy thud. He lay unmoving. A bright white beam radiated from the centre of the trees and a tall, statuesque figure emerged, accompanied by a smaller form.

He moaned as the brilliant radiance enveloped him.

'Five more minutes and I'll get up,' he mumbled, blocking the glare with an arm.

'Evandros, you must rise.'

'Sheesh, five minutes' extra sleep, that's all I'm asking.' He propped himself on an elbow, shielding his eyes. 'Can't you switch off the light? It's too damn bright!'

Kronos chortled. 'Your champion is a blithering idiot.'

A hand touched his head. He flinched, slapping it away. 'Hey, off with you!' He heard a murmur and felt warmth radiate from their hand against his skin. He baulked and twisted away.

'Evandros, it is me, Alexina, your sister.'

'Huh? I don't have a sister called Alexina, her name is ...' He halted, his mind drawing a blank. He panicked—he could not remember what she looked like. 'Oh, dear gods, I've forgotten. What a shameful brother I am.' His stomach gurgled and face grew cold. 'I ... I ... uh ...' His eyes rolled and he blacked out.

CHAPTER 59

E van stirred and grimaced. Something rock-hard poked him in the spine, in the neck and across his shoulders.

'What the hell …?' His head was throbbing as if squeezed in a vice. He pressed the base of his palm against his forehead, relieving a little of the pain. His mouth watered and bile rose. It reminded him of the few times he had drunk too much, which never ended well. He gulped for oxygen; his stomach roiled, the saliva increased. He swung to the side and vomited.

'Evandros!' The High Priestess held him as he purged. He sagged, staring open-mouthed and glassy-eyed at her.

'Alexina?'

Kronos sniffed, lip curling. 'Weak and inferior beings.'

She pressed a cool hand against his forehead and said to the luminous figure in the aperture of the three trees, 'He has a fever and his skin is clammy.' She flinched, seeing blood on her palm.

Sweat soaked his khiton, clinging to his chest. He wheezed, unable to breathe. The ethereal being engulfed them in a white aura. He squeezed his eyes shut. The brilliant bright light cooled his fevered body. He recognised the gentle touch on his chest and his eyes popped open.

'Can I go home now? I have done everything you've asked.'

'Soon, Evandros. Before you leave, there is one more task you must complete.' The glowing figure cradled him like a baby. She covered his lips with hers, and a faint gold aura enveloped them. The two bodies shimmered as one, and then the nimbus dimmed. The Mother Goddess and Evan stood together. He had never felt so clear-headed and calm. The High Priestess joined them.

The Dark Master circled behind the log; Zeus and the gods closed in. Kronos stuck out his hand. 'Give me the figurine and talismans.'

Zeus snarled. 'Not now, not ever. Tartaros awaits your incarceration. There you will forever lament your failure to win, and there you shall languish, a forgotten old god of no importance.'

'That is thoughtful of you but not essential,' Kronos said in a mild tone, 'as I won't be going back to Tartaros.'

The God of War chortled. 'How do you propose to escape? You are alone, we are many.'

Kronos tossed his head at Ares and sneered at the Mother Goddess. 'Your misbegotten children are spouting senseless diatribe, and I have little patience for trite games. Give me the spurious objects.'

Ares' face grew thunderous. 'You irascible, ineffective and blithering—'

'Ares,' Zeus intervened, 'Kronos knows he cannot defeat us. Do not react to his clumsy attempts at diversion. Evandros, come.'

Evan sought out the Mother Goddess for affirmation. She nodded. He avoided the thick roots that spread out like the tendrils of an octopus, and weaved in and out between the immortals. Their power and aura emanated from them like the first electrical storm of the winter season, with a sweet, pungent zing. The austere stance of the Pantheon of Gods made the atmosphere bristle with unspoken violence. *This won't end well*, he thought.

'Are you going to set this pitiful mortal … against me?' Kronos barked, doubling over in laughter. 'Did you not see how I battered him senseless with scant force?'

'You forget, Evandros is of my blood and possesses both the strength and the virility of an immortal,' Zeus said.

Kronos' golden visage darkened and his voice lowered. 'Then his death is of your doing.'

'Not his death—his rebirth is of your machinations,' said Zeus. Poseidon and Hades moved behind Evan. They towered head and shoulders over him, making him feel short for the first time in his life. He had always been the tallest in class, through school to university, but his height was more noticeable when he interacted with the Phoenicians who had rescued him from the shipwreck and befriended Phameas. The Egyptians, when he and his companions had travelled through Egypt to locate the golden serpent, weren't tall and neither were the Greeks, Evan having met the philosopher Plato after arriving in Athens.

'Rebirth?' The Titan thrust his chin at Zeus.

Zeus nodded. 'Evandros was reborn and created with power, knowledge and skills no ordinary mortal possesses, a unique composite engineered with incomparable and extraordinary talents to prevent your treachery against all immortals.'

'I brought him to his knees with a single blow,' Kronos said with disdain. 'He cannot injure me any more than you or your infantile siblings. No one can hurt me.'

'That is not entirely true.' Eris sashayed to the fore with her companion, Ekhidna. Kronos hissed and bared his teeth, stark white against the shadowed cowl. She smirked. 'While you may deplore my erstwhile associates, you are frightened of them.'

'No, not frightened, disgusted by them and their contemptible natures,' he spat. 'They are unworthy and must be destroyed.'

Ekhidna bared her fangs and launched herself at him.

'No!' Eris screamed. Zeus restrained her as the serpent wrestled with the Titan. He snapped Ekhidna's neck and tossed her limp serpentine coils at the goddess' feet.

'That is what I intend to do to all the misaligned and aberrant monsters that traverse these hallowed grounds.'

Eris collapsed to her knees and stroked the dead she-serpent's brow. Her jaw hardened, and she stated in a cold, steely voice, 'I am ready.'

'As am I.' Ares whacked the blade of his sword against his shield.

'I am ready,' Hera and Demeter chimed.

'We are ready,' echoed the others, striding forward.

Evan lowered his chin, clasping the labrys tight, and understood what he had to do. 'I am prepared to finish my task.'

Kronos edged closer to the log. 'What fools. You are no challenge for a Titan, not one as powerful as I.'

He lifted the log and hurled it at them. Evan took in a sharp breath as the large projectile rushed headlong towards them. He detected a draft and a shift in the air, making his hair rustle, the log barrelling closer. He swung the axe and cleaved the thick trunk in half. The pieces splintered and transformed into sawdust, showering him and Zeus. A blue nimbus shrouded him as he levelled the weapon at Kronos.

The Titan seized the nearest tree, uprooting it, and flung it at him. Evan whacked the timber, reducing it to powder. Kronos ripped out more trees and lobbed them at him. Protected by the blue aura, he deflected each missile without missing a beat. Kronos continued his attack, oblivious to the younger gods as they encircled him. In desperation, the Titan picked up a boulder, comparable in size to the monolithic blocks found at the citadel of Mykenae. Evan did not flinch, striking the cyclopean rock. Sparks ignited, rendering the stone into tiny pebbles that rained over him and the gods.

'What trickery is this?' Kronos bellowed. 'Today, you die.' He dove, hands outstretched.

Evan braced for the impact. 'I'll take you with me.'

The Titan roared, fingers elongated, claw-like. Evan spun on his heel, twirling the axe. The blade whistled through the air and sliced through an appendage. Kronos howled, clutching his wrist, the severed hand quivering at his feet. He wheeled, his injured arm spewing golden blood, spraying Zeus, Poseidon and Hades. He walloped Evan, whose body arched into the air and landed with a thud. Evan lay dazed and winded. Glittering pinpoints filled his vision.

Zeus fired a bolt of lightning. Kronos ducked, the electric charge splintering a tree. He wheeled about, the cowl falling away to reveal his scarred face. Poseidon rammed his trident at him. A gale-force wind buffeted the old god, forcing him back. His feet skidded in the dirt, and he bared his teeth, his long grey hair billowing behind. He hooked an arm around a tree trunk and clung to it.

Hades pitched balls of fire. Kronos cast the blazing orbs into the forest, the scrub igniting in a firebomb. Evan cringed as wood exploded, the fire devouring the dry tinder. Athene and Zeus doused the ravaging flames with water. Kronos snarled at the gods as they closed in. Evan hurtled at him.

Kronos vaulted aside, but not quick enough. The blade sliced through his cloak, leaving a gaping hole. The Titan slammed into him. The two tumbled, Evan pinned beneath, the handle of the labrys pressing against his ribcage. He gritted his teeth and tried to force Kronos off, but the immortal was too strong. From the corner of his eye, he saw Poseidon take aim with his trident, water spewing from the prongs. Evan choked as he inhaled a mouthful of seawater. Kronos stuck his hand out, and the water crystallised and shattered on the ground, the shards cutting his skin.

'Stop!'

Evan saw the Mother Goddess approach with Alexina.

'Mother, we must rid ourselves of this harbinger of doom who intends to destroy us,' said Zeus, voice as cold as the Arctic pole.

She raised her hands. Deep crimson beams emanated from her fingers and engulfed Kronos. His torso arched and his head was thrown back. He squealed. The cords in his neck stuck out. Hephaistos limped over to drag Evan away, but Kronos dug his fingers into his biceps. Evan tried to shrink away from the scorching rays. He smelt skin burning. Before he realised what was happening, someone yanked him out from Kronos' clutches. An arrow speared the Titan's shoulder. Evan hobbled away, nursing his arm, and joined the High Priestess. Kronos, encased in the red light, convulsed, his writhing body sending plumes of dust and soil into the air and scattering leaves into a mini whirlwind.

The Mother Goddess loomed over him. 'You have engendered great turmoil and destruction in order to gain sovereignty over mortals and at the demise of our kind. Such betrayal cannot go unpunished.' She took the labrys from Zeus. With darkened pupils, the Mother Goddess addressed Evan. 'You have succeeded where no other could accomplish such feats, and for this you shall return home with my blessing. Leave now, and go back to those who are waiting for you.'

'What about him?' He poked his chin at Kronos, writhing on the ground.

Her temperament changed. 'He is mine to deal with. Your duty is done here.'

Evan shivered, grateful he was on the right side of the Titaness. As he and the High Priestess about-faced, he noted the gods formed an impenetrable circle around Kronos.

'What do you suppose they'll do to him?' he asked as they emerged from the forest.

'Eternal punishment.'

'Punished but not executed?'

A shrill resounded, the pebbles rolling and boulders quaking, the leafy canopies quivering. The howl of a pained animal continued, dissonant and strident.

He covered his ears. 'Great Mother ...'

The High Priestess, face impassive and hard-eyed, said, 'Best we do not linger.' Without another word, she marched on. He swallowed, the shrieks harrowing, and scampered after her.

CHAPTER 60

They crested the hill overlooking the coast, greeted by the red and orange hues of the setting sun. Diminutive figures dotted the coast, scurrying back and forth as ants forage. Small fires, tiny pinpricks to the eye, flickered a welcome beacon. Evan quickened his pace, impatient to see Antioche and the babies. It felt like a lifetime since they'd started out that morning, and between the elation he'd enjoyed at seeing the birth of his babies, and the subsequent battle with the Minotaur to the ugly confrontation with Kronos, it was the strangest day he had experienced.

'How is your arm?' she asked.

'It does hurt,' he admitted, inspecting the angry colour on his bicep.

'Perhaps the queen's healer can help ease the pain.'

'All I want to do is to eat and take a swim to rid myself of the stench of death.'

'It has been an arduous day fraught with peril and loss,' she agreed. 'Yes, swimming and food are comforting and restore normalcy; however, I suspect your increased urgency has another purpose.'

'Perhaps,' he said. 'What of you? Aren't you keen to see Leander? I'm certain he'll be relieved to see you.'

She grew thoughtful. 'I ... wish to greet Leander ...'

'But ...'

She averted her face. 'I am uncertain, after his exploits on the Isle of Hephaistos.'

'It wasn't his fault. We were all drugged, and no one was aware of what they were doing. Leander was devastated knowing he hurt you. He is a respectable man and wishes to make you happy, even if it means you do not want him in your life.' He flexed his arm and winced. 'Nothing is ever easy, but it is important to learn the lessons or deal with the consequences of our decisions.'

'Sage words, Evandros. Have you learnt your lessons?'

He pondered her question, torn between what his head wanted to do and the feelings he was experiencing regarding Antioche and the birth of their children. He wondered what would become of them when he left. 'I've a better understanding of some: not all is what it appears, you can't change fate, and when life gives you lemons, make lemonade.'

She asked, 'What is lemonade?'

'A beverage made from lemons.'

She grimaced. 'Wouldn't that be too tart to drink?'

'Not if you put a sweetener in it, such as honey.'

'Oh ... I do not quite understand what you mean.'

'I can't alter destiny or how people behave or the outcome of a situation, but I can change my thinking and attitude.'

'And what will that achieve?'

'I get to drink lemonade every day.'

They walked the next few minutes in silence, Evan lost in his thoughts, ruminating and torn.

'I would like to try the lemonade.'

He peeked across at her, noting her peaceful demeanour. 'I'm delighted for you and Leander—you both deserve happiness.'

'Haven't you earned the same joy?'

'I am content that everyone is safe and unharmed, free to fulfil their dreams. That is my lemonade.'

'Evandros, the Elders will accept your decision to remain with Antioche and your children. They are your reward after Sibyl's sacrifice.' She placed a hand on his forearm. 'She would tell you that your happiness is important to her, wherever it is and whomever it is with.'

He noticed Dexion, who was hovering near the path they had taken that morning.

'She was special, and devoted to you and the Mother Goddess.' He was all at once weary. 'Let's not talk about this again.'

'Phameas! Homer! It is Master Evandros and the High Priestess!'

Dexion sprinted towards them, with Lykeios loping alongside, tongue hanging out of his mouth. The boy flung himself at Evan, almost pitching him off his feet.

'Glad to see you too.' He smiled, wrapping an arm about Dexion's shoulders.

Phameas juddered to a halt, gasping, clasping his sides. He blew his cheeks out, turning to the High Priestess, his face crimson. She laughed and patted his hand.

'Dear Phameas, it is wonderful to see you too.'

The Phoenician, panting, bowed and beamed at her. 'We are so overjoyed you have come back alive!'

Evan tried to walk, but Dexion's grip around his waist prevented him. 'So are we.'

Homer moved at a slower gait, clasping his side, grinning at them. He embraced them. Evan winced.

'So pleased you are up and walking, Homer. We were

concerned about you after the Minotaur walloped you,' he said when Homer let them go.

'Queen Antioche ordered her physician to treat Homer and Hektor as soon as we arrived.' Phameas rocked on his heels. 'She waited until they responded to the medicines before asking what happened and where you were. She asked to be informed of your return.' He then gave the High Priestess a warm grin. 'Leander is waiting for you too. He's been fretting since leaving you.'

'I wouldn't mind a quick dip in the sea to refresh the body and mind,' Evan said, 'and then food.'

'Did you hear that strange sound earlier?' Phameas asked. 'It sounded like an animal being mauled in a fight.'

He and the High Priestess exchanged a look.

'Yes,' she replied.

Phameas and Homer raised their brows at them when neither commented any further.

'Is the Dark Master dead?' asked Phameas.

'I don't know,' he replied. 'The Mother Goddess, Zeus and the other gods have measures in place for him.'

Homer tapped his arm and pointed at his tablet.

'"Did we succeed?"' Evan paused. 'I guess we did. Kronos doesn't have the icons.'

'That is excellent news!' Phameas patted Evan on the back. 'I knew you would triumph.'

'I am glad you did. I had my doubts,' Evan said.

'How could you? We had the Mother Goddess and the gods on our side,' said Phameas. 'Besides, we have you, the greatest warrior, who cuts down men as if they were made from straw and is unafraid to fight monsters, and the High Priestess with her unique god-given powers. What chance did he and the Goddess of Discord have against such formidable adversaries?'

'We didn't do this alone,' Evan said. 'Everyone helped and contributed, or we would not be here now.'

'Ahoy! Evandros! I am happy to see you!' shouted Jason. He and the Argonauts were cheering and clapping, their jubilance and raucousness rousing the others on the beach. Leander started running but stopped. The High Priestess saw him, hurried over and flung her arms around his neck. Evan smiled.

'About time.' Phameas crossed his arms against his chest. 'I was despairing they would never get themselves sorted.'

'Agreed.'

Jason and his crew surrounded them, all speaking, shouting to be heard, rejoicing and congratulating him.

'My friend, you have the fortune of the gods,' laughed Jason. 'I did not expect to see you again when you and the High Priestess departed for the sacred tree.'

'Nor did I, nor did I.'

'Come on, we must drink and eat!' said Jason. 'It is time to celebrate our victory, and the return of our heroes.' The captain scanned his men's faces. 'Orpheos, compose a song to commemorate our quest and that of our heroic friends.'

'Already have begun, Captain.' Orpheos grinned.

'May Apollo's gift bring truth to your lyre and words to sing,' Jason said with a large smile plastered across his face.

Evan, surrounded by his friends, Jason and the Argonauts, stole a quick peek to where the queen and her retinue camped and saw her re-enter the tent. He was not sure whether to feel elated or anguished, except the pit in his stomach was getting bigger.

CHAPTER 61

The revelry continued late into the night. Merriment and singing carried across the bay, and the roasting of boar permeated the air. Evan joined in the festivities, glad it was over, but wondered when the Mother Goddess and Zeus would send him home. He laughed at Phameas' re-enactment of the moment they'd entered the king of Kyrene's palace and the ultimatum Evan had given him.

'The king soiled himself?' asked Jason, astounded. 'Drakon? The same king of Kyrene who imprisons his citizens who cannot pay taxes, who orders the beheading of individuals who denounce his tyrannical rules?'

Phameas nodded, long sweeping bobs. 'I saw it, as did Leander and Hektor.'

'That's not how it exactly happened,' Evan protested, wagging a finger. 'The king ordered his men to come after us. They weren't too eager to do that, but we had to retrieve the weaponry he took from Leander, Hektor and Homer, so we went back. Drakon didn't expect us to return—'

'He wasn't too pleased to see you saunter into the megaron.'

Leander grinned. 'Not alive, anyway.'

'True. I caught him off guard, as he yelled at his guards.'

'Evandros sat on the throne, insisted the king return our weapons and demanded a cart and horse, and supplies,' Leander finished.

'When did the king disgrace himself?' Jason guffawed, shaking his head in disbelief.

'On his way to hide behind his throne,' Phameas chortled.

'In all honesty, I did not see it happen,' Evan said.

'You were too busy making sure the king fulfilled your demands,' Phameas said, then pointed to the two Atlanteans, 'but we saw the damp stain on his clothes.'

There was an uproar of laughter. Jason wiped his tears with the back of his hands.

'Now, that I'd like to have seen.'

'I wonder if he is still in power?' Evan asked, running a finger around the rim of his cup.

They went quiet for a moment and then convulsed into further hysterics.

'Let me fill the cup of the man who made a powerful king soil himself.' Jason poured wine into his cup.

Later into the evening, Evan sat staring at the water. The night was still except for the heavy snoring after the lengthy bout of drinking, breaking the tranquillity. He got up and walked to the water's edge, yanked off his khiton and waded in. Television public service announcements about not swimming after consuming alcohol came to mind, and he dove in, water sluicing over his face when he broke through the surface. He contemplated the wine-dark sea, gentle ripples lapping against his torso, and let his body move with the ebb and flow of the tide. Now he truly understood why he had such an affinity with the sea, and that he was from this period. But was it where he belonged?

He swam ashore and halted, seeing a shadowy figure on the shore. His heart beat faster and his stomach did a somersault. He drew in a steadying breath and waded towards the waiting individual.

'Good evening, Evandros.'

'Good evening, Antioche.'

They gazed at each other. He then sidestepped to pick up his discarded clothes and shrugged his khiton on. It stuck to his soaked body, and he felt Antioche's soft hands against his as she helped tug it down. Her proximity and the heat of her body created a mix of longing and desire to be with her, but he squelched his feelings and thoughts.

'I'm sorry about not seeing you earlier. The men wanted to celebrate. It has been a difficult and protracted journey and we've had little—'

'No need to explain, Evandros, I understand. It is important to spend time with your companions and close friends.' She appraised him with her grey eyes and then glanced down to the water lapping at their feet. 'I, our babies and my retinue are leaving in the morning. I thought perhaps you'd wish to see them before we depart.'

'How will your people react when you arrive with our son?' he asked.

'It doesn't matter—I am their queen. It is time we, as a people, find and accept necessary changes if we are to survive.'

'That is true of all civilisations.' He ran his fingers through his wet hair and took a keen interest in his sand-encrusted feet.

Her chin lowered, and she rounded to leave. 'I shall retire to my shelter.'

'Wait.' Evan reached out to her. 'I'll come to say goodbye.'

She nodded. He let go of her hand and accompanied her to the Amazon campsite. Two sentries straightened, thrusting out their spears on their approach. One dragged aside the flap of the entrance and Evan followed Antioche inside. One of the queen's companions rose to her feet and shook awake another, pulling her upright.

'My deepest apologies, Queen Antioche.'

'How are our babies?' She strode over to the bed.

'They sleep well, undisturbed by the raucousness of the evening.' The queen's handmaiden gave Evan an accusatory glare. He offered a half smile, somewhat embarrassed, and shrugged.

'Leave us.'

'Yes, Queen Antioche.' The women bowed and exited the tent.

Now that they were alone together, she beckoned him. He tiptoed to the other side of the bed and gazed in wonder at the two small faces cocooned in bedding lined with fur. Evan knelt, his heart swelled and warmed as he gazed at them. He caressed their heads, their hair fine, golden and soft, their porcelain skin a stark contrast to his bronzed, sandpapered hands.

'They are beautiful, as is their mother.' He smiled at her. 'They are fortunate to have you for a mother.'

Her eyes glistened. 'As they are to have you as their father.'

She lay on the fur-lined bed next to the babies and reached out to him. He took her hand and lay down, careful not to waken them. Without a second thought, he kissed her. He wiped away her tears and tucked an errant strand of hair behind her ear.

'It'll work out, and you'll be fine,' he whispered.

'How do you know this?' More tears welled in her eyes, and he brushed them away with a thumb, cupping her cheek.

'Our children have a unique heritage and will be protected by the best guardians there are, and so will you.'

'What of you?'

He grinned. 'Oh, don't worry about me, I'm taken care of.'

'Evandros ...'

'Shhh ... go to sleep. I'll be here when you wake up.'

CHAPTER 62

'Master Evandros! Master Evandros, wake up!'

Evan stirred and yawned. 'Dexion ... what's the matter?'

'You need to go. Hurry!'

He sat up, careful not to disturb the sleeping forms of Antioche and their babies. 'Why? What's happened?'

Dexion grasped his arm and tugged. 'You must leave from here.'

'Dexion, wait a minute.' Evan held him by the shoulders and searched the boy's frantic face. 'You've seen something. What is it?'

Instead of answering, he pulled Evan to his feet. 'There is no time to waste!'

'Evandros, what is wrong?' asked Antioche, rubbing her eyes.

'I'm not sure, but stay here.'

He allowed Dexion to lead him from the warm shelter and out into the morning sun, Lykeios at their heels. He pulled to a stop. 'What have you seen, Dexion?'

'Danger is coming.' The boy pushed him.

'Wait.' He saw Jason and his men sitting idle, many of them nursing their heads and looking miserable. 'No one else is ready to leave.'

'We must go to the village and hide,' Dexion insisted. Lykeios barked.

'Just us? Why?'

'I will explain when we are safe in Amnissos.'

'What about my backpack and weapons? And your bow and arrows?'

Dexion hopped about, as fidgety and nervous as a bird. 'We need to be quick.'

'I'll meet you back here in a couple of minutes.'

Dexion fled as if Hades' hounds were after him, Lykeios matching his pace. Troubled by the young boy's odd behaviour, Evan went to retrieve his gear. On the way, Phameas hailed him.

'Morning, Evandros.'

'Morning, Phameas. Has Dexion confided in you about his vision?'

'No. What did he see?'

'That's the problem—he won't tell me, just that we need to hide in the village.'

'I'm going with you.' Phameas fell into step with Evan.

'Bring your weapon—not sure what we may encounter.'

Phameas nodded, and they parted, going in different directions. Evan picked up his belongings from where he had discarded them the night before.

'What is happening, Evandros?' called out Leander. He and the High Priestess were sitting close, shoulders and thighs touching.

'That's what I'm trying to find out.'

'We'll come with you.' Leander made to rise.

Evan waved for them to remain seated. 'No, Phameas and Dexion are coming with me. I'll talk to you later.'

A scream resounded across the bay.

'Antioche!' He sprinted, beach sand spraying under his feet.

An iciness coursed through his veins on reaching the tent. The two Amazonian warriors lay on the ground, staring glassy eyed at the sky. His pulse thundered in his ears. He heaved aside the flap and swore, not able to see anything.

'Antioche?'

He took a few steps deeper into the tent and froze.

'Melaina,' he hissed. 'What are you doing here?'

'That is not the way to greet a dear, intimate friend.' Melaina flounced towards him, leering at Antioche, who sat on a chair and struggled against unseen bonds. 'I told you he'd come. Our hero cannot help himself.'

'Your father banished you,' Evan said through clenched teeth.

'Yes, he did.' Melaina ran gentle fingers along his cheek and down his chest, hovering over his heart. 'However, those bonds broke, and I am free.'

'What? How?'

'Does that really matter? What is important is that I am here to rescue you and we can resume our relationship.'

'There is no relationship! There wasn't one and never will be one!'

'That is not true,' Melaina said to Antioche, then smirked at him. 'Don't you remember that first occasion we met? I saved you from falling to your death after the attack by the harpies. We kissed.'

'You kissed me,' he snarled.

Melaina circled behind him, her fingers trailing along his shoulders. 'And what of that day you searched for me in Pylos, first down at the beach and next in the city?' She wagged a finger at the queen. 'You cannot rely on men to remember the little details.'

'Oh, I remember everything, how you planted seeds of ideas, titbits of information, just enough to keep me on your leash. No surprise to learn of your deception and treachery, with your being the daughter of Kronos.'

'You are wrong. I sought to safeguard you from my father.'

'What of the situations where we were in trouble? You didn't help or keep us safe. People died, the attackers injured many. That is not protection.' He swung around, eyes the colour of onyx. 'Leave now and I won't tell Zeus you were here.'

Melaina cackled. 'I do not fear Zeus or Apollo. They cannot harm me.'

'I'm certain the Mother Goddess would love to make your acquaintance.' He grinned at the flicker of fear in her eyes. 'Go, before they arrive.'

The goddess sauntered away. 'I am not done yet.' She pointed at the gurgling infants, their arms and legs flailing in the air.

'No!' Antioche cried, struggling against her constraints.

'Oh, do shut up.' Melaina clicked her fingers, and Antioche's mouth closed over. She redirected her scrutiny at the twins.

He dove in front of the babies, holding out the shield. A flash of red light bounced off the embossed bronze layer and struck the table, blasting it into nothingness. He drew his sword and levelled it at her chest.

She clenched her fists. 'How dare you? You are nothing but an insignificant mortal! Your weapons are no match for a goddess.'

'Shall we find out then?' Evan made a strong sweeping cut, nicking her arm, and she gasped to see her silver blood ooze from the wound. He attacked again. 'It's apparent you are not invulnerable to a weapon forged by the god Hephaistos.'

Melaina pounced, shrieking. He back-pedalled out of the tent and into the open.

'Great Baal, it's that crazy goddess!' Evan heard Phameas shout.

'Help Antioche!' he bellowed, backing away from the tent.

The goddess lunged at him. He slashed at her. The air whistled as the blade missed. Melaina, screeching like a harpy, pelted balls of fire at him. He thrust out the shield, the flames licking over the rim, intense and lethal. He heard a thump, then a growl. Melaina spun around, a lance bursting into smithereens.

'Enough! You will die!'

His eyes widened and he hurtled towards Antioche as she readied to throw another spear. Melaina gathered a large fireball and launched it at the queen. He charged across and tumbled, crashing into the leather hide of the tent. He gulped, clutching his throat.

'*No!* Evandros!'

He heard the twang of a bow and the swishing of projectiles, followed by a screech and then nothing. Evan collapsed to the ground and writhed, mouth ajar and choking. Excruciating pain ripped through every part of his body. Worse than when the marauder had stabbed him in the skirmish in their fight against the motley assembled bandits. A wet sound met his ears as he inhaled and his lungs gurgled, battling to draw breath. He blinked as Antioche's face swam into his eyesight, tears coursing down her cheeks. She gathered him to her chest. He attempted to lift his arms, but they were like lead.

'Evandros, stay with me.' She wept, burying her face against his neck.

Dexion, sobbing, clung to his pet wolf, Lykeios, as he howled. Behind him was Phameas, sinking to his knees. The High Priestess, her eyes glistening with tears, clung to Leander, whose face was taut and white. Homer wailed, a silent, tormented howl. Jason and the Argonauts and the Amazons pressed in. The sound of weeping filled the bay.

Evan's vision fluttered. Everything was flittering between light and dark. The voices and crying faded. He couldn't feel anything, not being held or Antioche's tears splashing on his skin. He saw the Mother Goddess and Zeus and the other gods hovering above, clustered in a semi-circle, their countenances serious and solemn.

He gasped and stiffened. His breath rattled.

His eyelids closed.

Darkness.

EPILOGUE

Evan felt as if he were floating, no longer pinned to the ground by some unseen leaden weight. He tried to open his eyes but couldn't, and no amount of struggling against the invisible force allowed him to see. He strained to call out for help but could not speak. Evan panicked, heart thumping when he attempted to sit up but was incapable of moving.

A cool, soft hand caressed his cheek. 'All is well, Evandros. Now is not the time.'

Her voice was familiar to him, as was the touch of her hand. His pulse calmed, her presence easing his confusion and anxiousness. He settled into the nebulous realm and drifted into a dreamless state.

He stirred, eyelids fluttering.

'My goodness! Welcome back, Mr. Chronis.'

He stared at the ceiling. It was pristine white. His ears picked up another noise, a persistent and regular beeping. His nose twitched, and he drew in a breath. The scent of antiseptic and bleach wafted from the bedding and saturated his sense of smell. His head flopped to the side and he saw a nurse in blue scrubs standing at the foot of the bed, holding a clipboard. The nurse moved to the bedside and took his pulse. Evan was confused.

'Wh ... whe ...?' he croaked.

'You are in hospital. You've had brain surgery. The surgeon will be along now that you have wakened.' She placed his hand back on the blanket and scribbled notes down. 'I'll return with water.'

'Ho ... how ...?'

She smiled, a practised clinical one, and an expression he recognised when the prognosis wasn't promising. 'I'll bring you that water and tell the surgeon you are awake.' She left the room. Ten minutes later, she came back with a jug and a plastic cup with a straw. She used the remote to elevate the bedhead and held the cup of water for him. 'Drink as much as you can.'

Pure clean water filled his mouth, lubricated his dry tongue and soothed his throat. He swallowed and spluttered, then sucked in another mouthful, the taste sweeter than the first. After a few sips, he pulled away, exerted.

'Well done, Mr. Chronis.' The nurse put the cup on the white metal bedside table, next to the jug. 'I'll return later. We'll bring you soup for your first meal.'

First meal? His head lolled to the side as the nurse left the room. *What is going on? Where is everyone?*

He plucked at the hospital-grade white blanket and sheets, his hands and arms a rich bronze, the only colour against the starkness.

'I don't understand.' His voice was hoarse, and he coughed.

'Mr. Chronis.'

Evan started, consumed and confused by his surroundings.

'I am Dr. Claudia Benson, the neurologist who removed a benign tumour from your brain.'

His mouth dropped open. 'I ... what?'

'What do you remember?'

He gawked at her, his mind filled with experiences and sensory memories of the places he visited and the people he met. 'I ... ah ... working, having sleeping problems, visiting the sleep clinic, returning home ... that's all.'

'That is good,' the physician acknowledged. 'Do you recall collapsing at home?'

'No. When did this happen?'

'Two months ago, one of your employees was concerned when you didn't turn up for work. He went to your house and saw you through the window, lying on the floor by the front door, and called for an ambulance.'

'Two months?' That surprised him.

'Yes. After examination, and because of your physical fitness and general good health, we could not determine the cause of your coma.'

'I was in a coma?'

She nodded. 'We conducted an MRI and found a tumour growing and pressing against your central cortex.' She paused. 'This constant pressure would have caused blackouts, moments where you didn't recall what happened and had hallucinations.'

'Right, okay.' He reeled at the information. Was all he'd lived through and encountered a delusion? A mental breakdown? 'Is it possible for visions to be as real as this room?'

Dr. Benson replied, 'The brain is a complex organ, and while we have learnt a great deal about its workings and processes, there is a lot we still don't understand about how the mind operates in relation to what is real or abstract, such as hallucinations. I have removed the tumour and you won't experience any further blackouts or visions.'

'Can you guarantee that, Doctor?'

'No, I cannot,' she replied after a moment's pause.

He nodded at her. 'I am grateful for your honesty.' He raised his hands. 'Can you explain how I have a tan after two months of being in hospital?'

'A potential side effect of the medication we've administered.'

'Ah huh ... when can I leave for home?' He knew it wasn't the medication that had coloured his skin.

'We'll keep you in the ICU for another twenty-four hours and, if there are no complications, transfer you to the general ward. We'll conduct further tests on your memory and agility, and if there are no issues with the results, I will discharge you in a week's time.'

'Sunlight! It is a great feeling to be out of that hospital,' Evan said, standing outside the automatic doors with his parents. He closed his eyes, tilted his face to the sun and drank in the fresh air.

'Are you certain you don't want a wheelchair? They'll provide one and we can use it to wheel you to the car,' his mother fretted.

'No, I'm fine. I've been walking up and down the wards and exercising in the rehabilitation room.'

'Wait here. I'll bring the vehicle and pick you up at the entrance.'

'Okay, Dad.'

The hospital sat on the fringes of the central business district and had views of the river. He wandered to the grassy strip that separated the principal thoroughfare and the hospital; beyond the road was the Swan River. His mother remained next to him and kept asking if he was all right.

'I'm fine, Mum, just enjoying the space and fresh air.' He saw people engaged in either jogging, cycling, or walking on the footpath that ran along the waterfront. There was a constant stream of pedestrian traffic, even a few individuals fishing from the riverbank. He smiled, excited to be home. Yet he felt empty and lost. 'What was that, Mum?'

'Do you feel up to going out for lunch to our favourite Greek restaurant? Nico would be happy to see you.'

'That sounds nice.'

He took a step, hearing the approach of a slow-moving vehicle, but he had the sense someone was watching him and he turned around. Standing under a tree on the opposite side of the four-way main road were three people staring at him. An adult male, a boy about the age of twelve and a woman with a pram and two babies. His heart slowed and the surrounding noise—the traffic, the birds twittering overhead, and his mother's chatter—abated.

'It cannot be, can it?' He took a step.

'Evan! Stop!' shouted his mother, grabbing his arm and wrenching him backwards.

The woman raised a hand to her mouth.

'What in the name of the Mother Goddess were you thinking?'

'I ... there is a woman, a man and ...' He whirled about to his mother. 'What did you just say?'

'What woman?'

'Did you just say "Mother Goddess"?'

His mother's brow furrowed. 'Have you forgotten the teachings of the Great Mother? You, who studied ancient history and the spread of the goddess' religious tenets. Perhaps we should visit the temple and offer libations.'

'Temple? Libations?' He then noticed the facade of the hospital, built with the same features as the first ancient health facility and named after Asklepios, the God of Medicine. 'Oh, shit! We did it!'

'Evan! Language!'

He swept around with fresh eyes and noted new high-rise buildings mixed with ancient structures. 'We did it. We won.'

Evan turned to wave at the small group across the road, and

his heart sank. They had gone. He opened the car door, and as he was about to get in, he saw the Mother Goddess with Phameas, Dexion, Antioche and the babies standing in the same place. She beamed at him. All around her shimmered, revealing an exuberant Zeus and the Pantheon of Gods.

'Now is the time,' the Mother Goddess said.

THE END

LIST OF CHARACTERS

LIST OF MAIN CHARACTERS

ATLANTEANS

Evan/Evandros – Twenty-First century Architect/Master scribe
and scholar

Zeus – God of Gods and Father of Gods

Alexina – High Priestess to the Mother Goddess

Leander – Water Master

Homer – Master of Husbandry

Hektor – Master Engineer

Phameas – Phoenician sailor on the ship that rescued Evandros

Dexion – Sicilian slave boy, capture by the Carthaginians

LIST OF MINOR CHARACTERS IN ORDER OF APPEARANCE

Kronos/Dark Master – Titan and father of the Olympian Gods

Eris – Goddess of Discord
Queen Antioche – Amazon
Queen's Physician – Amazon
Mother Goddess – also known as GAIA; Serpent Goddess
Hephaistos – God of Fire and Forge, divine smith
Hermes – Messenger of the Gods
Lykeios – wolf cub rescued by Dexion
Ares – God of War
Jason – Captain of the Argo
Melaina – Goddess; daughter of Kronos
Apollo – Sun God; god of oracles, music and diseases.
Ekhidna – half woman, half serpent
Rusa – Elder of Amnissos
Kitane – Priestess of Maia in Amnissos
Nereos – resident of Amnissos
Athene – Goddess of Wisdom
Poseidon – God of the Sea
Demeter – Goddess of Earth and Harvest
Minotaur – half man, half bull
Olympian Gods
Nurse – hospital where Evan was in a coma
Doctor Claudia Benson – Neurologist
Evan's parents

PLAN OF THE PALACE OF KNOSSOS

West Court

Central Court

Theatral Area

To Little Palace

To Royal Villa

Scale of Metres

DEAR READER

Thank you for reading *Minotaur's Lair,* if you have time to spare, a short review on Amazon, BookBub, and Goodreads are always appreciated.

All my best,

Luciana

ABOUT THE AUTHOR

Luciana Cavallaro, genre-bending fiction author, is the multi award-winning author of *The Labyrinthine Journey* and *The Guardian's Legacy*. She has been nominated for book awards in the action/adventure and historical fiction genres, Silver Award in The Global Book Awards, Finalist in the 13th New Media Film Festival and Page Turner Awards, and Quarterfinalist in the ScreenCraft Cinematic Book Competition 2022.

She is also proud of her ambitious attempt at driving her first car at the age of three. (Just between us, this was when she gave her father high blood pressure ... and the beginning of her adventures). Visit her website at https://luccav.me/

For more information, visit our website.
Be sure to sign up to our e-newsletter to keep up to date with our
latest releases, news and upcoming events.